Dick Leslie's Luck

A Story of Shipwreck and Adventure

by

Harry Collingwood

Double 9
BOOKS

Dick Leslie's Luck
A Story of Shipwreck and Adventure
by Harry Collingwood

ISBN: 978-93-68098-18-8

Published by

DOUBLE 9 BOOKS

2/13-B, Ansari Road
Daryaganj, New Delhi – 110002
info@double9books.com
www.double9books.com
Tel. 011-40042856

ABOUT THE AUTHOR

Harry Collingwood was an English author best known for his adventure novels, particularly those with maritime themes. He was a prolific writer, producing a wide range of novels, short stories, and travel writings. Many of his works reflect his fascination with the sea and the lives of sailors, often emphasizing bravery, adventure, and moral integrity in the face of danger.

Collingwood's works were quite popular during his lifetime, and he became known for his detailed depictions of naval life and shipwrecks, as well as for his well-developed characters who often found themselves in life-or-death situations. His writing style is often direct and focused on action, making his novels appealing to readers who enjoyed adventure stories with strong plots and vivid settings. One of Collingwood's most famous works is *Dick Leslie's Luck: A Story of Shipwreck and Adventure*, which showcases many of the themes that ran through his writing—survival, resilience, and human endurance. His other notable works include *The Pirate Island and The Log of the "Flying Fish"*, which also explore nautical adventures, often with an emphasis on exciting exploits at sea.

CONTENTS

Chapter One
A Maritime Disaster

The night was as dark as the inside of a cow! Mr Pryce, the chief mate of the full-rigged sailing ship *Golden Fleece*—outward-bound to Melbourne—was responsible for this picturesque assertion; and one had only to glance for a moment into the obscurity that surrounded the ship to acknowledge the truth of it.

For, to begin with, it was four bells in the first watch—that is to say, ten o'clock p.m.; then it also happened to be the date of the new moon; and, finally, the ship was just then enveloped in a fog so dense that, standing against the bulwarks on one side of the deck, it was impossible to see across to the opposite rail. It was Mr Pryce's watch; but the skipper—Captain Rainhill—was also on deck; and together the pair assiduously promenaded the poop, to and fro, pausing for a moment to listen and peer anxiously into the thickness to windward every time that they reached the break of the poop at one end of their walk, and the stern grating at the other.

Now, a dark and foggy night at sea is an anxious time for a skipper; but the anxiety is multiplied tenfold when, as in the present case, the skipper is responsible not only for the safety of a valuable ship and cargo, but also for many human lives. For the *Golden Fleece* was a magnificent clipper ship of two thousand eight hundred tons register, quite new—this being her maiden voyage, while she carried a cargo, consisting chiefly of machinery, valued at close upon one hundred thousand pounds sterling; and there were thirty-six passengers in her cuddy, together with one hundred and thirty emigrants—mostly men—in the 'tween decks. And there was also, of course, her crew.

For a reason that will shortly become apparent, it is unnecessary to introduce any of the above-mentioned persons to the reader—with two exceptions. Of these two exceptions one was a girl some three and twenty years of age, of medium height, perfect figure, lovely features crowned by an extraordinary wealth of sunny chestnut wavy hair with a glint of ruddy gold in it where the sun struck it, and a pair of marvellous dark blue eyes. Her beauty of face and form was perfect; and she would have been wonderfully attractive but for the unfortunate fact that her manner towards everybody was characterised by a frigid hauteur that at once effectually discouraged the slightest attempt to establish one's self on friendly terms with her. It was abundantly clear that she was a spoiled child, in the most pronounced acceptation of the term, and would be likely to remain so all her life unless some extraordinary circumstance should haply intervene to break down her repellent pride, and bring to the surface those sterling qualities of character that ever and anon seemed struggling for an opportunity to assert themselves. Her name was Flora Trevor; her father was an Indian judge; and, accompanied by her maid, and chaperoned—nominally, at least—by a friend and former schoolfellow of her mother, she was now proceeding on a visit to some relatives in Australia prior to joining her father at Bombay.

The other exception was a man, of thirty-two years of age—but who looked very considerably older. He stood six feet one inch in his socks; was of exceptionally muscular build, without an ounce of superfluous flesh anywhere about him; rather thin and worn-looking as to face—which was clean-shaven and tinted a ruddy bronze, as though the owner had been long accustomed to exposure to the weather; of a gloomy and saturnine cast of countenance; and a manner so cold and unapproachable that, although on this particular night he had been on board the *Golden Fleece* just a fortnight, no one in the ship knew anything more about him than that he went by the name of Richard Leslie; and that he was—like the rest of the passengers—on his way to Australia.

Now, there is no need to make a secret of this man's history; on the contrary, a brief sketch of it will lead to a tolerably clear understanding of much that would otherwise prove incomprehensible in his character and actions. Let it be said, therefore, at once, that he was the second, and at one time favourite, son of the Earl of Swimbridge, whom the whole world knows to be beyond all question the proudest member of the British peerage. Amiable, generous, high-spirited, and with every trait of the best type of the British gentleman fully developed in him, this son had joined the British navy at an early age, as a midshipman, and had made rapid progress in the profession of his choice—to his father's unbounded satisfaction and delight—up to a certain point. Then, when he was within a few months of his twenty-fifth birthday, a horrible thing happened. Without a shadow of warning, and like a bolt from the blue, disgrace and disaster fell upon and morally destroyed him; and almost in a moment the once favoured child of good fortune found himself an outcast from home and society; disowned by those nearest and dearest to him; with every hope and aspiration blasted; branded as a felon; and his whole life ruined, as it seemed to him, irretrievably. In his father's house, and while enjoying a short period of well-earned leave, he was arrested upon a charge of forgery and embezzlement; and, after a short period of imprisonment, tried, found guilty, and sentenced to a period of seven years' penal servitude! Vain were all his protestations of innocence; vain his counsel's representation that there was no earthly motive for such a crime on the part of his client; the evidence adduced against him was so overwhelmingly complete and convincing—although the greater part of it was circumstantial—that his protestations were regarded as a positive aggravation of his offence; and the last news that reached him ere the prison gates closed upon him were that the girl who had promised to be his wife had already given herself to his rival; while his father, stricken to earth by the awful blow to his family pride, as well as to his affection, was not expected to live.

That so fearfully crushing a catastrophe should have fallen with paralysing effect upon the moral nature of the convict himself was only what might naturally be expected. With the pronouncement of that terrible sentence by the judge the victim's character underwent a complete and instantaneous transformation, as was evidenced by the fact that to him the worst feature of the case seemed to be that he was innocent! He felt that had he been guilty he could have borne his punishment, because he would have richly merited it; but that, being *innocent*, he should thus be permitted to suffer such abasement and disgrace seemed incomprehensible to him; the injustice of it appeared to him so rank, so colossal, as to destroy within him, in a moment, every atom of his former faith in the existence of a God of justice and of mercy! And with his loss of faith in God went his faith in man. Every good instinct at once seemed to die within him; while as for life, henceforth it could be to him only an intolerable burden to be laid down at the first convenient opportunity.

Feeling thus, as he did, full of rebellion against fate, full of anger and resentment against his fellow-man for the bitterly cruel injustice that had been meted out to him, and kicking hard against the pricks generally, it was scarcely to be expected that he would prove very amenable to the harsh discipline of prison life; and as a matter of fact he did not; he was very careful to avoid the committal of any offence sufficiently serious to bring down upon him the disgrace of a flogging—that crowning shame he could not have endured and continued to live—but, short of that, he was so careless and intractable a prisoner, and gave so much trouble and annoyance to the warders in charge of him, that he earned none of those good marks whereby a prisoner can purchase the remission of a certain proportion of his sentence; and as a result he served the full term of his imprisonment, every moment of which seemed crowded with the tortures of hell! And when at length he emerged once more into the world, he did so as a thoroughly soured, embittered, cynical, utterly hopeless and reckless man, without a shred of faith in anything that was good.

The first thing that he learned, upon attaining his freedom, was that although the Earl, his father, had, after all, survived the shock of his son's disgrace, he had made a solemn vow never to forgive him, never to see him again, and never to have any communication with him. He had, however, made arrangements with his solicitors that his son should be met at the prison gates and conveyed thence to London, where he was lodged in a quiet hotel until arrangements could be made for his shipment off to Australia. This was quickly done; and within a week of his release the young man, under the assumed name of Richard Leslie, found himself a saloon passenger on board the *Golden Fleece*, with a plain but sufficient outfit for the voyage, and one hundred pounds in his pocket to enable him to make a new start in life at the antipodes; the gift of the money, however, was accompanied by a request from the Earl that he would never again show his face in England, or even in Europe.

At the moment when this story opens the sound of the ship's bell—upon which "four bells" had just been struck—was still vibrating upon the wet, fog-laden air; the steerage passengers were all below, and most of them in their bunks; while the cuddy people, with one solitary exception, were in the brilliantly lighted saloon, amusing themselves with cards, books, and music. The exception was Leslie, who, having changed out of his dress clothes into a comfortable suit of blue serge, was down in the waist of the ship, smoking a gloomily retrospective pipe. The ship's reckoning, that day, had placed her, at noon, in Latitude 32 degrees 10 minutes North, and Longitude 26 degrees 55 minutes West; she was therefore about midway between the parallels of Madeira and Teneriffe, but some four hundred miles, or thereabouts, to the westward of those islands. The wind was blowing a moderate breeze from about south-east by South; and the ship, close-hauled on the port tack, and with all plain sail set, to her royals, was heading south-west, and going through the water at the rate of a good honest seven knots. The helmsman was steering by compass, and not by the sails, since it was impossible to see anything above a dozen feet up from the deck; hence the ship was going along with everything a-rap full.

Captain Rainhill was very far from being easy in his mind. Seven knots, he meditated, was a good pace at which to be sailing through a fog thick enough to cut with a knife, and would mean something very much like disaster if the ship happened to run up against anything, particularly if that "anything" happened also to be travelling at about the same speed in the opposite direction; from this point of view, therefore, the speed of the *Golden Fleece* just then constituted a decided element of danger. On the other hand, however, it enabled her to promptly answer her helm, and thus might be the means of enabling her to swerve quickly aside and so avoid any danger that might suddenly loom up out of the fog around her; and in this sense it became a safeguard. Then there was the fact that the *Golden Fleece* was no longer in a crowded part of the ocean; it was three days since they had sighted a craft of any description, and there might be at that moment nothing within a couple of hundred miles of them, in which case there was absolutely nothing to fear. Furthermore, his owners made an especial point of persistently impressing upon their captains the great importance of—nay, more, the urgent necessity for—making quick passages; there were two keen-eyed lookouts stationed upon the topgallant-forecastle, and between them a third man provided with a fog-horn, upon which he at brief intervals blew the weirdest of blasts. Taking into consideration all these circumstances the skipper finally decided to leave things as they were, and put his trust in the "sweet little cherub that sits up aloft to look after the life of poor Jack."

"Five bells" pealed out upon the dank air, and the responsive cry of "All's well" from the look-outs came wailing aft from the forecastle. Leslie's pipe was out. He knocked out the dead ashes, and turned to go below. Then, considering the matter further, he decided that it was full early yet to turn in, and, sauntering across the deck to the port rail, he stood gazing abstractedly out to windward as he slowly filled his pipe afresh. The man with the fog-horn was still industriously blowing long blasts to windward when, ruthlessly cutting into one of these, there suddenly came—from apparently close at hand, on the port bow—the loud discordant yell of a steam syren; and the next instant three lights—red, green, and white, arranged in the form of an isosceles triangle—broke upon Leslie's gaze with startling suddenness through the dense fog, broad on the port bow of the *Golden Fleece*. A large steamer, coming along at full speed, was close aboard and heading straight for the sailing ship!

Leslie's professional training at once asserted itself and, as a frenzied shout of "Steamer broad on the port bow!" came pealing aft from the throats of the two startled lookouts, he made a single bound for the poop ladder, crying, in a voice that rang through the ship, from stem to stern—

"Port! hard a-port, for your life! Over with the wheel, for God's sake!"

His cry was broken in upon by a mad jangling of engine-room bells accompanied by a perfect babel of excited shouts—evidently in some foreign tongue—on board the stranger, mingled with equally excited shouts and the sudden trampling of feet forward, and loud-voiced commands from Captain Rainhill on the poop. As Leslie reached the head of the poop ladder the steamer crashed with terrific force into the port side of the ill-fated *Golden Fleece*, just forward of the fore rigging. So tremendous was the shock that every individual who happened at the moment to be on his, or her, feet on board the sailing ship was thrown to the deck; while, as for the ship herself, she was heeled over by it until the water poured like a cataract in over her starboard topgallant rail; there was a horrid crunching sound as the ponderous iron bows of the steamer irresistibly clove their way through the wooden side and decks of the ship; a loud twanging aloft told of severed rigging; there was a terrifying crash of breaking spars overhead; and then, all in a moment, as it seemed, the main deck and poop became alive with shrieking, shouting, distraught people rushing aimlessly hither and thither, and excitedly demanding of each other what was the matter.

The skipper, confounded for the moment by the appalling suddenness of the catastrophe, quickly recovered himself and, turning to the chief mate, ordered him to go forward to investigate the extent of the damage. Then, finding Mr Ferris, the second mate, at his elbow, he said—

"Mr Ferris, muster the watches at once—port watch to the port side, and starboard watch to the starboard side—and set them to work to clear away the boats for launching. Where is the chief steward?"

"Here, sir," answered the individual in question, forcing his way through the excited crowd that surrounded the skipper.

"Good!" ejaculated Rainhill. "Muster your stewards, sir, and turn-to upon the job of getting provisions and water up on deck for the boats. And, as you go, pass the word for all passengers to dress in their warmest clothing, and make up in packages any valuables that they may desire to take with them in the event of our being obliged to leave the ship. But they must leave their luggage behind; there will be no room for luggage in the boats. And tell any of them who may be below to complete their preparations and come on deck without delay."

At this moment Mr Pryce, having completed his investigations forward, came rushing up the poop ladder and, wild with excitement, shouted to the skipper—

"We can't live five minutes, sir! We are cut down from rail to bilge; there is a hole in our side big enough to drive a coach and six through, and the water is pouring into her like a sluice!"

"And where is the steamer?" demanded the skipper.

"She has backed out, and vanished in the fog," answered the mate.

"My God! what an appalling mess," ejaculated the distracted skipper. "And all through the lubberly carelessness of those foreign fellows, who were too lazy to sound their syren until they were aboard of us! Now, Mr Ferris, what is the news of the boats? Hurry up and get them into the water as smartly as possible. Back the main-yard, Mr Pryce."

This mention of the boats, added to the ill-advised candour of the mate's loudly proclaimed statement as to the condition of the ship, took immediate hold upon the mob of anxiously listening people who were crowding round the two men, and galvanised them into sudden, breathless activity; hitherto they had only vaguely realised that what had happened *might* possibly mean danger to them; now, in a flash, it dawned upon them, one and all, that they were the victims of a ghastly disaster, and that death was actually staring them in the face! And therewith a mad, unreasoning panic took possession of them, and with one accord they made a rush for the boats.

"Stand back, there; stand back, I say, and leave the men room to work," yelled the skipper. "Do you hear, there, you people from the steerage? Stand back, as you value your lives! Do you want to drown yourselves and everybody else? Here, Mr Pryce, lend me a hand to keep these madmen in order. Back, every man of you; get off this poop—"

He might as well have appealed to and attempted to reason with the ocean that was pouring in through the gash in the ship's side! It is doubtful whether any one of those to whom he addressed himself heard him; if they did they certainly took no notice. In a moment the ship's crew were swept away from the davits and tackle falls, and in another the maddened mob, with a wild yell of "We're sinking, we're sinking!" were struggling together, striking and trampling down everybody who happened to be in the way, and fighting desperately with each other for a place in the boats, that had been swung out and were ready for lowering. The skipper and the mate dashed manfully into the thick of the *mêlée*, no doubt hoping that their authority, and the habit of discipline that was being gradually cultivated among the emigrants would enable them to stem the tide of panic that was raging, and restore order for at least the few minutes that were needed to get the boats into the water. In vain! the two men were visible for a moment, fighting desperately, side by side; then they went down before that maniacal charge—in which the cuddy passengers had by this time joined—and were seen no more.

As for Leslie, the nearest approach to happiness that had been his for more than seven years came to him now with the conviction that he was at last face to face with inevitable, kindly Death. He had endured seven years of physical misery and mental torment because he had too much grit to resort to the cowardly expedient of taking his own life; but now, *now* fate—he no longer believed in the existence of such a being as God—fate had taken pity upon him and, through no act of his own, he was going to be relieved of his intolerable burden. For he knew that, with that fighting mob of raging maniacs struggling madly round the boats, escape was a sheer impossibility, and that in a few minutes—or hours, at the outside—for he was a strong swimmer—he would go down inanimate into the dark depths, and his load of disgrace and humiliation would fall from him for ever.

So, serene and contented in mind, he stood well back beyond the outer fringe of that frantic, swaying, cursing crowd, and cynically watched its proceedings. The scene upon which he gazed was precisely what he had expected from the moment when those three ill-omened lights had burst through the fog and told him that the *Golden Fleece* was a doomed ship. Here was selfishness supremely triumphant, beating down and eradicating in a moment every nobler instinct of humanity. It was "Every man for himself" with a vengeance; women and children were struck out of men's way with horrid curses and savage, murderous blows; men were fighting together like furious beasts; knives were out, blood was flowing freely, and the air was clamorous with shrieks, groans, and imprecations; the whole accentuated and made still more dreadful by the loud clash of dangling wreckage aloft, and the awful creaking and groaning of the riven hull as it writhed upon the low swell to the gurgling and sobbing and splashing sound of the water alongside and under the counter; the weird and horror-inspiring effect being still further intensified by the hollow moaning of the night wind over the heaving surface of the deep. The struggling crowd was no longer human, save in shape; it had become a mob of senseless, raging demons!

Blind, insensate selfishness! Yes; that was the motive that dominated every individual in that seething crowd. Had they but kept their heads and listened to poor Captain Rainhill, had they but helped instead of hindered, all might have been well. Many hands make light and quick work; and had every man there devoted but a tithe of the energy he was now displaying to the task of helping the crew to launch the boats it is possible that every life on board might have been saved. But, as it was, the boats hung there at the davits, crowded far beyond their utmost capacity with men who ignorantly sought to lower themselves, while others fought and struggled with the occupants for the places that they had secured; and nothing useful was done.

Meanwhile, although not one of that crowd of mad folk seemed to be aware of the fact, the ship was settling down with awful rapidity. Already she was sunk to her channels, and was heaving heavily upon the swell with the slow, deadly sluggishness of movement that, to the initiated, told so plainly that her end was nigh.

Now, utterly hopeless as Leslie's future appeared to him, impossible as seemed to be the task of ever rehabilitating himself in the eyes of the world, crushed as he was by the burden of his disgrace, and glad as he was at the prospect of deliverance from all his misery through the kindly agency of death, it was characteristic of him that, even now, at the supreme moment of his impending deliverance, his self-respect imperiously demanded of him that at all costs must he eschew even the faintest taint of so cowardly an act as that of suicide; if death were really close at hand — as it certainly appeared to be — well and good; it was what he was hoping for, and would be thrice welcome. Nevertheless, he felt it incumbent upon himself that he should take full advantage of such slender aids to escape as happened to present themselves; and accordingly, as the bows of the ship became depressed, while the stern rose in the air, telling that the *Golden Fleece* was about to take her final dive, he mechanically sprang to the taffrail and, disengaging a life-buoy that hung there, passed it over his shoulders and up under his armpits. Then, climbing upon the rail, he leapt unhesitatingly into the black, heaving water below him at the precise moment when a loud wail of indescribable anguish and despair from the frantic crowd fighting about the boats told that to them, too, had at last come the realisation of imminent doom.

As Leslie struck the water and floated there, supported by the life-buoy, the rudder and stern-post of the ship hove themselves slowly out of the water close alongside him until the keel, for a length of some thirty feet, was exposed; then the huge hull began to slide forward and away from him with an ever-quickening motion until, with a rush, a weird whistling of air escaping from the ship's interior that mingled horribly with the shrieks of those on deck, and a dull booming as the decks were burst up, the fabric plunged headlong and was gone!

Then came the deadly suction of the sinking ship; the waters poured from all round, like a raging torrent, into the swirling hollow where the craft had been; and as Leslie felt himself caught and dragged irresistibly toward the vortex he instinctively drew a deep breath, filling his lungs to their utmost capacity with air in readiness for the long submergence that he knew was coming.

Another moment and it had come; the tumbling waters had closed over him, and he felt himself being dragged down, down, down, and whirled helplessly hither and thither as he clung resolutely to his life-buoy. As he continued to descend he was constantly reminded that he was not alone in this frightful plunge into the depths; he several times came into more or less violent contact with objects, some at least of which were certainly struggling human beings like himself. Once he felt himself strongly clutched by the hair for a moment, but the swirl of the water almost immediately tore him free again. And still that awful, implacable downward drag continued, until he began to wonder dreamily whether he would ever return to the surface alive, or whether, after all, deliverance from his wretchedness—which in some inexplicable way already seemed much less poignant to him—was coming to him down there in those black depths. The pressure upon his body was rapidly becoming unendurable; the air was being forced from his lungs; he was suffocating! Involuntarily he began to struggle, throwing out his arms and legs instinctively in a powerful effort to return to the surface. Then, in a moment, he lost all consciousness of his dreadful situation and found himself once more back among the scenes of his childhood, a multitude of trivial and long-forgotten incidents recurring to his memory with inconceivable rapidity. He was a dying man; the agony of drowning was over, and he had entered upon that curious phase of retrospection that most drowning people experience, and that so pleasantly precedes that form of dissolution.

But after an indefinite period of oblivion consciousness returned, and he found that he had somehow come back to the surface and was painfully taking in great gulps of air, clinging tenaciously, meanwhile, to what, so far as he could discover, in the intense darkness, was the body of a woman!

Whether that woman was alive, or dead, Leslie knew not; but, still animated by the old reckless disregard for his own safety that had become a part of his nature, as well as by that innate feeling of chivalry that even his great sorrow had not eradicated, his first impulse was to give his unknown companion the benefit of whatever slender possibility of ultimate escape might exist; and he accordingly lost not a moment in disengaging himself from the life-buoy that still supported him, and adjusting it beneath the unconscious body of the woman in such a manner that she sat within it almost as though it were an armchair; the buoy floating aslant in the water, with its lower rim supporting the weight of the body, while its upper rim, which rose several inches above the surface of the water, pressed against and supported the woman's shoulders. By this arrangement the woman's head was raised well above the water; and if she were not already dead there was some prospect that she would ultimately revive and recover consciousness. As for Leslie, he was so powerful a swimmer that he really needed no support, now that he was once more himself; he accordingly threw himself prone upon his back and, in that position, floated easily, retaining his hold upon the buoy by means of the beckets of light line that were looped around it.

The water was quite warm; there was therefore no hardship in being immersed in it; there was not much sea running, and such as there was seldom broke. Leslie felt therefore that the probability of several hours of life still lay before him; and he began, with a queer feeling of dismay and disappointment, to ask himself whether, after all, he might not ultimately be doomed to escape. He knew that the catastrophe had occurred right in the usual track of ships bound south; and it was quite upon the cards that one of these might come along at any moment and pass within hail of him, or, at all events, close enough to permit of his being seen. And if this should happen to occur between daylight and dark he would feel bound to adopt such measures as might be possible to attract the attention of her crew and cause himself to be picked up. Well, he argued, if such a thing should happen it could not be helped; perhaps there might occur some other occasion. Besides, there was his companion. She might possibly be alive; and if such should be the case she would doubtless be anxious to escape; she had, in an accidental way, come under his protection, and he must do everything he possibly could for her.

The question as to whether life still lingered in the occupant of the life-buoy was speedily determined; for while Leslie still lay floating tranquilly upon his back, weighing the *pros* and *cons* of the situation, a faint groan reached his ear, quickly followed by a second, louder and more sustained; then followed certain sounds indicative of violent sickness; the patient was getting rid of the very considerable quantity of sea water that she had swallowed.

Leslie waited patiently until this unpleasant episode appeared to have come to an end, when, raising himself upright in the water, he said cheerfully —

"That's capital; you will soon be all right now. Are you feeling tolerably comfortable in that buoy?"

"Oh Heaven!" moaned a voice that Leslie fancied was not altogether unfamiliar to him, "is it possible that there is some one else in the same horrible plight as my unfortunate self?"

"Nay," said Leslie, "do not speak or think of yourself as unfortunate, at least as yet. You have thus far escaped with life—which is, I fear, more than any one else except myself has done—and while there is life there is hope, you know."

"Surely not in such a dreadful situation as ours!" said his companion. "What hope dare we entertain? What possible prospect of escape have we? Is it not a certainty that we shall perish miserably by thirst and starvation if we succeed in avoiding death by drowning? I must confess that I shall bitterly regret the respite that has in some mysterious way come to me, if I am doomed to linger on and endure the protracted horrors of death from hunger and thirst."

"Naturally you will," assented Leslie; "I fully agree with you that, if one or the other fate must necessarily overtake us, that of drowning is much to be preferred. But it is early yet to despair. We are in a part of the Atlantic that is much frequented by ships; and if fate will only be kind to us, it is quite on the cards that we may be picked up in the course of a day or two. And surely, if this fine weather will but last—as I believe it will—we can hold out for that length of time. And let me reassure you upon one point: so long as we are fully immersed in the water, as we now are, we shall not suffer very greatly from thirst; the water penetrates through the pores of the skin, and, being filtered as it were in the process, alleviates to a very considerable extent the craving for liquid that must otherwise result from long abstinence. Hunger, of course, is another matter; but we must make up our minds to endure that as best we may. You will understand that I am now looking at the bright side of things; there is a dark side also, but we will not consider that at present. What we have to do just now is to be hopeful; to maintain one's hopefulness is half the battle. And, if the assurance will help in the least to encourage you, I should like you clearly to understand that so long as life—or at least consciousness and a particle of strength—remains to me, you may rely upon my doing my level best for you. And, being by profession a sailor, I may be able to do much that a landsman could not. Meanwhile, however, all that we can do at present is to wait patiently for daylight. One point is already declaring itself in our favour; I notice that the fog is lifting."

"Is it?" responded the girl, wearily. "I cannot say that I am able to detect any improvement. But, naturally, a sailor's trained eyes would be more quick to see such a change than those of a lands-woman like myself. And you spoke of yourself as a sailor. I seem to recognise your voice. Are you one of the officers of the *Golden Fleece*?"

"No," answered Leslie. "My connection with the ship was simply that of a passenger like yourself. But I used to belong to the British navy; and although I left it some seven years ago, I venture to believe that my knowledge of seamanship has not yet grown quite rusty. My name is Leslie—Richard Leslie, and unless my ears deceive me you are Miss Trevor."

"Yes," assented the girl; "you are quite right. I am that unfortunate individual—unfortunate, that is to say, in that I yielded to my poor aunt's persuasions and consented to embark in a sailing ship instead of going out to Australia in a mail steamer. I had not been very well for some months, and it was thought that the longer voyage by a sailing ship would benefit my health. And so you are Mr Leslie, the gentleman who held himself so rigidly aloof from all that he excited everybody's most lively curiosity as to his business, his antecedents, and, in short, everything about him. Well,

Mr Leslie, let me say at once that I am profoundly grateful to you for your promise to help me so far as you can. At the same time, I must confess that at present I quite fail to see in what way you can possibly be of the slightest assistance to me, excepting, of course, that your presence and companionship are a great comfort and encouragement to me. It would be awful beyond words to find one's self quite alone in such a frightful situation as this. By the way, do you think it likely that any others besides ourselves have survived this horrible accident—if accident it was?"

"Oh," answered Leslie, "there is no doubt as to its being an accident. But it was one of those accidents that might have been avoided. Rainhill was not to blame; he observed every possible precaution; the fault lay with the other fellow, who came blundering along through that dense fog at full speed. I take it he approached us so rapidly that he failed to hear our fog-horn until it was too late to avoid us. He ought, under the circumstances, to have been steaming dead slow. Then, upon hearing our fog-horn, he could at once have stopped his engines, and, if necessary, reversed them, until the danger of collision was past. As it is, it is quite upon the cards that he, too, has gone to the bottom. No ship could strike so terrific a blow as that steamer did without suffering serious damage herself. As to the probability of there being other survivors than ourselves, I doubt it. It is absolutely certain that nobody could possibly have escaped in either of the boats; and, watching the mad fight for them, at a distance, as I did, I imagine that when the ship went down, every one of those frantic people went under in the grasp of somebody else, and so lost, in another person's death-grip, whatever chance he might otherwise have had of coming to the surface. It is a marvel to me how *you* escaped. Where were you when the ship plunged?"

"I? Oh, I was down on what they called the 'main deck,'" answered Miss Trevor. "I heard the captain give orders that every one was to don their warmest clothing, so I slipped into my cabin and changed my evening frock for a good stout serge that I wore when I first came on board; and when I emerged from the saloon I found myself quite alone. I was just about to climb up on the poop when the ship seemed to slide from under me, and I found myself being dragged down beneath the surface. Then I lost consciousness, and knew no more until I awoke to find myself afloat in this life-buoy. I have been wondering how I came to be in such a singular position. Can you by any chance enlighten me?"

"Well, to be perfectly candid, I put you there," answered Leslie. "I recognised from the first that, with the mad panic prevailing on board, there would be no possibility of utilising the boats; so I took the precaution to provide myself with a life-buoy, in which I jumped overboard. Like you, I was of course dragged under by the suction of the ship, as she went down;

and, like you, I lost consciousness, though not, I think, for very long. And when I recovered my senses I found myself once more afloat, with a fold of your dress in my grasp. So, as the simplest means of relieving myself of the fatigue of supporting you, I placed you in the buoy, not needing it myself, since I am a strong swimmer, and can support myself for practically any length of time in the water."

"From which it would appear that I am indebted to you for the circumstance that I am alive at the present moment," commented Miss Trevor. "I suppose I ought to be profoundly grateful to you; but—"

"Excuse me for interrupting you," broke in Leslie, "but if I am not greatly mistaken there is something floating out there that may be of use to us. I will tow you to it. In our present circumstances we must avail ourselves of everything that affords us an opportunity to better our condition."

Chapter Two
Picked Up

The object that had attracted Leslie's notice proved to be one of the hencoops belonging to the *Golden Fleece*, that had broken adrift when the ship went down, and returned to the surface. There was another floating at no great distance, so, having towed Miss Trevor, in her life-buoy, to the first, and directed her to hold on to it for a few minutes, he swam on to the second, which, with some difficulty, he got alongside the first. The lashings of both were fortunately intact, the cleats to which the coops were secured having torn away from the deck; Leslie therefore temporarily secured the two coops to each other, intending, as soon as daylight appeared, to lash them properly together in such a manner as, he hoped, would form a fairly useful raft. During the progress of this small business, the conversation between the two people thus strangely thrown together had necessarily been interrupted; and as Miss Trevor did not appear to be very eager to renew it, Leslie thought it best to maintain silence, in the hope that his companion might be able to secure a little sleep.

Meanwhile, the fog had gradually been growing less dense, and within about half an hour of the incident of the hencoops a few stars became visible overhead. An hour later the fog had completely disappeared, revealing a star-studded sky that spread dome-like and unbroken from zenith to horizon.

To Leslie the night seemed interminable; but at length his anxious eyes were gladdened by the appearance of a faint paling of the sky low down on the horizon in the eastern quarter. Gradually and imperceptibly the pallor spread right, left, and upward toward the zenith, until a broad arch of it lay stretched along the horizon, within the limits of which the stars one after another dwindled in brightness and presently disappeared. Against this patch of pallor the heads of the running surges rose and fell restlessly, black as ink; and once, as Leslie and his companion were lifted on the top of the swell, the former thought he caught sight, for a moment, of a small toy-like object in the far distance. When next he was hove up he looked for it again, but for some few minutes in vain. Then came another unusually lofty undulation that for a moment lifted him high enough to render the horizon almost level, with only an isolated ridge here and there to break its continuity; and during that brief moment he once more caught sight of the object, and knew that it was no figment of his imagination; on the contrary, it was a clear and sharply defined image of the upper canvas—from the royals down to the foot of the topsails—of a barque, steering south. She was, of course, much too distant to be of any use to them, but her appearance just then was encouraging, inasmuch as it confirmed his conviction that they were fairly in the track of ships. He pointed the craft out to his companion, and said what he could to raise her hopes; but by this time the poor girl was beginning to feel so exhausted from her long exposure, and the intense emotions that had preceded it, that he found his task difficult almost to the point of impossibility.

During the brief period occupied by Leslie in watching the distant barque and endeavouring to deduce from her appearance substantial grounds for encouragement on the part of his companion, the sky had brightened to such an extent that the stars had all vanished, and presently, with a flash of golden radiance, up rose the sun; his cheering beams at once transforming the scene from one of chill dreariness to a blaze of genial warmth and beauty.

Leslie felt that, with the reappearance of the sun, it would be well to get his companion out of the water and up on the top of the hencoops as soon as possible, since dryness and warmth were what she now most urgently required; he accordingly at once went to work with a will to get his proposed raft into shape.

But, first of all, he made it his business to investigate the interiors of the coops, with an eye to the provision of a certain want in the not far distant future. He felt sure that in one, if not both, of the coops would be found a number of drowned fowls; and although the hunger of himself and his companion had not yet nearly reached the point of demanding satisfaction on a diet of raw, drowned poultry, he foresaw the speedy approach of a moment when even such unappetising fare as this would be welcome. He accordingly turned the coops over so that he could get at their contents; and found, as he had expected, that each contained a fair supply of food. Indeed there was more than they would be able to consume before it became unusable, one coop yielding fourteen fowls, and the other eight. These he abstracted and secured; then he turned the two coops over in the water so that they floated right side upward, and face to face—in order that their tops should afford something in the nature of a smooth platform upon which the pair could recline with the minimum of discomfort—and in that position he firmly lashed the two together with the lashings still attached to them. Then he helped Miss Trevor to get out of her life-buoy and clamber up on the top of the fragile structure; finding, to his satisfaction, when he had done so, that the raft possessed just enough buoyancy to support her comfortably, when reclining at full length upon it, although, unfortunately, not enough to keep her dry, since even in such quiet weather as then prevailed, the sea continuously washed over it.

It occurred to Leslie that, since the hencoops had broken adrift from the sinking ship, other wreckage might have done the same; and he accordingly proceeded to search the surface of the ocean with his gaze, in quest of floating objects. For a few minutes his quest was vain; but presently, just to the southward of the sun's dazzle on the water, his eye was caught by a momentary appearance of blinking light, as of the sun's rays reflected from a cluster of floating wet objects. The next instant he lost it again behind a heaving mound of swell; then he caught it again and, this time, for long enough to enable him to decide that it was about half a mile distant. For a moment he was doubtful whether, being so far away, what he saw could possibly be wreckage from the *Golden Fleece*; but a little reflection suggested to him that, if this wreckage should happen to be floating deep, it would be quite possible for him and his companion, with the hencoops—floating on the very surface as they all were—to have been driven quite this distance to leeward by the mere wash of the sea. Whether or no, however, it was certain that away there, some half a mile to windward, there was enough wreckage, apparently, to afford them a raft upon which they could be supported high and dry.

There was but one way of reaching this wreckage, and that was to swim to it, propelling the raft and its fair burden before him. This was a decidedly formidable task to undertake; for the raft, being rectangular in shape, and drawing about two feet of water, offered a very considerable amount of resistance to propulsion, especially under the unfavourable conditions which were the only ones possible; still there was no other task upon which Leslie could employ himself—and he felt that it was imperative to do *something*, if only to while the time away and interest his companion, thus diverting her thoughts and preventing her from dwelling too much upon the horrors of their present situation. He therefore set manfully to work and, shaping a course by the run of the sea, proceeded to propel the raft to windward, resting his hand upon its after end and striking out with his legs, in long, steady strokes that could be maintained for a considerable period without entailing undue fatigue.

Their progress was painfully slow, almost imperceptible, indeed; for when at the end of an hour's vigorous swimming Leslie paused to take breath and a look round, the utmost that he could say was that they were certainly not any further away from the wreckage for which he was aiming than they had been to start with. And, reasoning upon this, the conclusion forced upon him was that, after all, he had merely succeeded in retarding their own drift to leeward; while to actually force his unwieldy raft to windward and thus reach the desired *flotsam*, was quite beyond his unaided powers.

He had just rather ruefully arrived at this unwelcome conclusion when, clambering up on the raft to take a good look round, as the structure rose heavily upon the back of a swell he suddenly sighted, away in the northern board, a tiny speck of creamy white, gleaming softly out against the warm delicate grey tones of the sky low down in that quarter. It was but a momentary glimpse, for he had no sooner caught it than the raft settled down into the trough, while a low hill of turquoise blue water swelled up in front of him, hiding the horizon and the object upon which his eager gaze had been so intently fixed. Then the raft was once more hove up, and Leslie again caught sight of the object, which this time remained in view for a space of perhaps six seconds; and brief though this period may seem, it was sufficient to enable his practised seaman's eye to determine the fact that what he saw was the head of the royal of a ship steering to the southward.

"WHAT IS IT, MR. LESLIE, DO YOU SEE ANYTHING?"

So anxiously did Leslie await the next reappearance of the tiny object, and so tense was his attitude of expectation, that it attracted the notice of his companion, who was fast sinking into a state of torpor from exhaustion. She raised herself painfully into a sitting attitude and, in weak and some-what fretful tones, inquired:—

"What is it, Mr Leslie; do you see anything?"

"Yes," answered Leslie, still anxiously watching; "there is a vessel of some sort away out there; and she is steering this way. What I am anxious to determine, if I can, is whether she is likely to pass close enough to us to enable us to attract her attention."

"Oh, I pray Heaven that it may be so!" ejaculated Miss Trevor, brightening up perceptibly at the prospect of possible rescue. "Is there nothing that we can do to insure that she shall see us? You say that you are a sailor, and I have been told that sailors are amazingly ingenious creatures, surely you can think of something, some act that would better our position!" She spoke querulously, with an undertone of the old disdain that formerly marked her manner running through her speech.

"A man can do but little with only his two hands and no tools to help him," answered Leslie, gently; "yet you may rely upon my doing all that is possible under such disadvantageous conditions. From the position of that craft, and the course that I judge her to be steering, I fear that she will pass too far to windward of us to permit of our attracting her attention. The fact that we shall be to leeward of her when she passes will be against us; for a sailor looks half a dozen times to windward for once that he glances over the lee rail. And my efforts during the last hour have convinced me of the impossibility of driving this ungainly structure to windward by merely swimming. If I only had an oar, or a paddle of some sort, I might be able to do something; but then, you see, I haven't, so it is of no use to think further of that. The wind is dropping, which is a point in our favour, inasmuch as it will lessen the speed of yonder craft in coming down toward us, and so give us more time in which to act. I believe that, for instance, it would be possible for me, alone and unencumbered, to swim out to windward far enough to intercept her; but I certainly do not like the idea of leaving you here, alone, even on such an important errand as the one that I have in my mind; for if the wind should happen to shift, or I should by any other means fail to reach her, I might meet with some difficulty—it might perhaps even prove impossible—to find you again."

"Oh, pray do not allow consideration for me to interfere with your freedom of action," retorted the girl, bitterly. "If you can save yourself by leaving me here to die alone, I beg that you will not hesitate."

"Stop, if you please," answered Leslie, with some sharpness of tone. "You have no right to think or to suggest that I should do any such thing. Perhaps, however, you may have misunderstood me," he continued, more gently. "What I had in my mind was this. It occurred to me that it might not be difficult for me to swim out and intercept that ship, attract the attention of those on board her, and get picked up. Then I could explain to the skipper that you were down here to leeward, afloat upon a raft; upon learning which he would of course at once bear up and run down to look for you. And, as in all probability you would only be some two miles away at the moment when I should be picked up, there would be absolutely no possibility of missing you. Still," he continued, thoughtfully, "there remains the chance of my failure—as I said just now; and I scarcely like to risk it. If it were not for the fact that you are in so weak and exhausted a condition, I would suggest that you once more get into the life-buoy; when, abandoning this raft, and trusting to chance to find either it again, or the other wreckage that we have been trying to reach, I would endeavour to tow you far enough to windward to enable us to intercept that vessel and get her to pick us up."

"Do you really think that such a proceeding would be likely to prove successful?" demanded the girl, with a considerable access of animation in her voice.

"It might, or it might not," answered Leslie. "It is impossible to say with certainty; so much depends upon chance. Still I think the experiment is quite worth trying; we may have to do something very like it eventually, and it would be better to try it now, while we have a little strength left us. Only if we are to attempt it, we had better start forthwith, so that we may make as sure as we can of achieving success. By the way, I suppose you are fairly hungry by this time. Are you hungry enough to tackle a raw slice off the breast of a drowned chicken?"

The girl made a gesture of disgust. "If the most dainty meal imaginable were placed before me at this moment, I do not believe I could touch a morsel of it," she said, "But I beg that you will not allow my squeamishness to deter you from eating, if you feel the need of food."

"Thanks," replied Leslie, cheerfully. "I must confess that I am quite ready for breakfast. And although the fare can scarcely be described as appetising, I think I will attempt a morsel; it may prove useful to me, in view of the task before us."

And therewith, extracting his knife from his pocket, and selecting a fairly plump fowl, he hacked off a goodsized slice of the breast, from which he stripped skin and feathers together. Then, cramming the lump of flesh into his mouth, he masticated it well, extracting all the juice from it; after which he pronounced himself ready for the new adventure.

Hauling the life-buoy up on the raft, he showed Miss Trevor how to place herself in it in such a manner as to secure the maximum amount of support from it; and as soon as she had arranged herself according to his instructions he bade her plunge boldly in; which she did. He then at once followed her and, passing his left arm through one of the beckets, forthwith struck out, swimming with a long, steady stroke, in the direction which he had decided would be the most advantageous for him to take.

It was perfectly true that, as Leslie had remarked, the wind was falling light; it had dropped quite perceptibly since sunrise, and the state of the ocean was reflecting this change; the sea was going down; it no longer broke anywhere, and the conditions for swimming were improving every moment. The pair of strange voyagers were making excellent progress, as was evidenced by the rapidity with which they drew away from the raft; within half an hour, indeed, they had left it so far astern that it was with the utmost difficulty Leslie was able to locate it again when he paused for a moment to rest. And when a further quarter of an hour had elapsed it had vanished altogether; thus vindicating Leslie's previous doubts as to the wisdom of swimming out alone to intercept the ship, leaving Miss Trevor upon the raft, to be sought for and picked up later on.

As to the craft for which they were aiming, it was clear that she was but a slow tub, for she came drifting down toward them at a very deliberate pace. The wind had softened away to about a four-knot breeze; but Leslie was of opinion that, although she showed all plain sail, up to her royals, she was scarcely doing three knots. This was all in their favour, for while the smoothening of the sea's surface enabled Leslie to attain a much more satisfactory rate of speed with the same moderate amount of exertion, the low rate of sailing of the on-coming vessel rendered it certain that, apart from accident, they would now assuredly be able to reach her. And by the time that this had become an undoubted fact, Leslie had made out that the stranger was a small brig, of some two hundred and thirty tons, or thereabout. He would greatly have preferred that she had been a bigger craft, because the probability would then have been greater of her proving a passenger ship, and a passenger ship was what Leslie was now particularly anxious to fall in with, for Miss Trevor's sake—a change of clothing being an almost indispensable requirement on the part of the young lady, so soon as she should once more find herself on a ship's deck. That there were no passengers—or, at least, no women passengers—aboard the brig, however, was practically certain—she was much too small for that—and unless the skipper happened to be a married man, with his wife aboard, Miss Trevor would have to fall back upon her own resources and ingenuity for a change of clothing. He discussed this matter with his companion as he swam onward; but the young woman just then regarded the question with a considerable amount of indifference; her one consuming anxiety, for the moment, was to again find herself on the deck of a craft of some sort; all other considerations she was clearly quite willing to relegate to a more or less distant future.

Meanwhile, the brig was slowly drawing down toward them, and as slowly lifting her canvas above the horizon. And by the time that she had raised herself to the foot of her courses, Leslie had succeeded in bringing her two masts into line, so that the pair were now dead ahead of her. Having accomplished this much, the swimmer concluded that he might safely take a rest, for the brig, being close-hauled, would be certain to be making more or less leeway; and it was quite possible that she would drive to leeward at least as fast as they did, if not faster, he therefore threw himself over on his back, requesting his companion to keep an eye on the approaching brig, and report to him her progress from time to time.

The breeze, having begun to drop, continued to fall still lighter, until Leslie, raising himself for a moment to take a look at the brig, saw with some dismay that her lower canvas was wrinkling and collapsing occasionally for lack of wind. She was by this time, however, hull-up, and not more than half a mile distant; moreover the rest in which he had been indulging had refreshed him so considerably that he felt quite capable of further exertion. He therefore determined to shorten the period of suspense as much as possible by swimming directly for the craft—a resolution that was immensely strengthened by the sudden recollection that they were afloat in a part of the ocean where a shark or sharks might put in an unwelcome appearance at any moment. Accordingly, without mentioning this last unpleasant reflection of his to his companion, he recommenced swimming, this time shaping a course directly for the brig.

Although his own individual progress, and that of the brig, was slow, their combined progress toward each other rapidly shortened the distance between them, and within about a quarter of an hour of the time that Leslie had recommenced swimming he had arrived near enough, in his judgment, to commence hailing, with a view to attracting the attention of the brig's crew. Ceasing his exertions, therefore, he took a good long breath and shouted, at the top of his voice—

"Brig ahoy! *Brig ahoy*! Brig Ahoy!"

The hail, thrice repeated, exhausted the capacity of his lungs, and he paused, anxiously listening for a reply. He thought—and Miss Trevor thought, too—that in response to his last shout a faint "Hillo?" had come floating down to them; but the wash of the water was in his ears, and he could not be certain, he therefore again took breath, and repeated his hail.

This time there could be no doubt about it; the answering hail came distinctly enough, and immediately afterwards—so close was the brig to them—he saw first one head, then another, and another, appear in the eyes of the vessel, peering over the bows. Quick as light, and treading water meanwhile, he whipped the white pocket-handkerchief out of the breast-pocket of his coat and waved it eagerly over his head. The people in the bows of the brig stared incredulously for a moment; then with a sudden simultaneous flinging aloft of their arms they abruptly vanished.

"All right," ejaculated Leslie, in tones of profound relief, "they have seen us, and your deliverance, Miss Trevor, is now a matter of but a few brief minutes!"

"Oh, thank God; thank God!" cried the girl, brokenly; and then, all in a moment, the tension of her nerves suddenly giving way, she broke down utterly, and burst into a perfect passion of tears. Leslie had sense enough to recognise that this hysterical outburst would probably relieve his companion's sorely overwrought feelings, and do her good; he therefore allowed her to have her cry out in peace, without making any attempt to check her.

She was still sobbing convulsively when Leslie, who never took his eyes off the slowly approaching brig, saw five people suddenly appear in the vessel's bows, three of them pointing eagerly, while the other two peered out ahead under the sharp of their hands.

"Brig ahoy!" hailed Leslie; "back your main-yard, will you, and stand by to heave us a couple of rope's ends when we come alongside?"

"Ay, ay," promptly came the answer from the brig. The men in the bows again vanished; and, as they did so, the same voice that had just answered pealed out, "Let go the port main braces; main tack and sheet; back the main-yard! And then some of you stand by to drop a line or two, with a standing bowline in their ends, to those people in the water."

The main-yard swung slowly aback, the canvas on the mainmast pressed against the mast, still further retarding the vessel's sluggish movement; and as she drifted almost imperceptibly up to them, a few strokes of Leslie's arms took the pair alongside, where some half a dozen rope's ends, with loops in them, already dangled in the water. With a deft movement, Leslie seized and dropped one of them over his head and under his armpits; then, taking Miss Trevor about the waist, he gave the word "Hoist away, handsomely," and four men, standing on the brig's rail, dragged them up the vessel's low side, and assisted them to gain the deck.

The vessel, on board which they now found themselves, was a small craft compared with the *Golden Fleece*, measuring, as Leslie had already guessed, about two hundred and thirty tons register. That she was British the language of her crew had already told him; and he was thankful that it was so, for he might now reasonably hope for courteous treatment of himself and his companion—which is not always to be reckoned upon with certainty, under such circumstances, if the craft happens to be manned by foreigners. The vessel, moreover, appeared to be tolerably clean; while the crew seemed to be a fairly decent lot of men.

As he gained the deck, a tall, dark, rather handsome man—but with an expression of countenance that Leslie hardly liked—stepped forward. He was clad entirely in white, and was clearly the master of the brig.

"Good morning," he said, without offering his hand, or uttering any word of welcome. "Where the devil do you come from?"

"We are," answered Leslie, "survivors—the only two, I am afraid—of the passenger ship *Golden Fleece*, bound to Melbourne, which was run into and sunk by an unknown steamer last night about eleven o'clock, during a dense fog. My name is Leslie; I was one of the cuddy passengers; and this lady—who was likewise a cuddy passenger—is Miss Trevor."

The man's rather saturnine features relaxed as he gazed with undisguised admiration at the lovely girl, wet and bedraggled though she was; and, stepping up to her, he held out his hand, saying—

"Your most obedient, miss. Glad to see you aboard my ship. My name's Potter—James Potter; and this brig's the *Mermaid*, of London, bound out to Valparaiso with a general cargo. And this," he added, directing the girl's attention toward a slight, active-looking man who stood beside him, "is my only mate, Mr Purchas."

Miss Trevor bowed slightly, first to one and then to the other of the two men, as these introductions were made; then, turning once more to Potter, she thanked him earnestly and heartily for having picked up herself and her companion, and stood waiting irresolutely for what was next to happen.

"Oh, that's all right, miss; you're very welcome, I'm sure. Glad to have the chance of doing a service to such a beauty as you are." Then, turning abruptly about, he shouted, "Swing the main-yard, and fill upon her. Board the main tack, and aft with the sheet. Lively now, you skowbanks; and don't stand staring there like stuck pigs!"

The men hurried away to execute these elegantly embellished orders. And Leslie, who had stood impatiently by, with a slowly gathering frown corrugating his brow, stepped forward and said —

"I hope, Mr Potter, that our presence on board your brig is not going to subject you to inconvenience. And I hope, further, that we shall not need to tax your hospitality for very long. Sooner or later we are pretty certain to fall in with a homeward-bound ship, in which case I will ask you to have the goodness to transfer Miss Trevor and myself to her, as Valparaiso is quite out of our way, and we have no wish to visit the place. Meanwhile, we have been in the water for somewhere about twelve hours, and Miss Trevor is in a dreadfully exhausted condition, as you may see for yourself. If you could kindly arrange for her to turn in for a few hours, you could do her no greater service for the present. And to be quite candid, I should not be sorry if you could spare me a corner in which to stretch myself while my clothes are drying."

The skipper turned upon Leslie rather sharply and scowlingly.

"Look here, mister," he said, "don't you worry about the young lady, I'll look after her myself. She shall have the use of my cabin. The bunk's made up, and everything is quite ready for her at a minute's notice. You come with me, miss," he continued; "I'll take you below and show you your quarters. You can turn in at once, and when you've rested enough I'll have a good meal cooked and ready for you. This way, please."

And therewith, offering his arm to the girl, he led her aft toward the companion, without vouchsafing another word to Leslie. As for the girl, she was by this time so nearly in a state of collapse that she could do nothing but passively accept the assistance offered her, and submit to be led away below.

"Queer chap, rather, the skipper; ain't he?" remarked the mate, coming to Leslie's side as Potter and Miss Trevor vanished down the companion-way, "This is my first voyage with him, and, between you and me and the lamp-post, it'll be the last, if things don't greatly improve between now and our getting back to London. I reckon you'll be all the better for a snooze, too, so come below with me. You can use my cabin for the present, until the 'old man' makes other arrangements."

"Very many thanks," answered Leslie; "I shall be more than glad to avail myself of your kind offer. Before I do so, however, I wish to say that somewhere over there," pointing out over the lee bow, "about three miles away, there is some floating wreckage from the *Golden Fleece*, and, although I think it rather doubtful, there *may* be a few people clinging to it. I hope you will represent this to Mr Potter, and induce him to run down and examine the spot. It will not take him much off his course; and if the fellow has any humanity at all in him he will surely not neglect the opportunity to save possibly a few more lives."

"All right," said Purchas, "I'll tell him when he comes on deck again. Now you come away below and turn in."

Therewith the mate conducted Leslie down into a small, dark, and rather frowsy stateroom at the foot of the companion ladder, and outside the brig's main cabin; and having said a few awkward but hearty words of hospitality in reply to the other's expressions of thanks, closed the door upon him and left him to himself.

Five minutes later, Leslie was stretched warm and comfortable in the bunk, wrapped in sound and dreamless sleep.

Chapter Three
Captain Potter causes Trouble

When Leslie awoke the warm and mellow glow of the light that streamed in through the small scuttle in the ship's side prepared him for the discovery that he had slept until late in the afternoon; and as he lay there reflecting upon the startling events of the previous twenty-four hours the sound of eight bells being struck on deck confirmed his surmise by conveying to him the information that it was just four o'clock. He raised himself in the bunk, striking his head smartly against the low deck-planking above him as he did so. He looked for his clothes where he had flung them off before turning in, but they were not there; casting his eyes about the little apartment, however, he presently recognised them hanging, dry, upon a hook screwed to the bulkhead. Thereupon he dropped out of the bunk, and proceeded forthwith to dress, noting, as he did so, by the slow, gentle oscillations of the brig, that the sea had gone down to practically nothing while he slept, while the occasional flutter and flap of canvas, heard quite distinctly where he was, told him that the wind had dropped to a calm.

Dressing quickly, he hurried on deck, wondering whether he would find Miss Trevor there. She was not; but the skipper and mate were both in evidence, standing, one on either side of the companion; neither of them speaking. The sky was cloudless; the wind had dropped to a dead calm; the surface of the sea was oil-smooth, but a low swell still undulated up from the south-east quarter. The ship had swung nearly east and west; and the sun's beams, pouring in over the starboard quarter, bit fiercely, although the luminary was by this time declining well toward the horizon.

"Well, mister, had a good sleep?" inquired the skipper, with some attempt to infuse geniality into his voice.

"Excellent, thank you," answered Leslie, as with a quick glance he swept the entire deck of the brig. "Miss Trevor is still in her cabin, I take it, as I do not see her on deck. She has had a most trying and exhausting experience, and I hope, sir, you will afford her all the comfort at your command; otherwise she may suffer a serious breakdown. Fortunately, I am not without funds; and I can make it quite worth your while to treat us both well during the short time that I hope will only elapse ere you have an opportunity to trans-ship us."

"Is Miss Trevor any relation of yours?" asked Potter, his tone once more assuming a suggestion of aggressiveness.

"She is not, sir," answered Leslie, showing some surprise at the question. "She was simply a fellow-passenger of mine on board the *Golden Fleece*; and it was by the merest accident that we became companions, after the ship went down. Had you any particular object in making the inquiry, may I ask?"

"Oh no," answered Potter; "I just thought she might be related to you in some way; you seem to be pretty anxious about her welfare; that's all."

"And very naturally, I think, taking into consideration the fact that I have most assuredly saved her life," retorted Leslie. "Having done so much, I feel it incumbent upon me to take her under my care and protection until I can find a means of putting her into the way of returning to England, or of resuming her voyage to Australia—whichever she may prefer."

"Very kind and disinterested of you, I'm sure," remarked Potter, sneeringly. "But if she's no relation of yours there's no call for you to worry any more about her; she's aboard my ship, now; and *I'll* look after her in future, and do whatever may be necessary. As for *you*, I'll trans-ship you, the first chance I get; never fear."

The fellow's tone was so gratuitously offensive that Leslie determined to come to an understanding with him at once.

"Captain Potter," he said, turning sharply upon the man, "your manner leads me to fear that the presence of Miss Trevor and myself on board your ship is disagreeable or inconvenient—or perhaps both—to you. If so, I can only say, on behalf of the young lady and myself, that we are very sorry; although our sorrow is not nearly profound enough to drive us over the side again; we shall remain aboard here until something else comes along to relieve you of our unwelcome presence; then we will go, let the craft be what she will, and bound where she may. And, meanwhile, so long as we are with you, I will pay you two pounds a day for our board and accommodation, which I think ought to compensate you adequately for any inconvenience or annoyance that we may cause you. And Miss Trevor will continue to be under my care; make no mistake about that!"

The offer of two pounds per diem for the board and lodging of two people produced an immediate soothing and mollifying effect upon the skipper's curious temper; he made an obvious effort to infuse his rather truculent-looking features with an amiable expression, and replied, in tones of somewhat forced geniality—

"Oh, all right, mister; I'm not going to quarrel with you. You and the lady are quite welcome aboard here; and I'll do what I can to make you both comfortable; though, with our limited accommodation, I don't quite see, just at this minute, how it's going to be done. The lady can have my cabin, and I'll take Purchas's; you, Purchas," turning to the mate, "can have the steward's berth, and he'll have to go into the fo'c's'le. That can be managed easy enough; the question is, Where are we going to put you, mister?"

"Leslie," quickly interjected the individual addressed, who was already beginning to feel very tired of being called simply "mister."

"Mr Leslie—thank you," ejaculated the skipper giving Leslie his name for the first time, in sheer confusion and astonishment at being so promptly pulled up. "As I was saying, the question is, Where can we put you? We haven't a spare berth in the ship."

"Pray do not distress yourself about that," exclaimed Leslie; "any place will do for me. I am a sailor by profession, and have roughed it before to-day. The weather is quite warm; I can therefore turn in upon your cabin lockers at night if you can think of no better place in which to stow me."

"Oh, the cabin lockers be—" began Potter; then he pulled himself up short. "No," he resumed, "I couldn't think of you sleeping on the lockers; they're that hard and uncomfortable you'd never be able to get a bit of real rest on 'em; to say nothing of Purchas or me coming in, off and on, during the night to look at the clock, or the barometer, or what not, and disturbing you. Besides, you'd be in our way there. No, that won't do; that won't do at all. I'll be shot if I can see any way out of it but to make you up a shakedown in the longboat. She's got nothing in her except her own gear—which we can clear out. The jolly-boat is turned over on top of her, making a capital roof to your house, so that you'll sleep dry and comfortable. Why, she'll make a first-rate cabin for ye, and you'll have her all to yourself. There's some boards on the top of the galley that we can lay fore and aft on the boat's thwarts, and there's plenty of sails in the sail locker to make ye a bed. Why," he exclaimed, in admiration of his own ingenuity, "when all's done you'll have the most comfortable cabin in the ship! Dashed if I wouldn't take it myself if it wasn't for the look it would have with the men. But that argument don't apply to you, mister."

"Leslie," cut in the latter once more, detecting, as he believed, an attempt on the part of the skipper to revert to his original objectionable style of address.

"Yes, Leslie—thanks. I think I've got the hang of your name now," returned Potter. "As I was saying, that argument don't apply to you, seein' that the men know how short of accommodation we are aft. Now, how d'ye think the longboat arrangement will suit ye?"

"Oh, I have no doubt it will do well enough," answered Leslie, although, for some reason that he could not quite explain to himself, he felt that he would rather have been berthed below. "As you say, I shall at least have the place to myself; I can turn in and turn out when I like; and I shall disturb nobody, nor will anybody disturb me. Yes; the arrangement will do quite well. And many thanks to you for making it."

"Well, that's settled, then," agreed the skipper, in tones of considerable satisfaction. "Mr Purchas," he continued, "let some of the hands turn-to at once to get those planks off the top of the galley and into the longboat, while others rouse a few of the oldest and softest of the sails out of the locker to make Mr—Mr Leslie a good, comfortable bed. And, with regard to payment," he continued, turning rather shamefacedly to Leslie, "business is business; and if you don't mind we'll have the matter down on paper, in black and white. If you were poor folks, now, or you an ordinary sailor-man," he explained, "I wouldn't charge either of ye a penny piece. But it's easy to see that you're a nob—a navy man, a regular brass-bounder, if I'm not mistaken—and as such you can well afford it; while, as for the lady, anybody with half an eye can see that she's a regular tip-topper, thoroughbred, and all that, so she can afford it too; while I'm a poor man, and am likely to be to the end of my days."

"Quite so," assented Leslie. "There is not the least need for explanation or apology, I assure you. Neither Miss Trevor nor I will willingly be indebted to you for the smallest thing; nor shall we be, upon the terms that I have suggested. I shall feel perfectly easy in my mind upon that score, knowing as well as you do that we shall be paying most handsomely for the best that you can possibly give us. And now, at last, I hope we very clearly understand each other."

So saying, he turned away and, walking forward to where Purchas was superintending the removal of the planks referred to by the skipper, he asked the mate if he could oblige him with the loan of a pipe and the gift of a little tobacco.

"Of course I can," answered Purchas, cordially. "At least, I can give ye a pipe of a sort—a clay; I buys about six shillin's worth every time I starts upon a voyage. I get 'em at a shop in the Commercial Road, at the rate of fifteen for a shillin'! I find it pays a lot better than buyin' four briars at one-and-six apiece; for, you see, when you've lost or smashed four briars, why, they're done for; but when you've lost or smashed four clays—and I find that they last a'most as long as briars—why, I've still a good stock of pipes to fall back upon. If a clay is good enough for ye, ye're welcome to one, or a dozen if ye like."

"Oh, thanks," laughed Leslie; "one will be sufficient until I have lost or broken it; then, maybe, I will trespass upon your generosity to the extent of begging another."

"Right you are," said the mate, cordially. "I'll slip down below and fetch ye one, and a cake o' baccy. I'll not be gone a moment."

And away the man went, eager, as most British sailors are, to do a kindness to a fellow-sailor in distress. He speedily returned with a new short clay, and a cake of tobacco, which he handed to Leslie with the remark that he knew what it was to be without pipe or tobacco, and could therefore sympathise with him. Leslie was soon deep in the enjoyment of the first smoke that he had had for some eighteen hours; and while he was still at it he saw Miss Trevor emerge from the companion and gaze somewhat anxiously about her.

As she stepped out on deck, Potter, who had been leaning moodily over the quarter-deck rail, puffing away at a strong cigar, sprang upright and advanced eagerly toward her, with one hand held out, and his cap in the other. She returned his somewhat grotesque bow with a cold stateliness for which Leslie felt that he could have hugged her; and then, seeing that the man would not be denied, she allowed her hand to rest in his for just the barest fraction of a second. As Leslie approached, he heard Potter anxiously inquiring after her welfare, and doing the honours of his ship generally, with a ludicrous affectation of manner that amused him greatly, and even brought the ghost of a smile to the face of the girl.

Leslie made the polite inquiries demanded by the occasion, learning in return that Miss Trevor felt very much better for her long rest; and then he turned to the skipper, and said—

"Before going below I mentioned to your mate that some wreckage— apparently from the *Golden Fleece*—was floating at no great distance; and I left a message with him for you, suggesting that you should run down and examine it, upon the off-chance that there might be some people clinging to it. Did you do so?"

"I did not, sir," answered Potter. "I'd have you know, in the first place, Mister—Leslie—if that's your name—that I'm cap'n aboard my own ship, and take orders from nobody but my owners. In the next place, I took a good look at the wreckage through the glass, and saw that there was nobody on it; so, you see, there was no use in running the brig away off her course."

"But, my good fellow—" remonstrated Leslie.

"Now, look here," broke in Potter, "don't you try to come the officer over me, and dictate to me what I shall do, or what I shan't do; because I won't have it. I satisfied myself that there was nobody upon that wreckage; and that's enough."

"I presume you have no objection to my satisfying *myself* also that there is nobody upon it?" returned Leslie, keeping his temper admirably in face of the other's offensive manner. "If you will kindly lend me the ship's glass, I will go up into the main-top and have a look for myself."

"So you don't trust me, eh?" sneered Potter. "Well, you'll just have to, whether you like it or not. I refuse to let you use the ship's glass; I forbid you to touch it; it's the only glass aboard; and I'm not going to risk the loss of it by trusting it to a man who may clumsily drop it overboard for aught that I can tell."

"Very well," said Leslie; "if you choose to be uncivil and offensive, I cannot help it. At all events, I will take a look for myself."

And, so saying, he sprang into the main rigging and danced up the ratlines at a pace that made the shellbacks on deck stare in wonderment.

"Come down out of my rigging, you; d'ye hear?" roared Potter. "Come down, I say. How dare you take such liberties aboard my ship? D'ye hear what I say?" as Leslie grasped the futtock shrouds and lightly drew himself over the rim of the top. "If you don't come down at once I'll send a couple of hands aloft to fetch ye."

Taking not the slightest notice of the man's ravings, Leslie stood, lightly grasping the topmast rigging in one hand while he shaded his eyes with the other, gazing intently away to the westward meanwhile. At first he could see nothing; but presently, being remarkably keen of sight, he caught what he was looking for, some three miles away. At this distance it was of course quite impossible to discern details with the unaided eye; but as he gazed the impression grew upon him of something moving there; the suggestion conveyed was that of a fluttering or waving movement, as though some one were endeavouring to attract the attention of those on board the brig. And the longer he gazed, the stronger grew the conviction that there really was some living thing upon that floating mass of wreckage. He stared at it until his eyes ached; and finally he hailed—

"On deck there! I am almost certain that you are mistaken in your supposition that there is no one on that wreckage. I cannot of course be absolutely sure without the glass; but *with* it, there could be no possibility of mistake. Captain Potter, I appeal to you, as one sailor to another; I appeal to your humanity; send me up the glass that I may set this question at rest. Surely you would not willingly or knowingly leave a fellow-creature to perish miserably, rather than take the trouble to investigate—"

"Will you come down out of that, or won't you?" demanded Potter, angrily:

Then, seeing that Leslie was again gazing eagerly out across the glassy surface of the water, the skipper shouted—

"Bill and Tom, up with you both into the main-top and fetch that man down. If he won't come peaceably, heave him down! I'm cap'n of this ship, and I don't mean to allow anybody aboard her to disobey my orders. Now, hurry, you swabs; no skulking, or I'll freshen your way for you with the end of this fore-brace." And he threateningly threw a coil of stout rope off a belaying-pin by way of hastening the movements of the two men.

Looking down on deck, Leslie saw the seamen spring with some alacrity into the main rigging, and then continue their ascent with exaggerated deliberateness, mumbling to each other meanwhile. And as they did so, he saw Miss Trevor step quickly to Potter's side and lay her hand upon his arm as she spoke to him—pleadingly, if he might judge by her whole attitude, and the low-toned accents of her voice. He saw Potter seize her hand and tuck it under his arm, patting it caressingly for an instant ere she snatched it away indignantly and walked from him to the other side of the deck; and then the heads of the two men, Bill and Tom, showed over the rim of the top.

"Better come down, sir," said one of them. "The skipper 've got a very queer temper, as you may see, sir; and if you don't come he'll lay the blame on to us; and'll think nothin' of takin' it out of us with a rope's-end."

"Come up here into the top, both of you," commanded Leslie. "Never trouble about your skipper and his temper. I believe there is some one alive, on that wreckage away yonder, and I shall be glad to have your opinions upon the matter. Now," as they joined him in the top, "there is the wreckage, about two points on the starboard quarter. Do you see it?"

"Ay, ay sir; I sees it, plain enough," answered the man named Bill; while his companion, Tom, replied, "Yes; I can see something afloat out there, certingly; but I wouldn't like to take it upon me to say what it is."

"Very well," said Leslie, turning to Bill; "you appear to have tolerably good eyes—"

"Main-top, there," interrupted Potter, "are you coming down out of that, or aren't you? If you're not, say the word, and I'll come up myself and start the lot of you."

"For the Lord's sake, sir, go down, I beg ye; or there'll be something like murder up here in a brace of shakes, if the skipper keeps his word," exclaimed Tom, in accents of consternation.

"Leave your skipper to me; I will undertake to keep him in order if he is ill-advised enough to come up here. Now," he resumed, turning again to Bill, "you seem to have reasonably good eyes. Look carefully at that wreckage, and tell me whether you can see anything having the appearance of a man waving a shirt, or something of the kind."

The man looked long and intently, gazing out under the sharp of his hand; and presently he turned to Leslie and said—

"Upon my word, sir, I do believe you're right; there *do* seem to be something a wavin' over there—"

The sharp crack of a pistol and the whistle of a ballet close past them interrupted the man's speech; and, looking down, they saw Potter standing aft near the lashed wheel with a smoking revolver in his hand, which he still pointed threateningly at the top.

The two men, without another word, flung themselves simultaneously over the edge of the top and made their way precipitately down the rigging, while Leslie, swinging himself on to the topmast-backstay, slid lightly down it, reaching the deck some seconds ahead of them. He alighted close alongside Miss Trevor, who, with her hands clutched tightly together, stood, the image of terror, gazing with horrified eyes at the skipper.

In two bounds Leslie reached Potter's side.

"You scoundrel! you infernal scoundrel!" he exclaimed, as with one hand he wrenched away the revolver, while with the other he seized the fellow by the throat and shook him savagely. "What do you mean by such infamous conduct? Do you realise that you might have killed one of us? Have you gone mad; or what is the matter with you? Answer me, quick, or I will choke the life out of you!"

And, with a final shake that went near to dislocating Potter's neck, Leslie flung the fellow furiously from him, dashing him against the rail with such violence that, after staggering stupidly for a moment, he sank to the deck, sitting there in a dazed condition.

The mate and three or four of the crew came running aft at this juncture, with some indefinite idea of interfering; then paused, gazing uncertainly from one to the other, evidently undecided as to what action, if any, they ought to take. They looked at the mate; and the mate looked at Leslie.

"You had better take him below, and let him lie down for a while, Mr Purchas," said Leslie, assuming quite naturally the direction of affairs. "And when you have done so," he continued, "I shall be obliged if you will kindly afford me the opportunity for a few minutes' conversation."

"All right," answered the mate, "I will. Yes, that'll be best; let's take him below into my cabin. Lay hold here, Bill, and give me a hand to get the skipper down the companion ladder."

With some difficulty they got Potter below and into the mate's cabin, where they laid him in the bunk and, making him as comfortable as they could, left him to recover his scattered faculties. Meanwhile, Leslie, catching sight of the ship's telescope hanging in beckets in the companion-way, took possession of it and, slipping the revolver into his jacket pocket, again ascended to the main-top; from which elevation, and with the aid of the telescope, he quickly satisfied himself that there certainly *was* at least one living person clinging to the wreckage and intermittently waving what looked like a strip of canvas, with the evident design of attracting the brig's attention.

By the time that he had assured himself of this fact, Purchas had returned to the deck; seeing which, Leslie beckoned him up into the top.

"Look here, Purchas," he said, as the mate scrambled over the rim and stood beside him, "I was right in my surmise, there *is* some living person, or persons, on that wreckage. Take the glass and satisfy yourself of the truth of my statement."

The mate took the glass, and presently, removing the instrument from his eye, turned to Leslie.

"You are right, Mr Leslie," he said, "there *is* somebody there, I can see him wavin' something. Now, the question is, what's to be done? The sun's pretty near settin', and it'll be dark in half an hour or thereabouts."

"The more need that you should arrive at a prompt decision," interrupted Leslie. "Now, if I may advise, what I would suggest is this. Let me have the quarter-boat and four hands. I will go down to the wreck and bring off anybody who may be upon it, and if it falls dark before we return, hoist a lantern to the peak, as a guide to us, and we shall then have no difficulty in finding the brig."

The mate considered for a moment. Then—

"All right," he said, "I'll take upon myself the responsibility of agreein' to that. The skipper'll be madder than ever when he finds out what we've done; but I don't care for that, I'm not goin' to leave a feller-creature to die on no wreckage, if I can help it. And if the skipper makes a fuss about it, the authorities at home 'll bear me out."

"Of course they will," assented Leslie. "And now that we have settled that point, the sooner a start is made the better. So please call for four volunteers to go with me in the boat, and I'll be off."

Then, while Purchas went forward to muster a boat's crew, Leslie walked over to where Miss Trevor stood.

"Oh, Mr Leslie," she exclaimed, "what a *dreadful* man the captain of this ship is! Is he mad; or what is it that makes him behave in so horribly violent a manner?"

"Simply overweening conceit of himself, and an enormously exaggerated opinion of his own importance as master of this ridiculous little brig; together with, perhaps, an unusually violent and ungovernable temper, I imagine," answered Leslie, with a smile. "I am afraid," he continued, "that those mad antics of his with his revolver must have been rather terrifying to you. However, that sort of thing will not occur again—unless he happens to have another of them—for I have the weapon now, and intend to retain possession of it until we are able to take our leave of him, which I hope will be ere long. Meanwhile, I am going away in a boat, for about half an hour, to take a man—or, it may be, a woman—off that wreckage that we were trying to reach this morning when we sighted this brig. It is still quite close at hand, and I shall not be gone very long. And during my absence Purchas will look after you and see that you come to no harm. He is a good fellow, in his way, and will not allow our mad friend to interfere with you."

"Thank you," she answered, with a shade of the old hauteur in the tones of her voice; "I am not in the least afraid. Mad though the man may be, I do not think he will attempt to molest me."

"No," acknowledged Leslie, who had not failed to observe Potter's undisguised admiration of the girl, "to be perfectly frank with you, I do not think he will. Ah, here come the men who are going with me in the boat. I must say *au revoir!*"

"Good-bye, for the present," answered Miss Trevor; "I hope you will be successful."

"Now then, lads," said Leslie, as the men came aft and began to cast off the gripes, "we have no time to lose. The sun will set in another ten minutes, and then it will very soon be dark. We must look lively, or we shall not reach that wreckage without having a troublesome search for it. Ah, that is all right," as he stood on the rail and looked into the boat, "I see that her gear is all in her, and that you have kept her tight by leaving some water in her. We may as well get rid of that water before we lower her."

And so saying, he stepped into the little craft, and, pulling out the plug, allowed the water to run off.

"We are all ready for lowerin', sir," sang out one of the men, presently.

"Then lower at once," answered Leslie, as he pushed back the plug into its place, "and then jump down into her as quickly as you like."

In another moment the boat squelched gently into the water; the men tumbled over the brig's low side into her and unhooked the tackle blocks; the man who was going to pull the bow oar raised it in his hands and with it bore the boat's bow off the ship's side; the other three men threw out their oars; and Leslie crying, "Give way, men," as he grasped the yoke lines, the little craft started on her errand of mercy, heading straight for the wreckage, the bearings of which in relation to the fast setting sun, Leslie had very carefully taken just before the boat was lowered.

It was at this moment absolutely a flat calm; there was not the faintest breath of air stirring anywhere in the great dome of cloudless sky that overarched the brig; the swell had subsided until it was scarcely perceptible; and the whole surface of the sea gleamed like a polished mirror, faithfully reflecting the rich blue of the sky to the eastward—against which the commonplace little brig, illumined by the brilliant ruddy orange light of the setting sun, glowed like a gem of exquisite beauty—while away to the westward it repeated with equal fidelity the burning glories of the dying day.

The sun was just vanishing beneath the horizon when Leslie caught his first glimpse of the raft from the stern-sheets of the boat, in which he stood, instead of sitting, in order that he might extend his horizon as much as possible. For the next five minutes he was able to steer by the glow of the sunset in the sky; but by the end of this time the glow had faded to a tender grey, and the night descended upon them almost with the rapidity of a falling curtain. The western sky no longer afforded a beacon to steer by, and Leslie found himself obliged to turn round and steer backwards, as it were, by the brig. But in the fast gathering gloom she soon became too indefinite an object to be reliable, Leslie was therefore obliged to face about once more and select a star for his guidance.

The men had been pulling with a will for a full half-hour when suddenly the man who was wielding the bow oar arrested his movements, holding his dripping blade just clear of the surface of the water, as he cried—

"Hark! did ye hear that, sir?"

"What?" demanded Leslie.

The other three men suspended their efforts as the first man replied—

"Why, I thought I heard somebody singin' out, somewheres. Ay, I was right," he continued, as a faint "Hillo!" came pealing softly across the darkling surface of the water.

"Hillo!" answered Leslie, sending a stentorian shout ahead through his hollow hands.

"Boat ahoy!" came the answering shout.

"Give way briskly, men," cried Leslie; "the sound seems to be coming from straight ahead. We shall get a sight of something now in a few minutes."

The men resumed their pulling with a will, encouraged by the fact that the shouts kept up by the unseen man were rapidly becoming clearer, more audible, and evidently nearer. Suddenly a dark mass loomed up ahead and another cry told them that they were close aboard the wreckage.

"Oars!" commanded Leslie. The men ceased pulling, and the individual upon the wreckage shouted—

"Boat ahoy! you'll have to pull right round this raffle, and come up on t'other side afore you'll be able to take me off. You can't get alongside of me from where you are; there's too much yard-arm and splintered spar stickin' out in that direction. And I daren't jump overboard and swim to you, for I've been blockaded all day by sharks—see, there's one of them now, close alongside of ye!"

And looking over the side, the crew of the boat beheld, revealed as a shape of fire in the highly phosphorescent sea, a monster of fully twenty feet in length or more, swimming rapidly along, a few feet below the surface; while, some half-a-dozen yards away, a second suddenly revealed his presence.

"All right," answered Leslie, "stay where you are; we will pull round to the other side."

So said, so done; and five minutes later they had got the man—the only occupant of the wreckage as it proved—safe aboard the boat, and were pulling back towards the brig, now barely discernible as a small, faint, indistinct dark blot against the blue-black, star-spangled sky, with her anchor light hoisted to the gaff-end as a guide to the returning rescue party.

The rescued man proved to be—as Leslie had already guessed from the fellow's manner of speech—one of the foremast hands of the *Golden Fleece*. Like Leslie, he had been dragged under when the ship went down, but in his downward journey had encountered what proved to be a loose cork fender, to which he had clung desperately. The buoyancy of the fender was sufficient to immediately check his descent into the depths, and ultimately to take him back to the surface, where he found himself close alongside a mass of top-hamper, consisting of the ship's fore-topmast with all attached, that had torn itself adrift from the wreck when she went down; and to this he had at once swam, and taken refuge upon it. He told a pathetic tale of the despair that had seized him, when, at dawn, he had found himself the sole survivor, as he supposed, of the catastrophe; and of the alternations of hope and despair that had been his throughout the day when the brig appeared in sight, drifted up to within three short miles of him, and there lay becalmed. The most distressing part of his experience, perhaps, consisted in the fact that, although an excellent swimmer, and quite capable of covering the distance between himself and the brig, he had found himself beset by a school of sharks, and therefore dared not forsake the refuge of the wreckage, and take to the water.

Upon the return of the boat to the brig, Leslie learned from the mate that Potter was still in his bunk, and that the dazed feeling resulting from the blow that he had sustained when thrown against the rail still seemed to be as acute as ever. Purchas, indeed, seemed to be growing rather anxious about him; and eagerly inquired of Leslie whether the latter happened to know anything about medicine; as he thought the time had arrived when something ought to be done to help the man back to his senses. Medicine, however, was a branch of science about which Leslie happened to know little or nothing; but he readily acceded to Purchas's suggestion that he should have a look at the patient; and accordingly—although by this time a substantial meal was set out upon the brig's cabin table, and the ex-lieutenant felt himself quite prepared to do ample justice to it—he forthwith descended to the cabin in which the skipper was lying; and, having knocked at the door without getting a reply, entered.

It was the same cabin in which he himself had enjoyed some hours of sleep after his long spell in the water, and Potter was lying stretched at full length upon the bunk that he had previously occupied. A small oil lamp, screwed to the bulkhead, afforded a fairly good light, by the aid of which Leslie saw that the man was lying with his eyes wide-open, and the eyeballs turned slightly upward, apparently staring at the deck above him. But the gaze was without intelligence; and the fellow appeared to be quite unconscious of his surroundings, for he took no notice whatever of Leslie's entrance; nor did the eyes waver in the least when the latter spoke to him, Leslie laid his hand upon the forehead of his late antagonist, and found it cool to the touch, although clammy with perspiration. Then he laid his fingers upon the man's wrist, and felt for his pulse, which appeared to be normal. Beyond the dazed condition which the man exhibited, there did not appear to be much the matter with him; and when at length Leslie left him and entered the main cabin—at the table of which he found Purchas and Miss Trevor seated, discussing the viands before them—he said as much; adding his opinion that the condition in which he found the skipper would probably end in sleep, and that the man would no doubt be all right in the morning. The conversation then turned to other matters, the mate remarking that he supposed the skipper's indisposition meant an all-night job on deck for him (the mate); whereupon Leslie expressed his readiness to take charge of a watch until Potter should be able to resume duty—an offer which Purchas gladly accepted. It was arranged that, as the preceding night had been a very trying one for Leslie, he should take the middle watch; and accordingly, when the meal was over, as Miss Trevor, pleading fatigue, retired to the cabin that Potter had given up to her, Leslie sought the seclusion of his quarters in the longboat, which had been made ready for him, and was soon wrapped in sound and dreamless sleep.

He was called at midnight by Purchas, who reported to him with some uneasiness that there was no change in the skipper's condition. The night was still beautifully fine, and the weather a flat calm; there was therefore nothing calling for Leslie's immediate attention, and he readily assented to Purchas's urgent solicitation that he should take another look at the patient, and say what he thought of his condition. Upon descending to the stuffy little cabin he found that, as the mate had reported, there was no marked change in Potter's condition; he still lay, as before, without movement, his unseeing eyes upturned, and apparently quite unconscious of the presence of the two men who bent over him. The only difference noticeable to Leslie was that the man's breathing seemed to be somewhat stertorous.

"Well, what d'ye think of him?" anxiously demanded Purchas, when at length Leslie raised himself from his examination.

"To be quite candid with you, Purchas," answered Leslie, "I scarcely know what to think; but I am afraid the man's condition is somewhat more serious than I thought it to be when I last visited him. I must confess that I do not like this long spell of wakefulness combined with unconsciousness of his surroundings. What is actually wrong I am sorry that I cannot say, but the symptoms appear to me to point to an injury of the brain. You have a medicine-chest on board, I suppose?"

"Oh yes," answered Purchas. "It is in the skipper's cabin."

"Um!" remarked Leslie. "That is awkward. We cannot very well gain access to it just now without disturbing Miss Trevor; and I do not think that the case is urgent enough to demand that we should do that. But to-morrow morning, as soon as the young lady is out of her cabin, we will get that medicine-chest and overhaul the book of directions that I have no doubt we shall find in it; and perhaps we shall discover a description of symptoms somewhat similar to those exhibited by your skipper. And, if so, we will try the remedies recommended. Now I would advise you to turn in; and don't worry about the skipper, for I have no doubt that we shall be able to pull him round all right. And perhaps this will be a lesson to him to keep his temper under somewhat better control."

"Well, I'm sure I hope it will," answered Purchas. "If it does that, I shan't be sorry that this has happened; for I can tell you, Mr Leslie, that when the 'old man' gets his back up, as he did this afternoon, things grow pretty excitin' aboard this hooker. Well, good night; and if anything happens atween this and eight bells, you might give me a call—not but what I expect you're a far better sailor-man than what I am."

"Oh, that's all right," laughed Leslie; "I think you may trust me to take care of this three-decker of yours. But if anything happens, and I find myself at a loss, I will not fail to call you. Good night!"

And, so saying, Leslie left the cabin and, making his way up on deck, took a sailor-like look at the brilliantly star-lit sky that stretched cloudless all round the brig from zenith to horizon, as he thoughtfully filled and lit his pipe.

To tell the truth, he was less easy in his mind touching Potter's condition than he had allowed Purchas to see. That the man was something more than merely stunned was now undeniable; and although the injury might not in itself be serious, the complete ignorance of Purchas and himself in relation to medical and surgical matters might possibly lead to wrong treatment that, in its turn, might result in complications ending, who could say where? Of course the man had only himself to thank for it; his conduct had been provocative to the last degree; yet Leslie had been animated by no vindictive feeling when he had attacked the man, still less had he intended to inflict any serious injury upon him; he had, indeed, acted solely in self-defence in taking the fellow's revolver away from him; and as to the violence that had accompanied the act—well he himself considered it perfectly excusable under the circumstances; and so, he believed, would any unprejudiced person. Nevertheless, he regretted the incident; he would much rather that it had not happened; and while dismissing the subject from his mind, for the moment, he resolved that henceforth he would keep himself much better in hand in his dealings with the man.

The calm continued throughout Leslie's watch; and when at eight bells he turned over the charge of the deck to Purchas, the brig, save for an occasional lazy and almost imperceptible heave on the now invisible swell, was as motionless as a house.

When, however, Purchas called him at seven bells—thus allowing him time to wash and dress in readiness for breakfast at eight o'clock, Leslie found, upon turning out, that while the morning was as gloriously fine as the preceding night had been, the brilliant blue of the sky overhead was streaked here and there with light touches of cirrus cloud, the forerunners of a breeze that was already wrinkling the surface of the azure sea and causing it to sparkle as though strewed with diamond dust in the wake of the sun, while it just filled the brig's sails sufficiently to keep them asleep and give the old tub steerage-way. The watch were just finishing off the task of washing decks; the men going over the streaming planks with swabs and squeegees, to remove the superfluous water, while Purchas, sitting on the stern grating, was drying his bare feet with a towel preparatory to drawing on his socks and shoes. Miss Trevor was not visible.

The mate, having bade Leslie good morning, proceeded to inform him that the breeze, which was breathing out from the eastward, had come up with the sun, and that he hoped it would freshen as the day grew older; winding up with an earnest aspiration that it would last long enough to run them into the "Trades." Then, having donned his foot coverings, he drew Leslie aside, out of hearing of the helmsman, to impart the information that, having visited the "old man's" cabin an hour previously, he had found him no better, and that he was beginning to feel "downright anxious" about him.

Hearing this, Leslie proposed that they should both go down together, to investigate Potter's condition; and Purchas eagerly acquiescing, they presently found themselves once more bending over the sick man.

As the mate had said, there was no perceptible change in the skipper's appearance, save that, as Leslie thought, his breathing was a trifle more stertorous. He was lying in precisely the same attitude that he had assumed when first placed in the bunk; indeed, the two men agreed that, so far as they could see, he had not moved a limb from that moment. While they stood there together, discussing the man's disconcerting condition, faint rustling, as of garments, outside the cabin door, accompanied by light footsteps upon the companion ladder, apprised them of the fact that Miss Trevor was moving, and had gone on deck; whereupon Leslie went out and followed her. He found her standing just to windward of the companion, gazing with visible delight at the brilliant and sparkling scene around her. She had evidently rested well, for she looked as fresh and wholesome as the morning itself; and although her costume was somewhat shrunken, and showed here and there patches of whitish discolouration from its long immersion in the sea, she still presented a picture of grace calculated to charm the most fastidious eye.

Lifting his cap, Leslie stepped forward and greeted her, bidding her good morning, and remarking that he hoped she had slept as well as her appearance seemed to suggest; to which she replied, laughingly, that she had, and that she hoped she could return the compliment.

"Oh yes," answered Leslie; "I have slept admirably, thanks. I have had eight hours in, and four hours—the four hours of the middle watch—on deck, having undertaken to stand watch and watch with Purchas during the skipper's indisposition, the mention of which brings me to the point of asking you, Miss Trevor, whether you will permit me to enter your cabin for the purpose of removing a medicine-chest that, I understand from the mate, is there."

"Yes, certainly," assented the girl, "you may enter it at once, if you wish, Mr Leslie. I have tidied it up myself this morning, and intend to do so regularly in future; it will provide me with something to do. But you spoke of Captain Potter's indisposition. Is he unwell, then?"

"Why, yes," said Leslie; "he appears to be. The fact is, that he has not yet recovered from the blow that he received yesterday evening when he forced upon me the disagreeable necessity to disarm him. He has lain unconscious the whole night through, without moving so much as a muscle, so far as one can see; and, to tell you the whole truth, Purchas and I are beginning to feel more than a trifle uneasy about him. Hence my request for permission to have access to the medicine-chest."

"Oh dear, I am *so* sorry," exclaimed the girl, a note of concern at once entering her voice. "Pray go at once, Mr Leslie, I beg, and do whatever you may deem necessary. I *hope* it will not prove that the captain is seriously injured; it will be so—so—very—embarrassing for you."

"Well," answered Leslie, "of course I should be very sorry if, as you say, anything serious were to happen; but, even so, the man will only have himself to thank for it."

And, with this attempt to justify himself, Leslie raised his cap again, and vanished down the companion-way.

As his footsteps sounded on the companion ladder, Purchas emerged from the cabin occupied by Potter, and joined him.

Chapter Four
Death of the Skipper

"Well, Mr Leslie," inquired the mate, "is there any chance of our coming at that medicine-chest? To speak plainly, I don't half like the look of the skipper, and that's a fact. It ain't natural for a man to lie like that, hour a'ter hour, without movin'; and the sooner we can bring him back to his senses, the better I shall be pleased."

"Yes," answered Leslie, "I quite understand how you feel about the matter, and I feel quite as anxious as you do about it; more so, possibly, since it is I who am responsible for the man's condition. I shall be bitterly grieved if he proves to be seriously injured; but in any case I hope you will understand that it was impossible for me to allow him to retain possession of his revolver. He had clearly conceived an extraordinary aversion for me, and exhibited it without restraint. I believe that when he fired at me he fully intended to kill me, if he could, and I was compelled to act in self-defence. If a man allows his temper to get the better of him to that extent, he must take the consequences. But here we are," as he threw open the door of Miss Trevor's cabin, "and that, I take it, is the medicine-chest;" pointing to a fairly large chest standing against the bulkhead.

"Yes," assented Purchas, "that's the chest. Better have it out of this into the main cabin, hadn't we? Then we shan't be obliged to disturb the lady whenever we want to get at it."

"Certainly," agreed Leslie; "I was about to suggest it."

And therewith the two men seized, each of them, a handle and carried the box into the main cabin, placing it conveniently for pushing it under the table, out of the way, when not required. The chest was unlocked, and they threw it open, disclosing an interior fitted with a tray on top, which contained a long tin tubular case labelled "Diachylon Plaster," surgical scissors, surgical needles, rolls of bandage, and numerous other surgical instruments and appliances; while, underneath the tray, the body of the chest was full of jars and bottles containing drugs, each distinctly labelled, and each fitted into its own special compartment. There was also in the chest a book setting forth in detail the symptoms of nearly every imaginable disease, with its appropriate treatment, and also the proper course to pursue in the event of injury. The book was furnished with a very complete index, to facilitate prompt reference.

This book they took out and laid open upon the cabin table, now spread with the breakfast equipage. Anxiously they pored over its pages, finding more than one reference that seemed fairly to fit the case; and at length Leslie, to whose judgment the mate seemed disposed to defer, decided upon a treatment, which they proceeded forthwith to act upon. It consisted in the administration of a draught, and the application of a blister; and owing to the absolute insensibility of the skipper and his consequent powerlessness to assist in any way it was a somewhat lengthy job; but they completed it at last, and then went to breakfast.

As it was not expected that any visible result of their treatment would become apparent for the first hour or so, they did not visit the skipper at the conclusion of the meal; but Purchas went to his cabin and turned in, leaving Leslie in charge of the deck—the latter undertaking to call the mate at seven bells, in time to take the meridian altitude of the sun at noon, for the determination of the brig's latitude.

During the time that Leslie had been occupied below he had been conscious of the fact that the breeze was freshening, as was evidenced by the increasing heel of the brig and her growing liveliness of movement; and when at length he went on deck and relieved the carpenter, who had been temporarily in charge, he found quite a smart breeze blowing from about due east, and the brig, with her weather-braces slightly checked, and everything set, to her royals, staggering along, with a great deal of fuss and much churning up of water about her bluff bows, at a speed of some six knots. He glanced aloft and saw that her topgallant-masts were whipping and buckling like fishing-rods.

"Hillo, Chips," he said good-humouredly, "so you are one of the carrying-on school, I see. But what about those sticks aloft; aren't you trying them rather severely? Of course you ought to know their condition better than I do; but it looks to me as though you are giving them rather more than they ought to be asked to do."

"Oh, they're goodish sticks, sir, are them topgallant-masts, and the skipper's a rare hand for carryin' on; she ain't no clipper, as I dare say you've noticed, sir; but the cap'n makes a p'int of gettin' every inch out of her as she's capable of doin' of. All the same, sir, I believe it's about time them royals was took in."

"So do I," agreed Leslie, as a somewhat fresher puff took the brig and caused the spars to buckle still more ominously. "Royal halliards, let go! Clew up and furl!" he shouted to the men who were lounging on the forecastle over some tasks that they were performing in the leisurely manner usual with merchant seamen.

The carpenter sprang to the main royal halliards and let them run; a man forward dropped the serving-mallet that he was using, and did the same with the fore royal halliards; and while two other hands started the sheets and began to drag upon the clewlines, a third shambled aft and helped the carpenter to clew up the main royal.

This relieved the brig a trifle; but there was a hard look about the sky to windward that promised still more wind; so Leslie said—

"The breeze is coming still stronger before long, Chips; you had therefore better make one job of it, and take in the topgallantsails as well. And when that is done, if the men are not better engaged, let them get to work and set up the topgallant and royal rigging fore and aft; it is shockingly slack—hanging fairly in bights, in fact—and is affording practically no support to the spars."

"Ay, ay, sir!" answered the carpenter, who was acting also as boatswain. "I've had my eye on that riggin' for the last day or two; it wants settin' up badly, and I'll attend to it at once."

The men had got the canvas clewed up, and were aloft furling it when Miss Trevor emerged through the companion-way; and Leslie, with a word of greeting, hastened to arrange a deck-chair for her accommodation on the lee side of the deck, within the shadow of the main trysail; for although there was a slight veil of thin, streaky cloud overspreading the sky, the sun shone through it with an ardour that made shelter of some sort from it very acceptable, especially to a girl who might be supposed to set some value upon her complexion. She accepted Leslie's attentions with a brief word or two of thanks, uttered in tones that suggested an inclination to revert to her former unapproachable attitude; and the ex-lieutenant at once left her to herself, passing over to the weather side of the deck and devoting himself strictly to his duties as officer of the watch.

At seven bells he called Purchas, who presently made his appearance on deck, with an old-fashioned quadrant in his hand. He looked aloft, and then to windward, noted the changes that Leslie had affected, and graciously expressed his approval of them. Then he said—

"I s'pose, Mr Leslie, you're a first-class navigator and know all about shootin' the sun?"

"Naturally, I do," answered Leslie; "navigation is, of course, an essential part of the education and training of a naval officer; and I learned all in that line that they thought it necessary to teach me a good many years ago."

"Ay, so I supposed," returned Purchas. "As for me, I've learned what was required to enable me to get my certificate; but, after all, I don't really understand it properly. I can take the sun at noon, of course, and work out the ship's latitood; but, even at that, I've got no very great faith in myself; and as to the longitood—well, there; I always feels that I may be right or I may be wrong. I never was much of a hand at figures. So, if you've no objections, I'd take it very kind of you if you'd lend me a hand at this job while the skipper's on his beam-ends. He's got a real dandy sextant in his cabin that I'll take it upon me to let you have the use of; and the chronometer's in there too. We might as well have them things out of there too, then we shan't have to disturb the young lady every time we wants 'em."

Leslie quite agreed as to the desirability of this, and he also cheerfully undertook to check and assist Purchas in his navigation. The latter therefore went below to make the necessary transfer, and presently returned to the deck, carrying Potter's sextant—a very handsome and valuable instrument—in his hand. This he handed to Leslie; and as the time was now drawing well on towards noon, the two men betook themselves to the forecastle—the sun being over the jib-boom end—and proceeded to take the meridian altitude of the luminary. This done, "eight bells" was struck, the watch called, and Leslie and the mate returned aft to work out their calculations. As a result, there proved to be a difference of two miles between them; nothing very serious, but enough to prove that Purchas's doubts of himself were fully justified.

Upon being called by Leslie, the mate had looked in upon Potter for a moment on his way up on deck, but had failed to discover any improvement in his condition. He now suggested that they should both go below and subject their patient to a closer examination—which they did.

As Purchas had already remarked, there was no apparent improvement in Potter's condition; on the contrary, when Leslie felt his pulse it seemed to him that it was weaker. This, however, might be accounted for by the fact that the man had taken no nourishment from the moment that he had sustained his injury, and owing to his absolute helplessness, it seemed impossible to administer any to him. A further study of the book of directions accompanying the medicine-chest, however, instructed them how to overcome this difficulty; and, summoning the steward, the mate forthwith gave him instructions to kill a chicken and have some broth prepared as quickly as possible. Meanwhile the blister was snipped and dressed, another dose of medicine administered, with considerable difficulty, and the man was once more left to himself, the self-constituted physicians having then done all, for the moment, that was possible.

"I wish something big would come along—a man-o'-war, for instance," observed Leslie, as he and the mate left the cabin together; "we could then signal for medical assistance. A properly qualified doctor could soon say precisely what is wrong, and what would be the proper treatment to adopt. And if the case is really serious—as, to be frank with you, Purchas, I am beginning to fear it is—we might even trans-ship him, and thus give him the best chance possible for his life. You, of course, in such an event, would fully report all the circumstances of the case, and I should accompany the man to the other ship, to take the responsibility for whatever might happen. And Miss Trevor would go with me, since she, of course, now wishes to return home—failing an opportunity to continue her voyage to Australia or India—as soon as possible. What do you think of my plan?"

"Why," answered Purchas, "it seems a good enough plan, so far as it goes. And if that there ship that you're talkin' about could spare me a navigator to help me take the brig to Valparaiso, why, I'd be perfectly satisfied. But there don't seem to be much chance of our fallin' in with nothin'; we haven't spoke a single craft of any sort this side of Finisterre."

"The greater the likelihood of our doing so soon," remarked Leslie. "It may be quite worth while to keep an especially bright look-out, with a view to the intercepting of anything that may happen to heave in sight."

On board small craft of the *Mermaid* type it is usual to have dinner served in the cabin at midday; and accordingly, the steward having already announced that the meal was on the table, and summoned Miss Trevor, Leslie and Purchas entered the cabin and proceeded to dine. It was Leslie's afternoon watch below and his eight hours out that night, so he decided to lie down on the cabin lockers and get an hour or two's sleep after he had smoked his pipe on deck. Before doing so, however, he went forward to the galley to inquire how the chicken broth was progressing, and finding that it was ready, he took it aft, and, on his way below, requested Purchas to accompany him, and assist him to administer it.

The two men entered the cabin together, and stepped to the side of the bunk. The figure of Potter still lay exactly as they had left him; but as Leslie stood for a moment gazing, he gradually became aware that a subtle change in the man's appearance had taken place; through the swarthy tints of the sunburnt complexion an ashen grey hue seemed to have spread. He bent closer, and laid his hand upon the wrist, feeling for the pulse. There was no beat perceptible. He moistened the back of his hand and laid it close to the lips, waiting anxiously to feel the breath playing upon the moistened skin. He could detect nothing. Then he laid his hand upon the man's chest, over his heart. The chest had ceased to heave; and there was not the faintest throb of the heart, so far as he could feel. Finally, he snatched a small mirror from the nail on which it was hanging, and laid it gently, face downward, on Potter's mouth. He left it there for fully two minutes; and when at length he lifted it again its surface was still bright and undimmed as before. He carefully hung the mirror upon its nail again, and, turning to the mate, said—

"Mr Purchas, I regret to inform you that Captain Potter is dead!"

"Dead!" ejaculated Purchas. "No, no; he can't *be*! there must be some mistake."

"I very greatly fear that there is *no* mistake about it," returned Leslie. "I have seen death, in my time, too often not to recognise it. You will observe that breathing has ceased; neither can I find any trace of a pulse, or the slightest flutter of the heart-beat. All these symptoms are, I believe, quite consistent with a state of trance; and, remembering that, we must of course be careful to do nothing precipitately. But I am convinced that the man is really dead—a very short time will suffice, in this climate, to demonstrate whether or not that is the case—and I would advise you to give immediate instructions to have the necessary preparations made for his burial. Should my surmise prove correct, you are now the master of this brig; and as such you will of course adopt such measures with regard to me, as the immediate cause of this misfortune, as you may deem fit. But there is no necessity to put me in irons; I cannot very well escape."

"Put you in irons!" ejaculated Purchas; "I should think not. No, Mr Leslie, you had no intention of killin' the skipper; I'll swear to that. It was an accident; neither more nor less. How was you to know that a great strong man, like he was, was goin' to stagger back and hit his head again' the rail, same as he did? And he provoked you; all hands 'll bear witness to that; he shot at ye, and you was quite justified in takin' his revolver away from him. Oh no, there'll be no puttin' of you in irons so long as I'm skipper o' this brig. But of course I shall have to make a hentry of the whole affair in the official log-book; and now you'll have to go on with the brig to Valparaiso, whether or no, to hear what the British Consul there have got to say about it."

"Certainly," assented Leslie, "I shall make no difficulty about that. And I have not very much fear as to the result. But, as to Miss Trevor, I hope you will seize the first suitable opportunity that occurs to trans-ship her. She, poor girl, will now be more anxious than ever to get away from this vessel."

"Yes, yes; of course she will," agreed Purchas. "And I suppose, Mr Leslie," he continued, "you won't have any objections to continue lending me a hand to work and navigate this brig? Now that the skipper's gone I shall need help more'n ever."

"You may rely upon me, Mr Purchas, to do everything in my power to help you," answered Leslie. "And now," he continued, "while you are making the arrangements of which I just now spoke, I will go on deck and make Miss Trevor acquainted with the news of our misfortune."

Miss Trevor received the news of Potter's demise with a few expressions of well-bred regret, but she did not appear to be very greatly concerned at the event. It could scarcely be otherwise. In the first place, she had only been in the man's company a very few hours; and although he had certainly picked her and Leslie up—thus saving them in all probability from a lingering and painful death—he could scarcely have acted otherwise, seeing that he had nothing to do but give orders for a few rope's ends to be dropped over the side to them. Then, although she had given no sign of it, his manner toward her had been such as to fill her with vague fear; while his behaviour toward Leslie, when that individual had unavailingly attempted to convince him of the presence of another survivor upon the floating wreckage, was scarcely of a kind to inspire a woman with confidence or respect.

By eight bells in the afternoon watch there was no longer room for doubt that Potter was really dead; and this being the case, Purchas very wisely decided to bury the body at once, and get rid of it. At his summons, therefore, the carpenter and another man came aft with a square of canvas, palm, needle, and twine to sew up the body, and a short length of rusty chain—routed out from the fore-peak—wherewith to sink it. Meanwhile the brig's ensign was hoisted half-mast high, and the men were ordered to "clean" themselves in readiness for the funeral—all work being knocked off for the remainder of the day. Upon being apprised of what was about to take place, Miss Trevor retired to her cabin.

The process of sewing up the body and preparing it for burial occupied about half an hour, by which time the men were all ready. Meanwhile Leslie had been coaching Purchas—who frankly confessed his ignorance—as to the part he was to perform; it being of course his duty, as master of the ship, to read the burial service.

The carpenter having reported that the body was ready, two more men came aft, bearing with them a grating which they laid down on the deck alongside the companion. They then descended to the berth wherein the dead man lay and, assisted by the carpenter and the man who had helped to sew up the body in its canvas shroud, carried the corpse, with some difficulty—owing to its weight, and the cramped dimensions of the berth and the companion-way—up on deck, where it was laid upon the grating, and a spare ensign spread over it as a pall. Then the four men raised the grating and its burden to their shoulders, and with Purchas in front reading the burial service, and Leslie following behind, all, of course, uncovered, the little procession moved slowly along the deck to the lee gangway, where the rest of the crew, also uncovered, awaited it. Arrived at the gangway, the grating was laid upon the rail, with the feet of the body pointing outboard; the carpenter and his assistant supporting the inner end of the grating.

Shorn though the ceremony necessarily was of most of the solemn formalism that characterises an interment ashore, and further marred in its effectiveness by the droning tones in which Purchas deemed it proper to read the beautiful and solemn words of the prescribed ritual, it was, nevertheless, profoundly impressive, the peculiar circumstances of the case, and the setting of the picture, so to speak—the small brig out there alone upon the boundless world of waters, the little group of weather-beaten bare-headed men surrounding the stark and silent figure upon the grating, who a few brief hours before had been the head and chief of their small community; the man to whose knowledge and skill they had willingly committed their fortunes and themselves, who had ruled them as with a rod of iron, whose will was their law, who had held their very lives in his hands, at whose caprice they were either happy or miserable, and who now lay there without the power to move so much as a finger either to help or hurt them, and whose lifeless clay they were about to launch to its last resting-place, there to repose "till the sea gives up her dead,"—this, with the wailing moan of the wind aloft, the sobbing of the water alongside, and the solemn glory of the dying day all uniting to imbue the scene and the occasion with a profundity of sadness and a sublimity that would have been impossible under other circumstances. And so deeply was Leslie moved by it that, for the first time since the words of his cruel and unjust sentence had fallen upon his ears, he once more felt, to conviction, that God the Creator, God the Ordainer, God the Father was and must be an ever-living and omnipotent entity. And for the first time, also, since then he followed the prayers that Purchas droned out with an earnest and heartfelt sincerity at which he felt himself vaguely astonished.

At length the mate reached the words in the service, "we therefore commit his body to the deep," whereupon the two men who supported the inner end of the grating tilted it high, and the heavily weighted body, sliding out from beneath the outspread ensign, plunged with a sullen splash into its lonely grave. The remainder of the service was quickly gone through; and as the little party of mourners rose from their knees with the pronouncement of the last "Amen," the sun's disc vanished in a blaze of indescribable glory beneath the horizon, while at the same moment "four bells" pealed out along the brig's deck.

"Go for'ard, men," ordered Purchas, replacing his cap upon his head; "and see that that gratin' is stowed away again in its proper place. Haul down that ensign, one of you. And whose trick at the wheel is it?"

For the next three or four days nothing worthy of mention occurred on board the brig, save that the breeze which had sprung up on the morning of the day of Potter's death held good, and ran them fairly into the Trades. Our next vision of the *Mermaid*, therefore, shows her bruising along under all plain sail, including fore and main royals, together with port topgallant and topmast studding-sails on the main, and topmast and lower studding-sails on the foremast; the rigging having in the interim been properly set up, so that the brig could carry that amount of canvas without jeopardy to her spars.

The death and burial of the late skipper had permitted of a certain modification of arrangements aft. Thus, while Miss Trevor was, by Purchas's natural courtesy, allowed to retain possession of the late Potter's cabin, as the best and most commodious berth in the brig, Purchas had transferred the chronometer, charts and other paraphernalia appertaining to the navigation of the brig, to his own cabin, which he once more occupied; Leslie moving from the longboat into the steward's cabin, now vacated by Purchas. With the permission of the latter, also, Leslie had appropriated to his own use Potter's somewhat extensive kit—the two men being much of a size, although Potter had been of considerably stouter build. This, of course, conduced greatly to Leslie's comfort, as it afforded him, among other advantages, a much-needed change of linen; although the ex-lieutenant did not assume possession of these articles without certain inward qualms that, under the circumstances, were not to be wondered at.

Then it presently transpired that Potter—who had possessed a shrewd eye for a money-making speculation—had, before leaving London, invested a considerable sum in articles of various kinds that he knew, from experience, he would be able to dispose of at a huge profit, upon his arrival at Valparaiso; and among these there happened to be a capacious case of ladies' clothing. This case Leslie also commandeered, giving to Purchas, in exchange, a signed agreement to pay to Potter's heirs, executors, or assigns— if such could be found upon their return to England—the full value of the goods, as well as of the clothing that Leslie had appropriated to his own use. This case of clothing, together with the other goods included in the speculation, were, as Purchas happened to know, stowed in the after hold, on top of the cargo; Leslie therefore lost no time in having the hatches lifted and the case hoisted on deck, and opened. Then he summoned Miss Trevor upon the scene, and invited her to overhaul the case and help herself freely to the whole or such part of the contents as she might find of service to her; with the result that the lady soon found herself in possession of an ample if somewhat showy wardrobe, to her infinite comfort and contentment.

During the whole of this time, it may be remarked, not a single sail of any description had been sighted; although Leslie, keenly anxious to meet the wishes of Miss Trevor in the matter of trans-shipment, had caused a bright look-out for ships to be maintained throughout both day and night.

A week, or maybe rather more than that, had elapsed since Potter's death when Leslie discovered what appeared to him a fresh cause for the apprehension of future trouble. It was Purchas who this time gave rise to the apprehension. The fellow had, from the moment when Leslie and Miss Trevor first came aboard the brig, been exceedingly civil and obliging to them both, cheerfully doing everything that lay in his power to make them comfortable. It is true that, perhaps in return for this, he had not hesitated to invoke Leslie's assistance in the matter of navigating the brig, and standing a watch—in fact, performing the duties of a mate; but this, under the circumstances, was perfectly natural, and quite in accord with Leslie's own inclination.

But later, within a few days of Potter's death, indeed, Leslie thought he detected in Purchas an inclination to shirk some of the more important duties of the ship, such as the navigation of her, for instance, and relegate them entirely to him. Even this, however, did not greatly worry Leslie. In any case, he always took the necessary observations for the determination of the brig's latitude and longitude, independently of Purchas; and whether the latter checked his observations or not was a matter of indifference to him, since he had the fullest confidence in the accuracy of his own work—a confidence, indeed, that Purchas appeared to fully share, since, in the event of any discrepancy between them, the new skipper always accepted Leslie's results in preference to his own. This, however, was not the chief cause of Leslie's disquietude, which arose from the fact that on more than one occasion, when it had been his "eight hours out," he had noticed, when calling Purchas at midnight, that the latter's breath had smelt strongly of rum, and that the man, upon taking the deck, had appeared to be strongly under the influence of drink. So markedly, indeed, was this the case upon a recent occasion that Leslie had taxed him with it.

"Look here, Mr Purchas," he had remarked, "you have been mixing your 'nightcap' too strong to-night, and are scarcely in a fit condition to have charge of the brig. Go below and sleep it off. I will take your watch for you, with pleasure."

"Oh, will you?" Purchas had retorted disagreeably. "Le' me tell you, shir, tha' you'll do nothin' o' short; I'm qui' cap'le lookin' after thi' ship or any other ship that ever was built; and I won' have you or any other man tryin' take my charac'er away. You go b'low an' leave me 'lone. D'ye hear?"

Seeing at once that the man was in much too quarrelsome a condition to be satisfactorily reasoned with, Leslie had at once left him and gone below; only to return, however, within the next ten minutes to find Purchas stretched at full length upon a hencoop, fast asleep and snoring stertorously.

On the morning following this incident Leslie, finding the skipper once more sober and, as usual under those circumstances, quite genial and friendly, tackled him again upon the subject.

"I want to talk to you very seriously, Purchas," he said, as the two walked the weather side of the deck together, smoking, after breakfast. "You are now the skipper of this brig, you know; and, as such, are accountable to nobody but your owners for your conduct. But this, as I have understood you to say, is your first command; and whether you retain it or not after the termination of this voyage must necessarily depend to a very great extent upon your behaviour *now*. Insobriety is, as I need hardly tell you, the one unpardonable sin in the eyes of a shipowner. No man will knowingly entrust his property to the care of another who, even only occasionally, permits himself to take too much liquor, because he can never know just when that overdose may be taken. He is always ready to believe that it may be imbibed at the most inopportune moment, and that the master of his ship may be under its influence at the precise instant when the safety of the ship, crew, and cargo demand his utmost vigilance and most intelligent resource. And although you may imagine that what you do out here in mid-ocean cannot possibly reach the ears of your owner, you must not forget that sailors have a keen eye for what goes on aft; a skipper cannot get drunk without the fact reaching the sharp ears of those in the forecastle. It is one of the easiest things in the world for an officer to acquire, among his crew, a reputation for insobriety; and, once they get ashore, you may trust them to talk about it freely, very often adding embellishments of their own. The reputation of a ship-master is in the hands of his crew; and if he is foolish enough to afford them the opportunity, they may be depended upon to ruin it for him. Besides, I want you to remember your responsibilities as master of this brig. I will undertake to look after her and see that nothing goes wrong during the time that I have charge of the deck; but I cannot *always* be on deck, you know; and if you should happen to be intoxicated and incapable—as you were last night—while I am below, what would be the result of a sudden squall, for instance? Or how is the craft to be kept clear of possible collision on a dark and dirty night? There are a thousand sudden emergencies constantly threatening the seaman, any one of which may arise at a moment's notice."

"Yes, yes," answered Purchas, somewhat impatiently; "I know all about that. I've heard it all a thousand times before; heard it until I'm sick of it. But there's no call to make a fuss about it; I own up that I was just a little bit 'sprung' last night; but what of it? The night was fine and clear, the 'glass' was steady, and there wasn't nothin' anywheres within sight of us; so where was the danger?"

"There was none, as it fortunately happened," admitted Leslie. "But who is to know what will occur within the limits of a four-hours' watch? Suppose, for instance, that I had not chanced to notice your condition, and had turned in; and that while you were lying unconscious upon that hencoop a sudden squall had struck the brig, what would have happened? Why, the craft might have been dismasted, or even, perhaps, capsized! And where should we all have been, in that case?"

"Well, ye see, we warn't dismasted, let alone capsized, so there's no harm done," answered Purchas, testily. "All the same," he added, in more moderate tones, "I'm willin' to admit that there's a good deal of reason in your argufication, so I'll go slow in future; I don't say that I won't take a glass or so of grog of an evenin' if I feels to want it; but I'll take care not to swaller enough of it to capsize me again."

"You would do far better to swear off it altogether," asserted Leslie. "You would be glad, afterwards, that you had done so. You are an excellent seaman; and I shall be more than glad to help you to perfect yourself in navigation, if you will allow me, so that there should be nothing to stand in the way of your getting your master's certificate upon your return to England. And with that, and a reputation for reliability such as you can acquire during this voyage, there should be nothing to prevent your continuing in the command of this brig, or even of your getting something very much better. And now, I think, it is about time for us to get our sights for the longitude."

Chapter Five
A Tragedy; and a Narrow Escape

For the next two or three days Purchas faithfully adhered to his promise to refrain from taking enough liquor to "capsize" him; when, again at midnight, on going below to call him, Leslie found the fellow so completely intoxicated that it was impossible to arouse him; and he had perforce to remain on deck the whole night through. And when at length, at the expiration of the morning watch, he again went below, hoping to find that the man had at all events so far slept off the effects of his over-night debauch as to be capable of coming on deck and sobering himself by taking a douche under the head pump, he discovered, to his intense disgust, that this glib maker of promises had somehow obtained a further supply of rum during the night, and was at that moment in a more helpless state than ever! The brig was, however, by this time within a day's sail of the equator, where Leslie felt tolerably certain that they would fall in with one or more homeward-bound ships, and so be able to transfer Miss Trevor to safer and more eligible quarters; so he did not allow the incident to worry him greatly. He remained on deck long enough to secure sights for his longitude; and then, turning over the care of the brig to the carpenter—a very steady and trustworthy man—he went below and turned in, giving orders that he was to be called at seven bells; adding, in explanation of Purchas's non-appearance, that he was not very well.

It seemed that he had been asleep but a few minutes when the carpenter, in pursuance of his instructions, knocked at his cabin door, with the information that seven bells had gone. He accordingly rose, plunged his head into a basin of cold water, and within ten minutes was once more on deck, with Potter's sextant in his hand, ready to take the sun's meridian altitude, from which to deduce the latitude.

This done, his calculations completed, and the brig's position at noon pricked off on the chart, he once more hied him to Purchas's cabin, only to find the door locked from within. For the moment he felt very strongly inclined to burst his way into the cabin, and haul the man up on deck, drunk or sober; but upon further reflection he realised that by the adoption of such a course he would be irretrievably "giving the man away" to his crew—which it was eminently undesirable to do—so, muttering to himself, "Let the brute drink himself out; he will perhaps be better afterwards!" he entered the main cabin and seated himself at the table, upon which the noonday meal was already spread.

Miss Trevor and he were of course the only persons present, with the exception of the steward, who was waiting upon them; and presently the girl, noticing the absence of Purchas, inquired whether he was ill.

"He is not very well, I am sorry to say," answered Leslie, briefly; and then he turned the conversation into another channel.

But later on, when the steward had left the cabin, he said to Miss Trevor—

"You were just now inquiring about Purchas; and I told you that he was not very well. That reply, I must now explain to you, was not strictly accurate, but I gave it because the steward was present, and I did not wish to state the actual facts in his presence; for, had I done so, it is certain that he would have carried the news forward to the men, which would have been eminently undesirable. The truth, however, is that Purchas has lately given way to drink, and is at this moment locked in his cabin, helplessly intoxicated. It is a thousand pities; for the man has now an excellent opportunity of confirming himself in the command of this brig, and so establishing himself in the position of ship-master, if he will but make use of it. That, however, is his affair; not ours. My reason for telling you this is, that if the present breeze holds we shall reach the equator by this time to-morrow, at a point where we may hope to fall in with homeward-bound ships; indeed we may meet with them at any moment now; I would therefore advise you to pack up your belongings forthwith, in order that you may be ready to be transferred to the first suitable craft that comes along."

"Thank you very much for telling me this," answered the girl. "I shall be more than glad, for many reasons, to once more find myself 'homeward-bound,' as I believe you sailors term it. And although, thanks to your never-ceasing kindness and consideration, I have been quite comfortable and happy on board this vessel, it will be a relief to me to leave her, for the memory of that terrible man, Potter, oppresses me. I should think that you, too, will be very glad to get away from a ship that must be fraught, for you, with such unpleasant memories."

"I shall, indeed," assented Leslie. "But my deliverance, as I suppose you know, must come later. The misfortune by which I became, most unwillingly, the primary cause of Potter's death, renders it imperative that I should go on to Valparaiso with this brig, there to surrender myself to the authorities and answer for my action. I do not suppose," he continued, in answer to the expression of consternation that suddenly leapt into her eyes, "that they will be very hard upon me; Purchas and the whole of the crew can of course testify that I acted under extreme provocation and in self-defence; so that probably, if I have to stand a trial at all, the verdict will be one of 'misadventure.'"

"Oh, but this is dreadful!" ejaculated the girl.

She pulled herself up suddenly, and appeared to consider the situation for some moments; then she said very quietly—

"So, if I am to go home, it appears that I shall have to go alone?"

"I fear so," answered Leslie. "But," he continued reassuringly, "you must not run away with the idea that I intend to pack you off aboard the first ship that happens to come along, suitable or otherwise; I reckon upon falling in with several ships within the next thirty-six hours, we shall therefore be able to pick and choose; and you may rest assured that I will not put you aboard a vessel until I have thoroughly satisfied myself that you will be quite comfortable and happy in her. And although we have been speaking only of homeward-bound ships, thus far, we must not forget that, if we should happen to run into a calm on the Line, it is quite on the cards that we may encounter something *outward-bound*, either to the Cape, India, or Australia, into which to trans-ship you; in which case you will be able to continue your original journey with practically no loss of time."

"Yes," answered Miss Trevor, slowly. "That would be an advantage, certainly. On the whole, Mr Leslie, I think I should greatly prefer an outward-bound to a homeward-bound ship, if you please."

"All right," laughed Leslie; "we will see what can be done. And now I must go on deck to keep a lookout for a suitable craft."

He paused at Purchas's cabin, on his way on deck, and tried the door, but it was still locked from the inside; so he ascended the companion ladder and went out on deck. It was a most gloriously brilliant and sparkling afternoon; the sky an intense blue, save where it was flecked here and there with woolly-looking patches of trade cloud sailing solemnly up out of the east; the sea, too, was as brilliantly blue as the sky, but of a deeper tint; there was not very much swell on, although the breeze was blowing fresh from the eastward; and the brig, with her weather-braces well checked, was staggering along under every rag of canvas that would draw. Leslie glanced keenly ahead and then all round the crystalline clear horizon in search of a sail; but there was nothing in sight save a school of porpoises that were gambolling alongside, racing the brig and chasing each other athwart her fore-foot, each fish apparently rivalling all the rest in an endeavour to see which could shave the brig's stem most closely without being touched by it.

Thinking that the sight might amuse Miss Trevor, he ran quickly down the companion ladder and entered the main cabin, with the object of inviting her to come on deck and witness it. He entered the cabin just in time to catch sight of her effecting a distinctly hasty retreat into her own private berth; and although it was only, a momentary glimpse that he caught of her ere she slammed the door behind her, he could almost have sworn that she had her pocket-handkerchief to her eyes, as though she were, or had been, crying. Vaguely wondering what was the trouble, he paused uncertainly for a few seconds; then, in pursuance of his original intention, he knocked at her door, and shouted—

"Miss Trevor, there is a school of porpoises at play alongside, if you would care to come on deck and watch them. It is a pretty sight, and, I think, would amuse you."

There was no reply for a moment or two. Then, in a strangely muffled tone of voice, the girl answered—

"Thank you, Mr Leslie. I will be up in a few minutes."

It was fully ten minutes after this that the girl, clad entirely in white, made her appearance on deck; and as Leslie stole a covert glance at her face, and noted its absolute composure, he told himself that he had been mistaken; she had certainly *not* been crying; and he wondered what in the world it was that could have put so ridiculous an idea into his head. She appeared to be frankly and unfeignedly interested in the gambols of the porpoises, laughing heartily from time to time; and altogether seemed so absolutely happy and free from care that Leslie, while he could have kicked himself for being such a fool, felt quite reassured.

At sunset, that night, the breeze still held as fresh as ever; but no sail had yet been sighted, either meeting or overtaking the brig; a circumstance that somewhat disconcerted Leslie, for he was aiming to cross the equator in the longitude of 30 degrees West, at which point it is quite usual for a number of outward and homeward-bound ships to meet; and the *Mermaid* was now so near that point that, with the wind holding so fresh and steady as it did, he would not have been in the least surprised to fall in with quite a procession of craft proceeding in either direction. It was disappointing, this bareness of the horizon in every direction; for he felt that his companion and charge must be intensely anxious to exchange into something that would be taking her either back to her home, or out to her friends; and he was keenly desirous to relieve her anxiety at the earliest possible moment. And yet, at the back of his mind, behind his earnestness of desire, he was ashamed to discover that there existed a certain feeling of satisfaction that the moment for parting with the girl was still deferred. He had found his connection with her very pleasant—the strong and virile man always *does* find it pleasant to have something or somebody to protect and be dependent upon him—she was the only intellectual companion now left to him; and with her would go the only individual with whom he could exchange an idea worth uttering. Yes, he admitted to himself, he would miss her when she was gone, miss her badly; ay, and more than badly. Well, it couldn't be helped; she must go, of course; and this curious feeling of depression that was worrying him at the thought was but an additional imperative reason for her departure with the least possible delay. If by any chance her departure were to be delayed much longer it might be that by then he would feel that he did not want to part with her at all! He stamped his foot on the deck in impatient anger at the novel and unpleasant turn that his thoughts were taking; and sprang into the fore-rigging on his way to the royal-yard, to take a last look round ere darkness fell. He soon reached his destination, and swept the whole circle of the horizon with an eager intensity of gaze. And so clear and transparent was the air that had there been anything in the nature of a sail within thirty miles he could have seen it. The horizon, however, was as bare as it had been from the deck; and he presently descended from his post of observation with an obstinate feeling of relief that made him intensely angry with himself.

Three times, that evening, during the dog-watches, did Leslie try the door of Purchas's cabin, in an endeavour to gain access to the man and ascertain his condition. On the first two occasions he failed, the door remaining locked against him; but when for the third time he found the door still fastened, he lost patience and, setting his shoulder to the obstruction, burst it open; having arrived at the conclusion that the fellow ought not to be left to himself any longer.

He found the cabin, as he had quite expected, reeking with the fumes of rum, and Purchas still insensible in his bunk. It had been a matter of astonishment to him how the man had contrived to keep himself supplied with drink; for although Leslie, Miss Trevor, and the steward were constantly in and out of the main cabin—from which alone access was to be gained to the lazarette, wherein the ship's stores and the spirits were stowed—no one had seen him moving about. Stifling therefore the feeling of loathing and nausea that possessed him, he proceeded to institute a search of the cabin with the object of ascertaining whether the drunkard had secreted a supply therein. The search resulted in the speedy discovery of twelve bottles, seven of them empty, an eighth about a quarter full, and four still unbroached. The whole of these he at once got rid of by opening the port in the side of the cabin, and launching them through it into the sea. Then, leaving the port wide-open to sweeten the air somewhat, and assist in the revivification of the man in the bunk, he retired from the cabin, closing the door behind him, and went on deck.

The prolonged incapacity of the new skipper rendered it necessary for Leslie to make some arrangement whereby he could secure a proper amount of rest; and therefore, the carpenter being a steady and fairly reliable man, he arranged with him that the latter should take charge of the starboard watch during Purchas's "indisposition." It was Leslie's eight hours in, that night, and consequently he was free to retire to his cabin between the end of the second dog-watch and midnight; but the weather was now so hot that the comparative coolness of the night air on deck proved irresistibly attractive to Miss Trevor, who, "sleeping in" all night, was naturally indisposed to go to bed at so early an hour as eight o'clock in the evening; and as she evinced a disposition to keep the deck for an hour or two, Leslie also remained on deck to bear her company.

For some time the two walked the weather side of the brig's flush deck, between the stern grating and the mainmast, conversing more or less intermittently upon various topics, until at length Leslie's attention was attracted to the man at the wheel, who, he noticed, was continually glancing over his shoulder with a perturbed air at the water astern, instead of keeping his eyes upon the compass card. It seemed also to Leslie that the man was trying to attract his attention, although he was too bashful, in Miss Trevor's presence, to speak.

So when the pair next reached the stern grating in the course of their promenade, Leslie paused, and said—

"What is the matter, Tom? You seem to be bestowing quite an unusual amount of attention on the wake of the ship; is there anything remarkable to be seen there?"

The man straightened himself up with the satisfied air of one who, after much striving, has at length achieved success.

"Well, I don't exactly know, sir, as you would call it *remarkable*" he answered; "but there's something visible over the starn as perhaps the lady might like to see."

"Oh!" answered Leslie. "Then let us have a look at it."

And offering his hand to Miss Trevor, he assisted her to mount the grating and led her to the taffrail, over which they both leaned, gazing down into the black profundity beneath them.

The brig was travelling at the rate of about six knots; at which speed she was wont to create a considerable amount of disturbance in the element through which she ploughed her passage; the water was brilliantly phosphorescent, and as a result of this the wake of the brig was on this occasion a mass of sea-fire, the foam that she churned up on either side of her glowing and sparkling with luminous clouds interspersed with thousands of tiny stars that waxed and waned with every plunge of the vessel. The water was almost as transparent as air itself, and by leaning out over the taffrail it was possible to see the rudder, the brig's "heel," and a considerable amount of her "run," all aglow with bluish white light that streamed away far astern like a miniature Milky Way. It was a beautiful spectacle, and one at which an imaginative person might have gazed for a full hour or more without tiring. But Tom, the helmsman, was not an imaginative man, and the spectacle of a ship's wake glowing and scintillating with sea-stars was one that he had beheld so often that it had long ceased to appeal to him as anything at all uncommon. It was something else that had attracted his attention, and that he had thought might interest "the lady." For there, in the very thickest of the swirling mass of clouds and discs and circles and stars of sea-fire, at a depth of perhaps six feet below the surface, was to be seen, brilliantly illuminated by its own movement through the water, the glowing shape of an enormous shark, fully twenty feet in length, keeping pace with the brig as steadily as if he were being towed by her. The whole bulk of the monster was clearly, startlingly, distinct, much more so than would have been the case at daytime, for his body showed against the black water like a shape of white fire, while with every sweep of his powerful tail he scattered a trail of glowing sparks behind him that constituted of itself quite a respectable wake.

"Oh, what a dreadful creature!" exclaimed Miss Trevor, shrinking back in dismay at the sight. "It is like a nightmare! That must surely be a shark; is it not? It is the first shark I have ever seen, Mr Leslie; and I am certain that I never wish to see another. I had no idea that sharks were such monstrous creatures; I always thought that they were about the same size as the porpoises that we were looking at this afternoon."

"Yes," laughed Leslie, "very possibly. This, however, is rather an exceptionally fine fellow, although I have seen even bigger specimens than he. Do not look at him too long," he continued, "or possibly you may dream of him, in which case he would be likely to prove a nightmare to you indeed."

"He've been followin' of us for the last hour, sir," remarked the helmsman. "And they *do* say that when a shark hangs on to a ship like that, somebody's goin' to die aboard of her."

"Yes," answered Leslie, carelessly, "I have heard that story myself; but I don't believe it, for I have been in ships that have been followed for days on end by sharks, without anything coming of it—except that we have generally managed to catch the sharks themselves at last. No; this fellow is following us because he happens to be hungry, and hopes that the cook will heave overboard enough scraps to take the sharp edge off his appetite. But the dew is falling very heavily, Miss Trevor; had not you better fetch up a wrap?"

"No, thanks," answered the girl, as she moved away and extended her hand for him to help her down off the grating on to the deck; "it is growing late, so I will bid you good night and go to my cabin."

"Sorry to hear that Mr Purchas is bad, sir," observed Tom, tentatively, when Miss Trevor had vanished down the companion ladder. "Hope it ain't nothin' serious?"

"Oh dear, no," answered Leslie, perceiving with annoyance that the man was connecting the presence of the shark under the counter with Purchas's invisibility; "merely a rather sharp bilious attack, which is now over, I am glad to say. He will probably be on deck again to-morrow."

Then, as the carpenter—who had been keeping out of the way during Miss Trevor's presence on deck—came aft, Leslie gave over the charge of the brig to him, and turned in.

The remainder of the first watch, and the whole of the middle watch, passed without incident save that, when Leslie went on deck at midnight, he found that the wind had softened down somewhat—as was indeed to be expected, with the brig drawing so near to the equator—the vessel's speed having dropped to about four knots. But the weather held superbly fine, and the barometer remained absolutely steady; Leslie therefore retired to his bunk at the end of the middle watch with a perfectly easy mind, and the fixed determination to have Purchas on deck and under the head pump at seven bells, when he himself would be called.

It was still quite dark when he was startled out of a profound sleep by a sudden loud outcry on deck, followed by a rushing and scuffling of feet overhead accompanied by the flapping of canvas, as though the brig had been suddenly luffed into the wind.

Leslie was well acquainted with the vagaries of equatorial weather, and therefore, under the apprehension that a squall was threatening, he sprang from his berth and dashed up on deck without waiting to exchange his pyjamas for other clothing. As he emerged from the companion he came into violent contact with some one who was evidently about to make a hasty descent of the ladder; and when the pair had recovered from the shock, he discovered that he had collided with the carpenter, who betrayed every symptom of the most violent agitation; while the entire crew, apparently, shouting to each other excitedly, were grouped upon the stern grating. The brig had been luffed into the wind, and everything, including studding-sails, was flat aback. It was well for the craft, and all concerned, that the wind had fallen light, or there would have been mischief up aloft, and plenty of wreckage among the lighter spars.

"What in the world is the matter, Chips?" demanded Leslie testily, as with a single glance he took in the full condition of affairs.

"Oh, Mr Leslie, sir, something awful has just happened!" exclaimed the man addressed, stammering with agitation and excitement. "I were standin' as it might be just there," pointing to a spot on the deck about midway between the skylight and the mainmast, "fillin' my pipe, when out of the corner of my heye I seen somebody step out of the companion on deck; and fust of all I thought 'twas you; but, lookin' again, I see as it was the skipper—not Cap'n Potter, you'll understand, sir, he bein' dead and buried; but Cap'n Purchas. I were just goin' up to him to say how glad I were to see 'im about again, when he steps over to the binnacle, takes a peep into the compass-bowl, and then, afore a man could say 'Jack Robinson,' up he jumps on to the starn gratin', from there to the taffrail—an' overboard! Scotty, there, who was at the wheel, owns that he more'n half guessed, from the queer look in the skipper's heyes, that somethin' was wrong, and made a grab at 'im as 'e passed; but Mr Purchas were miles too quick for 'im, and Scotty on'y reached the taffrail in time to see the pore man strike the water. And the next second that devil of a shark that have been followin' of us had 'im!"

Leslie reeled as though he had been struck a heavy blow. Here was another tragedy; the second that had happened within the short space of time that had elapsed since he had joined this unlucky brig. And even as he had blamed himself for being in some sort responsible for the first, so now he reproached himself as being in a measure responsible for this. He felt that he had been remiss. In his anxiety to shield the unhappy man from the observation and unfavourable comment of the crew, he had carefully concealed from everybody the true cause of Purchas's retirement, leaving the man alone to recover from his drunken bout instead of telling off somebody to watch him. Had he done this, he reflected in self-reproach, this dreadful thing would not have happened. The need for concealment was now past, however; so, rallying his faculties, he called all hands to group themselves round him, as he had something to say to them.

"My lads," he began, "I believe that you all profoundly regret the awful thing that has just happened; for Mr Purchas was a most kind and considerate officer to every one of you. But none of you can regret his terrible end so much as I do; for I feel that I am to some extent to blame for it. A certain wise man has said, 'Of the dead speak nothing but good;' and it is well to carry out this precept, so far as is possible. There are occasions, however, when the truth—the whole truth—must be told, even though it reflect discredit upon those who are gone; and this is one of them. I am sorry to be obliged to tell you that what really ailed Mr Purchas was—drunkenness! Very little more than a week had elapsed after Captain Potter's death when I discovered in Mr Purchas a tendency to take rather too much rum. I spoke to him about it, with the result that he promised to be more moderate in his potations. But he did not keep his promise, and upon one occasion, at least, he was so thoroughly intoxicated that he slept through his entire watch, stretched out upon a hencoop."

"Ay, ay, sir; that's gospel truth. I remember it perfectly," murmured two or three of the men, interrupting.

"Of course," assented Leslie, "you could not have avoided noticing it. It was after that occurrence that I remonstrated with him; and for a few days thereafter he was better. Then he began again, finally giving way altogether, with the melancholy result that you have all witnessed. I knew how injurious to his interests it would be, and how seriously it would weaken discipline if you men should once come to understand that your skipper was a drunkard; so I let it be understood among you that Mr Purchas was confined to his cabin through a slight illness; while, as a matter of fact, he was all the time lying there in a drunken stupor.

"*Now*, when it is too late, I feel that I committed an error of judgment in attempting to conceal from you all the actual facts. Instead of being so keenly anxious to shield him that I could think of nothing else, I ought to have anticipated the possibility that upon his return to consciousness he might be tempted to do something foolish; and, anticipating this, I ought to have told off a man from each watch to sit with and keep an eye upon him."

"Ay," observed the carpenter, "it might ha' been a good thing to ha' done that, certingly. But you haven't got nothin' to reproach yourself with, sir; you done what you did with a good and kind intention; and you wasn't to know that the fust thing he'd do when he come back to his senses 'd be to up and jump overboard. Oh no, sir, you ain't to blame in noways for what's happened. What do *you* say, bullies?"

"No, no; in course the gen'leman ain't to blame; nobody what's seen how the land lay—like we have—and how Mr Leslie have been a-doin' all he could to help the skipper, could ever say as he's any way to blame. Not he!" answered one and another of the men, each of them in one way or another endorsing the carpenter's verdict.

"Thank you, men," returned Leslie; "it is a great relief to me to feel that you think as you do in this matter. Now, that being disposed of, there is a further point to be considered; and it is this. The shocking fate of Mr Purchas leaves us with no navigator on board save myself. I have no great desire to proceed in this brig all the way to Valparaiso; but, nevertheless, there are reasons that, to me, seem to make it desirable that I should do so. I may tell you that we are now very near the Line; so near, indeed, that we may fall in with other craft, aiming to cross it at the same point as ourselves, at any moment. Now if we should fall in with a ship, would you wish me to communicate with her and ask her captain to place a navigating officer on board this brig, to take her to Valparaiso; or would you prefer that I should take charge—with Chips, here, as mate—and navigate you to Valparaiso myself?"

"Speakin' for myself," answered the carpenter, promptly, "I don't want nobody better'n what you are, Mr Leslie, in command of this here hooker. We knows you, sir; and we've seen what you can do—we've took your measure, sir—if you'll forgive the liberty of my plain speakin'—and we're all agreed as you're a prime seaman—one o' the best as I've ever sailed under—and I'd a precious sight sooner see you in command than what I would a stranger. And, if I ain't mistook, that's the feelin' with all hands of us. Am I right, mates, or ain't I?"

"Right you are, Chips; no stranger for me."

"Mr Leslie's the skipper for us; we don't want nobody else." Thus, and in similar terms, the entire crew expressed their perfect agreement with the view enunciated by the carpenter; and there and then the matter was settled.

It was with a very considerable amount of trepidation that, next morning, Leslie undertook the task of communicating to Miss Trevor the news of Purchas's death—taking care to suppress the full horror of the tragedy by simply stating that the unfortunate fellow had committed suicide by jumping overboard, omitting all mention of the shark. But although the girl was naturally much shocked at the occurrence of a second death on board, following so quickly upon that of Potter, this was the full extent of her emotion; Purchas was not at all the sort of man to appeal to her or to arouse in her any sort of interest or feeling beyond that of disgust at his weakness in surrendering himself to the seduction of so degrading a vice as that of drink; and she received the information quite calmly, much to her companion's relief.

Meanwhile, and quite contrary to expectation, the breeze again freshened an hour or so before sunrise, with the result that when Leslie took his observation at noon he found that the brig was within a mile of crossing the equator. And, what was a much more remarkable circumstance, the horizon was still absolutely bare, not a single sail of any description being in sight, even from the main royal-yard!

Upon ascertaining this last disconcerting fact, Leslie turned to Miss Trevor, who was on deck, and said—

"Fate appears to have a grudge against you, and to be determined that you shall not yet leave us. I had confidently reckoned upon falling in with something hereabout to which I could transfer you; but the continuance of this breeze—which most sailors would regard as a stroke of marvellous good fortune—has enabled everything bound south to slip across the Line without suffering the exasperating experience of a more or less prolonged period of calm; while, as your ill-luck will have it, there happens to be nothing northward-bound on the spot just when we are most anxious to meet it. Furthermore, every mile that we now sail will lessen your chance of effecting a trans-shipment, because our course will be ever diverging from that of northward-bound shipping. Of course, now that I am in command, I can continue to steer for a day or two longer in such a direction as may enable us, with luck, still to fall in with a homeward-bounder, but—"

"Is my presence on the ship then, so *very* embarrassing to you, Mr Leslie?" she interrupted with the ghost of a smile. "It would certainly appear so; for the burden of your conversation, ever since we came on board, has been my trans-shipment!"

"Embarrassing!" ejaculated Leslie, in extreme surprise. "Most certainly not; on the contrary—" he interrupted himself. "That is not the point at all," he continued. "I have assumed—very naturally, I think—that you are anxious either to return home and make a fresh start, or else to continue your outward journey, according as circumstances may determine; and I, on my part, have been most anxious to meet what I conceived to be your wishes. But, as to your presence aboard the brig being an *embarrassment* to me, I assure you that the longer you are compelled to remain here, the better I shall be pleased."

"Thank you," answered the girl; "I suppose I must accept that admission as a compliment. Well, Mr Leslie, of course you are quite right in assuming that, if a favourable opportunity should offer, I would gladly avail myself of it. But my greatest anxiety is to allay that of my friends; which, I imagine, they will not begin to experience until some little time has elapsed after the date at which the *Golden Fleece* might reasonably be expected to reach Melbourne. And about that time I should think we ought to be at Valparaiso, ought we not? Very well. In that case, it will be easy for me to despatch from there a reassuring cable message to my Australian friends, following it up with a letter of explanation, and all will be well. Moreover, though you would perhaps never suspect it, I am of a decidedly roving and adventurous disposition, and I shall not at all object to visiting Valparaiso; you need, therefore, worry yourself no further upon that feature of the matter. But, of course, if you would rather not have me—"

"Pray say no more, I beg you," interrupted Leslie. "Your continued presence on board this brig can only be a source of the keenest pleasure and satisfaction to me; and if you can be content to remain, I shall be more than content that you do so."

And thus was settled a matter that was destined to exercise a most important influence upon the lives of these two people.

Singularly enough, within an hour of the occurrence of the above-recorded conversation, a sail was sighted ahead, steering north; which upon her nearer approach proved to be a South Sea whaler, homeward-bound. She was steering a course that promised to bring the two craft close alongside each other; and at Leslie's suggestion Miss Trevor at once went below and hurriedly penned three letters—one to her people at home, one to her father in India, and one to her friends in Australia—briefly detailing the particulars of the loss of the *Golden Fleece* and what had subsequently befallen the writer, together with her intention to proceed to Valparaiso, if necessary; after which she would act according to circumstances. At the same time Leslie wrote to the owners of the *Golden Fleece* apprising them of the loss of the ship, and the fact that, as far as his knowledge went, there were but three survivors, namely, Miss Trevor, himself, and the seaman whom he had taken off the wreckage.

By the time that these letters were ready, the whaler was close at hand, upon which the brig's ensign was hoisted, and the signal made that she wished to communicate. Thereupon both craft were brought to the wind, and hove-to; the brig's quarter-boat was lowered, and the carpenter, with three hands, pulled alongside the whaler, taking the letters with him, with the request that the skipper would kindly post them at the first port arrived at. This the man readily agreed to do—such little courtesies among seamen being quite usual; and then, with mutual dips of their ensigns, the two craft proceeded upon their respective ways.

The *Mermaid* was singularly fortunate in the weather experienced by her on this occasion of crossing the Line, as it often happens that ships in these latitudes are detained—sometimes for weeks—by persistent calms, during the prevalence of which, by constantly box-hauling the yards and taking the utmost advantage of every little draught of air that comes along, they may succeed in gaining a mile or two in the course of every twenty-four hours; whereas she carried a breeze with her that ran her, without a pause, from the north-east trades, across the calm belt, right into the south-east trade winds, which happened just then to be blowing fresh. She therefore made excellent progress to the southward after parting from the friendly whaler.

It was about a week later that the brig, thrashing along to the southward, close-hauled, and with her fore topgallantsail and main royal stowed, experienced a thrillingly narrow escape from destruction.

It was just two bells in the first watch, that is to say nine o'clock p.m. The night was fine, with bright starlight, and no moon, that luminary happening then to rise late. The wind was piping up strong and sending the trade clouds scurrying across the spangled sky at a great pace; and there was a fair amount of sea running, into which the *Mermaid* dug her bluff bows viciously, smothering her forecastle with spray and darkening the weather clew of her fore-course with it halfway up to the yard. Miss Trevor was on deck, taking the air, and graciously favouring Leslie with her company for an hour or two prior to turning in for the night. The pair were promenading the deck together, fore and aft, between the stern grating and the mainmast, the girl availing herself of the support of Leslie's arm to steady her upon the dancing deck.

Suddenly, as they were in the act of wheeling round abreast the main rigging, a flash of ruddy light illumined the tumbling surface of the sea, the deck they trod, the sails, and every detail of the brig's equipment; and glancing skyward, they beheld a meteor trailing a long tail of scintillating sparks behind it, high aloft over the brig's port quarter. With inconceivable rapidity the glowing object increased in size, its light meanwhile changing as rapidly from red to a dazzling white, until the light became almost as intense as that of the noonday sun. It was a magnificent spectacle, but one also full of unspeakable horror for those aboard the brig who stood gazing in speechless fascination at it; for it was evident that it was not only falling through the air at a speed far surpassing that of a cannon shot, *but was also coming straight for the brig*. A deep humming sound that, as it seemed, in the space of a single moment increased to an almost deafening scream, marked the speed of its flight through the air; and as Leslie grasped the fact that in another second that enormous glowing mass—weighing, as he conceived, some hundreds of tons—must infallibly strike the brig and smash her to atoms, he instinctively interposed his own body between his companion and the gigantic hurtling missile—as though such frail protection could have been of any service to her! Then, while it was still some two hundred yards from the brig—at which distance the heat of it fell upon their white upturned faces like the breath of a suddenly opened furnace—the dazzling white-hot mass burst with a deafening explosion into a thousand pieces, some of which flew hurtling over and about the brig, but happily without touching her; and the danger was over. It had come and was gone again in the brief space of some seven seconds.

"That is the narrowest shave I have ever had in my life," ejaculated Leslie, catching his breath. "And you, Miss Trevor, have had an experience such as falls to the lot of few people, I imagine—the experience of being threatened with destruction by a falling meteor, and surviving to tell the tale! I wonder how many others, beside this little ship's company, have ever beheld so appalling and magnificent a sight as we have this night witnessed?"

"Have you any suspicion, Mr Leslie, that this brig is especially marked out and chosen as the theatre for exceptionally thrilling experiences?" quaintly demanded the girl. "Because if there is a probability that such is the case, I really think I shall be obliged to reconsider my decision to proceed to Valparaiso in her, and ask you to land me at the nearest port. The tragic deaths of those two men, Potter and Purchas, were quite thrilling enough to upset the nerves of any ordinary girl; but when it comes to being bombarded by meteors, I would really very much rather be excused."

"Of course you would," assented Leslie, laughingly. "All the same," he continued, "although I must confess that I have never heard of such a thing happening, it might as probably have occurred in the heart of London itself as out here at sea. That meteors actually fall to the earth we know, for there are numerous records of such happenings; they have been seen to fall, and have immediately afterwards been found partially buried in the ground and still hot from the friction of their flight through the air. Precisely where they will fall and strike is necessarily a matter of the merest chance; you are, therefore, so far as falling meteors are concerned, quite as safe here as anywhere else."

"Thank you," answered Miss Trevor, gravely, "it is reassuring to learn that, no matter where I am, I am liable to have a huge incandescent mass of meteoric stone hurtling at me out of space at any moment—for that is what your statement really amounts to, you know—isn't it? And now I will bid you good night and retire to my cabin, with the fixed resolution not to dream of falling meteors."

And therewith she gave him her hand for a moment, and then vanished down the companion-way.

Chapter Six
The Mermaid's Crew witness a Catastrophe

The *Mermaid* carried the south-east trade winds until she was well south of the parallel of Rio de Janeiro; and then she ran into the Doldrums; these being belts of calm, broken into at intervals by light baffling airs from various directions, with occasional violent squalls, or terrific thunderstorms, just to vary the monotony. These belts of exasperating weather are to be met with to the north of the north-east and the south of the south-east trade winds, interposed between the trade winds and those outer regions where a steady breeze of some sort may usually be reckoned upon.

And here the unfortunate crew of the brig encountered their full share—and a little over, some of them said—of the annoyances that usually accompany a passage across these belts; their first experience being a calm that lasted five days on end without a break, save for the occasional cat's-paw that came stealing from time to time over the glassy surface of the ocean, tinging it here and there with transient patches of delicate evanescent blue. And as these cat's-paws were all that they could rely upon to help them across the calm belt, it was necessary to maintain a constant watch for them, and to trim round the yards in such a manner as to make the most of them during their brief existence. This constant "box-hauling" of the yards was no trifling matter, accomplished as it had to be under the fierce rays of a blazing sun; and as it often happened that after laboriously trimming the yards and sheets to woo a wandering zephyr, it either expired before reaching the brig, or capriciously turned in another direction, passing her by without causing so much as a single flap of her canvas, it is not to be wondered at that the grumbling among all hands was both loud and deep.

At length, however, with the dawn of their sixth day of these vexatious experiences, there appeared to be a prospect of something more helpful than mere cat's-paws coming their way; for although the calm still continued, the morning broke with a dark, lowering, and threatening sky through which the rays of the sun were unable to pierce. This last was in itself a relief to everybody; for although the heat was still so oppressive that the slightest exertion threw one into a profuse perspiration, the stinging bite of the sun was no longer to be reckoned with. Furthermore, the eyes of those on board the brig, weary of continually gazing upon a bare horizon since the day upon which the friendly whaler had vanished from their view, were now gladdened by the sight of another craft, a small barque, that had drifted above the southern horizon during the night, and now lay some five miles away from them.

As the morning wore on towards noon the aspect of the sky steadily, though by insensible degrees, assumed a more threatening character, the huge masses of cloud that overspread the entire dome of the visible sky darkening in tint to such an extent that the scene became enwrapped in a murky kind of twilight. That wind, and plenty of it, was brewing, seemed evident from the fact that the clouds, although not drifting across the sky, were working visibly, writhing and twisting into the most extraordinary and fantastic shapes, as though influenced by some powerful impulse within themselves. One of the most frequent of these manifestations was the sudden darting forth of long sharp quivering tongues from the bodies of the blackest and most lowering of the clouds. With the appearance of the first of these Leslie knew what to expect, for he had beheld the same phenomenon more than once before, and quite understood what it portended. So he turned to Miss Trevor, who was on deck interestedly watching the subtle changes in the aspect of the sky, and said to her—

"Have you ever seen a waterspout, Miss Trevor? No? Then the chances are that you will see several before you are many hours older. Have you noticed those long, black, quivering tongues that dart out and in from the bodies of the darkest clouds? Well, those are the forerunners of waterspouts. See, there is one now. Do you mark how it seems to be striving to reach down to the surface of the sea? Ah! it has shrunk back again. But sooner or later, unless I am greatly mistaken, one of those tongues will reach down, and down, until it begins to suck up a column of water from the ocean; and there you will have a full-grown waterspout."

He gazed round the sky intently; then went to the skylight and as intently studied the barometer—or "glass" as sailors very commonly call the instrument. The mercury in it had fallen somewhat since he had last looked at it, though not sufficiently to cause alarm. Nevertheless, short-handed as the brig was—such small craft are usually sent to sea with at least two hands too few in the forecastle—he deemed it best to err on the right side, if err he must; so as it was by this time noon he ordered eight bells to be struck; and when the watch had come on deck he set them to work to clew up, haul down, and stow everything save the two topsails and the fore-topmast staysail; after which he ordered them to go to dinner.

Dinner in the cabin was served at the same time as in the forecastle on board the *Mermaid*; when Leslie and Miss Trevor, therefore, went below, the deck was left in charge of one man only, namely the carpenter. This, however, did not particularly matter, since the brig was well snugged down, while Chips might be trusted to keep a sharp look-out and give timely warning of the approach of anything of an alarming nature. Nothing, however, occurred; and Leslie and his companion were allowed to finish their meal undisturbed.

It was now Leslie's watch below, and in the ordinary course of events he would have retired to his cabin for the purpose of securing an hour or two of rest. But, with such a lowering and portentous sky as that overhead, he scarcely felt justified in entrusting the carpenter with the sole responsibility and care of the brig for so long a time; and he accordingly accompanied Miss Trevor on deck again.

They found the aspect of the sky more gloomy than ever; the clouds had formed themselves into heavier masses, and donned a deeper tinge of black than they had worn during the forenoon, and they were displaying a still greater degree of activity. Tongues of cloud were still darting out and back again, but they seemed no nearer to the formation of waterspouts than during the morning; and Leslie began to think that, perhaps, for once in a way he was going to prove a false prophet. Meanwhile, although during the whole of the morning and up to that moment, there had not been the faintest breath of wind, the two craft—the barque and the brig—had closed on each other to within a distance of some three miles, in the mysterious manner characteristic of craft becalmed within sight of each other. The barque, Leslie noticed, had followed his own example, and stripped to precisely the same canvas as that exposed by the brig.

The conditions were not conducive to animated conversation; and judging from Miss Trevor's brief replies to his remarks, that she would prefer to be left to her own thoughts for awhile, he presently left her leaning over the rail gazing at the barque—which the swing of the brig had now brought abeam—and seating himself upon the short bench alongside the companion, proceeded to fill a pipe. He was lighting it with an ordinary match, the unshielded flame of which burned as steadily as though he had been in a hermetically scaled room, when Miss Trevor suddenly cried out—

"Oh, look, Mr Leslie, look! Surely there is one of your waterspouts at last!"

Leslie sprang to her side and looked in the direction toward which she pointed, where, at a distance of some eight miles away, he beheld a fully formed waterspout moving very slowly and majestically in a southerly direction.

"Yes," he agreed, "that is a real, genuine waterspout, and no mistake. But it is too far off for you to see it to advantage. Did you actually behold it come into existence?"

"No," she answered; "I was watching the ship yonder, and only caught sight of it accidentally, after it had become fully formed. I should really like to witness the genesis of a waterspout."

"Then keep your eye on that cloud," he recommended her, pointing to an especially black and heavy one that hung a few degrees from the zenith and apparently about half a mile astern of the barque. "If I am not greatly mistaken it is about to develop a very fine specimen in a few minutes. Do you note that black tongue that is slowly stretching down from it? Although it lengthens and shortens you will observe that it does not shrink back altogether into the cloud; on the contrary, every time that it lengthens it becomes perceptibly longer than it was before; and observe how steadily its root—where it joins the cloud—is swelling. Now watch, see how it continually stretches down, further and further towards the water. Ah, and do you see that little mound forming in the sea immediately beneath it? See how the water heaps itself up, as though striving to reach up and join the down-stretching tongue of cloud. Ah! there the two unite and you have the perfect waterspout. And a very noble example of its kind it is. They will be having a splendid view of it from yonder barque, for, see, it is moving in her direction, and is about to pass close to her, rather too close to be altogether pleasant, unless my eyes deceive me!"

He sprang to the companion, and seizing the telescope, applied it to his eye.

"Why," he exclaimed excitedly, after a moment or two, with his eye still glued to the instrument, "what are they about aboard that barque? Why don't they fire at the thing and break it? It will be upon them in another moment, to a dead certainty, unless it changes its course! No—yes—yes, it is going to hit her! Heavens! look at that!"

And as he stood there gazing he saw that vast column of water sweep steadily down upon and over the barque, completely hiding her from view for a moment. Then it suddenly wavered in the middle and broke, collapsing with a tremendous splash and commotion of the sea, the sound of which came drifting down to the brig with startling distinctness some ten or twelve seconds later. And there, in the very midst of the tumbling circle of foaming whiteness left by the vanished waterspout there floated the barque, no longer trim and all ataunto as she had shown a few seconds before, but a dismasted, mangled wreck, with bulwarks gone, boats swept from her davits, all three masts snapped short off at the level of the deck and lying alongside with all attached, a mere tangled mass of wreckage still fast to the hull by the standing and running rigging.

Leslie stamped his foot upon the deck in sympathetic vexation at the ruin thus wrought in a moment, and again applied his eye to the telescope. The carpenter, whose watch on deck it now was, stood beside him, eagerly impatient to discuss with him the details of the catastrophe that they had just witnessed; while the watch, forward, leaned over the bows alternately muttering to each other their opinions, and glancing round in apprehension lest a waterspout should steal upon the brig unawares and treat them as the crew of the barque had been treated.

It was this same crew—or rather the entire absence of any sign of them—that was now disturbing Leslie.

"I can see nothing of them," he muttered impatiently, searching the wreck with the lenses of his telescope. "Here, Chips, take a squint, man," he continued, thrusting the instrument into the eager hands of the carpenter. "His decks are as bare as the back of my hand; there is not enough bulwark left standing to make a matchbox out of—nothing but the stumps of a few staunchions here and there. I can see the coamings of the hatches rising above the level of the planking; I can see the windlass; I can just make out the short stumps of the three masts, and I can find where the poop skylight stood; but hang me if I can see anything *living* aboard her!"

The carpenter in turn applied his eye to the telescope, and gazed through it long and anxiously.

"No, sir," he agreed at length, "what you says is perfekly true; there ain't nobody a-movin' about on that there vessel's decks. Question is, what's become of 'em? Be they down below? Or have they been swep' overboard? Stan's to reason that when they found theirselves onable to steer clear o' that there spout they'd go below and shut theirselves up as best they could, knowin' as nothin' livin' could surwive a waterspout tramplin' over 'em, as one may say; but where be them there chaps *now*? If they was all right they'd be out on deck by this time—wouldn't they?—lookin' roun' to see the extent o' the damage. Would the bustin' o' the thing kill 'em, d'ye think, sir—they bein' shut up below?"

"It is difficult to say," answered Leslie, meditatively. "It would depend almost entirely upon the strength of their defences. We can see for ourselves what it has done to the craft herself; it has made a clean sweep of everything on deck, and reduced her to the condition of a sheer hulk. Hang this weather! I don't like the look of it; it is not to be trusted! If it were only a shade or two less threatening I should feel strongly tempted to send away a boat to see just what has happened aboard there. There may be a number of poor fellows somewhere on that wreck just dying for want of assistance. But—"

He paused, and again glanced anxiously round the horizon, noting that the aspect of the sky was still as full of menace as ever.

"No," he continued, "I dare not do it; it would be risking too much. Ha! look there; here it comes! Fore and main-topsail halliards let go, and man your reef-tackles!" he shouted, as a long line of white foam appeared on the western horizon, slowly widening as it advanced.

The men sprang to their stations in an instant, galvanised into sudden and intense activity by the urgency that marked the tone of the commands, and the next instant there was a rattling and squeaking of blocks and parrells as the topsail-yards slid down the well-greased topmasts and settled with a thud upon the caps. Then, as the men began, with loud cries, to drag upon the reef-tackles, Leslie shouted—

"Call all hands, carpenter, to close-reef topsails. Look alive, lads; if you are smart you may have time yet to get those reef-points knotted before the squall strikes us. Well there with the reef-tackles. Belay! Now away aloft with you all, and hurry about it. You, too," he added to the man who had been standing by the useless wheel, "I will look after her."

And, so saying, he mounted the wheel-grating while the whilome helmsman slouched along the deck, and, climbing the rail, began to claw his deliberate way up the main rigging.

It took the hands about five minutes to pass the weather and lee earings, by which time the squall was close to the brig, its approach being heralded by a smart shower of rain that drove Miss Trevor to the shelter of the cabin. Then, while the men were still upon the yards, tying the reef-points, the wind came roaring and screaming down upon the brig—fortunately from dead astern—and, with a report like that of a gun, her topsails filled and, with the foam all boiling and hissing around her and her bluff bows buried deep in the brine, the *Mermaid* gathered way and was off, heading south-south-west; which was as nearly as possible her proper course.

The men aloft, meanwhile, although nearly jerked off the yards by the violence and suddenness with which that first puff struck them, stuck manfully to their work until they had tied their last reef-point, when they leisurely descended to the deck, squared the yards, took a pull upon and belayed the halliards, and then went below to change into dry clothes and oilskins—an example which Leslie quickly followed as soon as he was relieved at the wheel.

The squall lasted for a full half-hour—during which the dismasted barque vanished in the thickness astern—and then it settled down into a strong gale that swept them along before it to the southward for nearly thirty hours, moderating on the following day about sunset.

The following morning dawned brilliantly fine, with a light breeze out from the westward that was just sufficient to fan the brig along, under everything that would draw, at a bare four knots in the hour over a heavy westerly swell.

"Why, what is the meaning of this, Chips?" demanded Leslie, as he emerged from the companion-way, at seven bells, clad in bathing-drawers only, on his way forward to take his matutinal douche under the head pump; "is this swell the forerunner of a new gale, or has it been knocked up by something that we have just missed?"

"Well, sir," answered Chips, "I'm inclined to think as your last guess is the proper answer. We struck the beginnin's of this here swell about two bells this mornin', and the furder south we goes the heavier the run seems to be gettin'—as though we was gettin', as you may say, more into the track of a breeze that have passed along just about here. Besides, the glass have gone up a goodish bit durin' the night, and is still risin'!"

As the day progressed, appearances seemed to favour the correctness of the carpenter's theory, for the weather remained fine, with less wind rather than more; while, after a time, the swell appeared to be dropping somewhat. It happened, that after the men had taken their dinner that day, it being the carpenter's watch on deck from noon until four o'clock p.m., he—acting now in the capacity of boatswain—took it into his head to go aloft, with the object of examining the brig's upper spars and rigging, to see how they had fared in the late blow. Taking the foremast first, he ascended to the royal-yard, and from thence worked his way conscientiously down to the slings and truss of the lower yard. While on his way aloft, however, he was observed to pause suddenly in the fore-topmast crosstrees and gaze intently ahead, or rather in the direction of some two points on the lee bow. He remained thus for nearly five minutes, and then proceeded in the execution of his self-appointed duty, taking first the foremast and then the mainmast, and subjecting everything to a most scrupulous and thorough overhaul; with the result that everything was found satisfactory aloft, except that certain chafing gear looked as though it would be all the better for renewal.

Meanwhile the watch on deck, who were engaged upon sundry odd jobs which they were able to execute on the forecastle, had noted the action of the carpenter, and had come to the conclusion that his keen eyes had detected some distant object of more or less interest ahead; and they accordingly snatched a moment from their tasks, at fairly frequent intervals, to cast an inquiring glance over the bows. And their watchfulness was at length rewarded, just as seven bells was striking by the sight of something that showed for a moment as it and the brig were simultaneously hove up on the top of a swell. It bore about a point on the lee bow; was some two miles distant; and, so far as could be judged from the momentary glimpse they had obtained of it, appeared to be a floating mass of wreckage. Its appearance was to them ample justification for a general knocking-off of work to watch for its next appearance, one of the more energetic of them even exerting himself to the extent of ascending the fore-rigging high enough to get a view over the fore-yard. From this elevation an uninterrupted view of the object was to be obtained; and after long and careful scrutiny the man made it out to be the dismasted hull of a ship that was either water-logged, or upon the point of foundering.

"Deck ahoy!" he hailed, in approved fashion; "d'ye see that dismasted craft out there on the lee bow?"

"Ay, Jim," growled the carpenter, "I've seen her this hour an' more. Ye may come down an' get on wi' your work, my lad; you'll get a good enough view of her from the deck afore long."

At eight bells the carpenter went below and called Leslie, who had been lying down in his cabin, and at the same time reported the sighting of the wreck, which was by this time clearly visible from the deck, except when hidden from time to time by an intervening mound of swell. Knowing exactly where to look, Leslie caught sight of her immediately over the lee cathead, the instant that he stepped out on deck. She was by this time about half a mile distant, and clearly distinguishable as a craft of some six hundred tons register. She was submerged almost to her covering-board, and the whole of her bulwarks being gone between her topgallant forecastle and long full poop, the sea was making a clean breach right over her main deck, leaving little to be seen above water but a short length of her bows and about three times as much of her stern. Seen through the powerful lenses of the brig's telescope, Leslie made out that she had once been a full-rigged ship, and from the little that showed above water he judged her to be American-built. Her three masts were gone by the board, also her jib-booms, which were snapped close off by the bowsprit end. There was no sign of any floating wreckage alongside her, from which Leslie was led to surmise that her masts must have been cut away; a circumstance that, in its turn, pointed to the conclusion that she had been hove over on her beam-ends—probably by a sudden squall—and had refused to right again. But what had become of the crew? A glance at the craft's davits answered that question. There were no boats to be seen, while the davit-tackles were overhauled and the blocks in the water. This clearly pointed to the fact that the boats had been lowered; the presumption therefore was that the crew had abandoned the craft, fearing that she was about to founder. Nevertheless, the weather being fine, and the condition of the sea such that the craft could be boarded without much danger or difficulty, Leslie determined to give her an overhaul; and accordingly the brig, having by this time arrived almost directly to windward of the seeming derelict, he gave orders to back the main-yard, and instructed the carpenter to take the lee quarter-boat, with three hands, and go on board.

"Well, Miss Trevor," said Leslie, as the two stood together near the binnacle, watching the boat rising and falling like a cork over the long hummocks of swell as she swept rapidly down toward the wreck, "what think you of that for a sight? Is it not a very perfect picture of ruin and desolation? A few days ago—it can scarcely be more—that craft floated buoyantly and all ataunto, 'walking the waters like a thing of life,' her decks presenting an animated picture of busy activity, as her crew went hither and thither about their several tasks; while yonder poop, perchance, was gay with its company of passengers whiling away the time with books, games, or flirtations, according to their respective inclinations. And over all towered the three masts, lofty and symmetrical, with all their orderly intricacy of standing and running rigging, and their wide-spreading spaces of snow-white canvas; the whole combining to make up as stately and beautiful a picture as a sailor's eye need care to rest upon. And now look at her! There she lies, clean shorn of every vestige of those spacious 'white wings,' that imparted life and grace to her every movement; her decks tenantless and wave-swept; her hull full of water, and the relentless sea leaping at her with merciless persistency, as though eager to drag her down and overwhelm her! Can you conceive a more sorrowful picture?"

"I could, perhaps; although I grant you that it must be difficult to imagine any sight more grievous than that to a *sailor's* eye," answered the girl, gazing upon the scene with eyes wide and brilliant with interest and excitement. "How fearlessly that little boat seems to dance over those huge waves! She reminds me of one of those birds—Mother Carey's chickens, I think they are called—that one reads about as sporting fearlessly and joyously on the tops of the wave-crests during the height of the fiercest storms. Ah, now they have reached her," she continued, clasping her hands on her breast unconsciously as she watched the wild plunges of the boat compared with the deadly slow heave of the water-logged hulk. "Oh, Mr Leslie, how could you order those men to undertake so desperately dangerous a task? They will never do it; they cannot; their boat will be dashed to pieces against that great, ponderous wreck!"

"Never fear," responded Leslie, cheerfully; "Chips knows what he is about. See, there; how keenly he watched for his chance, and how neatly he took it when it came. He saw that rope's-end hanging over the stern long before he came to it, you may depend; and now inboard he goes, and there he stands on the poop without so much as a touch of the boat against the wreck. And there goes the boat round into the sheltered lee of the hull, where she will lie quite comfortably. And thither we will go, too, in readiness to pick them up when they shove off again."

The brig bore up and, wearing round, came-to again quite close under the lee of the wreck; so close, indeed, that it was quite easy to see with the unassisted eye everything that was going on aboard her, as well as to obtain a more comprehensive and detailed view of the havoc that had been wrought on her by the combined effects of wind and sea.

Their attention, however, was for the moment attracted rather to what was happening on board, than to the condition of the wreck herself; Miss Trevor being an especially interested spectator. After all, it was not very much: simply this, that under the lee of a hencoop on the poop, that had somehow resisted the onslaughts of the sea, Chips had discovered a very fine Newfoundland dog crouching—or perhaps lying exhausted; and he was now endeavouring to induce the animal to leave his shelter with the view of coaxing him into the boat. But for some reason or other the brute refused to move, responding to the carpenter's blandishments only by a feeble intermittent beating of his tail upon the deck.

"Oh," exclaimed Miss Trevor, when she grasped the state of affairs, "I *hope* he will be able to rescue the poor creature! He is a beautiful animal; and I am so fond of dogs."

"What is the matter with him, Chips? Won't he trust you?" hailed Leslie, sending his powerful voice to windward through the palms of his hands.

The carpenter stood up and faced about. "Seems to be pretty nigh starved, so far as I can make out, sir," he replied. "The poor beggar's just nothin' but skin and bone, and too weak to stand, by the looks of 'im."

"Then take him up in your arms and drop him overboard," suggested Leslie. "And you, there, in the boat, stand by to pick him up. He'll have sense enough to swim to you."

So said, so done; Miss Trevor watching the apparently somewhat heartless operation with tightly clasped hands. Leslie's conjecture as to the creature's sagacity was fully justified; for upon finding himself in the water the dog at once began to paddle feebly toward the boat, and in less time than it takes to tell of it a couple of men had seized him and dragged him into the boat, in the bottom of which he lay shivering and panting, and rolling his great trustful eyes from one to the other of his rescuers.

After this there was little more that the carpenter could do on board. It was impossible for him to pass along the main deck from the poop to the forecastle, for the sea was sweeping that part of the derelict so continuously and in such volume that, had he attempted any such thing, he must inevitably have been washed overboard. Nor could he, for the same reason, enter the poop cabin from the main deck; but he peered down into it through the opening in the deck that had once formed the skylight; and presently he swung himself down into it and disappeared from view. Meanwhile the brig, being buoyant, was settling rapidly to leeward, and soon drifted out of hailing distance. In about ten minutes from the time of his disappearance the carpenter was seen to climb up out of the cabin on to the deck and beckon to the men in the boat, who at once paddled cautiously up alongside; when, watching the roll of the hull and the heave of the boat alongside, Chips seized a favourable opportunity and lightly sprang into the smaller craft. The men in her at once shoved off and, pulling her bows round, gave way for the brig, the carpenter carefully watching the run of the sea as he sat in the stern-sheets and steered.

"Here they come!" exclaimed Leslie, watching them. "Lay aft here, men—all hands of you—and stand by to sway away as soon as they have hooked on. See that those tackles are well overhauled—give them plenty of scope to come and go upon!"

Coming down before wind and sea, the boat took but a few minutes to traverse the distance between the derelict and the brig; and presently, slipping close past under the stern of the latter, she rounded-to in the "smooth" of the brig's lee, and shot up alongside. As she did so, the man who pulled "bow," and Chips, respectively made a lightning-like dash for the bow and stern tackles, which they simultaneously got hold of and hooked into the ring-bolts, flinging up their arms as a signal to those on board to haul taut. Meanwhile the remaining two hands in the boat laid in their oars and, rising to their feet, cleverly sprang into the main chains as the brig gave a heavy lee-roll.

"Haul taut fore and aft, my hearties," shouted Leslie, balancing himself on the lee rail and grasping a backstay, as he anxiously watched the dancing boat. "Out you come, Chips, and you also, Tom. Capital! Now, hoist away fore and aft; up with her smartly, lads, while this lee-roll is on! Good! very neatly done! Catch a turn, now, for a moment; and you, Chips, jump into her again, and pass out the dog. Take care that you don't drop him overboard! Well done! Now hoist away again, men. Well, there; two blocks; Belay! Haul taut and make fast your gripes. Good dog, then; poor old fellow! Why you are just skin and bone, as Chips said. Never mind, old chap, your troubles are over now, and we will soon set you on your pins again. Here, steward, bring along some water for this dog—not too much to start with; and give him a little food. Now, carpenter, what were you able to make out aboard there? Fill your main-topsail, lads, and bring her to her course."

Meanwhile, Miss Trevor was on her knees beside the dog—a magnificent black Newfoundland—patting his head, and speaking loving words to him; to which attentions the poor beast responded by whining pitifully as he licked her hands and slapped the deck feebly with his tail. When the steward brought the food and water she took them from him and herself gave them to the dog, allowing him first to drink a little, and then to take a mouthful or two of food; then another drink, and then more food, and so on, until he had taken as much as she thought good for him for a first meal.

"Well, sir," responded the carpenter, as he turned to walk aft with Leslie, "there wasn't much to learn aboard that there hooker beyond what you could see for yourselves from the deck of this brig. I 'low she was hove down upon her beam-ends in a squall, some time durin' the night, most likely; and then they had to cut away her masts to right her again. Anyhow, her masts was cut away, that's sartin', because the lanyards of the riggin' showed the clean cuts of the tomahawks clear enough. And I reckon that, when she was hove over, she started butt, or somethin' o' that sort, because she was full o' water, and it was only her cargo—whatever it may ha' been—that kept her afloat. She'd been a fine ship in her time, her cabin bein' fitted up most beautiful wi' lookin' glasses and white-and-gold panels, velvet cushions to the lockers, and a big table o' solid mahogany, to say nothin' of a most handsome sideboard wi' silver-plated fittin' up agin' the fore bulkhead. Then, on each side of the main cabin, there was a row of fine sleepin' berths—six on side—and four others abaft the after bulkhead, all of 'em fitted up good enough for a hemperor. But there weren't nobody in 'em, in course; they and the main cabin bein' up to a man's waist in water, all loppin' about wi' the roll o' the ship, and fine cushions and what not floatin' about fore and aft and athwartships. I couldn't find no papers nor nothin' worth bringin' away wi' me—unless it were the aneroid, tell-tale, and clock what was fixed to the coamin's where the skylight had been, and I couldn't unship none o' them without tools; but the tell-tale and the clock bore the name o' *Flying Eagle*—Philadelpy; that I take to be the name an' port o' registry o' the craft."

"No doubt," agreed Leslie. "And how long do you think the craft had been as you found her?"

"Well, not so very long, sir, I should say," answered Chips. "Everything looked fairly fresh aboard of her; the paintwork weren't noways perished-like wi' the wash of the water, and the polish on the mahogany was pretty nigh as good as a man could wish; but the cushions was certingly a good bit sodden. I should say, sir, as he'd been desarted a matter o'—well, perhaps three or four days."

"Ah," commented Leslie, speaking to himself rather than to the carpenter, "then it could not have been the same squall that struck us. No, certainly not, the distance is altogether too great for that. It means, however, that there has been bad weather in these regions of late; so we will keep our weather eyes lifting lest we should be caught unawares by a recurrence of it. Thank you, carpenter; you have done very well. And now, if you will keep a look-out for a few minutes, I will go below and enter a full account of the matter in the log-book while the particulars are fresh in my memory."

Miss Trevor had all this time been looking after the dog, petting him and making much of him, until the animal, revived and strengthened by the food and drink that he had taken, had struggled to his feet and was now staggering after her along the deck, as she slowly and carefully induced him to take a little exercise. Then, after the lapse of about an hour, she fed him again, somewhat more liberally than at first; until by dint of care and assiduity on her part the poor beast was once more able to walk without much difficulty.

The sun went down in a clear sky that night, and although the breeze held, the swell rapidly subsided, thus clearly indicating that it was not the forerunner of an approaching gale, but the last remaining evidence of one already past—in all probability the same gale the initial outfly of which had worked the destruction of the *Flying Eagle*.

The life of a sailor is usually one of almost wearisome monotony, despite what landsmen have to say as to its excitements. True, the individual who is fortunate enough to possess an eye for colour and effect, and the leisure to note the ever-varying forms and tints of sea and sky—especially if he also happens to be endowed with the skill to transfer them to paper or canvas—need never pass an uninteresting moment at sea. Such fortunately circumstanced people are, however, few and far between, and it is more especially to the ordinary mariner that reference is now made. To him there are, broadly speaking, only two experiences, those of fine weather and of storm. Fine weather means to him usually little more than the comfort of dry clothes, his full watch below, and perhaps not quite such hard work; while bad weather means sodden garments, little and broken rest, and— unless the ship be snugged down and hove-to—incessant strenuous work.

To him the constantly changing aspects of the sky appeal in one way only, namely, as forecasts of impending weather.

And the incidents of sea-life, apart from the changes of weather, and the sighting of occasional ships, are few. Derelicts are not fallen in with every day; nor is the overwhelming of a ship by a waterspout a frequent occurrence. Yet extraordinary events—some of them marvellous almost beyond credence—unquestionably do occur from time to time, and nowhere more frequently than at sea. And it is quite within the bounds of possibility for one craft to circumnavigate the globe without encountering a single incident worth recording, while another, upon a voyage of less than half that length, will fall in with so many and such extraordinary adventures that there will not be space enough in her log-book to record the half of them.

This, it would almost appear, was to be the experience of the *Mermaid*; for upon the afternoon of the day following that of their meeting with the *Flying Eagle*, her crew were privileged to witness a sight that a man may follow the sea for years without beholding.

Chapter Seven
Dismasted!

It was about one bell in the first dog-watch; the weather was fine, the water smooth, the breeze light; and the brig, with little more than bare steerage-way upon her, was laying her course, with squared yards, both clews of her mainsail hauled up, and studding-sails set on both sides, her topsails occasionally collapsing and flapping to the masts for lack of wind to keep them "asleep." Miss Trevor was, as usual, on deck, seated in a deck-chair, with a book on her lap and the fingers of one hand playing abstractedly with an ear of the great dog that lay stretched contentedly upon the deck beside her. Leslie, also with a book in his hands, was seated right aft upon the taffrail, with his feet upon the stern grating, in such a position that he could look past the helmsman right forward and command the entire starboard side of the deck, as far forward as the windlass-bitts— and, incidentally, study the varying expressions that flitted athwart Miss Trevor's face as she read. The carpenter, with the rest of the men, was on the forecastle, looking after them and busying himself upon some small job that needed attention. The stillness of the peaceful afternoon seemed to have fallen upon the vessel; the men conversed together intermittently in subdued tones, that barely reached aft in the form of a low mumble; and the only sounds heard were the occasional soft rustle and flap of the canvas aloft, with an accompanying patter of reef-points, the jar of the rudder upon its pintles, the jerk of the wheel chains, and the soft, scarcely audible seething of the water alongside.

Upon this reposeful quietude there suddenly broke the sound of a gentle "wash" of water close alongside, then a long-drawn, sigh-like respiration, and a jet of mingled vapour and water shot above the port bulwark to a height of some ten or twelve feet, so close to the brig that the next instant a small shower of spray came splashing down on the deck in the wake of the main rigging.

So totally unexpected was the occurrence that it startled everybody. Leslie sprang to his feet and looked with mild surprise down into the water; Miss Trevor dropped her book as she shot out of her chair; the dog, who had manifested a readiness to respond to the name of Sailor, leaped up and rushed to the bulwarks, where he reared himself upon his hind legs, emitting a succession of deep, alert barks; and the crew forward shambled over to the port bulwarks, staring curiously.

"Come up here, Miss Trevor," said Leslie, extending his hand to help the girl up on to the grating beside him. "Here is a sight that you may never have an opportunity to behold again—at least, under such perfect conditions as these."

The girl, closely attended by Sailor, sprang lightly upon the grating, and following with her eyes Leslie's pointing finger, gazed down into the blue, transparent depths, where she beheld the enormous black bulk of a large sperm whale, lying right up alongside the brig—so close to her, indeed, that his starboard fin was right under her bilge, about a third of his length—from his blow-holes aft toward his tail—showing shiny as polished ebony, some six inches above water, while his ponderous tail stretched away some forty feet or more beyond the taffrail, where it could be clearly seen gently rising and falling to enable him to keep pace with the brig.

"What a veritable monster!" exclaimed Miss Trevor, gazing down with wide-open eyes of mingled astonishment and dismay at the huge creature, as she clung unconsciously to Leslie's supporting arm. "Is it dangerous? I hope not, because it looks big enough and strong enough to destroy this ship at a single blow if it chose to do so!"

"You need not be in the least alarmed," answered Leslie, reassuringly. "He will not hurt us if we do not interfere with him. These creatures are only dangerous if attacked; then, indeed, they have been known to turn upon their assailants, with dire results. But ah! look there!—there is another one!"

And sure enough, up came another of the monsters, breaking water with a rush that showed nearly half his length, at a distance of only some fifty yards from the brig.

"And there is another!" cried Miss Trevor, with unmistakable trepidation, as a third came to the surface and blew close under the brig's counter.

"Pity as we ain't a whaler, sir," remarked the helmsman. "If we was, here 'd be a chance to get fast to two of 'em at once, without so much as havin' to lower a boat!"

"Yes," responded Leslie, good-naturedly. "Such chances do not, however, seem to come to whalers. Why, there blows another!" as a fourth whale broke water about a hundred yards on the brig's starboard beam. "We seem to have fallen in with a whole school of them!"

And so indeed it proved, for within ten minutes there were no less than seventeen of the monsters in view at the same moment within a radius of a quarter of a mile of the brig, which craft appeared to possess a fascination for them; for they not only swam round and round her, but approached her so closely and so persistently that Miss Trevor became seriously alarmed; while even Leslie began to grow somewhat uneasy lest the brutes, whose temper he knew to be rather uncertain, should develop an inclination to attack the craft. To the relief, however, of all hands, the curiosity of the creatures at length appeared to be satisfied, and they drew off from the brig a little, still remaining upon the surface, however. And presently the huge brutes began to develop a playful disposition, that commenced with their chasing each other hither and thither, first of all in a leisurely manner, then, as their excitement grew, their rapidity of movement increased until they were rushing through the water—and round the brig—with the speed of a fleet of steamers. And finally they took to "breaching," that is, throwing themselves completely out of the water, to a height of from ten to twenty feet, coming down again with a splash, that soon set the water boiling and foaming all round them, and creating a commotion that caused the brig to roll and pitch as though she were in a choppy sea. This exhibition of strength and activity lasted for a full three-quarters of an hour, when the creatures disappeared as suddenly as they had come, much, it must be confessed, to the relief of all hands aboard the brig.

From this time nothing of moment occurred until the *Mermaid* arrived off Staten Island, the eastern extremity of which she sighted at daylight on a cold, bleak morning some ten weeks after the date when Leslie and Miss Trevor had become members of her ship's company. The weather had, in the interim, been fine upon the whole, with occasional calms and contrary winds; but, taking everything into consideration, Leslie felt that they had done by no means badly.

On this especial morning, however, appearances seemed to point to the probability that they were about to experience an unpleasant taste of typical Cape Horn weather. The sky was gloomy and overcast, the entire firmament being obscured by a thick pall of cold, leaden-hued cloud lying in horizontal layers, and presenting the appearance described by sailors as "greasy"—an appearance that usually forebodes plenty of wind and, not improbably, rain. The breeze was blowing fresh from the westward, having hauled round from the north-west during the night, and the brig was pounding through a short, lumpy sea under single-reefed topsails. The air was damp and raw, with a nip in it that sent everybody into their thick winter clothing, and called for a fire in the cabin stove; and the deck, as far aft as the waist, was streaming with water that had come in over the weather rail in the form of spray. Everybody on deck, except Miss Trevor, had donned sea boots and oilskins, and the only creature who appeared to enjoy the weather was Sailor, the dog, who trotted about the deck and through the heavy showers of spray with manifest delight. There was no hope whatever of getting a sight of the sun that day; but this was a matter of comparatively slight importance, since Leslie had very carefully taken the bearings of the land, and had thus been able to verify his reckoning.

As the day wore on the wind freshened perceptibly, while with every mile that the brig made to the southward the sea grew longer and heavier, and the air more bleak and nipping. At noon, when the watch was called, Leslie seized the opportunity to take a second reef in the topsails, and to haul up and furl the mainsail; an arrangement that was productive of an immediate change for the better, since the brig went along almost as fast as before, while she took the seas more easily, and was altogether drier and more comfortable. The barometer, however, was falling steadily; a circumstance that, combined with the look of the sky to windward, led Leslie to the conclusion that they were booked for a regular Cape Horn gale. All through the afternoon the weather steadily became more unpleasant, and about one bell in the first dog-watch, it came on to rain—a cold, heavy, persistent downpour—while the wind piped up so fiercely that Leslie decided to haul down the third reef in his topsails, brail up and stow the trysail, and take in the inner jib without further delay, thus snugging the brig down for the night.

The next morning dawned dark, gloomy, and so thick with driving rain that it was impossible to see anything beyond half a mile from the brig in any direction. But within that radius the scene was depressing enough, a steep, high sea of an opaque greenish-grey tint sweeping down, foam-capped and menacing, upon the brig from to windward, while the air was thick with spindrift and scudwater. The foresail had been taken in during the middle watch; and the brig was now under close-reefed topsails and fore-topmast staysail only, under which canvas she was making a bare three knots in the hour, leaving behind her a short wake that streamed out broad on her weather quarter. So unpleasant were the conditions that, except for brief intervals during the fore and afternoon, Miss Trevor remained below, whiling away the time as best she might with a book; disregarding Sailor's importunate invitations to accompany him on deck.

Meanwhile the gale was steadily increasing, and between five and six bells in the afternoon watch the main-topsail suddenly split with a loud report, and immediately blew out of the bolt-ropes; with the result that, despite the utmost efforts of the helmsman, the brig at once fell off into the trough of the sea. Hearing the report, and the subsequent commotion on deck, Leslie, who had been snatching a little rest in his cabin, dashed up on deck and, taking in the position of affairs at a glance, gave orders for the fore topsail to be at once clewed up, and the spanker to be set; which being done, brought the brig once more to the wind, and extricated her from her dangerous situation. Then he ordered a new main-topsail to be at once brought on deck and bent; having no fancy for leaving the brig all night under such low and ineffective canvas as the spanker—a sail that, with the heavy sea then running, was half the time becalmed.

By the time that the remains of the burst main-topsail had been unbent, and the new sail brought on deck, it was eight bells, and all hands were set to work to bend the sail. This, under the existing weather conditions—with the wind blowing at almost hurricane strength, and the brig flung like a cork from trough to crest of the mountainous, furious-running sea, with wild weather rolls as the seas swept away from under her, succeeded by sickening rolls to leeward that at times laid her almost on her beam-ends as she climbed the lee slope of the next on-coming sea—was a long, difficult, and perilous job for the hands aloft; and Leslie heaved a sigh of relief when at length, having bent and close-reefed the sail, the little party laid in off the yard, and descended to the deck to assist in sheeting it home. This delicate job was happily accomplished without mishap; and, the trysail being brailed in and stowed, the brig was then hove-to under close-reefed main-topsail and fore-topmast staysail.

All through the night and the whole of the succeeding day the gale continued to rage furiously, and although the *Mermaid* proved herself to be an unexpectedly good sea-boat in such exceptionally heavy weather, riding easily the mountainous sea that was now running, she rolled with such terrific violence that it was impossible to move anywhere on board her, whether on deck or below, without incurring the risk of serious injury. As for Miss Trevor, acting on Leslie's advice, she kept to her own cabin, and passed the disagreeable time in the comparative safety of her bunk, which she left only at meal times.

The morning of the fourth day brought with it a change. The gale broke about the time of sunrise, and soon afterwards the sky cleared, the canopy of cloud broke up, and drifted away to the eastward in tattered fragments, revealing a sky of hard pallid blue, in which the sun hung low like a ball of white fire. The sea went down somewhat, and no longer broke so menacingly, while it changed its colour from dirty green to steel-grey. Far away on the southern horizon a gleam of dazzling white betrayed the presence of a small iceberg, and the air was piercingly cold.

Gladly welcoming the change, Leslie—who had spent the whole of the preceding night on deck—ordered the close-reefed fore topsail to be set, as well as the foresail and main trysail; under which considerable increase of canvas the brig was soon once more moving with comparative rapidity through the water, and looking well up into the wind. Then, watching for a "smooth," they wore the craft round, and brought her to on the port tack, during the progress of which evolution the wind shifted a couple of points to the southward, enabling them to lay a course of north-west by west, which Leslie hoped would suffice him to draw out clear of everything, and carry him into the Pacific Ocean.

This hope was strengthened as the day wore on, for the wind continued to draw gradually still further round from the southward, while it steadily decreased in force—though growing colder every hour—thus enabling Leslie to shake out first one reef in his topsails, then a second, and finally the last, also to set his jib and main-topmast staysail; so that by sunset the brig, under whole topsails and main-topgallantsail, was booming along famously, with an excellent prospect of finding herself fairly in the Pacific in the course of the next twenty-four hours.

A disconcerting circumstance, however, that rather tended to damp Leslie's hopes, was the fact that the barometer persistently refused to rise, although the wind was subsiding so rapidly that it threatened to dwindle to a calm, and as the evening faded into night the stars grew dim and finally disappeared. Still, there was nothing that could be called actually alarming in the aspect of the weather; and as Leslie had been almost continuously on deck during the entire duration of the gale—snatching a brief half-hour of rest from time to time as best he could—and it was now his eight hours in, he decided, after deliberating the matter until four bells in the first watch had struck, to go below and turn in until midnight; leaving instructions with the carpenter to instantly call him in the event of anything occurring to necessitate his presence on deck.

It seemed to him that he had scarcely laid his head upon his pillow and closed his eyes ere he was awakened from a profound sleep by a sudden screaming roar of wind; the brig heeled over to port until she appeared about to capsize; and as Leslie, dazed for the moment by his sudden awakening, sprang from his bunk, a loud crash on deck, immediately succeeded by a lesser one, told a tale of disaster. The brig righted as the harassed man sprang up the companion ladder, clad only in his pyjamas, and dashed out on deck to find everything in confusion, the mainmast gone by the board and hammering viciously at the ship's side, while a furious banging forward told that the fore-topmast also had gone, and, with everything attached, was hanging to leeward by its rigging. Moreover, a howling gale from the *northward* was sweeping over the brig and deluging her with showers of cutting spray.

"Where is the carpenter?" was Leslie's first cry as he emerged from the companion and groped blindly about him in the blackness of the starless night.

"Here I be, sir," answered Chips, close at hand. "Oh, Mr Leslie, here's a dreadful business! And I be to blame for it, sir—"

"Never mind, just now, who is to blame," exclaimed Leslie. "Call all hands, and let them get to work with their tomahawks upon that main rigging. Cut everything away, Chips, and be smart about it, my man, or we shall have the mast punching a hole in the ship's side, and there will be an end of us all."

And so saying, without waiting for an answer, Leslie made a spring for the rack in which the tomahawks were kept, and, seizing the first of the small axes that he could lay hands upon, he set an example to the rest by hacking away at the lanyards of the main shrouds. It was a heart-breaking business, that blind hewing and chopping at the complicated gear that held the wreck of the mainmast fast to the hull; but it was accomplished at last, and then, the brig having paid off almost dead before the wind, it drifted astern and went clear, with much scraping and a final bump under the counter that made the old hooker tremble, and must have infallibly destroyed the rudder had it chanced to hit it. Then all hands went to work and attacked the topmast rigging, which, being less complicated, was soon cleared away.

The harassed crew now had a moment in which to collect their energies for fresh efforts, and take stock, as it were, of the extent of the disaster that had befallen them. And the first matter into which Leslie made particular inquiry—after he had gone below and got into his clothes—was the state of the crew; it had been impressed upon him—although he had hitherto been too busy to mention it—that some men seemed to be missing—or rather, he had vaguely felt that there were not so many men on deck as there ought to be.

So he now turned to the carpenter, and said—

"Muster all hands, Chips, and let the steward give them a good, generous tot of grog; they will be all the better for it after their hard work in the wet and cold. Moreover, I wish to satisfy myself that they are all right; it has struck me more than once since I came on deck that some of them are missing."

Dick Leslie's Luck: A Story of Shipwreck and Adventure | 97

"I pray to God that you're wrong, sir," answered the carpenter; "but, now that you comes to speak of it, the same thing have struck me too. Here, lay aft, bullies, all of yer, and let's have a look at ye," he continued, sending his voice forward to the forecastle, where the men were now grouped, awaiting further orders.

They came aft, slouching along the deck after their usual manner, and grouped themselves about the binnacle, "Why, where's the rest of ye?" demanded the carpenter, glaring angrily from one to the other; "where's Bill—and Jim—and Joe? Jump for'ard, one of ye, and tell 'em to lay aft here for a tot o' grog."

"We're all here, Chips—all that's left of us, that is. Bill, and Jim, and Joe are all missin'; ain't to be found nowheres. Anyhow, they ain't in the fo'c's'le; I'm ready to swear to that!" answered one of the little crowd that grouped themselves round the binnacle, their eyes gleaming in the dim light of the binnacle lamp with that transient horror that sailors feel at the sudden loss of a shipmate.

"Not in the fo'c's'le!" ejaculated the carpenter, staring wildly about him, "Oh, my God! three men gone, and all of 'em in my watch!" he cried, flinging his clenched fists above his head in his agony of self-reproach. "You're sure that they ain't in the fo'c's'le? Then they ain't nowhere else aboard this unlucky hooker; they're overboard—that's where they are— went when the squall struck us and very nigh throwed us on our beam-ends. And it's my fault—all my fault; it's *I* that have lost them three men. Ye see, Mr Leslie, it's like this here. I'm a man what can't do without his proper 'lowance of sleep, and this here last gale have fair knocked me up and made me that stupid that I haven't knowed what I've been doin' latterly. And the fact is, that in this here last watch of mine I was fair overcome wi' want of sleep, and I dropped off without knowin' it, and without wantin' to; and this here's the consekence," —flinging his right hand wildly out to indicate the crippled state of the brig—"this an' the loss o' three good men."

"Well, Chips, it is a pity," said Leslie, soothingly and sympathetically; "if you had but told me how completely you were knocked up, I would have taken your watch for you, although I am pretty well knocked up myself. The mischief, however, is done and cannot now be helped, so it is useless to worry any more about it. We must not, however, allow the ship to run further to leeward than we can help; so clew up the foresail, lads; we will let her scud under bare poles until daylight. Then we will see what can be done to mend matters. Now take your grog, men; and when you have clewed up and furled the foresail, go below. You, too, Chips. I have had a little rest, and can doubtless hold out until the morning. I will look after the brig until then."

As the men shambled away forward, leaving Leslie at the wheel, the latter dimly caught sight of something huddled up in the companion-way, at the top of the ladder; and while he stood staring at it in an endeavour to make out what it was, it moved; and the next moment Miss Trevor, enveloped in a dressing-gown, stepped out on deck, and, with teeth chattering with cold, exclaimed—

"Oh, Mr Leslie, what dreadful thing has happened? I was awakened by the terrible noise and confusion—the crashing and thumping, the thrashing of the sails, the howling of the wind, and the shouting of the sailors—and I feared that the ship was sinking—for it seemed just as bad as on the night when the *Golden Fleece* was run into; so I wrapped myself in this dressing-gown, and have been to and fro between the top of the stairs and my own cabin for quite an hour, I should think. But I would not come out on deck, for I saw at once that you were all extremely busy; and I knew that, if I did, I should only interrupt you, and be in your way."

"You would, indeed," answered Leslie, bluntly. "And even now," he continued, "the deck is no place for you on this wild and bitter night; you will get wet through and 'catch your death of cold,' as they say ashore. Therefore I beg that you will forthwith go below and turn in; there is no further danger at present; the brig is scudding quite comfortably, as you may see; and there is nothing that we can run up against between this and the morning; you may therefore finish your sleep in comfort and with an easy mind."

"But please tell me exactly what has happened," the girl persisted; "I shall be better able to rest if you will let me know the worst."

"Well, if you insist on knowing, the brig was caught aback by a sudden shift of wind, and we have lost our mainmast and fore-topmast," answered Leslie, saying nothing about their further loss of three men, as he did not wish to harrow her mind with such a distressing detail until it became impossible any longer to conceal it, Miss Trevor was not, however, to be so easily put off.

"But I heard the carpenter crying out that he had lost three men," she said. "What did he mean by that?"

"Precisely what he said," answered Leslie, reluctantly. "The poor chap was overcome with the fatigue of the last three days, and fell asleep in his watch on deck. The result is the loss of our spars, and—worse still—of three men, who, there can be no doubt, somehow got washed or knocked overboard when the squall struck and dismasted us."

"Oh, how dreadful!" exclaimed the girl in tones of horror. "This is indeed an unfortunate ship! We have met with nothing but tragedy since we came on board. I wish now—oh, I wish most fervently!—that we had met some other ship into which we could both have changed; we should then have escaped all these horrors."

"Possibly," agreed Leslie. "Yet '*quien sabe?*' as the Spaniards say, who can tell? We might have trans-shipped into some craft quite as, if not even more, unfortunate than ourselves. In any case, it is too late now; and even were it not so, you appear to have forgotten that we could not *both* have trans-shipped; *I* at least am bound to go on to Valparaiso in this brig. This, however, is not the moment to discuss these matters; you are shivering and your teeth chattering with cold; I must therefore *insist* that you go below and turn in at once. And as you pass through the cabin, mix yourself a good stiff glass of grog; it will do you good. I prescribe it."

"Very, well doctor, I will obey you," answered the girl. And forthwith she disappeared down the companion, without saying "Good night!" somewhat to Leslie's chagrin.

The apparent discourtesy was, however, soon explained; for a minute or two later she reappeared, bearing in her hand a tumbler of generously stiff grog, which she handed to Leslie, saying—

"*I* 'prescribe this.' Please drink it at once; for I am certain that you need it far more than I do. Oh yes, I will take some myself, since you so strenuously insist upon it. There, now you will feel better," as she received the empty tumbler from him. "And now, good night. I wish I were a man, for then I could stay here and help you."

"God forbid!" ejaculated Leslie, fervently. "Not even to secure the benefit of your help would I have you other than as you are. A thousand thanks for the grog; and now good night; let me not see you again until the morning!"

The disaster to the brig had happened shortly before midnight; and for the rest of that wild and bitter night, until seven bells in the morning watch, Leslie stood there alone at the wheel, keeping the brig stern-on to the fast-rising sea. Then the carpenter and the remainder of the crew appeared on deck, and one of them came aft to his relief. The cook lighted the galley fire; the steward presently brought him aft a cup of smoking hot cocoa; and then, when he had stripped to the skin, been pumped on copiously under the head pump, rubbed down vigorously with a rough towel, and invested in a complete change of dry garments, he felt a new man, ready for another arduous day's work, if need be. He, however, insisted that all hands should take a thorough good breakfast before starting the day's work; and the wisdom of this revealed itself immediately that the work began.

Meanwhile it is necessary to say that during those long weary hours of Leslie's lonely vigil at the wheel, the wind, that at the first outfly had come away from about due north, had gradually veered round until, by sunrise, it was a point south of east, in which quarter it seemed disposed to stick. Furthermore, with the coming of dawn it had evinced a disposition to moderate its violence somewhat, while the sky had cleared for a few brief minutes in the eastern quarter, revealing a glimpse of the sun; and upon examining the barometer, Leslie had noticed that the mercury in the tube showed a convex surface—a sign that it was about to rise; he therefore suffered himself to indulge the hope that with improving weather, they would ere nightfall be enabled, by good steady hard work, to get the brig into such shape as to once more have her under command.

Seen now, in broad daylight, the poor little brig presented a truly pitiful sight as compared with her appearance on the previous evening. She was then all ataunto, with every spar, rope, and sail intact; a thing of life, obedient to her helm, responsive to the will of her commander, and as fit as such a craft could be to cope with any and every possible caprice of wind or weather. *Now*, she was a poor maimed and disfigured thing; her mainmast gone, leaving nothing of itself but a splintered stump standing some ten feet above the deck; her fore-topmast also gone—snapped short off at the cap; and, of her normal spread of canvas, nothing now remained save her fore-course. And her loss was not confined to that of her spars only, although that of course was serious enough. But, in addition to this, she had lost a complete suit of canvas, and practically all her running and standing rigging—the latter item being one that it would be quite impossible to replace until her arrival at a port. Fortunately for all concerned, her owners had been prudent enough to provide her with two complete suits of sails; and she also carried a fairly liberal equipment of spare spars; it would therefore be no very difficult job to extemporise a "jury rig" for her; but the trouble would be to find the wherewithal to replace the lost standing and running rigging, blocks, and all the other items that would be needed to make that jury rig effective.

Needs must, however, when there is no alternative; and the British sailor is, with all his faults, an ingenious fellow, not altogether devoid of the inventive faculty, and possessed of a pretty turn for adaptation; give him but the idea and he will generally find the means to carry it out.

So while Leslie and Chips went the round of the deck immediately after breakfast, inspecting their stock of spare spars, and the navy man prepared a rough sketch illustrating his idea of the manner in which those spars could be most effectively made use of, the rest of the crew turned-to with a will to overhaul the boatswain's locker, the sail locker, and the fore-peak, routing out therefrom and bringing up on deck every article and thing that could conceivably be of use in the task that lay before them. Then, when Leslie had completed his arrangements with the carpenter, the latter brought his tools on deck; the spare spars were cast loose and placed conveniently at hand for working upon; and in a very short time everybody but Leslie, Miss Trevor, the cook, and the steward, was busily engaged on the forecastle, measuring, cutting, splicing and fitting rigging, while the carpenter trimmed the spars and otherwise prepared them to go into their destined positions.

As for the others, the cook and steward had their usual duties to attend to, and could not therefore be spared to lend a hand in re-rigging the brig, even had they possessed the necessary knowledge—which they did not; although later on, perhaps, when it came to mere pulling and hauling, their strength would be found useful, and would be unhesitatingly called for. Meanwhile the brig, although under her fore-course only, and running before the wind, needed to be steered; and this job Leslie undertook to personally attend to throughout the day, thus sparing another man for the pressing work on the forecastle.

Luckily for everybody concerned, the half-hearted promise of finer weather that the morning had given was more than fulfilled; for about four bells the sky cleared, the sun shone brilliantly, and the air became pleasantly mild, while although the wind still blew strongly from the east, the sea grew more regular, so that the dismantled brig now scudded quite comfortably, not shipping a drop of water, and forging ahead, at the rate of about three knots per hour, on her proper course.

Miss Trevor had not made her appearance at the cabin table when Leslie had been summoned below to breakfast by the steward, nor had she responded when the former had gently knocked at her cabin door. This circumstance, however, had not aroused any very serious alarm in the breast of the ex-Lieutenant, who, remembering the incident of the night before, when the young lady had come on deck after the accident to the brig, thought it quite probable that, in consequence of her rest being so rudely broken, she was now oversleeping herself. And in the confidence of this belief he had ordered the steward not to attempt to disturb her, but to prepare breakfast for her immediately upon her appearance. And he furthermore instructed the man to notify him if she failed to put in an appearance before four bells. As it happened, the young lady appeared on deck, fresh and rosy as a summer morning, and with Sailor in close attendance, a few minutes before that hour.

"What!" she exclaimed, lifting her hands in dismay as she saw Leslie standing at the wheel, precisely as she had left him on the previous night, "still at that dreadful wheel! Do you mean to say that you have been standing there all this time?"

"By no means, madam," answered Leslie, cheerfully. "I have since then had a most refreshing bath, changed my clothes, taken breakfast, and done quite a useful amount of very necessary work. It is scarcely needful to inquire after *your* health, your appearance speaks for itself; yet for form's sake let me say that I hope you are none the worse for your very imprudent behaviour last night."

"Oh no," she answered, with a laugh and a blush that vastly became her—so Leslie thought; "I am perfectly well, thank you. I took the grog that you prescribed, and then went dutifully to my cabin, in obedience to orders, where I at once fell asleep, and so remained until an hour ago. Then I rose, dressed, and had my breakfast; and here I am, ready and anxious to do anything I can to help."

"Help!" echoed Leslie, with a laugh. "You talked of helping last night—and most kind it was of you to have and express the wish—but in what possible way could a delicately nurtured girl like you help? And yet," he continued more soberly, "you *could* render me a little help, once or twice a day, if you would. It is not much that I would ask of you—merely to note the chronometer times for me when I take my observations of the sun for the longitude. I have sometimes thought that Chips has been a little erratic in his noting of the time; and I have more than once had it in my mind to ask you to undertake this small service for me."

"Why, of course I will," assented the girl, eagerly. "Why did you not ask me before? And there is another thing that I can do for you, now—this moment—if you will only let me. I can steer the ship for you while you go downstairs and obtain a few hours' much-needed rest. Your eyes are heavy and red for want of sleep; you look to be half dead with fatigue! And if you should break down, what would become of the rest of us? Please let me try at once, will you? I am quite sure that I could manage it; it looks perfectly easy."

Leslie laughed. "Yes," he assented; "I have no doubt it does; because, you see, I happen to know just how to do it. But *you* would find it very hard work, and would soon be terribly tired. No; you could not possibly steer the craft in this heavy sea, especially as we are running before the wind—which constitutes the most difficult condition for steering. But, if you wish to learn to steer, I shall be delighted to teach you as soon as we again get fine weather and smooth water."

And with this promise the girl had to be content, although she persisted in believing it to be quite easy to turn the wheel a few spokes either way, and so keep the brig sailing on a perfectly straight course. Meanwhile, the crew got to work and rigged a pair of sheers over the stump of the mainmast, firmly staying it with guys leading aft to the taffrail and forward to the windlass-bitts. Then they rigged at the apex of the sheers the strongest threefold tackle that they could extemporise; and with the assistance of this they swayed aloft a spare main-topmast, that had been carefully prepared by the carpenter for fishing to the stump of the mainmast. This spar was accurately adjusted in the precise position that it was intended it should occupy, and its heel was then firmly secured to the stump of the mainmast by means of strips of stout planking about eight feet long, closely arranged all round and secured in position by a long length of chain wound tightly round, and further tightened by driving in as many wedges as possible. Then the spar was further secured by shrouds, stays, and backstays; thus providing a very respectable substitute for a mainmast. The sheers were then struck; a spare main-yard, fitted with brace-blocks and all other necessary gear, was next swayed aloft and firmly secured to the head of the extemporised mainmast; a spare main-course was bent and set; and by sunset that same evening Leslie had the satisfaction of seeing the brig once more in condition to be brought to the wind when occasion should arise. What the crew had accomplished that day constituted a most excellent day's work, especially taking into consideration the fact that they were almost worn-out with fatigue, Leslie therefore resolved to call upon them for nothing further in the shape of work that day; but he foresaw that it would be a great help to the craft to have a fore staysail that could be set when sailing on a wind; and a main trysail might also prove useful; he determined therefore that the next day should see these two sails in place, if possible. He would then have accomplished the very utmost that lay in his power, and sufficient, he hoped and believed, to enable him to take the brig to Valparaiso.

His observations, taken at noon and at three o'clock that day, showed him that the *Mermaid* was far enough to the southward and westward to justify a shift of the helm; and accordingly at four bells in the first dog-watch he altered the course to north-west by West, which he hoped would enable him to just clear Desolation Island and carry him fairly into the Pacific. It also afforded him an opportunity to test the efficiency of his jury rig; and his satisfaction was great at finding that with the yards braced forward the brig, under main and fore-courses only, behaved in a thoroughly satisfactory manner; although what she would do when hauled close on a wind still remained to be proved.

Happily for him the weather had by this time again become quite fine; the wind had softened down to merely a fresh breeze, and the sea had gone down considerably. He was therefore enabled to secure a few hours' sleep—a refreshment that he now absolutely needed, for he was by this time so completely worn-out and exhausted that he felt he could do no more.

The next day was nearly as busy an one as that which had preceded it, for it saw the completion of Leslie's plans, and left the brig under fore and main-courses and fore staysail; with main trysail bent and ready for setting when occasion should require. This achievement brought the ex-lieutenant to the end of his resources; but, on the other hand, he felt that the brig was now once more in reasonable trim for facing any contingency except a recurrence of really bad weather; and this last he hoped he would have done with when once the brig had fairly entered the Pacific. Luckily, the weather was now as fine as he could wish; the sky clear enough to enable him to get all his observations; not very much sea running; and a spanking fair wind driving the brig along upon her course at a speed of nearly five knots. Moreover, the fine weather would enable his crew and himself to get a sufficient amount of rest to thoroughly recuperate their exhausted energies, and prepare themselves for future contingencies. On the following morning, just as he had completed his forenoon observations for the longitude, land was sighted broad on the starboard bow, that proved to be the south-eastern extremity of Desolation Island; and at six bells in the afternoon watch the brig had arrived in the longitude of 75 degrees West, and was therefore at last ploughing the waters of the vast Pacific Ocean, to Leslie's profound satisfaction. He now shifted his course another point to the northward; and began to calculate the probable date of their arrival in Valparaiso.

It was his intention to maintain a north-west course for the ensuing twenty-four hours, in order to obtain a good offing, and then to haul up to the northward; but, to his disgust, when he turned out on the following morning he found that the wind had shifted and was blowing strong from about north-east, and that, with her yards braced right forward, and main trysail set, the brig would look no higher than north-west. It was, however, comforting to reflect that although the hooker was taking a wider offing than was at all necessary, she was edging up to the northward, in which direction lay their port of destination. And sooner or later they would be certain to get a westerly slant of wind that would help them. So, being in fact unable to do better, Leslie kept his starboard tacks abroad, and went driving along to the north-westward. And with every mile of progress that they now made there came an improvement in the weather; the air growing ever softer and more balmy, the water more smooth, and the skies clearer and more deeply and exquisitely blue.

Thus the brig drove steadily and pleasantly enough along, day after day, until the wondering voyagers seemed to have arrived in the lotus-eaters' region, "where it is always afternoon;" and still the wind hung inexorably in the north-east quarter, and the brig's bows obstinately refused to point higher than north-west, until Leslie's patience wore thin, and he grew moody and morose with long waiting for a shift of wind. For this condition of affairs lasted not only for days, but at last mounted to weeks; a circumstance that was practically unique in the history of those waters.

Chapter Eight
The Wreck of the Mermaid

At length, however, the inevitable change came; the wind died away to a breathless calm; the ocean took on the semblance of a sea of gently undulating glass; and the hitherto cloudless sky imperceptibly lost its intensity of blue as a thin, streaky haze gradually veiled it, through which the sun shone feebly, a rayless disc of throbbing white fire. The heat and closeness of the atmosphere were intense, even on deck, while the temperature below was practically unendurable. The brig lost steerage-way about two o'clock in the afternoon; and when the sun sank beneath the western horizon that night, looming through the haze red as blood, distorted in shape, and magnified to thrice his normal dimensions, there was little if any perceptible change in the atmospheric conditions, although the mercury in the barometer had been falling slowly but steadily all day.

The brig was now within the tropic of Capricorn, and not very far to the eastward of the Paumotu Archipelago, in which region night succeeds day with such astounding rapidity that the stars become visible within ten minutes of the sun's disappearance. Yet no stars appeared on this particular night; on the contrary, a darkness that could be felt settled down upon the brig almost with the suddenness of a drawn curtain. The darkness was as profound as that of the interior of a coal-mine; it was literally impossible to see one's hand held close to one's eyes; and movement about the deck was accomplished blindly and gropingly, with hands outspread to avoid collision with the most familiar objects, whose positions could now be only roughly guessed at. And the silence was as profound as the darkness; for the swell had subsided with almost startling rapidity, and the brig was so nearly motionless that there was none of the creaking of timbers or spars, none of the "cheeping" of blocks and gear that is usually to be heard under such circumstances. Even the men forward were silent, as though they were waiting and listening for something, they knew not what. So intense was the silence that even the striking of a match to light a pipe became almost startling; while its tiny flame burnt steadily and without a semblance of wavering in the stagnant air.

Gradually, however, a subtle and portentous change took place. The darkness slowly became less intense, giving place to a lurid ruddy twilight that appeared to emanate from the clouds, for by imperceptible degrees they grew visible and became streaked and blotched with patches of red that suggested the idea of their being on fire within, the incandescence showing through here and there in the thinner parts. This red light grew and spread until the whole surface of the sky was aglow with it; and it was an uncanny experience to stand on the stern grating, close up to the taffrail, and look forward along the brig's deck to her bows, and note every detail of the craft and her equipment showing distinctly and black as ebony against that weird background of red-hot sky and its ruddy reflection in the polished surface of the water.

Leslie scarcely knew what to make of this lowering and portentously illuminated sky. He had never seen anything quite like it before; but he instinctively felt that it foreboded mischief; and he accordingly kept a sharp eye on the barometer. It was still falling, and now with considerably greater rapidity than at first. At eight bells in the second dog-watch he came to the conclusion that the time for action had arrived; and before allowing the watch to go below he ordered everything to be clewed up and furled, leaving only the fore staysail standing. Then he settled himself down to wait doggedly for developments, determined not to leave the deck until a breeze had come from *somewhere*. For he had a suspicion that when it arrived, it would prove to be something stronger than ordinary; and he wanted to satisfy himself as to the manner in which his jury rig would withstand such an outburst as appeared to be impending.

Hour after hour went by, however, and nothing happened; until at length Miss Trevor, whose stay on deck had been unusually prolonged by curiosity—and perhaps a dash of apprehension—bade Leslie good night and retired to her cabin, the port of which he particularly requested her to keep closed, despite the stifling heat. At length the strange and alarming glow in the heavens faded as imperceptibly as it had come, until the darkness had become as intense as before; and Leslie was beginning to think that after all nothing was going to happen, when the whole scene became suddenly illuminated by a vivid flash of sheet lightning that for an infinitesimal fraction of a second seemed to set the entire visible firmament ablaze, and caused every detail of the brig's hull and equipment to imprint a clear and perfectly distinct picture of itself upon the retina. They all listened for thunder, but none came. Suddenly, however, a few heavy drops of rain pattered upon the deck, and an instant later down came a perfect deluge with the sound of millions of small shot roaring and rattling on the deck and hissing into the sea. The rain ceased as suddenly as it had come, as suddenly as the flow of water is stopped by the turning of a tap; and for about a quarter of an hour nothing further happened. Then the sheet lightning began to quiver and flicker among the clouds once more; and presently the pall immediately overhead was rent apart by a terrific flash of sun-bright lightning that struck straight down and seemed to hit the water only a few yards from the brig. Simultaneously with the flash came a crackling crash of thunder of absolutely appalling intensity; and before its echoes had died away another flash, and another, and another, tore athwart the heavens; until within the space of less than a minute the entire vault of heaven was ablaze with flickering and flashing lightnings, steel blue, baleful green, rosy red, and dazzling white, accompanied by a continuous crash and roar of thunder that was both deafening and terrifying. This tremendous manifestation continued for about ten minutes, when down came the rain again, in an even fiercer deluge than before; and in the very midst of it, while the thunder still crashed and boomed overhead, and the rain descended in such sheets and masses that everybody gasped for breath, as though drowning, away came the wind with a howling scream that in an instant drowned even the sound of the thunder. It struck the brig flat aback; and had she happened to have had any of her square canvas set she must undoubtedly have foundered stern first. As it was, Leslie, who happened to be the only man near the wheel, sprang to it and put the helm hard over, causing her to pay off as she gathered stern-way, and thus saving the craft. But even as he stood there, in the very act of putting the helm over, a crash reached his ears out of the midst of the terrific hubbub; he was conscious of receiving a violent blow on the head; and then he knew no more.

When Leslie again recovered consciousness, his first distinct sensation was that of racking, sickening, splitting headache, accompanied by a feeling of acute soreness and smarting. He also felt dazed, confused, and harassed by a vague but intense anxiety about something, he knew not what. Then he became aware that he was lying recumbent on his back, with his head propped high by pillows; and presently he also became aware that his head was heavily swathed in bandages. He stirred uneasily, and attempted to put his hand to his head; but was shocked to find that his hand and arm felt heavy as lead, so heavy, indeed, that after a feeble effort he abandoned the attempt. As he did so, a fluttering sigh, and a whispered "Oh, thank God; thank God!" fell upon his ear; a handkerchief saturated with eau-de-cologne was applied to his nostrils; and, as in a dream, he heard a voice murmur—

"Are you better, Mr Leslie? Tell me that you are feeling better."

Feeling better! Had he been ill, then? He supposed he must have been; otherwise, why was he lying there—wherever he might be—on his back, with his head bandaged and racked with pain, and with no strength in him?

Ill! of course he was; every nerve in his body bore testimony to the fact. But where was he? what was the matter with him? and whose was this gentle, tender voice—that somehow seemed so familiar—that questioned him? Everything was vague, confused, and incomprehensible, with a dominating impression that there was pressing, urgent need for him to be up and attending to something without an instant's delay.

As he lay there, painfully cogitating in a vain endeavour to disentangle the threads of mingled thought that seemed to be inextricably wound together in his throbbing, struggling brain, two warm drops splashed upon his face, and the same low voice that he had heard before, cried—

"Spare him, O God; spare him; have mercy!" and the handkerchief was again applied to his nostrils.

The tide of life ebbed back for a moment; he again sank into oblivion; and presently revived to the consciousness that soft arms were supporting him—arms that quivered and shook with the violent sobbing that fell upon his ears—while a shower of hot tears bathed his face. And then, all in an instant, recollection, vivid, intense, complete, came to him, and he opened his eyes.

For a moment he could see nothing. Then he became aware that the sun was streaming brilliantly in through the open port-hole near the head of his bunk, while a soft, warm, yet refreshing breeze was playing about his temples; and that Miss Trevor was bending over him with streaming eyes that gazed down upon him wild with anxiety and grief.

"Why, what is this? what is the matter? and why am I lying here idle when I ought to be on deck looking after the ship?" he murmured, attempting at the same time to rise.

But the imprisoning arms held him firmly down; the streaming eyes met his in an intensity of gaze that seemed to devour him; and the tender voice gain cried with indescribable fervour—

"Thank God; oh, thank God for this great mercy! You *are* alive! And you will continue to live. Yes, you *must* live; promise me that you will. Here; drink this, quickly." And she held to his lips a tumbler containing a liquid that, pungent to the taste, at once revived him.

"Thanks; a thousand thanks!" murmured Leslie, gratefully. "I feel better now. Please let me get up; I must go on deck at once."

"No; no, you must not; indeed you must not; there is no need," answered Miss Trevor; and Leslie thought he detected a tone of sadness mingled with relief in the accents of her voice.

"No need?" ejaculated Leslie; "but indeed there *is* need—" and then he paused abruptly; for it had suddenly dawned upon him that the brig had a distinct list to port, and that she was *motionless*; not with the buoyant motionlessness of a ship afloat in a calm, but with the absolute absence of all movement characteristic of a ship in dry dock, or *stranded*!

"Good heavens! what has happened?" he ejaculated. "Tell me, please, at once!" and he again attempted to rise.

But again his self-constituted nurse restrained him.

"Oh, please, *please*, do not move," she entreated. "You *must* obey me, now; or you will *never* get better. I will tell you everything; but indeed you must not attempt to rise; for, as I said just now, there is no need. The ship is quite safe; I am sure that nothing further can happen to her, at least not for some time to come; and long ere that time arrives you will, please God, be well again, and in a fit state to do whatever seems best to you."

"Nevertheless," answered Leslie, "I should like to see the carpenter, if you will have the goodness to call him to me. I perceive that the brig is ashore—though *where*, I have not the remotest notion; and he will be able to tell me, far more clearly than you can, exactly what has happened."

The girl leaned over Leslie, and looked down at him with eyes full of trouble.

"Mr Leslie," she said, the tears welling up into her eyes again, "I must ask you to prepare yourself to hear bad news—very bad and very *sad* news. I cannot bring the carpenter to you; I cannot bring him, or any other of the crew to you; for, my poor friend, you and I—and Sailor—are the only living beings left on board this most unfortunate ship!"

"You and I—the only people left aboard?" gasped Leslie. "Then, in Heaven's name, what has become of the real?"

"I cannot tell you—I do not know," answered the girl. "But if you will let me tell my story in my own way, I have no doubt that your knowledge of seafaring matters will enable you to judge with sufficient accuracy just what has happened.

"You will remember, perhaps, that on the night before last there was a terribly violent storm of lightning and thunder—"

"The night *before last*?" interrupted Leslie. "You mean *last* night, surely?"

"No," answered Miss Trevor; "I mean the night before last. You have lain here unconscious nearly thirty-six hours."

"Thirty-six hours!" ejaculated Leslie, with a groan. "Well, go on, please."

Dick Leslie's Luck: A Story of Shipwreck and Adventure | 111

"That storm," continued Miss Trevor, "was so violent and terrifying that I found it not only impossible to sleep through it, but even to remain in my cabin. I therefore rose, dressed, and stationed myself in the place you call the companion, at the head of the cabin stairs where, sheltered by the cover, I could at least watch what was going on. Crouched there, I saw everything that happened. I saw you spring to the wheel when the gale struck the ship; I saw you felled to the deck by the falling mast; and I was the first to spring to your assistance and drag you out from the midst of the tangle of ropes and broken spars. Then the carpenter and one or two other men came running up, and they helped me to bring you down here to your own cabin, where I have been attending to you ever since, and striving, oh, so earnestly and so hard, to restore you to consciousness."

"My poor, brave girl," murmured Leslie, "what courage, what devotion you have shown!"

The young lady resumed—

"The carpenter and the others left me immediately that we had got you laid comfortably on your bed, and the lamp lighted, explaining that it was necessary for them to be on deck to take care of the ship—as I could readily understand; for the frightful roar of the wind and the violent motion of the ship bore eloquent witness to the fury of the storm that was raging outside. They accordingly retired; and I heard them close the doors at the top of the stairs and draw over the cover—to keep the water from coming down into the cabin, I suppose; for I could hear it falling heavily on the deck with alarming frequency; while the hoarse shouts and calling of the men up above were truly terrifying.

"You were quite insensible, and bleeding freely from a wound in your head," resumed the young lady; "and my first thought, naturally, was the medicine-chest that I had seen under the cabin table. I made my way to this as best I could; and, finding the book of directions, turned to the part treating of wounds, where I found full instructions how to proceed.

"Acting upon these, I carefully clipped away the hair from all around the gash; bathed the place, washing away the blood as well as I could; and then applied a dressing, as directed, securing it in place with plaster, and then swathing your head with a bandage to preserve the dressing from displacement.

"I had just completed this task, and was sitting on the box under your lamp, trying to discover some way of restoring you to consciousness, when the ship suddenly struck with awful violence against something, and I heard a crash as of a falling mast on deck, accompanied by a terrible outcry among the men. Then the ship was lifted up, to come down again with another crash, even worse than the first; then she was thrown violently over on her side, and I heard a fearful fall of water on the deck, accompanied by more rending and crashing of timber. This was continued for, I should say, quite half an hour, the shocks, however, becoming less and less violent until they ceased altogether, and the ship seemed to remain stationary, save for a slight rocking movement that eventually also ceased; and I have not since then felt the slightest movement or tremor of any kind. The gale, however, continued to rage with unabated fury until midday yesterday, when it quickly died away, and the sun came out.

"Meanwhile, I continued my efforts to restore you to consciousness, but without success. And finally, when at length the gale had passed away and the weather had again become fine, I ventured to go up on deck to see what had happened to the ship, and what had become of the men; for, to my great surprise and alarm, none of them had come near me, or made any attempt to inquire after you, from the moment when they had helped to bring you down into the cabin!"

"And what did you find?" demanded Leslie, anxiously.

"I found," answered Miss Trevor, "that the ship is lying stranded on an immense reef of rocks, and is within about two miles of *land*—a large island, I take it to be, for I can see the sea beyond each end of it. But that is not the worst of it. The ship is a complete wreck, both her masts being broken and lying in the water beside her, most of her bulwarks broken and gone, and not one of the crew to be found!"

"I must get up; I really *must*!" insisted Leslie. "*Please* do not attempt to keep me here," he continued, as his companion strove to dissuade him from his purpose. "I *must* go on deck and take a look round, if only for a few minutes, just to satisfy myself as to the actualities of our situation. If I cannot do that, I shall simply lie here and worry myself into a fever, thinking and fearing every imaginable thing."

"Well," remarked the girl, doubtfully, "if that is to be the result of confinement to your cabin, perhaps I had better yield to your wish and allow you to go on deck, just for a few minutes. But you must promise to be very good and obedient, to do exactly as I tell you, and—in short, to leave yourself entirely in my hands. Will you?"

"Oh, of course I will," assented Leslie, with an eagerness and alacrity that were not altogether convincing to his companion, who saw, however, that she would have to yield somewhat to this headstrong patient of hers if she wished to retain any control at all over him.

She accordingly assisted him first to sit up in his berth and then to climb out of it—he still being dressed in the clothes that he was wearing when the accident happened to him—and eventually, with very considerable difficulty—Leslie finding himself curiously weak, and so giddy that he could not stand without support—she contrived to get him up the companion ladder and out on deck, where Sailor accorded them both a boisterous and effusive welcome.

Arrived there, Leslie sank upon the short seat that ran fore and aft alongside the companion cover, and cast his eyes about him. It was a melancholy sight that met his view. The brig, with a list of about four strakes to port, was hard and fast upon the inner edge of a reef that seemed to be about a mile wide, and stretched for many miles in either direction, ahead and astern, she lying broadside-on to the run of the reef. The jury mainmast had snapped short off immediately above the lashings that bound it to the stump of the original spar, and had gone over the stern, some of its gear having evidently struck Leslie down as the spar fell. The foremast was also over the side, having gone close to the deck; and all the wreckage was still floating alongside attached to the hull by the rigging. The bulwarks had all disappeared save some ten or twelve feet on either side extending from the taffrail, forward, and a few feet in the eyes of the ship. The decks had been swept clean of every movable thing, including the longboat and the jolly-boat that had been stowed on the main hatch; and both quarter-boats had also vanished from the davits, leaving only fragments of their stem and stern-posts hanging to the tackle blocks to show what had happened to them.

No part of the reef showed above water, but its extent and limits were very clearly defined by the ripples and agitation—gentle though this last was—of the surface of the water above it. The surf was breaking heavily on its outer margin in clouds of gleaming white that flashed and glittered in the brilliant sunshine; and an occasional undulation of swell came sweeping in across the reef, causing a thousand swirls and eddies to appear as it traversed the vast barrier of submerged rock—coral, Leslie judged it to be—but it did not affect the brig in the least, sending not even the faintest tremor through her, by which the sick man judged that she must have been deposited in her present position at a moment when the level of the sea was considerably higher than it was just then. The craft was lying so close to the inner edge of the reef that had she been carried another fifty yards she would have been swept right over it; in which case she would undoubtedly have at once sunk in the deep-water that lay between this outer barrier reef and the island some three miles away—not two miles, as Miss Trevor had estimated the distance.

But, oh, that island! When Miss Trevor had spoken of it Leslie pictured to himself some tiny, obscure, bare atoll of perhaps a mile in length, and not more than a dozen feet high at its highest point—knowing from his reckoning that, at the time of the fatal outbreak, the brig had not been near enough *any known* land to render wreck upon it possible. But the land upon which he gazed with wondering eyes measured fully three miles from one extremity to the other—with a promise of considerably more beyond the points in sight. And instead of being only a few feet in height above the sea-level, it rose in a gentle slope for about half a mile from the beach of dazzlingly white sand that fringed its margin immediately opposite where the brig lay, and then towered aloft to a bare truncated peak that soared some six thousand feet into the beautifully clear air. The whole island, except some two hundred feet of its summit, appeared to be densely clad with vegetation, among which many noble trees were to be seen, some of them being resplendent with brilliant scarlet blossoms.

The fresh air had exercised a distinctly revivifying effect upon Leslie who, after some quarter of an hour's rest, felt strong enough to move about the deck, with Miss Trevor's assistance and support; and he accordingly proceeded forward as far as the galley which, to his profound satisfaction, he found to be undamaged and with all its paraphernalia intact. Then he went on to the fore scuttle—the hatch of which was on and secured. Throwing back the cover, he peered down into the dark and evil-smelling place, and called several times, without eliciting any reply. He would fain have investigated further, to the extent of descending into its interior; but his companion considered that he had by this time done quite as much as was good for him, and flatly refused to render him the least assistance toward this further adventure. He was perforce compelled therefore to abandon his intention and retreat to his own end of the ship. Here, availing himself of the support of the short remaining length of the bulwarks, he leaned over and peered down into the clear, transparent water, through which he could clearly see the white surface of the reef upon which the brig rested; and its colour and the comparative smoothness of its surface convinced him that he had been right in his conjecture that it must be of coral formation.

"Well, sir," demanded his companion, as she carefully assisted him to his former resting-place alongside the companion, "what think you of our surroundings, as a whole?"

"To be perfectly candid with you," he replied, "I regard them as decidedly promising; although I quite admit that we are in a very distinctly awkward predicament. In the first place, I fear that we shall have to reconcile ourselves to the prospect of a somewhat lengthened sojourn, for unless I have made some very serious error in my calculations—which I do not believe— we are far out of the usual tracks of ships, and our only hope, therefore, of being seen and taken off rests in the possibility that some wandering whaler may put in here for water. That, however, is a prospect upon which it will be unwise for us to reckon overmuch; and we must consequently pin our faith upon our ability to devise a means of escape for ourselves. That, in a few words, means that I shall have to set to work forthwith upon the task of constructing some craft big enough and seaworthy enough to convey us to some spot from which we can take passage home again. I see that such a prospect appears sufficiently alarming to you, and I will not attempt to conceal from you the fact that it means—as I just now said—a rather lengthy stay here. But, fortunately for us, the materials for the construction of such a craft are all here to our hand; this brig will afford us all the timber that we require for such a purpose, with plenty to spare; and I am not altogether ignorant of the arts of naval architecture and ship-building. Then we shall probably find that there is a sufficient stock of provisions still left on board here to sustain us during the period of our detention here, to say nothing of the resources of the island itself, which looks as though it might be capable of affording us an ample subsistence of itself. Then there is a beach ashore there that looks quite good enough to serve as my shipyard; with a nice little plateau adjoining it upon which I purpose to erect a tent for our accommodation—for I do not think it would be wise to remain aboard here longer than may prove absolutely necessary."

"Why," exclaimed the girl, "you appear to have planned everything out already. How fortunate I am in having you as my companion! If you had not been hurt, I suppose you would have been on deck when this disaster occurred, and the chances are that you would then have been drowned with the rest of the poor fellows; and I should have been left alone here to die miserably."

"Yes," agreed Leslie, dryly, "my accident was certainly a blessing in disguise, from that point of view. If I can succeed in getting you safely away from here, and putting you in the way of returning to your friends, I shall at least have accomplished something useful before I die."

"Oh, Mr Leslie," exclaimed the girl, "you know I did not mean that! I simply meant—well—I mean—oh dear, how am I to express myself so that you will understand? Surely you do not believe me to be such an utterly selfish and heartless creature as to be glad that you have escaped the fate of the others merely because, by so doing, you are left alive to be my helper and protector?"

"No, indeed," answered Leslie, heartily, "I assure you, Miss Trevor—" He paused abruptly, thought for a moment, and then resumed: "Look here, we have been thrown together—you and I—and our fates intermingled in a very extraordinary manner, and we are likely to remain together for some time longer in fairly intimate association, each of us the sole companion of the other. Do you not think that, under the circumstances, we might as well drop the formality of 'Mr' and 'Miss?' My name is Richard; but my friends call me Dick, and I should be glad if you would do the same."

"Very well," answered his companion, "I will willingly do so, if you really wish it; it would be only prudish to object—under the circumstances, as you put it. And you, in your turn, may call me Flora, if the name commends itself to your ear. And now, sir, please go on again from where you left off."

"Let me see," mused Leslie, "what was it we were talking about? Oh yes, I remember. You were explaining to me that you were glad I had escaped drowning not so much because of the use I could be to—"

"Ah," interrupted his companion, "I can see that you are rapidly getting better, because you are beginning to tease. But, seriously, Mr Les—well, Dick, then—I want you to tell me something more of your plans. What do you propose to do first—when you are well enough to work again, I mean?"

"The first thing I propose to do," answered Leslie, "is to overhaul the carpenter's chest and satisfy myself as to what tools are at my command. That done, I shall at once begin to break up the brig, confining myself, in the first instance, to the removal from her of just sufficient material to admit of the construction of a raft. The next thing will be to convey ashore such canvas, rope, and other matters as may be needed for the erection of a comfortable and commodious tent for our accommodation ashore; together with all necessary furniture, the galley stove, pots and pans, and all the rest of it. I am rather anxious to carry out this much of my plans with as little delay as possible; because, you see, the weather is one of those things upon which one can never depend—another gale may spring up at any moment, and when it does the brig will most probably go to pieces. I am therefore exceedingly anxious to get you comfortably established ashore before this happens. Then, if all goes well, I shall at once proceed to pull the poor old *Mermaid* carefully to pieces, damaging the planking as little as may be in the process, because that is the material out of which I purpose to build my boat. I shall do this, transferring it, and everything on board that may be likely to be of use to us, to, the shore before I do anything else; because, should the brig break up of herself, much valuable material is certain to be lost. Then, when I have got everything safe ashore, I shall begin upon the boat."

"I see," remarked Flora, with animation, "that we have a kind of Crusoe existence before us—a sort of perpetual picnic. Very well; I shall undertake the house-keeping part of the work; keep the tent clean and tidy; prepare nice appetising meals for you when you come home tired from your work;

keep your clothes in repair; do the washing; and generally look after domestic affairs. Oh, you may smile as much as you like. I dare say you think that I know nothing about such matters; but I do; and I flatter myself that I shall astonish you."

"Yes," laughed Leslie, "I expect you will; I am fully prepared to be astonished. No," he continued, as he saw a pout rising to his companion's lips, "I did not quite mean that. True, I have before me a vision of a very charming young lady, always somewhat haughty and unapproachable, and always most elegantly costumed; who used to be the awe and admiration of everybody aboard the *Golden Fleece*; and I have been endeavouring—I must confess with not altogether brilliant success—to picture her doing the cooking and washing, ashore there. But I know—or at least I have been told—that woman's power of adaptability surpasses belief, and I have already seen that you possess it to a marvellous degree; therefore, despite what I said just now, I shall be astonished at nothing you do, or prove yourself able to achieve."

"Thank you," answered Flora, with a touch of annoyance in her tone. "I know I was perfectly horrid in those days—oh, how far away they seem, now—and I am afraid that I have not done much since then toward giving you a better opinion of me; but you shall see! Oh, Dick, please do not think badly of me! You have done so *very* much for me, and have been so invariably kind and considerate to me, that I cannot bear the idea that you should think ill of me. I owe my life to you. You must remember that I did not know you, then—"

"I know; I know," answered Dick, laying his hand reassuringly upon hers. "You acted quite rightly in keeping us all at arm's-length; for, as you say, you knew none of us then, and could not be expected to discriminate between one and another. For my own part, I would not have had you act otherwise than you did; so let us say no more about it. And now, if you will kindly help me, I think I had better go below and lie down for awhile. I must take care of myself for both our sakes."

So they went below again; and after Flora had dressed Leslie's wound afresh, the latter stretched himself out on the cabin lockers and sank into a refreshing sleep, while the girl busied herself in the preparation of such nourishing dishes, against his awakening, as the resources of the wreck afforded.

The following day found Leslie much stronger, and more like himself again; so much so, indeed, that, despite his fair companion's protestations, he set to work and got the carpenter's tool-chest on deck, and busied himself upon the light task of sharpening chisels, gouges, planes, adzes, axes, and so on; and generally putting everything in good order against the time when he would want to use them. This, with occasional periods of vest, occupied him through the whole of that day; at the end of which he declared himself to be none the worse but rather the better for his exertions.

The next day Leslie devoted to the task of lifting off the fore hatches and rigging a light pair of sheers over the hatchway by means of two pieces of the rail that he detached from the short length of bulwarks that still remained standing abaft. It was his purpose to give this part of the brig a thorough overhaul prior to attempting anything else; hoping that he might find therein something that would enable him to construct a raft without having recourse to the timber of the ship. And in this he was successful beyond his utmost hopes; for, among other matters, he found two stout packing-cases—measuring twenty feet long by three feet wide by two feet deep—containing long strips of gilt moulding, such as are used in house decoration. The moulding he carefully stowed away again—prudent man—not knowing whether in the future they might not, despite their gaudy appearance, come in useful for something. Then carefully taking the packing-cases apart, he shaped the bottom planking of each somewhat after the semblance of the bow and run of a ship—that is to say, he pointed the two square ends of each by sawing them to the required shape. Then he put the cases together again, curving the sides to fit the curves of the bottom planks; and when this was done he found himself in possession of two boat-like boxes, or flat-bottomed boats, of very respectable shape and size. These he next strengthened by nailing stout timbers, walings, and stringers to the bottom and sides, inside; when a careful caulking and paying of the seams completed them by rendering them watertight. So pleased was he with these two contrivances of his—the firstfruits of his labours—that although he had not originally intended to use them as boats, either of them was quite sufficiently large to convey himself and his companion across the tranquil waters of the lagoon that stretched between the brig and the island; and he accordingly determined that, before applying these structures to their ultimate purpose, he would make use of one of them in which to effect a preliminary exploration of the island. Accordingly he fitted the interior of one of them with a couple of seats—one in the middle for himself, and the other near the "stern" for Miss Trevor's accommodation; secured to each side a stout cleat in a suitable position, and suitably bored for the reception of a pair of rowlocks; and a length of three-inch planking sawn down the middle and shaped with a spokeshave into a pair of paddles completed the equipment of what turned out to be a very serviceable and handy boat.

The construction of these two "pontoons," as Leslie called them, together with the supplementary labour of fitting up one of them to serve as a boat, consumed nearly a week; but they were so thoroughly satisfactory when finished that their constructor regarded his time as well spent. The last item of his task, the making of the pair of paddles, or short oars, was completed as the sun was sinking below the horizon on the ninth day after the stranding of the *Mermaid*; and it was arranged that, if the weather held fine and the barometer continued steady, the next day should be devoted to a visit to the island.

Chapter Nine
An Island Paradise

The next morning dawned as fine as heart could wish, with a cloudless sky of matchless blue, and a "glass" that showed a rising rather than a falling tendency. Immediately after breakfast, therefore, Leslie emerged from the brig's cabin provided with a basket of provisions neatly packed by the fair Flora's hand and daintily covered with a spotlessly white cloth. This he deposited in the stern-sheets of his boat; and then addressed Sailor, who stood at the gangway watching the proceedings with eager interest.

"Now, Sailor, come along down, boy; that's a good dog, then. Come down, you sir, I say!"

Sailor wagged his tail excitedly, and barked in response, making a great show of being about to jump down into the boat, but baulking at the last moment and looking round anxiously to see whether his beloved mistress were coming, then approaching the side again and barking a response to Leslie's blandishments, but dexterously avoiding the efforts of the latter to capture and drag him down into the boat; and so on *ad infinitum* At length, however, Miss Trevor made her appearance, a radiant vision in white, and armed against the assaults of the too-ardent sun with a white lace parasol — one of the many spoils of the late skipper's speculative investment — and approached the head of the side-ladder that Leslie had rigged for her accommodation. Then, as she began to descend, Sailor hesitated no longer but, fearing lest he should lose his passage, sprang down into the frail craft with an *abandon* that nearly capsized her, and placed himself in the eyes of the boat, obediently to a signal from Leslie's hand. Another moment and Flora had taken her place in the stern, and Leslie was bearing-off from the brig's side.

With her load of three — for Sailor was nearly as heavy as his mistress — the boat proved to be somewhat crank, and Leslie had a momentary spasm of regret that he had not tied up the dog and left him aboard the brig, instead of bringing him with them; but the water was quite smooth, and they all sat still. The passage was consequently accomplished without mishap; and in about an hour from the moment of starting they all three stood safely on the dazzlingly white beach of coral sand that stretched for about a mile in either direction from the spot where they had landed. From here the hull of the brig looked little more than a small inconspicuous spot against the snow-white cloud of surf that broke eternally upon the outer edge of the barrier reef; and Leslie made a mental note to pull off aboard again betimes in the afternoon, for it would be practically impossible to hit off her position in the darkness.

The beach on which they stood was of no great width, some sixty or seventy feet wide, perhaps, from the water's edge to the spot where it abruptly met the luxuriant growth of thick guinea-grass that seemed to form the turf of the island. Immediately opposite the spot where they had landed there stretched a clear space of this turf, measuring about a quarter of a square mile in area, entirely unencumbered by bush, or tree, or shrub of any kind. Leslie recognised this as the spot that he had already fixed upon, while aboard the brig, as the site for his camp; and his nearer inspection of it now satisfied him that it was eminently suitable for the purpose and indeed could not be improved upon. Beyond the confines of this open space, to right, left, and rear of it, shrubs and small bushes grew at first sparsely and, further on, in greater profusion, until ultimately this more or less scattered growth merged into the dense and apparently impenetrable bush and forest with which the entire island appeared to be clothed.

When Leslie's eyes had first fallen upon this island an uneasy suspicion had arisen within him that so comparatively large and important an area must almost of necessity be inhabited; and he had not been altogether free from doubt as to what, in such a case, the disposition of its inhabitants might be toward him and his companion. He had an idea that he had somewhere heard or read that the natives of certain of the Pacific islands were addicted to cannibalism; and he felt that if by any evil chance this particular island should happen to be inhabited by such a race, the cup of their misfortunes would be full. Consequently, the work of constructing his pontoons had been frequently broken into by long and anxious examinations of the island through the telescope, in a search for indications of the presence of inhabitants.

These examinations had entirely failed to reveal any such indications; and the hope had gradually arisen in his mind that, after all, the island might prove to be uninhabited. But he was not yet by any means satisfied that this hope was well-grounded, and he determined that this first visit of his to the place should be mainly devoted to a further search and examination. Before doing anything further, therefore, he suggested to Flora that they should walk the entire length of the beach—keeping to the grass as far as possible, in order to leave the surface of the sand quite undisturbed—so that he might be able to carefully and systematically scrutinise it in search of footprints. For he argued that if savages really existed on this island, they could scarcely have failed to discover the existence of the wreck during the week that she had lain upon the reef; in which case they would most probably have gathered at the water's edge, at the nearest possible point, for the purpose of examining her. And since this particular strip of beach happened to be nearer the wreck than any other point of the island, he felt tolerably certain that footprints would be found upon it, if anywhere. A strong point in favour of the assumption that the island was uninhabited was the fact that the wreck had not been approached by canoes; for Leslie felt that if she had been seen by natives, they would scarcely have left her unvisited for an entire week.

The careful and systematic inspection of the entire length of beach consumed an hour, and was without result; no human footprints were anywhere to be seen; and Leslie was confident that if any person had walked upon that sand within the week, he would have left plain indications behind him, for the wind throughout that time had been too gentle to obliterate marks of any kind, as was evidenced by the fact that the footprints of birds were everywhere clearly distinguishable. Once, indeed, he thought he had found what he sought; but upon closer inspection the signs proved to be the track of a turtle that had come up on the sand to lay her eggs, as was evidenced by the fact that the eggs themselves were found, and a few of them appropriated.

Although his investigation thus far was reassuring, Leslie was not yet by any means satisfied. He wished to obtain a much clearer idea than he yet possessed of the actual extent and general shape of his island; and the only way by which this was to be accomplished, and at the same time a general survey of it effected, was to ascend to the summit of the mountain. This promised to be a decidedly arduous task, in that climate, especially as they had been cooped up for so long a time within the narrow confines of a small vessel, with very limited space for taking exercise. But he determined nevertheless to attempt it, feeling that he could never be perfectly easy in his mind until he had done so, and they accordingly set out forthwith on their way.

Path, of course, there was none; but this was of little moment, for they knew that so long as they continued to ascend every step took them so much nearer to the summit; and they were agreeably surprised to find that the bush and undergrowth that, at a distance, had appeared to be absolutely impenetrable, was not nearly so dense as it had looked. They were consequently enabled, by adopting a somewhat serpentine route, to make very fair upward progress, although they occasionally encountered spots where a passage had to be forced, and where Flora's dainty white costume suffered somewhat.

They had not gone very far upon their way before Leslie discovered, to his great relief and satisfaction, that they certainly need have no fear of starvation, even in the event of their being doomed to remain where they were for the rest of their lives. For, as they went, fruit-bearing trees of many kinds were found in great profusion, growing luxuriantly, and many of them loaded with most luscious fruit. Mangoes, bananas, plantains, limes, custard-apples, and bread-fruit were among the varieties that Leslie recognised; and there were many others with which he was unfamiliar, and which he therefore regarded with more or less suspicion. They saw no signs of animals of any kind; but the forest seemed to be alive with birds, the extraordinary tameness—or rather fearlessness—of which seemed to argue an unfamiliarity with man.

SHE SPREAD THE CLOTH ON THE GRASS AND SET OUT A DAINTY
AND ENTICING LUNCHEON.

Two hours of arduous climbing brought the adventurers to a most romantic spot, where a small stream of deliciously pure and cold fresh water gushed out from under a huge overhanging moss-grown rock, the banks of the rivulet being clothed with ferns of the most lovely and delicate varieties, while the surrounding sward was gay with flowers of strange forms and most exquisitely delicate and beautiful combinations of colouring. A huge tree, bearing large blossoms of vivid scarlet instead of leaves—which Leslie identified as the "bois-immortelle"—overhung the spot; and as the pair were by this time feeling somewhat tired and hungry, they seated themselves upon the yielding sward, and Leslie surrendering the lunch-basket to Flora, the latter spread the cloth on the grass and set out as dainty and enticing a luncheon as, supplemented by the fruit with which Leslie had filled his pockets, two hungry people need ever desire to find before them.

A narrow vista through the trees afforded the travellers a glimpse of the sea stretching blue and foam-flecked below them and right out to the horizon; and as Leslie judged from this glimpse that they must have accomplished considerably more than half their climb, the pair lingered for some time over their meal, resting their tired limbs and enjoying the loveliness of their surroundings. Then, after an interval of about an hour and a half, they again proceeded on their way, making better progress now than they did at first, as the undergrowth and trees became from this point steadily thinner as they progressed, until at length they were able to catch occasional glimpses of the summit for which they were aiming. Finally they emerged from the bush altogether, to find themselves breasting a steep slope, the soil of which was composed of fine scoriae and ashes.

"Just as I anticipated," ejaculated Leslie, as he stooped to examine the ground. "This island is volcanic; and yonder peak—the top of which, you will notice, appears to have been broken off—is the crater. But do not be alarmed," he continued, seeing a startled expression leap into his companion's eyes, "the volcano is undoubtedly extinct, and has probably been so for ages; for if you will but look around you at all this vegetation you will notice that it bears no remotest sign or indication of ever having been disturbed by volcanic action. I am not botanist enough to be able to judge the ages of those trees that we see below us; but thousands of them must be considerably more than half a century old; and as it is evident that no eruption has taken place since they started to grow, I think we may rest satisfied that no disturbance is in the least likely to occur during our occupation of the place. But let us push on; it is nearly one o'clock, and I am anxious to get up there to have a good look round and make a complete survey of our dominions."

They accordingly resumed their climb; and after a further three-quarters of an hour of arduous labour—the steepness of the acclivity and the looseness of the soil rendering progress exceedingly slow and difficult—they finally reached their goal, to find themselves standing, as it were, upon the rim of a huge basin about a third of a mile in diameter and some three hundred feet deep, the inner sides sloping almost perpendicularly, and the bottom forming a small lake. The perfectly bare sides were much too steep and the soil altogether too loose and treacherous to render an attempt at descent advisable, even had they wished it—which they did not—it sufficed Leslie that the whole appearance of the place confirmed his previous conviction that the volcano was extinct; and without wasting a second glance upon it he at once turned his attention to the scene beneath him.

They had happened, by a stroke of good luck, to hit upon the very highest point in the lip of the crater, and they were thus enabled to see, from the spot on which they stood, the entire extent of the island, to its uttermost limits; and they found it much bigger than they had anticipated.

In plan it bore a rough resemblance to a right-angled triangle, the body of which had been so twisted as to cause its apex to bear to the right. The base of this triangle, opposite to which the wreck of the brig could be seen as a tiny toy almost immediately beneath them, faced south-east, and appeared to measure between three and four miles across between its two extreme points, while the side corresponding to the perpendicular of the triangle was, according to Leslie's estimate, nearly, if not quite, ten miles long. The crater was situated not in the centre of the island, but quite close to its south-eastern side, which accounted for the steepness of the acclivity that the explorers had been obliged to climb. Northward of the crater, after the first five hundred feet of steep decline that formed the summit proper, the ground, undulating picturesquely, fell away in quite a gentle slope to the most northerly extremity of the island, which Leslie judged to be a fairly bold headland. The barrier reef, upon which the brig lay stranded, was visible with startling distinctness throughout its entire length from this point; and Leslie observed that it formed a natural and most efficient breakwater to the lagoon that stretched along the entire south-east shore of the island, curving gradually round in a crescent form until it joined the island itself at its most westerly extremity, while away to the eastward there was a deep-water passage, between the reef and the island, of about an eighth of a mile in width.

Turning his attention once more to the island itself, Leslie observed that it was wooded to its uttermost extremity, and that no beach was to be discovered in any direction save that upon which they had landed, the ground appearing everywhere else to slope precipitously to the sea, in the form of bold cliffs. And, as savages would naturally build their villages close to a beach, to secure facilities for their fishing operations, Leslie was further confirmed in his hope that his island was uninhabited; especially as he looked carefully in every direction for the smoke of fires, and found none.

Then he allowed his eyes to wander farther afield, and intently scanned the entire visible surface of the ocean, in search of a sail, but without success. He was not surprised at this; for he knew the island to be situated far out of the track of all ships, save perhaps whalers, and craft that might be driven by adverse winds out of their proper course; and although it is the first instinct of the castaway sailor to maintain a ceaseless watch for a sail, the ex-lieutenant knew that the chance of rescue for himself and his companion by a passing ship was altogether too slight to be seriously given a place in his plans for the future. Nevertheless, for a moment he entertained the idea of erecting a flagstaff on the summit and hoisting a flag upon it for the purpose of attracting the attention of any ship that might perchance pass the place; but a very brief consideration of the project sufficed to convince him that the benefit to be derived therefrom was much too problematical to justify the expenditure of so much labour and time as it would involve. Moreover he had a conviction that any ship sighting so conspicuous an object as the island in a spot shown upon the charts as clear sea, would approach and give the place an overhaul.

But although Leslie's most careful scrutiny failed to reveal any sign of the presence of ships, he was astonished to discover that there was other land in sight from his lofty lookout. He clearly saw two other eminences peering above the horizon to the westward, one bearing as nearly as possible due west, and the other about south-west, while away in the north-western quarter he believed he detected the loom of land at a very great distance. The two islands in clear view were apparently about the same distance away—a distance which, from their delicate, filmy appearance, he estimated to be quite a hundred miles; and he knew that they must be, like his own, mountainous, from the fact that they showed above the horizon.

The sun was by this time settling perceptibly in the western sky, and, lovely as was the prospect that stretched around them, Leslie felt that the time had arrived for them to be moving once more; they accordingly threw a final parting glance around them, and began the descent of the mountain. To ascend was one thing; to descend, quite another; and in a little more than an hour from the moment of leaving the summit they found themselves once more on the beach and beside their boat. Then, greatly fatigued by their unwonted exertions, but with the memory of a thoroughly enjoyable day fresh upon them, they paddled leisurely off to the brig, reaching her just as the sun was dipping below the horizon.

Their experiences of that day only whetted Leslie's—and, it must be confessed, Flora's—appetite for further exploration and adventure; the former in particular felt that he would never be satisfied until he had circumnavigated his island and critically examined every yard of its coast-line. To do this, a boat was of course necessary, or at least something of a much more seaworthy character than the "pontoon" in which he had adventured the passage to the island. And they had nothing of the kind. After Flora had retired to her cabin, however, Leslie spent an hour or so on deck, smoking his pipe and pondering upon the problem of how to supply the deficiency; and when at length he turned in, he believed he saw his way.

The following morning accordingly found him astir bright and early, eager to put his ideas into immediate execution. He first got on deck again the pontoon that he had used on the previous day, and proceeded to considerably strengthen her by the addition of further wales, stringers, and beams; and when he had got her to his liking, he proceeded to treat the other in a precisely similar fashion. Then he fitted them both with rudders. Next, having carefully disposed the two pontoons on deck, with their longitudinal centre-lines parallel and nine feet apart, he first decked them both completely in, leaving only a manhole eighteen inches square in the middle of each deck; and then proceeded to frame and fit together a thoroughly strong platform, twelve feet square, so arranged that it could be securely bolted to the gunwales of the two pontoons in the positions they occupied relatively to each other. This done, he launched the whole arrangement overboard; and found himself the proud and happy possessor of what, for want of a better and more appropriate name, he called a "catamaran;" the structure consisting, of course, of the two pontoons arranged parallel to each other, with a water space of six feet between them, and firmly and strongly connected with each other by the platform; the whole forming a very buoyant and commodious raft, capable of being rigged, and promising to behave exceedingly well under sail in smooth and even in moderately rough water. To rig this singular-looking craft with an enormous mainsail and jib was no very difficult matter, the wreckage alongside furnishing him with the requisite spars, canvas, and rigging. Each of the rudders was then furnished with a tiller; and these two tillers being connected together with a cross-piece, were controlled by a central tiller that actuated both rudders simultaneously. The construction and completion of this catamaran cost Leslie three whole weeks of arduous labour; but when she was finished he felt that the time had been well spent.

The next thing in order was to subject the craft to a sea-trial; and this Leslie at once proceeded to do. He left Flora on board the brig, with Sailor as her companion and protector, not caring to risk the girl's safety on the catamaran until the reliability and sea-going qualities of the latter had been tested; but he promised her that he would not be absent more than two hours at the utmost, when, if everything proved satisfactory, he would return and take her for a cruise; and he suggested that she might devote the interval to the preparation of a luncheon-basket to serve them for the day. Then, hoisting his sails, he pushed off, and got the craft under way.

His first act, after getting away from the brig, was to test the behaviour of the catamaran under sail by putting her through a series of evolutions, such as tacking, jibing, and so on; and then, finding that she proved to be marvellously handy, he tested her speed off and on the wind. The trade wind happened to be piping up quite strong that day, and it was therefore a very favourable occasion upon which to subject the craft to such a test as Leslie desired; and he was not only delighted but astonished at the quite unexpected turn of speed that the craft developed, this being doubtless due to the enormous spread of canvas that her peculiar form of construction enabled her to carry. She skimmed down-wind with the speed of a swallow, and was scarcely less swift when close-hauled and looking up within four points of the wind.

More than satisfied with the behaviour of his catamaran in smooth water, Leslie next headed her to the north-east, steering for the passage between the island and the reef that led to the open sea. The distance to be traversed was about four miles, and this the quaint-looking craft covered in seventeen minutes by Leslie's watch, passing in an instant from smooth water out on to a tumbling surface of sapphire-blue creaming and foaming sea, with a long and rather formidable swell under-running it. This was the sort of sea to find out for Leslie the weak points in his structure, if it had any; and for the next half-hour—while "carrying-on," and driving his craft full tilt against the sea under the heavy pressure of her enormous unreefed sails—he watched his craft carefully and anxiously, ready at the first sign of weakness to up-helm and run back to the shelter of the lagoon. But no such sign revealed itself; on the contrary, she not only stood up to her canvas "as stiff as a house," but slid along over the high-running sea as buoyantly as an empty cask, hanging to windward with a tenacity that filled her happy owner with wonder; throwing a little spray over her weather bow occasionally, it is true, but otherwise going along as dry as a bone. Her speed, too, was truly astounding; had the poor old *Mermaid* been all ataunto and alongside her, the catamaran could have sailed round and round her. At length, thoroughly satisfied with his trial, and fully convinced of the absolute seaworthiness of his craft, Leslie tacked—the catamaran working like a top, even in the heavy sea that was running—and, putting up his helm, bore away back for the lagoon, reaching the brig once more after an absence of about an hour and a half.

He found Flora awaiting him, attired in a good serviceable and comfortably warm serge gown—for he had warned her that she would find the strong breeze a trifle chill out at sea—and with the lunch-basket packed and ready. It was the work of less than a minute to transfer her and the basket from the deck of the brig to that of the catamaran, when, leaving Sailor to take care of the former—much to his disgust—they once more pushed off, and headed straight out for the passage skirting the inner edge of the reef, and noting, as they slid rapidly along, that this inner margin of the reef was simply teeming with fish. Then, almost before they had time to realise it, they were in the open sea once more, and heading away to the northward and westward with the mainsheet eased off to its utmost limit, and the main-boom square out to starboard. Leslie allowed himself an offing of about a mile, as this would enable him not only to get a very good general idea of the island as a whole, but would also enable him to carefully examine the coast-line.

The easternmost extremity of the island—between which and the barrier reef the deep-water passage lay—was a bold headland thickly overgrown with tall and stately forest trees, and terminating in a rocky cliff about one hundred and fifty feet high, that dipped sheer down into the sea; and beyond this, to the northward, the coast-line curved inward somewhat to the most northerly point on the island, forming what might almost be termed a shallow bay—shallow, that is to say, in point of depth of itself, but not of its depth of water, for the whole north-easterly coast-line of the island consisted of precipitous cliffs averaging about a hundred feet in height, with water enough alongside to float the biggest ship that was ever launched, if one might judge from its colour. There was no sign or possibility of a beach anywhere along here, which was comforting to Leslie, whose mind somehow still clung rather tenaciously to the idea of possible savages. But nothing mortal could by any possibility land on that eastern seaboard, nor would savages be likely to establish themselves in a spot so completely inaccessible from the sea. Moreover, the entire country, from the ridge or backbone of the island, that ran from the crater down to the most northerly point of the island, was densely covered with vegetation, showing no faintest sign of clearing or cultivation, so that Leslie began once more to feel reassured.

The most northerly point of the island was reached and rounded in some forty minutes from the moment of leaving the lagoon and bearing away round Cape Flora—as Dick insisted on naming the bold headland that formed the eastern extremity of the island. This most northerly point was, like the other, a lofty vertical cliff, timber—crowned to its very verge and descending vertically into the sea; and Flora declared that the only possible designation for it was Point Richard.

Rounding Point Richard, then, and hauling in the mainsheet, the voyagers found themselves suddenly under the lee of the land and in smooth water, save for the long undulations of swell that came sweeping up to them from the southward. They were now coasting down the western side of the island; and here again Leslie was gratified to discover that the conclusions arrived at by him during his visit to the summit were correct; there was no beach throughout the whole length of the coast-line; nothing but sheer perpendicular cliffs everywhere, although in places these cliffs rose no higher than some twenty feet above the sea-level. Finally they arrived off the south-westerly extremity of the island—which they agreed to name Mermaid Head—and found themselves skirting the outer edge of the reef, at a distance of about one hundred yards from the surf-line, lost in wonderment and admiration of the great wall of snowy foam and spray that leapt, sparkling like a cloud of jewels, some forty feet into the clear sunlit air. Then they re-entered the lagoon and ran alongside the brig— to the exuberant delight of Sailor—some three hours from the moment of starting, having had a most enjoyable sail, and satisfied themselves definitely that, since no savages existed on their own side of the island, the place must of necessity be altogether free from their unwelcome presence. And thenceforward Leslie's mind was completely free from at least that one anxiety.

And now, having provided himself with the means not only to pass freely and rapidly between the brig and the shore, but also to venture out to sea in chase of a ship, should occasion to do so arise, Leslie felt himself free to proceed with the execution of his great plan for the establishment of a dockyard ashore, and the construction of a craft sufficiently substantial and seaworthy to convey him and his companion back to the world of civilisation.

The first part of his task consisted in the erection of a spacious tent on shore for the accommodation of his companion and himself; and this he proposed to do with the aid of the old sails on board the brig, reserving the new ones and such canvas as he could find for the making of a suit of sails for the proposed new boat. He accordingly got out all the old sails, and deposited them on the deck of the catamaran, together with a quantity of cordage, blocks, and other gear, a crowbar, pickaxes, hammer, and shovel, an axe, and a number of miscellaneous odds and ends that he thought would be useful, and conveyed the whole to the shore. Then entering the woods, he selected the first nine suitable saplings that he could find, and cut them down, afterwards conveying them, one at a time and with considerable labour, to the site that he had chosen for his tent. He next dug six holes in the ground—three for each gable-end—and in four of these holes he reared four of his stoutest saplings to form the four corners of the tent, setting them carefully upright by means of temporary stays, and ramming the loose soil round about their feet until they stood quite firmly. Then, midway between the poles that were to form the gable-ends of the tent, he reared two others, some ten feet longer than the first four, these last being intended to support the ridge-pole of the structure, which he next hoisted into position and securely lashed. Then he similarly raised the eaves-poles into position and lashed them, thus completing the skeleton of the tent. The sides and ends of the structure, together with a central partition, were formed of sails, laboriously hoisted into position by means of tackles, laced to the ridge-pole, and securely pinned to the ground with stakes; and a spare main-course drawn over the ridge-pole, sloping down over the eaves, and drawn tight all round by ropes spliced into the leeches and secured to the ground with stout tent pegs, completed the whole. To prevent the flooding of the tent in wet weather, Leslie took the precaution to dig a good deep trench all round it to receive the rain-water, and from this he dug another to carry it off.

The next matter demanding attention was the furnishing of the tent. The need of bedsteads was easily met by driving four stout stakes into the ground, connected at their tops by side and end poles, to which lengths of stout canvas were attached by a lacing; and the structure was then ready to receive the mattress and bedding generally. The cabin lamp efficiently illuminated Miss Trevor's half of the tent, while a lamp taken from the steward's berth afforded Leslie all the light he needed to undress by. Then the cabin table, the locker cushions, the deck-chair, the ship's slender stock of books, and a variety of odds and ends conducive to comfort were transferred from the brig to the shore, together with the galley stove and its appurtenances; and the pair then went into residence in their new abode—which, it may be said, they found much more roomy, airy, and comfortable than their former quarters aboard the brig. The galley stove, it should be mentioned, was set up outside and to leeward of the tent, all cooking operations being conducted in the open air. The erection of the tent, from start to finish, absorbed a fortnight of Leslie's time, and involved such a lavish expenditure of labour that, could he have foreseen it, he would, as he afterwards confessed, have started much less ambitiously.

And now the ex-lieutenant found himself confronted by a truly formidable task, compared with which all that had gone before was a mere trifle. This consisted in overhauling the cargo of the brig, with the view of appropriating everything that could by any possibility prove of use to them either during their—as they hoped—temporary sojourn upon the island, or in the construction of the boat that was to take them away from it. Leslie had become aware, from remarks made by Purchas, that the brig was taking out a very considerable quantity of machinery, but this was all stowed in the bottom of the ship. On top of this there was a vast miscellaneous assortment of mixed goods of almost every conceivable description, and this it was that Leslie wished to get hold of and overhaul.

Accordingly, he one morning went off to the brig and proceeded to lift off the main hatches, disclosing to view a number of bales and packing-cases, mostly of a size and weight that it would be impossible for him to deal with single-handed. He saw that before it would be possible for him to raise even a fourth part of them it would be necessary for him to have the assistance of certain appliances, such as sheers, tackles, etcetera; but he succeeded in dragging a few of the lightest of them on deck and opening them.

The first case opened proved to contain china—a breakfast, dinner, tea, and toilet service, very handsome, and apparently very expensive. This would be exceedingly useful to them, for, to tell the truth, the brig's pantry had never been too liberally stocked; and the carelessness of the steward, combined with the heavy weather experienced by the brig, had played havoc with it. He therefore fastened up the case again and lowered it carefully over the side on to the deck of the catamaran. Then he got hold of a bale of rugs. These, he told himself, would help to make Flora's half of the tent more comfortable; and they, too, went down over the side. The next case—a small one, bearing what appeared to be a private address—contained a dainty little sewing-machine—possibly useful also to Flora. It followed the rugs. The next case that came to hand, though a large one, was unexpectedly light, so Leslie roused it on deck and opened it. It contained a number of bird-cages, such as are used for canaries. Some of them were of large size—large enough to accommodate half a dozen of the little songsters—and all were very handsome and, apparently, expensive. But they were not in the least likely to be of service, and would therefore only be in the way, so overboard they went, ruthlessly; the case itself, however, Leslie kept, as the wood and the screws might possibly be useful. There were no more packages at hand that could be manipulated without appliances, so Leslie replaced the hatches, drew the tarpaulin over them and battened it down, and then made sail for the shore.

As the catamaran ran in and grounded on the beach, Flora came down to meet him.

"Well, Dick," she said—the name came glibly enough to her lips now—"what luck have you met with?"

"Not bad," answered Leslie. "I have not been able to do very much, for the cases are mostly too large to handle without a tackle, and I have not thus far found anything that will go toward building our little ship; but I have here a set of china that will gladden your heart and replenish your pantry; some rugs for the floor of your compartment; and a sewing-machine that you may possibly find handy later on."

"And what have you brought that will be useful for yourself?" she asked.

"Nothing," answered Leslie. "The only other case that I could get at contained bird-cages—"

"Bird-cages?" she repeated, with a burst of hearty laughter. "Why, the brig must be quite a general emporium!"

"Yes," Leslie assented soberly. "I quite expect she will prove so. You see, a place like Valparaiso imports every imaginable thing from Europe; and it would not surprise me to find even pianos, watches and jewellery, as well as clothing, books, and such like among the cargo."

"Pianos?" exclaimed Flora, with delighted surprise. "Oh, Dick, if you should find a piano, please—*please* bring it ashore for me. I am passionately fond of music, and a piano would be such a solace to us here."

"If there is a piano in the ship you shall have it," answered Leslie. "Poor little girl! it must be horribly slow for you, cooped up here, practically alone, as you are. I am but a poor companion, I know, at the best of times; and henceforth I shall be so busy that you will be left more alone than ever. Yes; you shall certainly have a piano, if there is one in the brig."

"Now, Dick, you *know* I did not mean that—about your being a poor companion," answered Flora. "On the contrary, you are the very best companion that a girl in my unfortunate situation could possibly have; for you are, before and above all else, a gentleman—a chivalrous, courteous, tender-hearted gentleman, with whom I feel as safe as though you were my brother. And then you are brave, strong, resourceful, and so utterly unselfish that you amaze me—"

"There, that will do, thank you," laughed Leslie. "Do you wickedly wish to make me conceited? Because you will, if you say much more in that strain. As to 'brothers,' I hope you don't look upon me as a brother, do you?"

"Why, yes—almost," answered the girl, a little doubtfully. "Do you not wish me to regard you as a brother, Dick?"

"Um," he meditated; "of course that would be better than nothing; but—oh no; on the whole I think I have no desire that you should regard me as a brother. There, now of course I have offended you. What an ass and a cad I am!"

"You are not; you are *not*! And I will not have you say so," exclaimed the girl, passionately. "And you have not offended me," she went on. "It is only that I am feeling a little depressed to-day; and your—I mean—oh, I cannot explain!"

And therewith she turned away abruptly, and beat a hasty retreat to the shelter of the tent.

Leslie looked after her as though for a moment he felt inclined to follow her. Then he thought better of it, and meditatively proceeded to land the things that he had brought ashore from the brig. This done, he hunted up the axe and wandered off to the woods in search of a couple of spars to serve as sheers for working the main hatchway. The cutting down of these, the conveyance of them to the shore, and the towing of them off alongside the brig provided him with plenty of work for the remainder of the day; he therefore did not again meet his companion until the day's work was over and they sat down to dinner. It was apparent that by that time the young lady had completely recovered her spirits; but she carefully avoided all reference to the little scene that had occurred earlier in the day, so Leslie thought it best to let the matter drop, although he continued to puzzle over it for several days thereafter.

The following day saw Leslie once again aboard the brig, where he busied himself in getting his spars in on deck, converting them into sheers, fitting them, and by means of tackles and stays rearing them into position and securing them. It was a long and heavy job, occupying him the entire day, and sending him back to the island at night completely fagged out. But on the succeeding day he went off to the brig early—in fact, before Flora made her appearance—and strenuously devoted himself to the task of breaking out the contents of the main hold. He spent the entire morning in rousing cases, bales, and packages of all kinds up on deck; and after partaking of a hurried lunch he carefully opened these and examined their contents. Two of the largest he found to contain respectively men's and women's clothing; another contained books and music; a fourth contained stationery and drawing-paper; a fifth contained rolls of silk, linen, drapery, ribbons, laces, and haberdashery; and all these he lowered on to the deck of the catamaran for conveyance to the shore. Others contained rolls of wall-paper, ironmongery, photographic materials, drugs—with the properties and uses of which he was unacquainted—lawn-mowers, garden rollers, and other matters that did not appeal to him; and these he sent over the side to keep the bird-cages company. Then, when the sun was within half an hour of the western horizon, he left the brig and returned to the island with his booty.

Flora seemed greatly amused when Leslie told her what he had brought ashore.

"Why, Dick," she exclaimed, "there is enough clothing in those two cases to last us for the rest of our lives; to say nothing of that third case which you say is full of unmade silks and linen. Surely it was scarcely necessary to cumber yourself with the last, was it?"

"Who knows?" answered Leslie. "It is impossible to say how long we may be compelled to remain on this island; and I intend to save every single article and thing that may by any possibility be useful to us. I am not going to take any chances. For aught that I can tell, it may be beyond my power to construct such a craft as I have in my mind; in which case we may be compelled to remain here until—it may be years hence—a ship comes along and rescues us. I have no wish to alarm you, dear,"—it was surprising how often that term now rose to his lips, and how difficult he found it to avoid letting it slip out—"but I cannot conceal from myself—and it would be unfair to conceal from you—the possibility that we may be obliged to spend a quite appreciable portion of our lives here; and I intend to make the very fullest provision possible for such a contingency. But do not be frightened," he continued, catching the sudden look of gravity that leapt into her face; "you shall not be detained here a moment longer than I can help."

"Oh, Dick, it is not so much *that*," she murmured; "it is the terrible anxiety that my poor father must be suffering that worries me."

"Ah, yes," agreed Leslie; "I can quite understand the poor gentleman's feelings. Why didn't I think of that before?" he suddenly ejaculated. "Look here. I will write a message, seal it up in a bottle, and set it adrift clear of the island to-morrow. There is just a chance in a thousand—or perhaps ten thousand—that it may be picked up; and in that case, not only will your father's anxiety be relieved, but help and rescue will be brought to us. I will write my statement immediately after dinner."

Chapter Ten
A Discovery—and a Confession

The statement that Dick Leslie that evening wrote ran as follows:—

"The finder of this document is earnestly requested to communicate its contents to Lloyds, the British Admiralty, the leading London newspapers, and Sir Ernest Trevor, K.C.M.G., Judge of Her Majesty's Supreme Court, Bombay.

"On the — day of —, in the year 18—, the ship *Golden Fleece*, Captain Rainhill, sailed from London for Melbourne, having on board, among other passengers, Miss Flora Trevor, daughter of the above-named Sir Ernest Trevor, and Mr Richard Leslie.

"On the night of the — day of —, in the same year, the ship's reckoning at noon on that day being Latitude 32 degrees 10 minutes North and Longitude 26 degrees 55 minutes West, the *Golden Fleece* was run into and sunk by an unknown steamer during a dense fog. The only known survivors of the wreck consisted of the above-named Flora Trevor, Richard Leslie, and a seaman named George Baker, belonging to the ship. These three persons were picked up and rescued on the following day by the brig *Mermaid* of London, James Potter, master, which sailed from the last-named port on the —th day of —, bound for Valparaiso.

"On the date of the rescue of the three above-named persons by the brig, Captain Potter met with an accident, from which he died on the —th day of —; and the mate, Thomas Purchas, succeeded to the command of the vessel. Then Purchas gave way to drink, and on the night of the —th day of — committed suicide by jumping overboard. Thereupon Mr Richard Leslie, who had at one time been an officer in the British navy, assumed command of the brig, with the intention of navigating her to Valparaiso. During the passage of Cape Horn, however, the *Mermaid* encountered contrary winds and very heavy weather, in which she was dismasted, with the loss of three of her crew. The brig was then put under jury rig, so far as the resources of the vessel permitted; but it was not of a sufficiently efficient character to permit of her being worked to windward, and a persistent succession of contrary winds drove her deep into the heart of the Pacific Ocean, where, during a gale that sprang up on the night of the —th of —, she was driven ashore, and became a total wreck on the outlying reef of an unknown island, not marked on the charts, but situate in Latitude 16 degrees 8 minutes South, Longitude 120 degrees 56 minutes West. During this gale the *Mermaid* was again dismasted, and Mr Leslie, who was at the wheel, was knocked down and injured on the head by the falling wreckage, in consequence of which he was conveyed below, where Miss Trevor remained in attendance upon him. He lay insensible for nearly thirty-six hours; and it was during this time that the brig struck on and was driven nearly the entire width of the reef, where she now lies. The only survivors of this disaster are Miss Trevor and Mr Leslie, who undoubtedly owe their lives to the fact that they were below when the brig struck. It is urgently requested that help be sent to them as quickly as possible, as the island upon which they have been wrecked lies quite out of the usual track of shipping, and their prospects of rescue by a passing vessel are consequently small.

"(Signed) Flora Trevor. Richard Leslie.

"Dated this — day of —, 18—.''

"There," exclaimed Leslie, as he read over the completed document, "that ought to bring us help if the bottle happens to be picked up. But we must not count upon it, for it may drift about for years before it is found. However, we will do what we can to attract attention to it. A mere floating bottle is a very inconspicuous object, and may be passed within a hundred feet without being noticed; but I will pack it in a good big packing-case before sending it adrift. A floating case, especially if conspicuously marked, stands a hundred times as good a chance of being picked up as does a mere bottle."

Accordingly, on the following day, the bottle, with the document hermetically sealed within it, was taken on board the brig and carefully packed away in the centre of a large packing-case filled with fine shavings from other cases; and then the entire exterior of the case was painted black and white in a bold chequer pattern, with the words "Please open" in bold red letters on each side, and as soon as the paint was dry Leslie put it on board the catamaran, and, running some three miles to leeward of the island, launched it overboard. The case, being light, floated high, and, with its bold chequer pattern, formed a conspicuous object, calculated to attract attention at any distance not exceeding a mile. Then he returned to the brig, and, with Flora's assistance, resumed his task of breaking out cargo.

There is no need to state in detail the contents of each case and bale that they hoisted on deck; suffice it to say that the cargo, being what is known as "general," comprised almost every imaginable thing, much of it being of a character that would either conduce to their present comfort or be possibly useful to them in the future. Only a small proportion of the whole, therefore, went overboard; and since the remainder would in any case be irretrievably lost to its proper owners, Leslie had no scruples whatever in appropriating it to their own use.

The goods thus appropriated comprised an infinite variety of articles, among which may be enumerated enough lamps to illuminate a small village; a few pictures, with which they adorned the interior of their tent; household furniture of all kinds, such as bedsteads, with their bedding, wardrobes, dressing and other tables, chests of drawers, domestic utensils of every kind, cutlery, china and glass, carpets, a huge pier glass, and, to Flora's infinite delight, a magnificent Kaps grand piano. Then there was more clothing—enough to last them both for the remainder of their lives—a case of repeating rifles and revolvers, another case containing ammunition for the same, and a quantity of valuable jewellery, watches, etcetera, cases of perfumery, handsome fans, bric-à-brac—in short, a sufficiency of everything to enable them to convert their humble tent into a most comfortable, elegant, and luxurious abode.

This, however, was not all, or even their most valuable find. There were cases containing picks, shovels, and other implements, some steel wheelbarrows, a case containing a large assortment of carpenters' and joiners' tools, cases of assorted nails and screws, and a very long packing-case, which, upon being opened, was found to contain a handsome and highly finished set of spars, evidently intended for a yacht of about fifteen tons measurement. Close to this was found another case, bearing the same marks as the first, and containing two complete sets of cotton canvas sails, clearly intended for the same craft. These valuable finds not only filled Leslie's heart with immeasurable delight, but set him eagerly searching for further cases, similarly marked. Nor was he disappointed, for the next day's search resulted in his finding a third case, the contents of which consisted of a complete set of gun-metal belaying-pins and other fittings, together with a number of patent blocks, single, double, and threefold, that he had no difficulty in identifying as intended for the same craft.

"Little woman," he exclaimed, "this find is worth more than all the rest of them put together. These spars and sails will save me months of work, and shorten our term of imprisonment here by just that much. They are intended for a craft of about the size that I had in my mind, and now, of course, I shall design her of exactly such dimensions as they will fit. Are you not glad?"

"Of course I am, Dick," she replied; "I am glad of anything that will ease your work for you, for indeed you have been making a perfect slave of yourself ever since we landed here. The discovery of these things has, I suppose, relieved your mind of a great deal of anxiety; and I hope that now you will be able to take matters more easily."

"I am afraid," said Dick, "there still remains a great deal to be done before I can think of 'taking matters easily.' I must complete my examination of this cargo, for one thing; and when that is done I must begin to pull the poor old brig herself to pieces for the sake of her timber, that being the only material available out of which to build our boat."

"But surely there is no such very urgent need for hurry over all this work, is there, Dick?" remonstrated Flora.

"Oh yes, there is," insisted Dick; "for the reason that, if another gale were to spring up, the brig would most probably go to pieces, and then everything in her would be lost, excepting, of course, such matters as might be washed ashore. And the timber of which she is built would be more or less smashed up and generally made less fit for use than it will be if I am afforded time to break her up carefully."

"I see," assented Flora, thoughtfully. "In that case I suppose we had better go to work again, hadn't we?"

So they resumed operations; Dick descending into the hold and slinging the cases, one by one, and then coming on deck and taking the tackle fall to the winch, and heaving the package on deck while Flora hung on to the tail-end of the rope to prevent it slipping round the winch barrel. It was easy work for the girl, and such as she could do without becoming greatly fatigued; but for the man it was hard labour indeed, and such as sent him back to the island at night almost too weary to eat.

But a day or two later he met with a find that more than rewarded him for all his toil, and rendered a further continuance of it unnecessary. Among the first cases that he came upon was a long and heavy one, marked like those containing the spars and sails, that, upon being opened, was found to contain copper sheathing, already cut to shape and carefully marked. There was also, in the same case, a small, light, flat box, containing two drawings to scale; one being a sheer, half-deck, and body plan of a very smart, handsome, and wholesome-looking cutter, thirty-five feet long on the water-line, and ten feet beam; while the other was a drawing similarly marked to the copper sheathing, showing exactly where and how every sheet ought to be applied. Near this case was another, similarly marked, a very large case as to length and breadth, but of no great depth. Wondering what this could possibly contain, Leslie eagerly opened it and found in it the complete set of steel frames for the cutter, packed one inside the other, and each marked and figured in accordance with the sheet of plans. And finally, not to dwell at undue length upon this discovery, important though it was, he also found the keel, stem and stern-posts, rudder and trunk, deck-beams, wales, stringers, skin and deck-planking—in short, every scrap and item of material and fittings required for the little vessel; so that nothing remained but to put the whole together. A more fortunate find could by no possibility be conceived for two people circumstanced as he and his companion were.

It goes without saying that the whole of this valuable material was most carefully and promptly transferred to the beach; and as the last item of it was unloaded from the catamaran Leslie flung himself down upon the sand and exclaimed, in accents of infinite relief—

"There, that is a good job well done; and I care not now though the old hooker should go to pieces to-morrow!"

"And now," returned Flora, "you will be able to give yourself a little holiday, and take some much-needed rest, will you not? Promise me that you will, Dick, please. You have been looking very anxious and worried of late, and have been toiling the whole day through, day after day, in the hot sun. I am sure such arduous work is not good for you; and indeed I have more than once been tempted to refuse to help you, because I knew that, if I did, you would be compelled to desist. But when I saw how eager you were I thought it would be cruel; and I could not bring myself to be that, even though I felt that it would be for your good."

"You have been infinitely good to me, Flora," answered Leslie, with deep feeling—"infinitely good, and infinitely patient; while I have been impatient and exacting. In my impatience—I can see it now—I have worked you cruelly hard—"

The girl put her hand over his mouth. "You shall not say another word until you talk sensibly," she declared. "The idea of saying that you 'worked me hard'! Why, what I did was child's play; a girl of fifteen could have done it without being distressed. Please do not let me hear you say such things again!" she insisted, imperiously; immediately adding, "Now, you will promise to take a day's rest to-morrow, will you not, Dick?"

"Certainly, if you wish it," assented Leslie. "We will both take a day's holiday, and go fishing along the inner edge of the reef, shall we?"

"By all means," agreed Flora. "I have often thought that I should like a little fish, as a change of diet; I am getting most horribly tired of salt beef and pork and tinned meats. But you have been so feverishly busy that I did not like to ask you."

"Then," said Leslie, with severity, "please do not do it again. How many times must I tell you that you have only to express a wish, to have it gratified, if I can do it, before you will believe me?"

"I do believe you, Dick; indeed I do," she answered softly. "I know that there is nothing I could ask you that you would not willingly and gladly do for me if you could. You are the kindest, most generous, most chivalrous gentleman that I ever met—"

"Stop, please!" exclaimed Leslie, with a sudden fierceness of energy that frightened the girl; "you must not say such things as that, or I shall some day forget myself and— But you have not yet heard my story; I must tell it you some day, Flora; yes, the time is drawing near when it will be imperatively necessary for me to tell you my story. Then we shall see what your opinion of me will be."

"So you really have a history?" remarked the girl. "The people on board the *Golden Fleece* suspected as much, and freely said so; and as I have watched you from time to time, and have observed your sudden fits of melancholy, I have often thought that they must have been right in their surmise. Yes; you shall tell me your story, Dick; I shall be profoundly interested in it, I am certain; and if it is a sad one—as I more than half suspect—you shall have my whole-hearted sympathy. But, whatever you may have to tell me, it will never alter my opinion of you; you may have met with misfortune, or suffered grievous wrong, but nothing will ever persuade me that such a man as you have shown yourself to be can ever have done anything of which you or your friends need be ashamed. Tell it me now, Dick, if you will."

"No," answered Leslie, resolutely, though he longed for her promised sympathy more intensely than he had ever longed for anything else in his life; "no; I will not tell you now; the time is not yet ripe. But it will be ere long; and then I will tell you."

"So be it," agreed Flora. "Until then I can wait. And now let us go to dinner, for I see by the appearance of the cooking-stove that it is ready, and I am sure you must need it."

On the following morning, in accordance with their over-night arrangement, they got on board the catamaran after breakfast and, sailing out to the reef, anchored on its inner edge, and started to fish. They appeared, however, to have chanced upon an unfavourable spot to start with, for after about half an hour their efforts were rewarded by the capture of only four fish, so small as to be quite worthless, except for bait; Leslie therefore tripped his anchor and, setting his canvas, determined to try his luck somewhat further to the north-eastward, and nearer the entrance channel.

They had been under way some ten minutes, slipping along over the very inner edge of the reef, with the deep-water of the lagoon on their port hand, when Flora, who was peering abstractedly down into this deep, pellucid water, suddenly cried out—

"Oh, look, Dick, look; what is that huge object over there? Is it another wreck?"

"Where away?" asked Leslie, gazing out over the reef.

"Down there in the water," answered the girl, pointing to a spot over the port quarter. "I cannot see it now, because of the light on the water; but I saw it most distinctly a moment ago. We sailed almost directly over it."

"And you thought it looked like a sunken wreck?" asked Leslie.

"Yes," answered the girl; "I certainly did. It was as large as a ship, and had somewhat the appearance of one."

"Well, we will go back and have a look at it," said Leslie; and, bearing up for a moment and then putting his helm down, he tacked, bringing the catamaran round in such a manner as to pass back over practically the same ground as before. And presently they both sighted the same object again—a huge something that certainly bore some resemblance to the hull of a ship, lying submerged upon the sandy bottom of the lagoon, about fifty fathoms from the inner edge of the reef. They were too far away from it, however, to distinguish it clearly, the light reflected from the surface of the water rendering their view of it indistinct; Leslie therefore this time wore the catamaran round, and, lowering her sails, allowed her to drift gently forward with the way that she still had on her. And this time they passed right over the object, when, as soon as the catamaran was fairly clear of it, he let go his anchor and allowed his craft to drive astern again until she floated fair and square over the mysterious thing. Then, lying down flat upon the deck of the catamaran, he peered straight down into the crystal-clear water, in the shadow of the craft, and saw beneath him what was unquestionably the weed-grown hull of a ship of antiquated model, of some four hundred tons measurement. She was heading straight for the reef, with her stern pointing toward the island. And as Leslie lay there intently studying her every detail, he presently made out a stout rope cable leading from her starboard hawse-pipe toward the reef, the end of it being buried in the sand. Her posture was such as to suggest to the experienced eye of the sailor that she had driven over the reef, somewhat in the same way as the *Mermaid* had done; but, unlike the latter craft, had cleared it altogether and had there been brought to an anchor, subsequently sinking where she lay. She seemed to have been a three-masted ship, for Leslie could see the stumps of the fore and main masts, and believed he could make out the stump of the mizzenmast broken close off at the deck. She had the appearance of a craft of somewhere about the Elizabethan period; being built with an excessive amount of sheer and a very high-peaked narrow poop, upon the after end of which the remains of what were probably three poop-lanterns could still be distinguished. She had a slight list to starboard, and had, in the course of her long submergence, either settled or become buried in the sand to the extent of about half the depth of her hull. What her nationality may have been it was of course impossible to tell, clothed as she was in a rankly luxuriant growth of weed. Leslie carefully noted in his pocket-book the exact bearings of the wreck; and then, lifting his anchor, they resumed their fishing, their efforts being rewarded with an excellent day's sport.

Leslie now set to work with earnestness and enthusiasm upon his great task of putting together the cutter, the component parts of which had so fortunately happened to form a part of the *Mermaid's* cargo. And the first thing he did was to name the prospective craft the *Flora*, as a compliment to his companion.

Now, the *Flora*, when completed, would be a craft of very respectable dimensions; far too bulky, indeed, to be launched by the simple process of pushing her off the beach into the water, as one would launch a small boat. The method of launching, therefore, was a matter requiring consideration, and would have to be arranged for before a stroke of work was done upon the boat herself. Leslie thought the matter over carefully, and at length arrived at the conclusion that there was nothing for it but to build the boat upon properly constructed launching ways. And for these he would require a considerable quantity of good stout timber properly squared; the provision of which involved a task of very considerable labour and difficulty. Trees there were in plenty on the island, of ample dimensions for his purpose; but how was he, single-handed, to get them down upon the beach, even after they had been trimmed and squared? And how was he to square them without a sawpit. The pit-saw itself he had, having found several among the other tools that formed part of the brig's cargo; but to work such a tool single-handed was an impossibility. Weighing all these difficulties in his mind, Dick at length came to the conclusion that there was no alternative but to draw upon the brig for the necessary material; and he accordingly went, rather reluctantly, to work upon the task of breaking up the poor old *Mermaid*. He decided that the deck-beams of the brig would be the most suitable for his purpose; and to obtain these it was necessary to break up the deck—a long and arduous job, only to be accomplished with hard labour and the assistance of an elaborate system of tackles.

It was while he was thus employed that the first break occurred in the fine weather that had prevailed ever since their arrival at the island. It began with the gradual dying away of the trade wind, followed by a heavy banking-up of dark thundery-looking clouds along the western horizon. With the cessation of the wind the temperature rose to such a pitch that work became an impossibility, and Dick was at length reluctantly compelled to knock-off and return to the shore, much to Flora's satisfaction—for she was continually in dread lest the untiring and feverish energy with which he laboured should result in his suffering a serious breakdown.

As it was too hot even to walk about, the pair were perforce compelled to remain inactive all the afternoon; and Flora inwardly decided that this would be a good opportunity for Dick to relate to her his promised story. It needed a very considerable amount of persuasion and coaxing to induce him to do so; but eventually he yielded and told her the whole miserable history from beginning to end, winding up with the words—

"And thus you find me here to-day, a disgraced and ruined man, under an assumed name, without prospects or hope of any description, with only a hundred pounds wherewith to begin a new career in an alien land, and no possibility whatever, so far as I can see, of ever being able to establish my innocence and so win reconciliation with my poor, proud, heart-broken father. Were it not for the fact that you are here, and must be restored to your friends with as little delay as may be, I could be well content to end my days here on this unknown island, alone and forgotten by all. Indeed, I think it more than likely that as soon as I have discharged my duty to you I shall return here."

"My poor Dick," exclaimed Flora, in tones of profound sympathy; "how you must have suffered! I am no longer surprised at your frequent fits of depression and melancholy; the wonder to me is that you did not go mad, or die of shame, in that horrible prison. But now that you have told me all you must put everything that is past behind you, and try to forget it; I believe your story implicitly; you could not be the man you have proved yourself to be to me, and be guilty of so mean an act as theft; oh no, nothing save your own admission could ever make me believe that of you. And you have all the sympathy of my heart, Dick; all my sympathy; all my esteem; all—oh, the thought of what you have been compelled to endure is terrible—terrible!"

And, to Leslie's unspeakable consternation, the girl suddenly buried her face in her hands and sobbed as though her heart would break. The expression of her whole-hearted sympathy and perfect faith in him touched him profoundly.

"Don't cry, darling, please don't; I cannot bear it—and I am not worth it," he protested. "I ought never to have told you. I was a selfish brute to extort your sympathy by the miserable recital of my own misfortunes; I have basely worked upon your feelings."

"You shall *not* say it," she answered, laying her hand upon his mouth; "I will not have you abuse yourself, you who have already suffered such unspeakable cruelty at the hands of others. You are *not* selfish; you are *not* base; you are nothing that is bad and everything that is good; you are a very king among men! Oh, Dick," she continued, taking his hand in hers, "do not think me forward or unmaidenly in speaking thus to you, dear; I am not. But do you think I do not know what your feeling is toward me; do you think I do not *know* that you love me? You poor, simple-hearted fellow, you are far too honest and straightforward ever to be able to deceive a woman, especially in such a matter as that; you may have thought that you were very successfully concealing your feelings from me, but I have known the truth—oh, ever since we have been on this island."

"It is true; God help me, it is true!" exclaimed Dick, smiting his forehead. "But it is also true that I never intended you to know. For what right have I, a disgraced and ruined man, to seek the love of any woman? And if I may not seek her love in return, why should I tell her that I love her?"

"You are looking at the matter with jaundiced eyes, Dick," answered Flora, still retaining his hand in hers. "I cannot wonder that you feel your humiliation cruelly; but the humiliation is really not yours; it is that of those who so shamefully plotted to ruin you. You are guiltless of this horrible charge—I am as sure of that as I am that I am a living woman. Besides, who is to know that Richard Leslie is one and the same man with him who stood in the dock charged with that shameful crime, and was pronounced guilty upon the strength of cunningly devised and manufactured evidence? No one, of course, except my father; he must know; because, Dick dear, it is my fixed determination that he shall help you in this matter; you will accompany me to Bombay, and personally deliver me over into my father's care. Then I shall tell him all that you have done for me, and been to me; and you will tell him your whole story, just as you have told it to me. And I am sure that, if only for the sake of his daughter, he will take up the matter and bring the truth to light. And, Dick, I am not going to allow your morbid feelings, or even maidenly reserve, to stand in the way of my happiness; you have confessed that you love me, and I know it to be true, for your eyes and your actions have told me so daily, for months past. It cannot be unmaidenly, therefore, in me to confess that I return your love with all my heart and soul."

"Oh, Flora, my love, my heart's darling, are you *sure* of this?" demanded Dick, laying his hands upon her shoulders and gazing into her eyes as though he would read her very soul. "Are you sure that you are not mistaking mere gratitude for a warmer feeling?"

"Yes, Dick," she answered, "I am quite, *quite* sure. My gratitude you won long ago; it was yours when we first stood on the deck of the *Mermaid* together, dripping from our long night's immersion in the sea—for had you not, even then, saved my life? And it grew even deeper as I noted day by day your thoughtful care and anxiety for my welfare. But gratitude and love are two very different feelings; and while I should of course have always been profoundly grateful to you for your unceasing care, I am sure that I should never have learned to love you had I not first seen that you loved me."

"Then God be praised for His unspeakable mercy in bestowing upon me this pricelessly precious gift of your dear love!" exclaimed Dick, fervently. "I will accept it, ay and I will moreover prove myself worthy of it. This blessed day marks a turning-point in my life; from this moment I leave my wretched past behind me; there shall be no more useless fretting and grieving for me. My work, now, is first to restore you to your father; next to free myself—by his help, if he will give it me, but anyway, to free myself—from the undeserved stigma that attaches to my true name; and, finally, to win for you such a home and position as you deserve. And, God helping me, I will do it!"

This was the second time within a few minutes that Dick Leslie had spoken the name of the Deity, and nothing could more clearly have indicated the change wrought in him by the knowledge of Flora's love. Hitherto he had felt himself to be an outcast, cruelly and unjustly deserted by his Creator; despised and condemned by his fellow-men; but now everything was different; he firmly believed that God had at last relented and had given him this girl's love to comfort and encourage him in his great trouble and humiliation; and he once more took hope into his heart. If God had relented, everything, he felt convinced, would yet be well with him.

And what is to be said of Flora; is any excuse needed for the extreme step that she took in forcing a confession of love from Leslie? Well, possibly there is; it may be that there are people who would assert that, despite her disclaimer, she was unmaidenly. If such there be, and if excuse for her be needed, then let it be found for her in the following facts. In the first place Leslie, despite his utmost caution, had betrayed his intense love for her in a thousand different ways, until the fact had become clear, unmistakable, and indisputable; a thing not to be doubted or gainsaid. And, in the next place, she saw that, for some unknown reason, he never intended to declare his love if he could possibly help it. A dozen times the declaration had trembled on his lips, yet he had resolutely withheld it. Why? Clearly for some reason that he deemed all-sufficient, and which, she fancied, must be intimately associated with those oft-recurring fits of gloom and depression from which she could not help seeing that he suffered. Finally, she loved him, and believed that—he also loving her—the knowledge of this fact might go far toward restoring his lost happiness. And when she had heard his story—told with all the bitterness and grief and indignation that had been eating into his soul and destroying his faith in God and man for over seven interminable years of suffering—she knew that she was right; that there was but one remedy for his misery; and, conscious of the nobility of her own motives, she fearlessly administered it. Who can or will blame her?

Meanwhile the brooding storm was slowly gathering its forces together for an outburst; the bank of cloud had piled itself so high above the western horizon that it had long ago obscured the sun; a weird twilight had fallen upon the scene; the stagnant air had grown even more oppressively hot than at first; not a bird uttered a single note; not an insect raised a chirp; not a leaf stirred; and in the profound silence the roar of the surf on the reef became thunderous in its resonance. They dined somewhat earlier than usual that night, and while they sat over their meal the darkness fell and they lighted the lamps. Then Leslie went out to see to the security of the catamaran, making her fast to the shore with additional moorings; and upon his return Flora insisted that he should lie down on the sofa while she sang and played to him. Then Leslie, in his turn, his heart lightened with returning hope and happiness, lifted up his voice, and for the first time since that terrible and memorable day, nearly eight years ago, broke into song. And finally they began to sing duets together, his clear, rich, mellow tenor blending well with Flora's sweet, sympathetic soprano.

The concert was interrupted by the distant muttering of thunder and the fitful flickering of lightning; and they went out together down to the shore to watch the gathering storm. It was a long time in coming, but by-and-by, as they stood together close to the water's edge, a sudden swishing sound, like that of wind stirring leaves, became audible, and in another moment the blast was upon them and tearing across the glassy surface of the lagoon, darkening its surface and lashing it into foam. Then, a minute or two later, down came the rain in sheets, and they had to beat a precipitate retreat to the tent, getting a thorough drenching on the journey, though it occupied them but a minute. The gale raged all through the night and up to nearly noon on the following day, when it broke, the sky cleared, and the wind gradually dropped to a moderate breeze, veering all the time round by north to east until the south-east trade wind was once more blowing, but very much more gently than usual. Upon going out, the next day, Leslie was delighted to find that the gale had done no damage whatever anywhere, all stores and materials having been effectually protected from the rain, while the direction of the gale had been such that it could not possibly harm the brig.

Although the gale actually broke—as has been said—shortly before noon, it moderated so gradually throughout the afternoon that it was not until the next day that the sea had gone down sufficiently to permit of the catamaran being taken alongside the brig without danger. As soon, however, as this was the case, Leslie went off again, accompanied by Flora, and resumed his task of breaking up the brig's deck. It was about the middle of the afternoon when Flora, who had been allowing her gaze to wander out over the sea to the southward and westward, called her companion's attention to a small object floating at a distance of about a mile in the offing. Leslie, ever on the alert, at once brought the telescope to bear upon the object, which appeared to be drifting helplessly before wind and sea toward the surf beating on the weather side of the reef, and immediately pronounced it to be a small canoe, apparently empty.

"We must have that craft; she will be very useful to us," he exclaimed, dropping the telescope and preparing to cast off the catamaran. "Will you come with me, sweetheart? You can be useful to me by taking the tiller, when we come alongside her, while I jump aboard and make fast a rope. But we must be smart or she will be among the breakers before we can reach her."

A minute later they were under way and slipping along toward the entrance channel, upon clearing which Leslie at once hauled his wind, standing to the eastward for about a mile, which took him far enough to windward to enable him to fetch the canoe on the next tack. He then hove about without a moment's delay, for the little craft was by this time perilously close to the surf, and it was questionable whether they would reach her in time to save her from being caught and dashed to pieces in it. So close, indeed, was she that Leslie began to seriously ask himself whether he was justified in taking the catamaran into a situation of such danger for the mere sake of an insignificant canoe; but reflecting that she was evidently light enough to enable Flora to paddle about in her without much exertion, and that it would afford the girl pleasure to do so; also that the little craft would be very useful for fishing and other purposes, he decided to risk it; and accordingly steered to shave just past her to windward. Then, when they were drawing close up to her, he handed over the tiller to Flora—who was by this time quite an expert helmswoman—instructing her to tack to the eastward the moment that he sprang into the canoe. Then, taking the end of a rope in his hand, he stood by to jump into the canoe as the catamaran shaved past her. Another moment and they were alongside the little craft, into which Dick nimbly leaped, with the rope's-end in his hand, crying, as he did so—

"Down helm, dear, and put her round!" A moment later he added, under his breath, "Hillo! here is a complication; a couple of naked savages in her! I wonder whether the beggars are dead!"

That, however, was not the moment in which to enter upon an investigation of the matter, for the two craft were on the very edge of the surf, and if by any chance the catamaran should miss stays nothing could save them. So Dick, with lightning-like rapidity, took a turn with his rope and made it fast to a sort of broad thwart in the centre of the canoe, and then, hauling quickly up alongside again, he regained the deck of the catamaran just as she was paying-off on the right tack.

As Leslie took the helm from her, Flora exclaimed—

"Oh, Dick, what does it mean? How came those two men—I suppose they *are* men?—in the canoe; and where have they come from?"

"From one of those islands, away out there to the westward, that we saw from the summit, without a doubt," answered Dick. "I suspect that they were caught unawares and blown out to sea by that gale of the day before yesterday. Once blown fairly away out of the lee of their own island they would have no choice but to keep their cockle-shell of a canoe dead before the sea, and to paddle for all they were worth, to avoid being swamped. I take it that they paddled until they were absolutely exhausted and could do no more, and then flung themselves down in the bottom of the canoe and dropped into a kind of lethargy."

"You think that they are still alive, then?" asked Flora.

"I have very little doubt of it," answered Dick. "These South Sea savages are pretty tough, I believe; and even were they not, it would take something more than, say, forty hours' exposure, in this climate, to kill them. Oh yes; they are alive, all right."

"And how will their presence on our island affect us, Dick?" asked the girl.

That was precisely the question that was worrying Leslie at that moment. He had no personal knowledge of the native inhabitants of the islands of the Southern Pacific, but had a vague recollection of having either heard or read that, while some of them were very gentle and inoffensive, others were extremely treacherous and ferocious; some of them even being addicted to cannibalism. He was not, however, going to alarm his companion unnecessarily, or say anything needlessly to raise her apprehensions; so he answered, with a great show of cheerfulness—

"Why, I hope it will very materially shorten the period of our sojourn here, sweetheart. They have the appearance of being good sturdy fellows; and I shall set them on to help me with my heavy work. It has gone to my heart to be compelled to ask you to do even the light work that you have hitherto done for me; although I could not have got on at all without your assistance. Now, however, with their help I shall be able to get on swimmingly, while you can amuse yourself in any way that you please. Now I am going to tack; look out for your head, dear; I cannot afford to have you knocked overboard by the main-boom. Helm's a-lee!"

Instead of returning to the brig, Leslie proceeded direct to the island where, having landed Flora, he proceeded, with some difficulty, to rouse the savages, and supply them with food and drink. They proved to be, as Leslie had said, a pair of fine, well-made men, naked, save for a kind of breech-clout round their loins, of sturdy physique, and apparently but little the worse for their adventure. Nor were they especially unprepossessing in appearance, although there was a certain character of ruthlessness in the expression of their eyes and about their mouths and chins that caused Leslie to determine that he would keep a very wary eye upon them, at all events until he had learned a little more about their character and disposition.

Chapter Eleven
Flora's Adventure

Leslie's two dark-skinned guests—for they were nearly black in colour—ate heartily of the food that was given them, their eyes wide-open with wonder, meanwhile, at the many strange objects—especially the tent and the catamaran—that they beheld around them; and the ex-lieutenant especially noted, with fast-growing distrust, the glances of hungry admiration that they bestowed on Flora when at length she emerged from the tent and approached the canoe to note their progress toward recovery. Leslie had already tested their knowledge of English, French, and German without success, from which he deduced the conclusion that they had not been brought into very intimate contact with the crews of vessels speaking any of those languages. Their own language, on the other hand was, as of course might be expected, merely unintelligible gibberish to him. This was unfortunate, since it would make intelligent communication between him and them difficult, at all events for a time; sailors, however, have a way peculiar to themselves of making their requirements understood by foreigners, and he had little doubt of his ability to overcome that difficulty ere long. Indeed, on that same day, after the men had eaten and drank to their hearts' content, Leslie contrived to convey to their understanding the fact that he expected them to build a hut for themselves; and he indicated the precise spot, at a considerable distance from the camp, where he wished it to be. As soon as they clearly understood what his desires were, they went off into the bush and, armed with a small tomahawk lent them by Leslie, proceeded to cut down some forty or fifty young and pliant saplings, the butt-ends of which they sharpened to a point, and then thrust vertically, into the ground in a circle some twelve feet in diameter. They then brought the tops of the saplings all together and bound them; thus producing a skeleton structure exactly shaped like a bee-hive. This skeleton they then strengthened by interweaving it with stout lianas—or "monkey-rope," as the sailors call the long, tough stems of the creepers that interlace themselves about the trees in tropical countries. This done, they again vanished into the bush; quickly returning with two generous loads of the leaves of a species of palm, wherewith they quickly and deftly thatched the entire hut, and thus completed it. The entire structure occupied but a couple of hours in the making; yet it had all the appearance of being a thoroughly comfortable and weather-proof dwelling. As soon as the hut was finished Leslie demanded back the tomahawk; but although he shrewdly suspected that they understood well enough what he wanted, they affected not to do so, keeping a tight hold upon the implement all through the discussion, until Dick simplified matters by seizing the holder by the arm and gently but firmly forcing it from his grasp. He then handed them a generous supply of fish, as an evening ration, and motioned them to withdraw to their hut, which they did, not over willingly, as Leslie thought. That same night he went to work and manufactured a canvas belt for Flora, to hold a brace of revolvers and a cartridge pouch; and the next morning early he took a small piece of board, some nine inches square, painted it to represent a target, and nailed it to a tree. Then, girding the fully equipped belt round Flora's waist, he led her to the target, having first initiated her into the mystery of loading and discharging a revolver, and said to her—

"As soon as you see that we have boarded the brig this morning, I want you to come up here and practise firing at that target until you have become a good shot. Begin your shooting at about this distance," marking off a distance of about five yards. "Standing as close to the target as this, you can scarcely fail to hit it. And when you are able to hit it three times in succession, I want you to retire one pace to the rear—so," suiting the action to the word, "and start shooting again until you have succeeded in hitting the target three consecutive times from the new position. Then retire another pace, and proceed as before, until you are able to hit the target time after time without missing, at this distance," indicating a peg driven into the ground at a distance of about fifty yards from the target. "When you can shoot straight at that range I think you will have attained a degree of proficiency sufficient for my purpose."

"Very well, Dick; I will do as you wish, of course," she answered; "and I think I shall not be long in attaining proficiency, for I believe I have a very 'straight' eye. Indeed, I gained several first prizes in archery competitions at home. But I wish, dear, you would tell me why you have suddenly taken this idea into your head. Has it anything to do with the arrival of the savages on the island?"

"Of course it has," answered Leslie, cheerily, thinking it best to be frank with his sweetheart—so far as it was possible for him to be so without alarming her. "You see, little woman, the matter stands thus. We know absolutely nothing about these fellows, whether their characters are bad or good; whether they are treacherously disposed, or otherwise. And while I have little doubt that in a fair-and-square, open, stand-up fight I should be able to give a reasonably good account of them, it will not be amiss for us to be on our guard against treachery. And there is no better way of dealing with savages than to inspire them with a good wholesome dread of one's powers and prowess. I propose, therefore, that, as soon as you have attained the necessary skill with your revolver, we shall indulge in a little pistol practice together, *allowing them to look on*. If they once get the fact thoroughly impressed upon them that we can both pot them, if necessary, at fifty yards, it will go a long way toward simplifying matters, by convincing them of the futility of attempting any tricks. But you must not let this very elementary precaution alarm you, sweetheart. As likely as not they will prove to be perfectly docile."

"I am sure I fervently hope and pray so," answered the girl. "But in any case," she continued spiritedly, "I shall not be frightened, because I shall always have you to take care of me."

Nevertheless, as soon as Leslie, taking the natives with him, had arrived on board the brig, she sedulously devoted herself to her shooting lesson, infusing into it that whole-hearted seriousness that women are wont to bring to any task set them; with the result that when Dick returned that evening she was able to report that she had attained to the desired degree of proficiency.

Meanwhile, Leslie found little difficulty in inducing the two blacks to accompany him aboard the catamaran and out to the brig. And when he reached the latter he had not much more difficulty in making them understand what he wanted them to do—this, by the way, consisting chiefly in heaving away upon the winch. He was careful to keep a watchful eye upon them all day, and especially when they first boarded the brig; being desirous to gather, if he could, some idea, from their looks and actions, whether they had ever seen a ship before. But although, as the catamaran drew up alongside the stranded vessel, he noticed that they regarded her with a considerable degree of curiosity and interest, these were hardly sufficiently marked to lead him to the conclusion that they had never seen such a craft before. This, however, was a comparatively unimportant matter. What concerned him most intimately was the fact that, after their night's rest, they seemed to exhibit a good deal more docility and intelligence than they had displayed on the night before. They worked well and—apparently—quite willingly, but did not appear to possess a very great amount of stamina, as they manifested every indication of being pretty completely exhausted before the day's work was over.

The next three days passed without the occurrence of anything worthy of record, save that Flora, acting upon Dick's advice, continued her pistol practice, with the view of further perfecting herself at the target, and acquiring even still greater dexterity. On the fourth day, however, feeling that she was tolerably proficient, and perhaps wearying somewhat of the monotony of perpetual shooting at a target, as soon as Leslie and the natives—one of whom now readily answered to the name of Cuffy, while the other did not disdain to be styled Sambo—had gone off to the brig, she resolved to treat herself to the luxury of a long ramble, with only Sailor for company. Accordingly, packing a small basket with a sufficient luncheon for herself and the dog, she set off.

She had not the least fear; for although they had taken many rambles together, neither she nor Leslie had ever seen the slightest trace of the existence of either animals or reptiles of any kind upon the island, and Dick had quite made up his mind not only that there were none, but that it was logically and physically impossible for any to get there. Besides, the natives were with Dick, and she had Sailor to take care of her; there was, therefore, nothing to be afraid of.

Now although, as has been said, Leslie and Flora had frequently indulged in rambles together, none of them had been very lengthy, or had carried them far afield, with the exception of the one that they had taken to the summit; and Flora's fancy now yearned to explore "fresh fields and pastures new;" a tantalising memory of a certain grove of especially noble and beautiful flower-bearing trees situate on the north-eastern slope of the peak dwelt persistently with her, she had conjured up a fancy picture of this particular spot that made it appear to her imagination a scene of enchanting and fairy-like beauty, and she longed to satisfy herself as to how closely her imagination approximated to the reality. Moreover, the walk promised to be an agreeably easy one, the slopes of the ground appeared to be gentle, and the face of the country finely broken; she therefore determined to wend her way in this direction.

Sauntering quietly along, she soon left the open savannah behind her, and plunged into the bush, heading generally in a northerly direction, but accommodating her route to the inequalities of the ground and the varying density of the undergrowth; naturally selecting a path that afforded her the easiest passage through the bush. In this manner, after a very pleasant and enjoyable walk for about an hour, she arrived at the crest of the eastern spur of the mountain, and, descending a gentle declivity, soon found herself in a region as romantically beautiful as even her vivid fancy had painted. Ravine succeeded ravine, each with its own tiny streamlet meandering through it, and each more picturesque and enchanting than the last, until at length, emerging from this broken ground, she reached a stretch of park-like country with practically no undergrowth, the greensward being studded with magnificent umbrageous trees, some of which were a mass of lovely blossom of the most exquisite tints, while others were lavishly draped with orchids of every conceivable shape and hue. She was by this time feeling somewhat fatigued and very hungry; she therefore selected the mossy roots of an enormous tree as a resting-place, and, seating herself, leisurely proceeded to eat her luncheon and to give Sailor his. The air of the place was exquisitely soft and balmy, the wide-spreading foliage shielded her from the too-ardent rays of the sun, and bathed the whole scene in a delicious golden green twilight; a profound silence reigned around, broken only by the soothing murmur of the wind through the topmost branches and the equally soothing rustle of the leaves—and it is not to be wondered at that the girl sank into a pleasant reverie that gradually merged into profound sleep.

When at length she awoke, the changed character of the light, and the deepened sombreness of the shadows, warned her that the sun was already low, and that she must hasten homeward if she would reach the camp ere nightfall; she therefore seized her empty basket, and set out upon her return journey, following her outward route as nearly as she could hit it off. But she had slept much longer than she suspected, and when at length she again reached the broken and romantic ground that she had traversed with such delight and enjoyment in the morning, the shadows had fallen so deeply that it was with the utmost difficulty only that she could discern her way, and she found herself obliged to proceed with the greatest circumspection. And now it was that, for the first time, she fully appreciated the advantage of having Sailor as a companion, for the dog appeared to remember the way by which they had come much better than she did, running on before her for a few yards, then pausing for her to come up to him, and again running forward. Several times he had persisted in adopting a certain route in preference to the one that she seemed disposed to pursue, and in each case had proved himself to be right; she therefore at length resigned herself blindly to his guidance, following him wherever he chose to lead.

In this fashion the pair hastened forward as rapidly as the rough and broken character of the ground would permit, Flora by this time being in a tumult of distress at the knowledge that Dick would already have returned from the wreck and be wild with anxiety at her unaccountable absence— for she had said nothing to him about her intentions when he left her that morning, the expedition being the result of an impulse that had come to her after his departure. The sun had by this time set, and even in the open the brief twilight was rapidly deepening into night, while where Flora now was, plunged in the heart of a wild ravine, thickly overgrown with trees and bush, it was so dark that she could with difficulty distinguish the form of the dog, even when he was close to her. But she had the comfort of knowing that Sailor was guiding her aright, for she presently, found herself making her way over a particularly difficult bit of ground that she had a vivid remembrance of having passed during the morning; find the difficulties that she had then experienced made her more than usually careful now, as she was fully aware that a false step would probably result in an ugly fall.

Yet, despite all her care, she took that false step, and instantly found herself plunging headlong over a low cliff into a dense tangle of undergrowth. She was not hurt in the least, but to her chagrin she found herself so completely involved in the tangle that, struggle as she would, it seemed impossible for her to extricate herself. Every movement of her body served but to involve her more completely, and to sink her more effectually into the heart of her leafy prison. Fortunate indeed was it for her that there happened to be no thorns on the bushes into which she had fallen, otherwise she must have sustained very serious injuries in her frantic efforts to free herself from the tough, cordlike lianas that entwined her body and limbs so completely that at length she found it practically impossible to further move hand or foot. As for Sailor, he seemed quite incapable of doing anything more useful than run to and fro along the narrow ledge from which his mistress had fallen, barking distractedly, and utterly disregarding Flora's imperative injunctions to go home. For she soon realised the exceedingly disconcerting fact that she was a helpless prisoner, as utterly unable to effect her escape, unaided, as though she were immured within the walls of a Russian fortress; and she further realised that unless the dog could be induced to return to camp and guide Dick to her rescue, she might actually remain where she was and starve ere her lover succeeded in discovering her.

Meanwhile Dick, too, had had an unfortunate day. For late in the afternoon, while breaking up the deck of the brig, the catamaran had in some inexplicable manner gone adrift, and, driving athwart the stern of the brig, snapped her mast short off at the deck, completely disabling her, of course. In consequence of this accident, Dick had at once knocked off work, and taken the craft across the lagoon to the camp, intending to procure a new spar from the woods forthwith, and immediately proceed with the repair of the damage. But the catamaran under sail was one thing, the same craft with her wings clipped was quite another thing; and in her disabled condition she proved so unexpectedly unhandy that the sun had set and darkness was already closing down when at length he got her to her usual berth.

It was Flora's invariable custom to stroll down to the beach to meet her sweetheart as soon as she saw the catamaran coming in from the wreck;

and Leslie was greatly surprised that on this night of all others—when the unusual lateness of his arrival and the dismantled condition of the catamaran might have been expected to excite her curiosity—she should fail to appear. Yet her absence aroused no shadow of anxiety within him; for what could possibly happen to her, alone there on the island, with the dog to protect her? Nor did the non-appearance of Sailor awaken any suspicion within him, for he knew that the dog and the girl were inseparable companions, and that wherever Flora might be, there would Sailor also be found. He concluded that Flora was somehow detained for the moment, and that she and Sailor would presently present themselves as usual. Meanwhile, he secured the catamaran, served out their supper rations to Cuffy and Sambo, and attended to one or two other matters.

But when, having attended to these matters, he at length made his way to the camp, and not only found the tent in darkness, but the cooking-stove in its rear unlighted, he began for the first time to feel uneasy. He whistled and called for the dog, knowing that if the animal were within hearing he would at once bark in response, even if he did not come bounding joyously to him, as was generally the case—for Sailor was almost as devotedly attached to Dick as he was to Flora. But on this occasion no Sailor appeared, nor did he afford any other manifestation of his near presence. Then Dick began to shout loudly for Flora, hoping to hear her sweet voice raised in reply.

He now began to feel seriously alarmed, knowing that she must have wandered away into the bush, and perhaps have lost herself in the darkness. Yet against this theory was to be set his knowledge of the sagacity of Sailor, who, he believed, was quite intelligent enough to find his way back to the camp from the uttermost extremity of the island in the darkest night. He entered the tent and, lighting the lamps, looked round the living-room compartment, thinking it possible that Flora might have left a note explaining her absence, or saying where she was going. But he knew that, had she written such a note, she would have left it in some conspicuous situation—as on the table—where it would at once be found. There was no letter, either on the table or elsewhere, so far as he could see. Then he instituted a thoroughly systematic search of the tent in quest of some sign or indication that might furnish him with a clue as to what had happened to her, or what had induced her to go off in this mysterious fashion, but without success. He even ventured to peep into her sleeping apartment, wondering whether perchance she had felt unwell and become unconscious. But a single glance sufficed to show him that nothing of that kind had happened. Finally, he hunted up a lantern, trimmed and lighted it, provided himself with a small flask of brandy, to meet a possible emergency, armed himself with a brace of revolvers and a small, keen tomahawk, and without remembering or being conscious of the fact that he was by this time fairly hungry—conscious of nothing, indeed, but an ever-growing feeling of keen anxiety and alarm—set out in search of the lost one.

The first question that now confronted him was, In which direction was he to search? There was no especially favourite spot, so far as he knew, to which she would be predisposed to wend her way; there were no roads or paths, or anything in the remotest degree approaching thereto, on the island: she would therefore be just as likely to head in one direction as another. The grass in the immediate neighbourhood of the tent was to some extent trodden down, it is true, by frequent traffic round it, and a path had gradually been worn into visibility between the tent and the cook-house; but beyond that everything was as fresh and trackless as upon the day of their landing. Then it occurred to Leslie to seek for traces of Flora's footprints in the grass, and he started to carefully quarter the ground beyond the worn area in the neighbourhood of the tent, carefully examining it with the aid of the lantern. And in this way he presently discovered one or two imprints of the heels of her boots, but it proved impossible to follow the track for more than half a dozen yards; moreover, upon a further search he found so many, leading in such a number of different directions, that he soon realised the impossibility of determining which of them he ought to follow. And all the time that he was thus engaged he never ceased to whistle and call Sailor, varying the proceedings occasionally by shouting the name of Flora, until he was so hoarse that he could scarcely articulate.

In this laborious and painfully unsatisfactory fashion he spent the entire night, carefully quartering the ground until he had covered the whole area between Mermaid Head on the one hand and Cape Flora on the other, and extending rearward toward the mountain to about a quarter of its height. The magnitude of such an enterprise as this, and its exhausting nature, can only be appreciated by those who have attempted a similar feat in a country overgrown with bush.

By the time that the sun had risen and Leslie was able to dispense with the aid of the lantern, he was so utterly weary that he could scarcely drag one leg after the other; his lips were so dry that he could no longer whistle, and his throat so sore that he could no longer shout, while he was sinking with exhaustion from hunger and thirst. Yet he pressed doggedly on, still prosecuting his search with grim determination and the same concentration as before until, close upon midday—when he was working over toward the eastern side of the island, he paused suddenly and listened as intently as though his life depended upon it. Yes; there it was again—the distant but faintly heard bark of a dog—he was sure of it! Gathering himself together, he once more strove to whistle, but failed; then he attempted to shout.

"Sailor! *Sailor*!! Sailor!!!"

He lifted up his voice in a steady crescendo until the last cry became a hoarse, cracked yell that was as unlike his own full, rich, mellow tone as any sound could well be. Yet the dog heard it, ay, and recognised it, for he immediately replied vigorously. Leslie continued to shout, dashing recklessly forward in the direction of the barking as he did so, and Sailor continued to reply; nay, more; now that he actually heard Leslie's voice calling him, he uttered a whining howl of excitement, hesitated for a few seconds, and finally bounded off to meet him in response to Flora's feebly uttered commands. Five minutes later he came dashing madly up to Leslie, looked up into his face, barked, wagged his tail energetically, and then dashed off back in the direction from which he had come, stopping at every few yards to assure himself that he was being followed. And in this way he led Dick forward, for about a quarter of an hour, over the rough, broken ground that Flora had traversed some twenty-four hours before, until the pair stood together on the spot from which the girl had fallen.

By this time Flora had become quite invisible from this spot; for she had continued her struggles at intervals all through the night until she had worked herself down into the very heart of the clump of scrub and creeper into which she had fallen, and which had now closed over her head. But there was a sort of indentation or sinkage in the surface of the scrub, presenting an appearance suggestive of some tolerably heavy body having fallen there, and at this indentation Sailor first steadfastly gazed, and then looked up into Leslie's face, barking continuously. And, peering intently down into this, Dick presently became aware of what appeared to be some tiny shreds of clothing clinging here and there to the bushes.

"Are you there, Flora?" he shouted.

There was no reply; for the moment that the sound of Dick's voice fell upon her ear, encouraging and talking to the dog, and she knew that rescue was at hand, the long-endured tension of her nerves relaxed, and she fainted. But Sailor's actions were not to be misunderstood; he continued to look alternately into Leslie's face and then down at the bushes, barking excitedly all the while and making as though he would leap down into the depression; so that even a very much less intelligent individual than Leslie could not have failed to understand that it was there that the missing girl would be found. He called once more, and, still failing to obtain an answer, wasted no further time in hesitation, but, seeing that the base of the declivity was the proper point to attack, scrambled down as best he could, closely followed by Sailor, and attempted to force a way into the heart of the bushes from that point. He soon found, however, that the tough tangle of creepers was not to be conquered by his unaided hands alone, and so set to work vigorously with his tomahawk, cutting away at the tangled and knotted mass, and dragging the severed ends apart and aside until after about ten minutes of arduous work he suddenly found himself at the mouth of what appeared to be a spacious cavern under the rock from which Flora had fallen; and there, prone upon the rocky floor, with her light clothing almost torn from her body by her long-continued efforts to free herself, he found his sweetheart lying insensible.

Kneeling upon the hard rocky floor, he raised the limp form in his arms and lost not a moment in applying his flask of brandy to her lips; and presently he had the satisfaction of feeling her stir in his arms.

"Ah, that is good! You are feeling better, darling, are you not?" he exclaimed encouragingly. "Tell me, sweetheart, are you very much hurt?"

"No, I think not," she answered, with a sigh of contentment as she realised that Dick was with her and that her troubles were now practically over. "I only feel very sore all over from my long struggle to free myself; and also rather cold. I have been here ever since sunset last night, Dick, fighting to escape from those dreadful entangling bushes; and I feel, oh, so utterly tired."

"My poor little girl," exclaimed Dick, tenderly, "you have had a very trying experience, and one that might have proved very serious, too, but for Sailor, here. Cold! of course you are. Here, let me wrap my jacket round you—so; that is better. Now, I am going to light a fire; the air of this place is chill as that of an ice-house. And while you are warming yourself and getting a little life into your body I will clear away the bush a trifle more, so that you can get out without difficulty."

There was plenty of wood to be had, suitable for building a fire, by simply cutting away the dry roots and tendrils of the bush in front of the cave; and in a few minutes Dick had a good fire blazing, by the light of which he saw that they were in the mouth of a cavern about eight feet high that seemed to reach back into the heart of the rock for a considerable distance. And some way back, lying just within the radius of the area that caught the illumination of the fire, he presently noticed something lying on the ground that bore an uncanny likeness to a human skeleton! He said nothing about it, however—having no wish that Flora's shaken nerves should be subjected to any further shock just then, especially as the imperfect view of the object that had been afforded him by the flickering light of the flames left him quite uncertain as to its identity—but at once went to work again with his tomahawk in a vigorous onslaught upon the bushes, managing, in another ten minutes or so, to make such a clearance of them as would enable his companion to pass out without difficulty.

By the time that he had accomplished this, Flora had so far recovered that she declared herself quite ready to essay the journey back to the camp; and they accordingly set out forthwith, Dick very carefully noting the surrounding landmarks, with the fixed determination to return at an early moment and thoroughly examine the interior of the cavern. As they went, Flora beguiled the way by relating to Dick, in full detail, all the particulars of her very unpleasant adventure; listening in return to Dick's account of his return to camp, his consternation at the discovery of her absence, and his long, arduous, and almost despairing search for her.

They reached camp about two o'clock in the afternoon; and after snatching a hasty meal made up of the first odds and ends that they could lay their hands upon, retired at once to their respective couches to get an hour or two of that rest of which they both stood in such urgent need.

It was within an hour of sunset when Dick awoke and turned out. His first care was to light up the cooking-stove and get some sort of a dinner under way; and, this done, he strolled over to the natives' hut to ascertain what these gentry were doing, as nothing was to be seen of them in the vicinity of the camp. They were not in the hut; and when he looked for their canoe he discovered that it had also disappeared. His first thought was that they might have gone off to the brig and attempted on their own account to continue the work of breaking up her decks; and he felt a trifle vexed at the idea, fearing that in their ignorance they might do a great deal more harm than good. But upon procuring his telescope and bringing it to bear upon the brig he soon satisfied himself that the canoe was not alongside her; nor, when he looked further, could he see anything of her anywhere along the inner edge of the reef, whither he thought they might have gone for the purpose of obtaining a few fish. It was then that, for the first time, the suspicion dawned upon him that they might have left the island altogether, with the intention of attempting to make their way back to their own people, and a further search at length convinced him of the accuracy of his surmise; for a second visit to the hut showed that not only were its usual occupants absent, but they had taken with them all their trivial belongings; while a further investigation led to the discovery that they had helped themselves to a few such trifles as a pair of tomahawks, a few yards of canvas, some light line, a small keg—presumably to hold a supply of water; a bag or two of assorted nails, a couple of fishing lines, and possibly a few other unimportant odds and ends. His first feeling at this discovery was one of vexation; for ignorant though these savages were, and difficult as he had found it to make them understand his wishes, they represented a certain amount of brute strength that he had already found most useful, and doubtless would have found even more useful later on, when he had succeeded in making them understand more clearly what he desired them to do. But a little further reflection enabled him to realise that in seizing the first favourable opportunity to get away from the island and attempt to return to their own kindred and people, they were only acting upon a perfectly natural and commendable impulse; they were, in fact, actuated by precisely the same feeling that had dominated himself ever since he had been on the island, and were doing precisely what he hoped eventually to do. And, having arrived at this conclusion, he dismissed the incident from his mind, and reverted to the same plan of life that had been his prior to the arrival of Cuffy and Sambo upon the scene.

The following day was devoted by Leslie to the task of procuring a suitable spar to serve as a new mast for the catamaran, and restoring that craft to her former serviceable condition. And it was while he was thus engaged that the thought first entered his mind that the accident by which the catamaran had become dismasted might possibly have been a blessing in disguise, since, but for that accident, the two savages might, by a not intricate process of reasoning, have arrived at the conclusion that such a craft would serve their purpose infinitely better than their own canoe, and forthwith appropriated her. That they did not do so was perhaps due to the fact that she was practically unmanageable except under sail, rather than to any innate sentiment of honesty on their part.

The catamaran having been once more rendered fit for service, Leslie decided to devote a few hours to the examination of "Flora's Cave," as he called it, while its situation and the landmarks in its vicinity were fresh in his memory; he accordingly set off immediately after breakfast on the following morning, telling Flora where he was going, but suggesting that she should remain in camp and take a thorough rest.

Going easily, he arrived at the cave in about an hour and a half after starting; and at once proceeded with his investigation. He had adopted the precaution to take a packet of candles along with him, and he commenced operations by lighting these, one after the other, and setting them up on the most convenient rock projections that offered. He thus succeeded in illuminating the entire interior of the cavern quite sufficiently for his purpose. Meanwhile, during the process of lighting up the cavern, he had already discovered that his first impression relative to the suspicious-looking object was well-grounded; it was indeed a skeleton; and his first act after completing his lighting arrangements was to subject this grisly object to a careful examination. He found it to be the skeleton of a man who must have stood about six feet high in his stockings, when alive. Attached here and there to the bones were fragments of clothing, while on the ground beside the ghastly framework were other fragments of fine linen, lace, gold-embroidered velvet, and silks, showing that the wearer must have been a man of some consequence. The waist was girded by a broad leather belt, so dry and rotten that it crumbled to powder in Leslie's fingers, and attached to this was a long, straight rapier with an elaborately ornamented hilt and sheath, all rotted and rust-eaten. To the same belt was also attached the sheath of what must have been a long and formidable dagger. And a couple of feet away from the head there lay a handsome steel casque very beautifully engraved and chased, but thickly coated with rust, like the rest of the steel accoutrements. A closer inspection of the skeleton disclosed the fact that the skull had been battered in, while a dagger that might have belonged to the empty sheath was found sticking up to its hilt in one of the ribs.

Turning from the skeleton, Leslie next proceeded to carefully examine a great pile of small cases, packages, and casks that had already come under his casual notice while engaged in lighting up the cave. He took these as they came most conveniently to his hand, the casks first claiming his attention. With the assistance of a small axe that he had taken the precaution to bring with him he soon forced off the head of one of these, revealing its contents. It consisted of a solid cake of some hard, black substance, moulded to the shape of the cask, that upon critical examination proved—as he had more than half expected—to be gunpowder, caked into a solid mass and completely spoiled by damp. Two similar casks were also found to contain powder in a like condition; and therefore, acting upon the justifiable assumption that the contents of all the casks was the same, he rolled the whole of them, sixteen in number, to the opposite side of the cave, out of the way, and turned his attention to a number of small black packages that, when he proceeded to handle them, proved to be unexpectedly heavy. His first thought was that they were pigs of lead, intended to be cast into bullets as occasion might require; but upon removing one of them to the open air, for greater convenience of examination, he discovered that the block—whatever it might be—was sewn up in what had once been hide, but was now a mere dry, stiff, rotten envelope that easily peeled off, revealing a dark-brownish and very heavy substance within. This substance he feverishly proceeded to scrape with the blade of his pocket-knife—for the presence of the hide envelope prepared him for an important discovery—and presently, the outer coat of dirt and discolouration being removed from that part of the surface upon which he was operating with his knife, there gleamed up at him the dull ruddy tint of *virgin gold*! It was as he had anticipated; the block upon which he was operating was one of the gold bricks that, sewn up in raw hide, were wont to be shipped home by the Spaniards of old from the mines of South America. He lifted the brick in his hands, and estimated it to weigh about forty pounds. The gold bricks were stacked together in tiers, twenty bricks long, four bricks wide, and four bricks high; there were therefore three hundred and twenty of them, and if his estimate of their weight happened to be correct, this little pile of precious metal must be worth—what? A short mental calculation—taking the gold to be worth three pounds fifteen shillings the ounce—furnished him with the answer; the handsome sum of close upon seven hundred thousand pounds sterling. Quite a respectable fortune!

But this was not all. There were other chests and cases still awaiting examination; and, fully convinced by now that he had accidentally stumbled upon one of those fabulously rich treasures that the Spanish galleons were reported to have conveyed from time to time from the shores of the new world to those of old Spain—how it had happened to find its way to this particular spot he did not trouble to puzzle out—Leslie went to work to break open and examine the remainder of the packages, heedless of the flight of time. Some of them he found to contain rich clothing, that fell to pieces as he attempted to lift the garments out of the receptacles that had held them in safe keeping for so long; others—two of the largest—were packed full of gold candlesticks, crosses, jewelled cups, and other vessels and articles of a character that seemed to point to their having been the spoils of some looted church—a circumstance that caused Leslie to suspect that his find represented the proceeds of some more than ordinarily successful oldtime piratical cruise. And finally the innermost chest of all, and consequently the last arrived at, disclosed to Dick's astounded gaze a collection of jewels, set and unset, that fairly made him reel with astonishment. There were great ropes of discoloured pearls, that would be priceless if they could by any means be restored to their pristine state of purity; diamond, ruby, emerald, and other necklaces, bracelets, rings, brooches, and other ornaments in more or less tarnished settings; heavy chains of solid gold; jewelled sword-hilts; and, last but not least, a great buckskin bag that was still in pliant and serviceable condition, containing a heterogeneous assortment of cut and uncut gems—principally diamonds, emeralds, rubies, and sapphires— every one of them apparently picked specimens, the whole constituting of itself a treasure of incalculable value.

As Dick, having pocketed a handful of these gems at random to show Flora, replaced the heavy bag in the chest and sank back on his haunches to rest himself while he mopped from his brow the perspiration of hard labour and excitement, the light that streamed in through the mouth of the cavern was momentarily obscured, and Sailor bounded in, barking joyously as he sprang at Dick and tried to lick his face. The dog was closely followed by Flora, who cried as she entered—

"Dick, Dick, where are you? Has anything—oh! there you are! Whatever has kept you so long, dear? Are you ill, or have you met with an accident? Oh! what is this horrible thing?" as she stumbled over the skeleton, which she had failed to notice, coming as she did straight from the brilliant outdoor light into the dimly illuminated interior of the cavern.

"That!" exclaimed Dick, lightly. "Oh, that is just a heap of bones that must have been left here by the original owners of this commodious abode." And with a sweep of his foot he unceremoniously transferred the poor remains to a dark corner of the cavern that he contrived to render still darker by dexterously extinguishing three or four of the candles in its immediate vicinity. "As to my being ill," he continued, "I am happy to assure you, my dear, that I never felt better in my life. And I have excellent reason for feeling well. Look at this!" And he pointed exultantly to the noble pile of treasure.

Chapter Twelve
Abduction and Pursuit

"Well, what is it, Dick? It looks like a number of very old boxes. Have you come upon a pirate's hoard?—as you ought to do, you know, in such a cunningly concealed cavern as this," exclaimed Flora, laughingly, as she peered inquisitively at the pile that even now she could only see very imperfectly.

"Ay," answered Dick. "You may laugh as much as you like, little girl, but that is precisely what I have done. Of course I am not prepared to assert positively that it is a *'pirate's* hoard,' although it looks uncommonly like it, I must confess; but that it is treasure, and very valuable treasure, too, is indisputable. Do you see this pile of black bricks here? Well, those are *gold* bricks; and I estimate their value at something approaching three-quarters of a million sterling."

"Three-quarters of a million?" repeated Flora, incredulously. "Oh, Dick, you cannot mean it; you are surely joking!"

"I assure you, dear, I never spoke more seriously in my life; what I am telling you is fact—plain, simple, indisputable, delightful *fact*! And the gold is only part of the story."

He lifted the covers of the other cases and held a candle while she looked at their contents, uttering exclamations of delighted amazement as she gazed. Then he withdrew the buckskin bag from the jewel-chest, and placed it in her hands.

"Lift that," he said simply.

"Oh, dear, how heavy!" exclaimed the girl. "I should not like to be obliged to carry this very far. What does it contain?"

Dick plunged his hand into his pocket and pulled out the handful of gems that he had abstracted from the bag.

"It is full of pretty little stones like these," he answered, displaying them to her astonished gaze. "Put your hand into the lucky-bag, dear, and see what you can find there."

She did so, and pulled out a similar handful to those which glittered in Dick's palm.

"Why, this is a perfect cave of Aladdin, Dick," she exclaimed, in delighted astonishment. "Where did it all come from, do you think?"

"It is impossible to say with certainty," answered Leslie; "but I have very little doubt that it was brought to this hiding-place from that old wreck that you discovered sunk in the lagoon. At all events it has lain here for many years—a hundred, at least, I should think; and its original owners have long been dead and gone, leaving no trace of their identity behind them. It is therefore now *ours*, sweetheart—our very own; so the fact of our being cast away upon this desert island has not been an unmitigated misfortune, after all, you see."

"No, indeed," agreed Flora, heartily. "There was a time when I certainly so regarded it; but I do so no longer, for it has given me you, and it has made you a rich man. Why, Dick, you must be a veritable millionaire!"

"Yes," agreed Dick; "there cannot be much doubt about that. At least, we are *jointly* worth quite a million, which practically means the same thing. And now, do you wish to adorn your pretty self with any of these gewgaws? Because, if so, you had better make your selection, and then we ought to be going, for I see that the sun is getting low."

"Yes, let us get away from here; it is a horrid place, notwithstanding the fact that it is a treasure-cave. And, as to wearing any of those things, I would very much rather not, Dick, please. They suggest to me all sorts of dreadful ideas—scenes of violence and bloodshed, the sacking and burning of towns, the murder of their inhabitants, and—oh no, I could not wear any of them, thank you."

"Very well," said Dick; "then I will just make everything safe here, and we will be off."

And, allowing Flora first to withdraw into the open air, he closed the chests again, extinguished the candles, and, rearranging the bushes in front of the cave so as effectually to conceal its entrance, left the spot.

For some time after this nothing of importance occurred to vary the monotony of existence on the island, Leslie devoting himself energetically to the important work of providing the material for and constructing the ways upon which he intended to build his cutter. This heavy task absorbed rather more than two months of his time; for it was laborious work, involving the handling of heavy masses of timber, which could only be done with the aid of tackles and other appliances, supplemented by the ingenuity of the highly trained sailor; moreover, Leslie was one of those individuals who believed in the wisdom of doing everything thoroughly well at first rather than incur the risk of being obliged to undo much of his work and do it all over again. But at length the ways were completed to his satisfaction; and, that done, the job of laying the keel and setting up the ready-made frames of the cutter in their correct respective positions and securing them there was comparatively simple and easy. This occupied exactly a month, at the end of which time the completed skeleton of the cutter stood revealed upon the stocks, to Dick's supreme gratification and Flora's wonder and admiration. And, indeed, Leslie had ample cause to be both satisfied and delighted; for this completed skeleton displayed the form of a remarkably handsome boat, possessed of exceptionally fine flowing lines, with a keen entrance and a perfectly clean delivery, yet with a splendidly powerful mid-section, and a depth of hull that promised great weatherliness with an ample sufficiency of freeboard. It was evident that her design had emanated from the drawing-board of a naval architect of quite unusual ability, for her shape seemed to promise the speed of the racer with the seaworthiness of the cruiser; indeed, as Dick was never tired of asserting, she could not have been more perfectly suitable for his purpose had she been specially designed for it. "Give me another hand to keep watch and watch with me, and I'll take her round the world!" he was wont to declare, when summing up the good points of the craft. It was at this stage of affairs, namely, when the skeleton framework of the cutter had been completely set up, and Leslie was preparing to commence the task of planking-up, that, upon emerging from the tent one morning after breakfast to wend his way down to the shipyard, he was amazed to see a cloud of smoke rising from the now partially dismembered hull of the brig, followed, even as he gazed incredulously, by an outburst of flame. Rushing back to the tent for the telescope, he brought the instrument to bear upon the craft, and then discovered that not only was she on fire, but also that there was a boat or canoe of some sort alongside her, and a moment later he saw a party of natives on board her!

"Look at that, sweetheart, the poor old 'Mermaid' is on fire, and we are about to see the last of her."

He stamped his foot on the ground with anger and vexation. Natives again, and this time in the form of wanton marauders; for he had no doubt that they had been plundering the wreck, and, having secured all that they required or could carry away, had maliciously set fire to her. And who were they, and where had they come from? Were they Cuffy and Sambo, returned to the island with a party of friends for the purpose of securing possession of some intensely coveted object—as seemed more than probable—or were they strangers, who had come upon the island accidentally? This last was scarcely probable, for there had been no bad weather to blow them out to sea, and the nearest land was so far distant that, assuming them to have come from it, they would scarcely have adventured the passage across so wide a stretch of ocean on mere speculation. At all events, let them be whom they might, and no matter where they came from, they must be driven off;

for the presence of a party of strange natives upon the island constituted an intolerable menace that must at once be put an end to.

These reflections flashed through Leslie's brain even as he lowered the telescope from his eye, and, calling to Flora, he pointed out to her the burning brig, saying—

"Look at that, sweetheart! The poor old *Mermaid* is on fire, and we are about to see the last of her. That, however, is not a matter of very great moment, for I believe I have got out of her practically everything that I need; the point that is of importance is that she has been set on fire, either wilfully or accidentally, by a party of natives, who are at this moment on board her. There are some ten or a dozen of them, so far as I can make out, and it seems pretty clear that they have come here on a looting expedition, organised, as likely as not, by those fellows Sambo and Cuffy, who seized the opportunity of my absence from the camp, in search of you, when you met with your accident at the treasure-cave, to return to their own island, taking along with them a few unconsidered trifles. Doubtless they have now been helping themselves again; and, although it is unlikely that they have taken anything of real value, I will not have them paying marauding visits to this island. They cannot again loot the brig, it is true, for they have set fire to her, and she must now burn until she burns herself out; but, unless I can very effectually convince them of the folly of such a proceeding, we shall next have a small army of savages descending upon the island itself, for the purpose of looting the camp, which will mean a big fight, involving heavy loss of life to them, and ending in my death and your captivity. Such a contingency as that will not bear thinking of; I am therefore about to go out to them and induce them, one way or another, to clear out. In plain language, I am going to drive them out to sea; and if harm comes to them, they will only have themselves to thank for it. They came here with a dishonest purpose, and they must take the consequences. You will, of course, remain here, with Sailor to take care of you. And do not be anxious if I do not return for a few hours; I intend to drive them so far to sea that they will find some difficulty in returning, especially as they must be fairly tired already with their long paddle to windward. And now good-bye, dear; I want to get afloat in time to prevent them from landing."

"Good-bye, Dick dear," answered Flora. "Be sure that you take the utmost care of yourself, and do not be away any longer than is absolutely necessary. I shall be anxious until you return."

"Ah, but that is just what you must not be," exclaimed Leslie, as he buckled on a belt containing two fully loaded revolvers, and began to stuff packets of ammunition into his pockets. Then, seizing a brace of Winchester repeating rifles from a rack in the corner of the tent, he started on a run for the beach, loading his rifle as he ran, for he saw that the blacks were in the act of leaving the brig.

Leaping aboard the catamaran, Dick cast off and made sail with all speed, for it looked as though the blacks meditated attempting a landing. As soon, however, as they saw the strange craft beating off to meet them, and making short tacks to keep between them and the beach, they whisked the canoe round and paddled desperately for the channel, with the catamaran in full chase.

The canoe—a big, wholesome-looking craft, propelled by ten paddles— reached the channel first, with a lead of about three-quarters of a mile, and at once, upon fairly reaching the open sea, headed away to the south-east, or dead to windward, her occupants having already apparently grasped the fact that the catamaran could only progress in the same direction by following a zigzag course. It was Leslie's intention to turn them, if possible, and drive them round the southern extremity of the reef, and so to leeward, reckoning upon the fact that they must already be considerably exhausted by their long paddle of something over one hundred miles to windward, and believing that if he could drive them far enough beyond the lee of the island to get them fairly into the full run of the sea and the full strength of the trade wind on that side, they would be in no mood or condition to paddle up to windward again; he therefore made a long board to the eastward on clearing the channel, hoping that on the next tack he would be able to near them sufficiently to execute the desired manoeuvre. But, to his disgust, upon getting into their wake, he found that he had gained upon them little or nothing, while they continued to paddle with a vigour that spoke well for their endurance.

Leslie now tacked again to the eastward, standing on until he could only see the canoe when she and the catamaran topped the back of a swell together, when he again hove about. Twenty minutes later he once more crossed the wake of the canoe, and now found that he had done much better, having neared her to within about eight hundred yards. He now lashed the catamaran's helm for a moment, leaving her to steer herself, and, picking up one of the rifles, took careful aim with it at the flying canoe, hoping to send a bullet near enough to her to spur her crew to renewed exertions, so tiring them out and compelling them to take the direction in which he desired them to go. He waited a favourable opportunity, and presently, when the canoe was hove up into plain view, brought both sights dead on her, and pulled the trigger. A moment later she sank into the trough and disappeared, but as she was on the point of vanishing he distinctly saw one of her occupants leap up, with a wild flourish of his paddle, and sink back into the bottom of the boat. Then he tacked once more to the eastward.

Altering his tactics now, and making short boards athwart the wake of the canoe, Leslie found that the chase was once more holding her own, this state of things prevailing until they had worked out an offing of about nine miles, when the catamaran again began to gain, until she had neared the chase to within about a quarter of a mile. Meanwhile Leslie had been carefully considering the whole situation. He was by nature a most humane man, one who would not willingly injure a fellow-being on any account, and, indeed, would go far out of his way to do even a total stranger a service; but there could be no two opinions upon the matter, he told himself—these savages *must* be made to understand that raiding expeditions to this particular island were too dangerous and unprofitable a pastime to be indulged in. He therefore once more opened fire upon them, and now in deadly earnest, his first three shots missing, while his fourth struck the hull of the canoe and made the splinters fly. Then he scored two more misses, followed by a hit that extorted a shriek from one of the crew. This last shot had the desired effect; the canoe bore up and headed away to the southward and westward with the catamaran hot in chase.

With wind and sea abeam, the chased and the chaser now went along with considerably accelerated speed, the catamaran, however, having very much the best of it; and within ten minutes from the moment of bearing up Leslie found himself closing fast upon the canoe, and less than a hundred yards astern of her. He now considered himself near enough to administer a final lesson to her crew of impudent marauders—who, to do them justice, were by this time looking scared out of their wits, and extremely sorry that they had ever molested him—so he put his helm down, hauled his fore sheet to windward, and dumped five raking shots into the canoe as he swept athwart her stern. Instantly the whole crew, dropping their paddles, flung themselves down into the bottom of the craft, and buried their heads in their arms, as though they would by that means protect themselves from the mysterious and terrible missiles wherewith they were being assailed; while three white spots that started into view on the hull of the canoe told that his shots had penetrated her close to the water-line. Leslie now held his hand, for he had no mind to take the lives of these savages unnecessarily; but he watched them carefully, nevertheless. And presently, one after another, eight black heads cautiously lifted themselves above the gunwale. The eyes in those heads stared wonderingly and apprehensively at the catamaran and her occupant, their owners evidently holding themselves ready to duck again at the first sign of danger; but at length, seeing that Leslie was indisposed to further interfere with them, they seized their remaining paddles—four only in number, the remainder having been lost overboard in their panic—and put the canoe dead before the wind.

It was clear to Leslie that, with only four paddles left, the savages could not possibly propel their canoe to windward and return to his island; they must perforce go to leeward and make their way back to their own island as best they could. He had therefore no more to fear from them—at least for the present; and he accordingly let draw his fore sheet and, getting way on the catamaran, tacked and bore away for the mouth of the entrance channel, leaving his enemies to paddle before the wind and sea, and find their way back home again if they could.

The catamaran had arrived within about six miles of the channel, and Leslie was already debating within himself the question whether, after all, it would not have been a wiser and more prudent thing to have put it beyond the power of his surviving antagonists to return to their friends, and possibly organise a very much more formidable expedition against him, and whether, even now, it would not be advisable to go in chase of and utterly destroy them, when his eye was attracted to a small triangular object of brownish yellow tint that, brilliantly illuminated by the bright sunlight, showed up strongly against the dazzling white of the surf breaking upon the weather edge of the reef. It was in shape like a shark's fin, but was not the same colour; it was hull down, and was sliding along at a rapid rate past the wall of surf. It needed but a single glance to enable Leslie to determine that it was a sail, ay, and undoubtedly the sail of a native canoe.

Sick with the sudden thought of the possibilities suggested by the presence of such an object just where he saw it, Dick took a hasty turn of a rope's-end round the tiller-head and with one bound reached the weather-shrouds, up which he shinned with an agility equalled only by the dread that struck like a knife at his heart. In a moment he was high enough to get a footing upon the throat of the gaff, from which elevation he was enabled to obtain a clear view of the craft. She was about three miles away, well to the southward of the dense column of smoke rising from the blazing brig, and was edging away round the curved outer margin of the reef, heading so as to pass to the southward of the island in a westerly direction. She was too far distant, of course, to enable Leslie to distinguish details with his unaided eye, but he could see that she was a big craft, capable, he thought, of carrying quite forty men, she showed a very large sail to the freshly blowing breeze, and was skimming along at a very rapid pace.

This was as much as Leslie could make out at that distance; but it was enough, and, groaning with dire apprehension of some dreadful evil, he slid down the shrouds and went aft to the tiller. He could see through the whole devilish scheme now. The gang who had set fire to the brig were evidently only a small contingent of the expedition, and it had been their duty to attract his attention and decoy him away from the island while the others—headed without doubt by those scoundrels Sambo and Cuffy—raided the camp.

That, Leslie savagely meditated, was undoubtedly what had happened. And, meanwhile, where was Flora? What had been her fate? Had she received sufficient warning to effect her escape to the Treasure-Cave, which, armed with her revolvers, she could hold for hours against any number of savages? Or had she been surprised? The thought of the latter alternative plunged Leslie into a cold sweat, and set him to muttering the most awful threats of vengeance. He had no room in his mind for thought of the possible extent of irremediable damage that the savages might have wrought in the camp; he could think of nothing but Flora; could only hope and pray that she might have made good her escape. The catamaran was sailing as well as ever, for there was a strong breeze blowing, yet Leslie ground his teeth in a fever of impatience at what he deemed her snail-like pace; for his first business now must be to ascertain the fate of the girl he loved. The very worst that could possibly have happened, apart from harm to her, was comparatively unimportant. Yet, all the same, his mind once set at rest about her, he would exact a terrible penalty from those daring marauders; he would pursue them, ay, to their very island itself, if need were; while, if he caught them at sea, not a man should survive to organise another expedition against him. He felt now that he had been a weak fool not to utterly exterminate the decoy party that he had just left.

At length, after what to Leslie appeared an eternity of suspense, the catamaran passed through the entrance channel and bore away for the camp, a raking view of which was to be obtained as soon as the veiling wall of surf was passed. To his inexpressible relief, the framework of the cutter still stood on the stocks, apparently uninjured; and inshore of it he could see the tent, also apparently uninjured. He had been cherishing a sort of half hope that he would also see Flora standing on the beach awaiting his arrival; but she was not there, and, upon reflection, he was not greatly surprised. No doubt she was still in hiding, and would probably not reappear until he had succeeded in making her aware of his return and of the fact that all danger was now past. As the catamaran sped along Leslie's keen glance roved anxiously over the various parts of the camp as they opened out, and he presently saw that his savage visitors had been busy with the varied items of the cargo that he had saved from the brig and stored under canvas, for the canvas cover was folded back, and boxes and bales were strewed here and there upon the sward. Ah, and there was Sailor—good dog!—lying down on the beach close to the water-line, waiting for him. But where, then, was Flora? She could certainly not be far off, or Sailor would not be there, lying so quietly and lazily stretched out in the sun. Leslie seized his rifle and fired a signal shot to let the girl know that he was at hand; but the echoes of the report pealed off the face of the mountain and still she did not appear, nor— stranger still—did Sailor leap to his feet with a welcoming bark. What, Dick wondered, was the matter with the old dog? Why did he lie there so utterly motionless? and what was that long thin shaft that looked almost as though its point were embedded in his body? Leslie gave vent to a bitter groan; for as he bore up to run the catamaran in upon the beach, he recognised only too clearly that the poor dog was dead—slain by the cruel spear that transfixed his body. And he saw, too—just in time to avoid grounding the catamaran upon the spot—that the sand of the beach was marked with many naked footprints, leading to and fro between the camp and a mark upon the sand that had evidently been left there by a canoe.

Leaping ashore, and taking care not to confuse the footprints by obliterating them with his own, Leslie examined the marks with the most anxious care; and presently his most dreadful fears were realised, for plainly to be distinguished here and there among the imprints of bare feet were the prints of Flora's little shoes, blurred in places, as though she had offered strenuous resistance to the coercion of her captors, but quite unmistakable for all that. Dick subjected the whole length of the track, from the water's edge to the boundary of the sward, to a most rigid examination, and at length satisfied himself that Flora's footprints all led in one direction, namely *toward* the water; and then, with a savage cry, he went to work to prepare for the pursuit. For there could no longer be a shadow of doubt that Flora had been carried off, and was at that moment aboard the canoe that he had seen under sail. Oh, if he had but known—if he had but known!

His preparations were few, and did not take very long to complete. He first dashed off to the tent, and, snatching the mattress and bedding from his bed, rushed down to the catamaran with it, and, flinging it down on deck, covered it with a tarpaulin. He would certainly be out one night, if not two, and Flora would need something softer than the bare planks to lie upon when he had rescued her. Then, returning to the tent, he flung into a basket all the provisions that he could lay his hands upon, together with half a dozen bottles of wine—there was no time to go to the spring for water—and this with a small case of rifle ammunition and a few others matters that he thought would be useful, he also conveyed on board the catamaran. He was now ready to start; but as yet he knew not in what direction the canoe was steering, except that she was undoubtedly bound to the westward. Now, there were at least three islands lying in that direction, and the canoe was probably bound to one or the other of these; but it was of the utmost importance to know *which* one, for any mistake upon this point would be fatal, as it must result in the canoe being missed altogether. So Leslie took a boat compass that had originally belonged to the brig, and the telescope, and, thus provided, made his way as rapidly as possible to Mermaid Head—as he had named the most southerly point of the island—hoping and believing that from the lofty cliffs of that headland the flying canoe would still be in sight.

To climb to this point cost him twenty minutes of precious time, although he did the whole distance at a run; but when he got there he felt that the time had been well spent. For there, some ten miles away, with the afternoon sun shining brightly upon her sail, lay the fugitive canoe, scudding away on a due westerly course, with the wind over her port quarter. He cast a hurried glance over that part of the ocean where he believed the second canoe ought to be, and at length thought he caught sight of her, but could not be certain, as the light of the sun lay strong upon the sea in that direction. But when at length he got into the field of his telescope the image of what he had seen, he found that it was some object, about the size of the smaller canoe, certainly, but floating awash. If therefore it was indeed the canoe that he had already pursued, she had either capsized or been swamped, and there was an end of her and her crew. He now carefully took the bearing of the big canoe, and, this done, at once set out on his journey back to the camp and beach.

The return journey was accomplished in about a quarter of an hour, for it was all downhill. Then, having reached the camp, Leslie hunted up one or two further articles that he anticipated might be useful, and, rushing down to the catamaran, got under way and headed her for the channel. The breeze had by this time freshened up somewhat, and the craft heeled over under the pressure of her enormous mainsail until her lee pontoon was buried to its gunwale, while the weather-shrouds were strained as taut as harp-strings; but Dick only smiled grimly as he heard the wind singing and piping through his rigging; he would scarcely have shortened sail for a hurricane just then. The queer-looking structure tore at racing speed across the smooth surface of the lagoon, shearing through it with a vicious hiss along her bends and a roaring wave under her lee bow, and so out to sea. Leslie was compelled to haul his wind for a short distance after shooting through the channel, in order to clear the northern extremity of the reef; but he tacked the instant that he had room, and stood away to the southward, skirting the outer margin of the reef as closely as he dared and gradually edging away as the reef curved round in a westerly direction. He found himself close in under the cliffs of Mermaid's Head about half an hour after clearing the entrance channel, and then at once shaped a course corresponding to the bearing of the canoe as taken from the summit of those same cliffs.

He calculated that the canoe had secured a fifteen miles' start of him, and, estimating as nearly as he could her speed from the glimpse that he had caught of her as she skimmed past the reef earlier on in the day, he doubted very much whether the speed of the catamaran exceeded that of the canoe by more than a couple of miles in the hour, to which might be added or subtracted a trifle according to the relative merits of the respective helmsmen. Knowing that in a stern-chase every trifle tells, Leslie steered as carefully as he knew how, and as one of the catamaran's merits happened to be that she would steer almost as well off the wind as she would on a taut bowline, he hoped that through this he might be able to gain a little extra advantage. Furthermore, he had a compass—which it was reasonable to suppose that the savages lacked—and that ought to prove a further help to him.

Being now, as he believed, fairly upon the track of the fleeing canoe, and having eaten nothing since breakfast, Leslie deemed the moment a fitting one wherein to snatch a meal; and this he did, steering with one hand and feeding himself with the other as he alternately eyed the compass and looked ahead on the watch for the first glimpse of the canoe's triangular sail, although he knew full well that several hours must elapse ere he might hope for that. And, meanwhile, what agonies of terror and despair would not that highly strung and gently nurtured girl be suffering! At the mere thought Dick set his teeth and carefully scrutinised the set of his canvas—already trimmed to a hair—to see if there was anything he could do to get a little extra speed out of his flying craft.

Meanwhile the sun slowly declined in the western sky, and finally sank, in a blaze of purple and crimson and gold, beneath the horizon; the glowing tints quickly faded to a dull purplish grey, a star suddenly glittered in the eastern sky, and was quickly followed by another and another, and two or three more, until the entire dome of heaven was spangled with them, and night was upon the solitary voyager. Dick lit the lantern that he had brought with him, and so arranged it that its light should fall upon the compass card, lit his pipe, and set himself to the task of endeavouring to work out a scheme for the recovery of his sweetheart without injury to her or—what was of almost as much importance, so far as her ultimate safety was concerned—himself.

It was a fortunate conjunction of circumstances that the savages had chosen—doubtless for their own convenience—the time of full moon for their raid, and night had scarcely fallen ere a brightening of the sky in the eastern quarter proclaimed the advent of the "sweet regent of the night." Leslie's island lay full in the wake of the rising orb; and for nearly half an hour the catamaran scudded along within the shadow of the peak, which stretched dark and clear-cut far over the ocean ahead of her. Little by little the shadow shortened, however, and by-and-by the catamaran slid over the edge of it as the gleaming disc emerged from behind the northern edge of the peak, and flooded the whole of the sea to the eastward with dancing streaks of glittering liquid silver.

It was about a quarter of an hour later that, as the catamaran rose upon the back of a somewhat higher swell than usual, Leslie's quick eye caught a momentary glimpse of a tiny white gleaming point straight ahead; and his heart leaped with joy, for he knew that what he had seen was the upper tip of the canoe's triangular sail. Greedily he watched for its next appearance, rejoicing meanwhile in the knowledge that the shadowed sides of his own sails were turned toward the flying canoe, and that behind them again loomed up the dark background of the peak; it would consequently need very sharp eyes—even though they should be those of a savage—to descry them.

For twenty minutes or so following upon the first sighting of the chase Leslie was able to catch only brief intermittent glimpses of the sail, as one or the other of the flying craft was swept up on the crest of a swell, but by the end of that time he had so far gained upon the canoe that even when they both sank into the trough together he was still able to see the upper part of the sail, while when both lifted simultaneously he could see the whole of it, right down to the foot, and even occasionally a glimpse of the heads of the savages; he estimated, therefore, that he had closed the chase to within a distance of about a mile.

Another quarter of an hour passed, at the expiration of which the canoe was in full view, and Leslie now took the two repeating rifles with which he had provided himself, and carefully loaded them both. But he had no intention of opening fire at long range, the motion of both craft was so lively that in the uncertain light of the moon accurate shooting would only be possible at a range of about a hundred yards, or less, and he was so fearful of the possibility of injury to Flora that he was quite determined not to shoot until he could make absolutely sure of his mark.

And now he suddenly became aware that he was no longer gaining nearly as rapidly as before upon the chase; indeed there were moments when he doubted whether he was gaining at all. For a few minutes he was puzzled how to account for this—for the breeze was still as fresh as ever, indeed he was rather inclined to believe that, if anything, it was slightly freshening—but presently, as he watched the canoe, he detected a kind of rhythmical glinting appearance on each side of her; and then the explanation occurred to him. His presence, and the fact that he was in pursuit, had at last been discovered by the savages, and they were now endeavouring to increase their speed by paddling. "Well," thought Dick, grimly, "let them paddle, if they will; at the speed at which that canoe is travelling they will be obliged to expend a great deal of strength to perceptibly increase it, and they *must* tire sooner or later. They may succeed in prolonging the chase somewhat, but I shall catch them, all the same."

But now a new cause for anxiety on Dick's part arose, for presently—whether in consequence of some subtle clearing of the atmosphere, or because of the gradual change of the moon's position in the heavens—the island that Dick knew lay somewhere ahead, and for which the canoe was obviously steering, suddenly loomed up ahead with such startling distinctness that Leslie feared that they must be very much nearer to it than was actually the case; and as the time sped on without bringing him very appreciably nearer to the chase, he became haunted by a dread lest the fleeing savages should after all reach the shore and gain the assistance of their friends before he could overtake them.

At length, however, he found that he was once more creeping up to the canoe, despite the fact that her occupants were still paddling apparently as vigorously as ever; it was obvious that, notwithstanding appearances, their long spell of exceptional exertion was telling upon them, and, consciously or unconsciously, they were gradually relaxing their efforts. Slowly, and foot by foot, the catamaran crept up; and at length Dick was convinced that not more than a bare quarter of a mile separated the two craft. Then an idea suddenly occurred to him: although he was still too distant to be at all willing to hazard a shot at the occupants of the canoe, there was no particular reason why he should not fire at the *sail*; he had with him an ample supply of ammunition, and a few lucky shots through it might cause the sail to split; nay, there was even the possibility that he might succeed in bringing it down altogether. Accordingly, planting himself firmly on the deck to leeward of the tiller, with the latter just pressing sufficiently against his left hip to keep the catamaran going straight and prevent her from broaching-to, he took one of the rifles in his hand, and, determining to devote himself entirely to the effort to bring down the sail, sighted the weapon to four hundred yards, raised it to his shoulder, and aiming carefully at the mast of the canoe, waited until he had got both sights dead on it, when he instantly pressed the trigger. He was still too far distant to be able to see the result of the shot, but he was inclined to believe that he had scored a hit somewhere, for he distinctly heard a loud shout that seemed to carry in it a note of alarm. Again, patiently waiting his chance, he fired; and this time he really fancied he saw some chips fly from the mast, close to the sling of the yard, at which point he was persistently aiming. Encouraged by this possible success, and still more by the fact that he was now distinctly overhauling the canoe, Leslie maintained a slow, careful, and deliberate fire upon her, always aiming for the same spot; and at length, at about the ninth shot, down dropped the yard into the canoe, to his mingled surprise and gratification, the fall of the sail eliciting a tremendous hullabaloo from the excited and astonished savages.

In the extremity of their consternation the flying raiders seemed unable to make up their minds what to do, and for a few minutes all was confusion aboard the canoe, during which the catamaran swept up to her hand over hand until the two craft were abreast, Dick taking the precaution to keep some fifty yards of water between him and the canoe, as he fully expected to be received with a shower of spears. Nor was he disappointed; for, as he ranged up alongside, the natives as one man rose to their feet, and in an instant some thirty spears were hurtling toward him. He had probably never been much nearer death than he was at that moment, for the spears flew all round him, one of them actually sweeping the cap off his head; but he remained untouched. Leslie at once raised his rifle to his shoulder, and selecting as a mark the individual who wielded the steering-paddle—in whom he instantly recognised the ci-devant Cuffy, with Sambo standing next to him—fired. The savage flung up his arms, staggered for a moment, and then fell backward overboard. Then, as the catamaran swept ahead, he caught a glimpse of something white lying in the stern of the canoe that he knew must be Flora's white-clothed body.

Quick as thought Leslie recharged both rifles, and hauling his wind, shot athwart the bows of the canoe; then he tacked, and, shaping a course that would enable him to cross the canoe's stern at a distance of about eighty yards, hauled his fore sheet to windward, checking the way of the catamaran and allowing her to cross quite slowly. Then he once more raised his rifle, and pointed it at Sambo. But the tragic fate of Cuffy had already produced its effect upon the now thoroughly terrified savages, who by this time realised that to remain in the canoe was but to court death. Yet what else could they do? There was but one alternative, and that was—to jump overboard, and trust to their ability to swim to the island that loomed ghostly in the moonlight ahead. And this they did, one after the other—the laggards being stimulated by another shot or two from Leslie's rifle—until the canoe, a fine big craft of about five feet beam and forty feet long, fitted with an outrigger, was empty of savages. Then, without troubling himself particularly as to what was likely to become of his beaten foes, Leslie gibed over, and shot alongside the canoe, jumping into her with the end of a rope that he had already made fast on board the catamaran. This rope's-end he deftly threw in the form of a half-hitch round the quaintly carved figure-head of the canoe, taking the end aft and making it fast round the heel of the mast, thus effectually securing the craft to the catamaran in a manner convenient for the towage of the former. This done, he strode aft, until he came to where Flora lay. And his blood rose to boiling-point as he bent over her; for he saw that not only had she been gagged, but that she had also been bound hand and foot so cruelly tight that she must have endured hours of untold agony.

Chapter Thirteen
The Drifting Raft

Without losing an instant Leslie whipped out his knife, and with a few strokes of its keen blade freed the unfortunate girl from her bonds; then, without saying a word to her, or wasting time in asking questions, he raised her tenderly in his arms, and, hauling the canoe alongside the catamaran, carried her aboard the latter and gently laid her upon the mattress that he had brought along with him for her especial benefit. The girl was practically in a state of collapse from her protracted sufferings; but by pouring a little brandy between her lips, and gently chafing her limbs where they had been compressed by the tightly drawn bonds, and thus restoring the arrested circulation of the blood, he at length brought her back to a sense of her surroundings. And then, as might have been expected, as soon as she fully realised that she had been rescued, and that she had nothing further to fear from her late captors, her tensely strained nerves suddenly gave way and she broke into a passion of weeping so violent that it thoroughly alarmed Leslie, who, poor ignorant creature, knew not what to do. Therefore, in the extremity of his ignorance, he did the very best thing possible; that is to say, he took her into his arms and soothed her with many tender and loving words. And as soon as she was calm enough to eat and drink, he placed food and wine before her, and set her a good example by eating and drinking heartily himself, chattering trivialities all the time to divert her mind, so far as he could, from her recent terrible adventure. Then, when she had taken all that he could persuade her to swallow, he insisted that she must lie down and endeavour to sleep.

The rescue of Flora having been happily effected, Leslie was naturally anxious to get back to the island as quickly as possible; for he dreaded lest the fearful shock that the girl had sustained, the long hours of intense physical suffering and of even more intense mental agony that she had endured, should seriously affect her health, and it was only on the island itself that he could afford her the requisite care and attention to ward off or battle with such a result. He therefore at once hauled his wind, and, with the captured canoe in tow, headed the catamaran on her homeward journey.

And now it was that for the first time he fully realised how strongly the trade wind was really blowing, for, close-hauled as the catamaran was, she felt the full strength of the breeze. It piped through her scant rigging with the clamour of half a gale, and poured into her canvas with a savageness of spite that threatened to tear the cloths clean out of the bolt-ropes, while it careened the craft until the lee gunwale was completely buried in the hissing turmoil of foaming yeast that roared out from under her lee bow and swept away astern at a headlong speed that made Leslie giddy to look at. And so furiously did the over-pressed catamaran charge into the formidable seas that came rushing at her weather bow that she took green water in on deck at every plunge, that swept aft as far as her mast ere it poured off into the dizzy smother to leeward, while her foresail and mainsail were streaming with spray to half the height of their weather leeches. Leslie knew that he was not treating his craft fairly in driving her thus recklessly in a strong breeze against a heavy sea; but he had perfect faith in her; he had driven every bolt and nail in her with his own hands, and was confident that there was not a weak spot anywhere about her; and the excitement and tension of the last few hours had wrought him into a condition of desperate impatience that would brook nothing savouring of delay. And, being completely dominated by this spirit of impatience, it was a vexation to him to find that he would be unable to weather the island without making a board to the southward, for as he stood there at the tiller the whole island—or at least as much of it as showed above the horizon—loomed out as a misty grey blot against the star-lit heavens clear of the luff of his foresail.

Leaning forward, Leslie gently raised the corner of the tarpaulin with which he had covered Flora to protect her from the moon's rays and the drenching spray, and found, to his intense relief, that she had fallen asleep, the sleep, probably, of complete exhaustion. Nor was he greatly surprised at this, for, as a matter of fact, now that the frightful danger was past and his excitement was subsiding, he also began to experience a sensation of weariness and a desire for sleep. But this it was of course quite impossible to indulge just then, so he lighted a pipe instead, and gave himself up to reverie, steering the craft mechanically, with his eye steadfastly fixed upon the luff of his mainsail, as a sailor will, although his thoughts may be thousands of miles away from his surroundings.

As Leslie stood there, gazing abstractedly ahead and puffing meditatively at his pipe, he was startled back to a consciousness of his surroundings by a violent shock that thrilled through the catamaran and caused him to look anxiously over the stern, under the impression that the craft had struck and run over a piece of floating wreckage. He could see nothing, however, and was still staring and wondering when the same thing occurred a second time; and Dick now noticed that the wind had suddenly fallen almost calm, also that the surface of the ocean appeared to be strangely agitated, the regular run of the sea out from the south-east having in a moment given place to a most extraordinary and dangerous cross-sea that seemed to be coming from all directions at the same moment, the colliding seas meeting each other with a rush and causing long walls of water to leap into the air to a height of from twenty to thirty feet. These leaping walls or sheets of water were in a moment flying into the air all round the catamaran, and falling back in drenching showers of spray that instantly flooded her. They at once awoke Flora, who started up in affright, crying to Dick to tell her what fresh danger had arisen.

"Oh, nothing very serious this time," answered Leslie; "It is quite a novel experience to me, I admit; but there can be only one possible explanation of it, and that is that we have just sustained a shock of earthquake. If I am right in my surmise, this extraordinary disturbance of the sea will subside almost as rapidly as it has arisen, and that will be an end of the whole business. But, by Jove, I am not so sure that it will be, after all," he added in quite another tone of voice. "Just look at that!"

And he pointed toward the island, over the peak of which there hovered a faint glow, like the reflection upon smoke of a hidden fire.

"Why, what does that mean, Dick?" demanded Flora. "It looks as though our volcano had become active again; but that is hardly likely, is it, after remaining quiescent for so many years?"

"Well, as to that," answered Dick, "its long period of quiescence constitutes no guarantee that it will not again break out into activity. And, as a matter of fact, it certainly has done so; that ruddy, luminous glow, hovering like a halo over the peak, can mean nothing else. So long, however, as it is no more actively violent than it now is, no very serious harm is likely to ensue; but, all the same, I would very much rather it had not happened. As it is, it is a hint to us to hurry up with our preparations and get away as quickly as may be from a region where such happenings are possible. And now, lie down, again dear, and get some more sleep, if you can. You need all that you can get. And it appears that the disturbance is all over, for the sea is smoothening down again, and here comes the wind, once more, back from its proper quarter."

When dawn broke, Leslie found himself within some ten miles of his island, but to leeward of it, Point Richard, its most northerly extremity, then bearing a good two points on his weather bow; he therefore tacked and made a board to the southward, with the object of getting far enough to windward to weather the reef on the next tack. Being now close enough to the island to get a distinct view of its general outline, he scrutinised it most carefully in the endeavour to discover whether the earthquake had seriously affected it; and it was with some concern and anxiety that he thought he could detect certain slight alterations of shape, here and there. Not, of course, that it mattered to him, in the abstract, how much or how little the island had altered in shape, provided—but this was a very big proviso—that it had not so seriously affected his dockyard as to damage the cutter, or caused the treasure-cave to collapse to such an extent as to obliterate its situation, or bury the treasure beyond the possibility of recovery.

Anxious now to get back to the camp at the earliest possible moment, Leslie was alternately watching the island and the luff of his mainsail, impatiently waiting for the moment to arrive when it would be possible to again tack to the eastward, when his eye was attracted by the appearance of an object some distance to the eastward and broad on his lee bow. Looking at it intently, it had to him the appearance of a mast with a fragment of sail fluttering from it, and keen though he was upon reaching camp with as little delay as might be, it was impossible for him, as a sailor, to pass such an object without examination. With a little stamp of impatience, therefore, he put up his helm and bore away for it.

It was not very far distant—a couple of miles, perhaps: certainly not more; and to reach it therefore involved no very serious loss of time. It was not long ere he was close enough to it to enable him to make out that it was a raft of some sort, rigged with a boat's oar, or a small spar, for a mast, upon which was hoisted the remains of what had once been a boat's lug sail. He noticed also that it was occupied by a little group of recumbent figures, whose attitudes were grimly suggestive of an ocean tragedy. They were mostly lying prone upon the raft, with the water washing round them; but one figure was seated with his back supported against the little mast. They were evidently all insensible, for though the catamaran was by this time quite close to them there was no attempt made by any one of them to signal her; there was nothing indeed to indicate that life still lingered upon that forlorn little ocean waif.

Taking room for the manoeuvre, Leslie tacked at the right moment, and, with fore sheet to windward, slid gradually and with steadily decreasing way up to the lee side of the raft, which he reached just as, with the main sheet eased full off, the catamaran lost way altogether. And as he glided up alongside the helplessly drifting fabric there came to his nostrils a whiff of poisoned air that told its own tale only too clearly. Still, although death was so obviously present, it was possible that life might be there too; so taking a rope's-end with him he sprang on to the little structure, and secured the two craft together. Then he rapidly examined the motionless figures, one after the other. There were five of them altogether, and of these five, three were undoubtedly dead; but in the case of the other two it seemed just possible that life was not quite extinct, and he therefore hurriedly removed them both to the catamaran, and as hurriedly cast the raft adrift again. Luckily Flora was once more asleep, and so escaped the dreadful sight presented by that little platform of broken planking and odds and ends of splintered timber, with its ghastly load, the empty water-breaker and entire absence of food on the raft telling at a glance the whole history of the tragedy.

The moment that the catamaran was again clear of the raft, Leslie turned his attention to the two pitifully emaciated and rag-clad objects that he had rescued, and commenced operations by administering a small quantity of brandy to each; his efforts being eventually rewarded by the discovery of signs of returning animation in both. Thus encouraged, he assiduously persevered, and presently one of them opened his eyes, and, staring vacantly about him, huskily murmured: "O God, have pity, and give me water—*water!*"

Leslie thereupon cautiously administered a further small quantity of the liquid, which the man eagerly swallowed, and at once asked for more; but gently laying him down on his back, with the promise that he should have more a little later on, Dick next turned his attention to the second man, and soon had the satisfaction of seeing him also restored to consciousness. Having achieved this much of success, Leslie now aroused Flora, and, briefly explaining to her the circumstances of the case, turned the two castaways over to her care, with instructions to give them, alternately and at brief intervals, small quantities of drink and food, while he devoted his attention to the catamaran and the task of navigating her back into the harbour. Meanwhile the little raft, with her ghastly cargo, went driving away to the northward and westward before the wind and the sea, and was soon lost to sight.

As the catamaran skirted close along the weather side of the reef, Leslie noticed that the brig had burnt herself out; for there was not the faintest whiff of smoke rising from the spot where she had lain. On the other hand, a thin pennant of light yellowish brown vapour was trailing away to leeward from the summit of the peak, showing that the eruption up there was still in progress. Dick was much comforted, however, to find that, even now, when he was so close in with the land, he could detect no evidences of disturbance by the earthquake on the southern slope of the mountain; and he began to cherish the hope that he would find the dockyard and camp uninjured. And this hope became a practical certainty when, upon passing through the entrance channel, the camp came into view, and he beheld not only the tent still standing as he had left it, but the framework of the cutter erect upon the stocks and apparently uninjured. Twenty minutes later the catamaran slid into her usual berth and gently grounded upon the sandy beach.

First assisting Flora to step ashore, and tenderly supporting her to the tent—to which he welcomed her back with a loving embrace—Dick next conducted the two rescued men to the hut that had originally been built and occupied by Sambo and Cuffy, into which he inducted them, with the intimation that they were to regard it as their future quarters. They were by this time so far recovered that both could walk, with a little assistance. Leslie therefore thought that he might now venture to give them a light meal, with a reasonable quantity of liquid to wash it down; and, this done, he recommended them to lie down and sleep for a while after they had refreshed themselves, and so left them.

As he walked from the hut down to the spot that he dignified with the name of The Dockyard, Leslie ruefully noted that the savages had played havoc with his belongings in their hurried search for booty; but as the havoc appeared to consist in a general capsizal of everything rather than in actual damage, and as the few matters that they had appropriated still remained aboard the captured canoe, he consoled himself with the assurance that, after all, there was not very much to worry about—excepting, of course, the terror and suffering to which Flora had been exposed, and the killing of poor Sailor, both of which filled him with bitter grief and anger.

As he passed on his way he detected evidences here and there of the fact that the island had not escaped altogether unscathed from the effects of the earthquake, small cracks in the ground showing here and there that had not heretofore existed; and when he reached the dockyard he found that two or three of his shores had been shaken down, leaving the cutter somewhat precariously supported; but to his infinite relief no actual damage had been done, and a couple of hours of hard work sufficed to put everything quite right once more. Then he returned to the tent, and, finding that Flora was lying down, he seized the opportunity to bury the body of the faithful dog out of her sight ere lying down himself to snatch an hour or two of much-needed sleep.

When he awoke, which he did of his own accord, the afternoon was well advanced; and upon emerging from the tent he discovered that not only was Flora up and stirring, but that she had routed out from their ample store of clothing a couple of suits to replace the rags in which the two castaways had been garbed when rescued; and that these two individuals, having washed and dressed, were now sitting in the sun, smoking—Flora having also supplied them with pipes and tobacco—and looking about them with mingled curiosity and surprise. As he approached them, with the view of eliciting from them the particulars of their story, they rose somewhat unsteadily to their feet, and while one lifted his cap in salute the other took his off altogether and lifted his finger to his forehead as he gave an awkward kick out astern with one leg, in true shellback style. That they were both English Dick had already ascertained; he therefore did not go through the formality of inquiring their nationality, but at once addressed them in his and their own language.

"Well, lads," he exclaimed cheerfully, "I hope you are feeling better?"

"Thank you, sir," answered the one who had lifted his cap, "yes, we are beginning to pull round again all right. And I am glad to have this early opportunity to thank you on behalf of myself and the bo'sun here for the service you've done us in taking us off the raft and bringing us ashore here. You've saved our lives, sir; there's no mistake about that, and we're both very much obliged to you, I'm sure."

"Ay, ay; right ye are, Mr Nicholls; very much obliged indeed we are; and that's puttin' the matter in a nutshell," supplemented the second man, with another sea-scrape of his foot.

Leslie was agreeably surprised at these men's appearance, now that they had removed from their persons the most repulsive evidences of their late misfortune, for whereas when he had taken them off the raft they were a pair of perfect scarecrows, mere skeletons, dirty, and in rags, they now—although still of course thin, haggard, and cadaverous-looking—wore the semblance of thoroughly honest, trustworthy, and respectable seamen. One of them, indeed, the younger of the two, who had been addressed by his companion as "Mr Nicholls," presented the appearance of a quite exceptionally smart young sailor, and Leslie at once put him down for—what he presently proved to be—the second mate of the lost ship. As for the other, Nicholls had spoken of him as "the bo'sun;" and he looked it—an elderly man, of burly build no doubt when in health, straightforward and honest as the day, and a prime seaman; "every finger a fish-hook, and every hair a ropeyarn." Leslie felt delighted beyond measure at the acquisition of two such invaluable assistants as these men would certainly prove so soon as they had recovered their lost strength.

"Oh, that is all right," said Dick, in response to their expressions of thanks; "I am, of course, very glad that it has fallen to my lot to render you such a service. And it was no doubt a lucky accident for you that I happened to be cruising outside the reef to-day. But for that circumstance I should certainly not have seen the raft, and in that case I am afraid there would have been no hope for you, for the raft would have passed some miles to the westward of the island, and your chance of being picked up would in that case have been remote in the extreme, for although I have now been here for some months I have not sighted a single sail since I arrived here. And now, if you have no objection, I should like to hear your yarn."

"Well, sir," answered Nicholls, "I don't know that there's very much to tell; but, such as it is, you're welcome to it. We belonged to a very tidy little barque—the *Wanderer*, of Liverpool—and sailed from Otago—which, as I suppose you know, sir, is in New Zealand—for London on—what's to-day?"

Leslie gave him the date.

"The dickens it is," ejaculated Nicholls; "then I've lost a day of my reckoning! Must have been a day longer on that raft than I thought. Well, anyhow, if what you say, sir, be true—and I'm sure I don't doubt your word—it's just a month ago, this blessed day, that we sailed from Otago, bound, as I say, for London, with orders to call at Callao on our way home. We sailed with a regular westerly roarer astern of us, to which the 'old man'—I mean the capt'n, sir,—showed every rag that would draw, up to to'gallant stunsails, and the skipper kept well to the south'ard, hoping to make all the easting that he wanted out of that westerly wind. And I reckon that he did, too, for we carried that same breeze with us to longitude 115 degrees, when we hauled up to the nor'ard and east'ard. Then about two days later—wasn't it, Bob?"

"Ay," answered the boatswain, who seemed to know exactly to what Nicholls was referring, "just two days a'terwards, Mr Nicholls."

"Yes," resumed Nicholls, "two days later we got a shift of wind, the breeze coming out at about east-north-east, and we broke off to about due north, which was disappointing, as we hoped to pick up the south-east trades just where we then were. But we held all on, hoping that the wind would gradually haul round. It didn't, however; on the contrary, it came on to blow hard and heavy, until we were hove-to under close-reefed topsails, and the sea—well *I* never saw anything like it in all my born days; the *Wanderer* was mostly a very comfortable little hooker when she was hove-to, but this time she rolled so frightfully—being in light trim, you must understand, sir—that I, for one, expected any minute to see her roll her masts over the side. And after we had been hove-to for twenty-six hours she scared the skipper so badly that he decided to up-helm and try whether she wouldn't do better at running before it. Well, we watched for a 'smooth,' but it didn't seem to come; and then, while we were still waiting, a sea came bearing down upon us that looked as big as a mountain. The skipper sang out for all hands to hold on for their lives, and some of us managed to get a grip, but others didn't. Down it came upon us, looking like a wall that was toppling over, and the next second it was aboard of us! I had took to the mizzen rigging, and was about ten feet above the level of the rail when that sea came aboard, and I tell you, sir—what I'm saying is the petrified truth—for half a minute that barque was so completely buried that there wasn't an inch of her hull to be seen, from stem to starn; nothing but her three masts standing up out of a boiling smother of foam. I made up my mind that the poor old hooker was done for, that she'd never come up again. But she did, at last, with every inch of bulwarks gone, fore and aft, the cook's galley swept away, every one of our boats smashed, and five of the hands missing—one of them being the chief mate.

"Well, as soon as she had cleared herself, the skipper sang out for the carpenter to sound the well; and when Chips drew up the rod he reported four feet of water in the hold! Of course all hands went at once to the pumps; but by the time that we'd been working at them for an hour we found it was no good, the water was gaining upon us hand over hand, and the craft was settling down under our feet. So we knocked off pumping and, our boats being all gone, went to work to put a raft together. But, our decks having been swept clean of everything, we hadn't much stuff left to work up, and it took us a couple of hours to knock together the few odds and ends that you took us off of this morning. We hadn't stuff to make anything bigger, and we hadn't the time, even if we'd had the stuff, for by the time that we had finished our raft the poor old hooker had settled so low in the water that we expected her to sink under us any minute.

"Then we got to work to scrape together such provisions as we could lay our hands on; but by this time the lazarette was flooded and not to be got at, while everything in the steward's pantry was spoiled, the pantry having been swamped by the sea that had broken aboard and done all the mischief. But it was the grub from the pantry, or nothing; so we took it—and there wasn't very much of it either—and also a small breaker of fresh water that the steward managed to fill for us, and then it was high time for us to be off.

"It wasn't a very difficult matter to launch the raft, for by this time every sea that came along swept over our decks, and the job for us was to avoid being washed overboard. Well, we got afloat; but, as luck would have it, a heavy sea swept over us just as we were launching and made a clean sweep of all the provisions that we'd got together, except one small parcel, and of course, once afloat, it was impossible for us to get back to the barque, even if there had been any use in our going back—which there wasn't.

"We had managed to find one oar and the jolly-boat's lug sail, and this we rigged up—as much by way of a signal as anything else, for of course we could do nothing but drive dead before the wind. And we hadn't left the barque above ten minutes when down she went, stern foremost, and there we were left adrift and as helpless as a lot of babies in that raging sea. There were ten of us altogether, and a pretty tight fit we found it on that bit of a raft, all awash as she was. It was within half an hour of sunset when we left the barque, and as darkness settled down upon us it came on to blow harder than ever, while the seas washed us to that extent that we could do nothing but hold on like grim death.

"The misery and the horror of that first night on the raft won't bear talking about; and if they would it would need a more clever man than I am to describe 'em. All I can remember is that I sat there the whole night through, in the black darkness, holding on for my life with both hands, with the sea washing over me, sometimes up to my neck, speaking to nobody, and nobody speaking to me.

"The gale broke about an hour before dawn; and when the sun rose he showed us a sky full of clouds that looked like tattered bunting of every imaginable colour one could think of, all scurrying across the sky in a westerly direction. And then we found that the wind had veered round and was coming out from about east-south-east. As soon as it was light enough to make out things, I took a look round to see how the rest of us had weathered out the night; and I tell you, sir, it nearly broke my heart to find that we mustered three less than we were when we left the barque, the poor old skipper being one of the missing. They had been washed off and drowned during the night; at least that's how I accounted for their loss.

"Then we opened our little stock of provisions—consisting mostly of cabin biscuit—that we had wrapped up in a bit of tarpaulin, intending to put a bit of food into ourselves and so get a little strength and encouragement. But when we came to open the bundle we found it full of salt water—and no wonder, seeing what clean breaches the sea had been making over us all night—so that our bread was just reduced to pulp, and no more fit to eat than if it was so much putty. And our water was pretty nearly as bad; the sea had got at it, too, and made it that brackish that it tasted more like physic than water. However, we took a drink all round, and tried to persuade one another that it wouldn't be so very long before something would come along and pick us up.

"The sea took a long time to quiet down; but by sunset it had smoothened so far that it only just kept the raft awash and the water up to our waists as we sat; so, as we had by this time got pretty well used to being wet through, we were feeling fairly comfortable, or should have been if only we had had a morsel of something to stay our hunger, and a drain of sweet water to quench our thirst—for we soon found that the more water we drank out of our breaker, the thirstier we grew.

"That night the steward went crazy, and started singing. First of all he began with the sort of songs that a sailor-man sings on the forecastle during the second dog-watch on a fine night; and from that he branched off into hymns. Then he fancied that he was at home once more, talking to his wife and the chicks, and it made my heart fairly bleed to listen to him. Then, after he had been yarning away in that style for more than an hour, he quieted down, and I thought he was getting better. But when daylight broke he was gone—slipped quietly overboard during the night, I reckoned.

"The next day was a terrible one. Our sufferings from hunger and thirst were awful; and about midday one of the men—an A.B. named Tom Bridges—went raving mad, and swore that he didn't intend to starve any more; said that one of us must die for the good of the rest; and presently set upon me, saying that I was in better condition than any of the rest, and that therefore I was the proper one to be sacrificed. He was a big, powerful man, and proved a match for the other five of us. We must have fought for a good twenty minutes, I should think, when he suddenly took hold of me round the waist and, lifting me off my feet as easily as if I was a baby, made to jump overboard with me in his arms. But another man tripped him up; and although we both went overboard, poor Tom struck his head as he fell, and must have been stunned, for I felt his grip slacken as we struck the water, and presently I managed to free myself and swim to the raft. But Tom went down like a stone, and we never saw him again.

"That adventure just about finished us all, I think; I know it finished me, for it completely took out of me what little strength I had left, and although I remember it falling dark that night, and also have a confused recollection of getting up once or twice during the next day to take a look round, I know nothing of what happened after that until I came back to my senses on the deck of that queer-looking craft of yours, and tasted the brandy that you were trying to pour down my throat."

"Well," remarked Leslie, "it has been a terrible adventure for you both, and one that you will doubtless remember for the remainder of your lives. But your time of suffering is now past, and what you have to do is to get well and strong as soon as possible. Yet, even here, although you run scant risk of perishing of hunger or thirst, and are in as little danger of drowning, there is another peril, namely, that of savages, to which we are all equally exposed; although I rather hope that certain action that I felt it incumbent upon me to take yesterday and last night may have averted it for a time at least. But perhaps, having heard your story, I had better tell you mine, and you will then understand our precise position—yours as well as Miss Trevor's and my own."

To this speech Nicholls replied in effect that, having already seen a great deal to excite his surprise and curiosity, it would afford him much pleasure to listen to anything in the way of explanation that Leslie might be pleased to tell them; a remark that Simpson cordially but briefly endorsed by adding—

"Same here, sir."

Now, it has been said that no man can do two things well if he attempts to do them both at one and the same time; but Leslie proved himself an exception to the rule. For he not only listened attentively to Nicholls' story of the loss of the *Wanderer*, but he at the same time succeeded in accomplishing the much more difficult feat of effecting a very careful appraisement of the characters of the two men whom he had rescued from the raft. And the result was to him thoroughly satisfactory; for ere Nicholls had arrived at the end of his yarn, Leslie had come to the conclusion that his new companions were thoroughly genuine, honest, steady, and straightforward men, upon whom he could absolutely rely, and whom he could take into his confidence with perfect safety. He therefore unhesitatingly told them the whole history of the loss of the *Golden Fleece*, and what had followed it, up to the moment of their meeting, judiciously reserving, however, for the present, all mention of the discovery of the treasure.

"Now," he said, by way of conclusion, "you see exactly how we are all situated here. I tell you frankly that I do not believe there is very much prospect of your getting away from here until the cutter is finished; although, should an opportunity occur, you will of course be at full liberty to leave the island, if you so please. But, so far as Miss Trevor and I are concerned, we shall now, in any case, stay here until the cutter is ready, and sail at least part of the way home in her. Now, it is for you to say whether you will throw in your lot with us, and remain until we are ready to go; or whether you will avail yourselves of any prior opportunity that may occur for you to escape. Whichever way you may decide, there is an ample supply of provisions and clothing—in fact, all the actual necessaries of life—for us all, to a due share of which you will be most heartily welcome. But, since I have made free use of the brig and her cargo, I shall of course feel myself bound to make good the loss to the underwriters upon my return to England; and I presume, therefore, that so long as you may remain upon the island, you will be willing to assist me in my work of completing the cutter, in return for your subsistence. Am I right in this assumption?"

"You certainly are, so far as I'm concerned, Mr Leslie," answered Nicholls. "I am not the man to loaf about here in idleness, and watch a gentleman like yourself working hard all day. I'd a precious sight sooner be doing a good honest day's work for my grub, than take all and give nothing in return. What say you, Bob?"

"Same here, Mr Nicholls—*and* Mr Leslie," answered Simpson.

"Very well," said Leslie; "then we will consider that matter as settled. You will not, of course, be in a fit state to turn-to for a few days; but as soon as you feel strong enough, let me know, and I shall be more than glad to have your assistance. Meanwhile, if there is anything that you require, you have only to say what it is, and if the resources of the island are equal to it, your wants shall be supplied."

It appeared, however, that all their immediate requirements had been met; so Leslie returned to the tent, where he found Flora awaiting him.

"Well, little woman," he remarked, greeting her genially, "have you had a good rest? Upon my word you are looking but little, if anything, the worse for your adventure. How are you feeling?"

"As well as ever, thank you, Dick," she replied, "excepting that my poor wrists and ankles still feel rather sore from the pressure of the ropes with which those wretches bound me. I have had a good rest, and although my sleep was disturbed at the outset by terrifying dreams, they passed off at last, and now I feel, as you say, really none the worse. But oh, Dick, it was an awful experience, and I expect I shall often see those dreadful savages' faces in my sleep for some time to come."

"Yes," assented Dick, "I fear you will. But you must try as hard as you can to forget your terror, dear; remembering that we are now two good men stronger than we were before, and that after the lesson I have given the natives they are not *very* likely to repeat their experiment in a hurry. And now, if you think you can bear to talk about it, I should like to learn just what happened after I left you."

"Well," said Flora, "there really is not very much to tell. I stood on the beach and watched you until you passed out through the channel, and disappeared behind the wall of surf; and then, accompanied by dear old Sailor—by the way, Dick, what has become of the dear old dog? I have not seen him since I returned; and I am afraid the poor fellow was hurt."

"Sweetheart," answered Dick, gently, "he did the utmost that a faithful friend can do; he died in your defence, and I have buried him."

"Dear old Sailor!" exclaimed the girl, the tears springing to her eyes at the intelligence of his death, "he fought bravely. I shall never forget him." She sat silent for a while, with her handkerchief to her eyes, and presently resumed—

"As I was saying, I walked back toward the tent, Sailor, as usual, keeping close beside me. I was within half a dozen yards of the tent when the dog suddenly stopped dead, growling savagely. 'Why, what is the matter, Sailor?' I said, patting him. He looked up at me for an instant, still growling, and his coat bristling with anger; then, with a quick yelp of fury he dashed off and darted behind the tent, and the next instant there was a dreadful outcry, mingled with the fierce barking and snarling of the dog. I was absolutely petrified with terror, for you were away, and already far beyond the reach of any sound or signal that I could make, while I was left alone on the island with I knew not who or what. Then the thought came to me to make a dash for the tent, and get the pistol that you gave me to practise with; but before I could carry out my idea, a perfect swarm of blacks, headed by Sambo and Cuffy, rushed out from behind the tent—with Sailor in the midst of them, fighting furiously; and in an instant I turned and ran for the beach, with them in pursuit.

"I have not the faintest idea what I intended to do; my one thought was to keep out of their clutches as long as possible; but, of course, I was almost instantly overtaken and seized, and my hands held behind me by Sambo, while Cuffy stood before me threatening me with a spear. Then, while some of the natives went off to the stack of stores and began to 'overhaul' them, as you call it, others disappeared in the direction of Mermaid Head.

"It was a horrible sensation, and made me deadly sick to feel myself actually in the clutches of those dreadful natives, and to see the look in Cuffy's eyes as he stood before me brandishing his spear in my face; but worse was yet to come, for presently one of the wretches came up with some pieces of rope in his hand, and then they bound my hands and feet together, rendering me absolutely helpless, as you found me.

"I suppose it would be about a quarter of an hour after this—although it seemed very much longer—when the second party of natives returned with a canoe, into which they flung me most unceremoniously; and then they all went off together, leaving me alone and so tightly bound that I was soon enduring agonies of torment. I bore the pain for perhaps an hour, and then I must have swooned, for I knew no more until I recovered my senses in your dear arms, and knew that you had saved me. Oh, Dick—"

Then she suddenly broke down again, and sobbed so violently and clung to Leslie in such a frantic paroxysm of terror that poor Dick became thoroughly alarmed, and, in his distraction, could do nothing but soothe her as he would a frightened child. This simple treatment, however, sufficed, for the sobs gradually diminished in violence, and at length ceased altogether; and presently Flora arose, declaring that she was herself again, and denouncing herself as a poor, weak, silly little mortal, who ought to be ashamed of herself.

Chapter Fourteen
Completion and Launch of the Cutter

On the day that followed the occurrence of the above exciting events, Nicholls and Simpson being still too weak to be fit for the somewhat laborious work of the dockyard, Leslie determined to pay a visit to his treasure-cave, being anxious to ascertain whether the earthquake had materially interfered with the configuration of the country in that direction, and, if so, to what extent. Upon learning his determination Flora announced her decision to accompany him; and accordingly, having packed a luncheon-basket, the pair set off together soon after breakfast, leaving Nicholls and the boatswain in charge of the camp.

The day was magnificently fine, but the temperature was somewhat higher than usual, the trade wind having softened down to a quite moderate breeze; so Dick and his companion proceeded on their way in a very leisurely manner, intending to take the whole day for their task of exploration. No very marked or important changes in the aspect of the landscape were noticeable until they reached the ridge or spur of the mountain that terminated in the headland that Dick had named Cape Flora; but as soon as this ridge, was crossed they saw that, for some unexplainable reason, the earthquake action had been much more violent on the northerly than on the southward side of it; so great indeed were the changes wrought that in many places the features of the landscape were scarcely recognisable, and Leslie had the utmost difficulty in finding his way.

At length, however, they arrived in the neighbourhood of the spot where they believed the cave to be situated, and here the changes had been so great that for some time Leslie was utterly at a loss. The surface was so twisted and torn, so utterly disfigured by landslides and upheavals of rock, that they might have been in another island altogether, so far as recognition of the original features was concerned. This was far worse than the worst Dick had anticipated, and for a time he was in a state of utter despair, fearing that his treasure had been swallowed up beyond recovery. Still, he felt convinced that he was in the immediate neighbourhood of the spot where the cave had been, and, bidding Flora to sit down and rest while he further investigated, he began to grope about here and there among the confused mass of rocks, studying them intently as he did so. For upwards of two hours Leslie searched and toiled in vain; but at length he came upon a piece of rock face that seemed familiar to him, and upon removing a number of blocks of splintered rock he disclosed a small hole, creeping into which he found himself once more, to his infinite joy, in the treasure-cave, with the treasure safe within it. He stayed but long enough to satisfy himself that everything was as he had left it, and then, emerging once more into the open daylight, he carefully masked the entrance again by placing the blocks very much as he had found them.

Pretty thoroughly fatigued by this time, he made his way to the spot where Flora was seated, and acquainted her with his success, while she unpacked the luncheon and spread it out invitingly upon the surface of the rock. This rock upon which they were seated occupied a somewhat commanding position, from the summit of which a fairly extended view of the surrounding country was to be obtained; and it was while the pair were leisurely eating their midday meal that Dick's eye suddenly caught the glint of water at no great distance. Now, he knew that when he was last on the spot there was no water anywhere nearer than the open ocean; yet this, as he saw it through the interlacing boughs and trunks of the trees, flickered with the suggestion of a surface agitated by an incoming swell. As soon, therefore, as they had finished their lunch, the pair made their way in the direction of this appearance of water; and after about ten minutes of easy walking found themselves standing upon the brink of a kind of "sink" or basin about a quarter of a mile in diameter, having a narrow opening communicating with the open sea. It was a strange-looking place, presenting an appearance suggestive of a vast hollow under the coast-line having fallen in and swallowed up a circular piece of the island, leaving two rocky headlands standing, the southern headland slightly overlapping the northern one and thus completely masking the basin or cove from the sea. The surrounding cliffs were about a hundred feet high, composed entirely of rock, and presenting an almost vertical face; but so rough and broken was this face, and so numerous were the projections, that not only Dick but Flora also found it perfectly safe and easy to descend by means of them right down to the water's edge, into which the cliffs dropped sheer, with a depth of water alongside so great that Dick could not discern the bottom, although the water was crystal-clear. And so narrow was the opening that what small amount of swell found its way into the cove was practically dissipated ere it reached the rocky walls, alongside which the water rose and fell so gently that its movement was scarcely perceptible. It was, in fact, an ideal harbour for such a craft as the cutter, and Dick at once determined to bring her round to this spot as soon as she was ready, in order to ship the treasure on board her.

Upon their return to camp that evening Dick found that Nicholls and Simpson were making such rapid strides toward recovery that they were not only able to walk about with something like an approach to their former strength, but that they also expressed their conviction that they would be perfectly able to begin work on the morrow. It appeared that they had been amusing themselves by prowling about the camp and investigating the condition of affairs generally. It was only natural that their chief interest should centre in the cutter, and the probable amount of work that lay before them all ere she would be completed and ready for sea. As has already been mentioned, her condition at this time was that of a completed skeleton, her keel, stem, and stern-posts having been joined up, the whole of her frames erected in position and properly connected to the keel, and all her wales and stringers bolted-to; she was therefore so far advanced that the next thing in order was to lay her planking. This planking, it may be mentioned, was of oak throughout, arranged to be laid on in two thicknesses, each plank of the outer skin overlaying a joint between two planks in the skin beneath it; and every plank had already been roughly cut to shape and carefully marked. All, therefore, that was now required was to complete the trimming of each plank and fix it in position. The inner layer of planking was much the thicker of the two, the intention of the designer evidently being that this inner skin should be attached to the steel frames by steel screws not quite long enough to completely penetrate the plank, the outer skin being attached to the inner by gun-metal screws carefully spaced in such a manner that there was always a distance of at least six inches between the steel and gun-metal screws, thus avoiding all possibility of even the smallest approach to galvanic action being set up between the two. And it was, of course, to the outer skin that the copper sheathing was to be attached.

Now the planking—even the comparatively thin outer skin—was much too stout and tough to be got into position without steaming; and this fact had occurred to Simpson while prowling about the dockyard that day. He had mentioned the matter to Nicholls, and the pair had at once looked about them to see whether Leslie had made any provision for the steaming of the planks; and, finding none, they had profitably amused themselves by sorting out, from the deck and other planking brought ashore from the brig, a sufficient quantity of stuff suitable for the construction of a steaming-trunk, and laying it aside ready for Leslie's inspection upon his return. They had not quite completed their self-imposed task when Dick got back to the camp, and, seeing them apparently busy, sauntered down to the spot where they were at work.

"Well, lads," said he, with a smile, "so you are getting yourselves into training, eh? I am glad to see that you are making such rapid advances toward recovery."

"Thank you, sir; yes, we're pulling round again all right," replied Nicholls. "We've been amusing ourselves to-day by taking a general look round, and so far as we can see, your cutter—a most remarkable fine little boat she is going to be—is just about ready to start planking-up. But we see no signs of a steaming-trunk anywhere about, Mr Leslie; so Bob and I have been putting in our time on the job of sorting out from among that raffle, there, enough stuff to make a trunk out of; and here it is, sir, if you don't happen to want it for anything else."

"No," said Leslie, "I do not require it for anything in particular; and as we shall certainly require a trunk we may as well work it up into one. That, I think, will have to be our next job."

"Yes, sir," agreed Nicholls; "it looks like it. But what about a boiler, sir, in which to generate the steam? I don't see anything knocking about ashore, here, that'll do for one."

"No," said Leslie; "and I am rather afraid we may have a hard job to find one. There is only one thing that I can think of, and that is one of the brig's water tanks. I had intended to bring one ashore for that especial purpose; but now that those rascally savages have burnt the craft we may find that her tanks have been destroyed by the fire."

"I should think not, sir," dissented Nicholls. "They will have been stowed right down in the bottom of her, perhaps; and if that's the case the fire won't have had a chance to get at 'em."

"I really do not know whether they were stowed in her bottom or not," answered Leslie; "but we will go off to-morrow, and have a look at the wreck. One thing is quite certain: we *must* have a boiler of some sort, or we shall never be able to get those planks into position—especially those about the head of the stern-post—without splitting them. And I would take a good deal of trouble to avoid such a misfortune as that."

The following day found Nicholls and Simpson so far recovered that they both declared themselves quite strong enough to turn-to, and accordingly Leslie—who, since the raid of the savages, was more feverishly eager than ever to get away from the island—took the catamaran; and the three men went off together to the wreck of the brig.

They found her burnt practically down to the water's edge, and everything not of metal that was in her also consumed down to that level. Below the surface, however, everything was of course untouched. But all the gear—sheer-legs, tackles, and the rest of it—that had been of such immense value to Dick in getting the various matters out of the brig, had been destroyed with her; and if any very serious amount of turning over of the cargo under water should prove to be necessary, he would be obliged to provide and rig up a complete fresh set of apparatus. Moreover, there was no longer the convenient platform of the deck to work from, instead of which they had to wade about on a confused mass of cargo beneath the surface of the water, affording them a most awkward and irregular platform with, in some spots, only a few inches of water over it, while elsewhere there was a depth of as many feet. A careful examination of the whole of the visible cargo failed to reveal the whereabouts of the water tanks, or of anything else that would serve the purpose of a boiler; and at length they were reluctantly driven to the conclusion that before the search could be further prosecuted it would be necessary to procure and rig up another set of sheer-legs, and to replace the lost gear with such blocks, etcetera, as they could find among the heterogeneous collection of stuff already salved from the brig.

To be obliged to expend so much time and labour all over again was decidedly disheartening; but, as Leslie said, it was quite useless to worry over it; it *had* to be done, and the sooner they set about it the better. So they returned to the shore, and while Nicholls and Simpson, armed with axes, went off into the woods in search of a couple of spars suitable for sheers, Dick proceeded to overhaul the mass of raffle brought ashore from the brig, and at length secured enough blocks and rope to furnish a fairly effective set of tackle wherewith to equip them. There was a tremendous amount of long-splicing to be done in order to work up the various odds and ends of rope into suitable lengths for the several tackles required; but four days of assiduous labour found the vexatious task completed and everything ready for the resumption of work. Then ensued an arduous and wearisome turning over of cargo—much of it consisting of heavy castings and other parts of machinery; but at length they got down to one of the tanks, which they hoisted out, emptied, and floated ashore.

Then came the building of the steam-trunk, which they erected close alongside the cutter and right down at the water's edge, for convenience in supplying the boiler with water; and this done, they were at length able to turn-to upon the important task of planking-up the hull of their little ship. And now it was that Leslie was able for the first time to appreciate the inestimable value of the carefully prepared and figured diagram of the planking that the builders had so thoughtfully included among the various matters appertaining to the construction of the cutter. For with it in his hand, all that was necessary was for Leslie to go over the pile of planking, noting the letters and numbers on each plank, and stack the whole in such a manner that the planks first required should be found on top of the stack, while those last wanted would lie at the bottom. And now, too, he found how great an advantage the possession of two able and intelligent workers was to him; for not only were the three men able to do thrice the amount of work possible to one man in a given time, but they were able to do considerably more when it came to such matters as lifting heavy weights, twisting refractory planks into position, and other matters of a similar kind where mere brute strength was required. Moreover, their steaming apparatus acted to perfection; and after the first two days—during which they were acquiring the knack of working together, and generally "getting the hang of things," as Nicholls expressed it—everything went like clock-work. They averaged six complete strakes of planking—three on either side of the hull—sawn, trimmed, steamed, and fixed, per diem; and as there happened to be thirty strakes up to the covering-board it cost them just ten days of strenuous labour to get the inner skin laid; and the laying of the outer skin consumed a similar period. Then there was the caulking and paying of the seams in the inner and outer skins—which was a task that needed the most careful doing and was not to be hurried—as well as the protection of the inner skin by a coat of good thick white-lead laid on immediately under each plank of the outer skin and applied the last thing before screwing each plank down; all this ran away with time; so that it took them a full month to complete the planking-up and advance the craft to the stage at which she would be ready for the laying of the decks. But before this was undertaken they painted her three coats of zinc white, and, as soon as this was dry, laid on her copper sheathing and hung her rudder.

The laying, caulking, and paying of the cutter's deck kept them busy for a fortnight; and she was then in condition for the fitting up of her interior. This, according to the original design, was divided up into a forecastle with accommodation for four men, abaft of which came a small galley on the port side, and an equally small steward's pantry on the starboard side. Then, abaft these again, came a tiny saloon, and finally, abaft this again, two little state rooms on one side, with a little bathroom, lavatory, and sail-room on the other. The saloon was entered by way of a short companion ladder leading from a small self-emptying cockpit, some five feet wide by six feet long, this cockpit being the only open space in the boat, the rest of her hull being completely decked over. The saloon was lighted by a small skylight and six scuttles—three of a side—fixed in the planking of the little craft. The staterooms, although very small, were still sufficient in size to enable an adult to sleep in them comfortably, and their interior arrangement was a perfect marvel of ingenuity, each being fitted with a small chest of drawers under the bunk, and a folding washstand and dressing-table. This was the arrangement set out in the plans and provided for in the materials for her construction; and as it happened to suit Leslie's requirements exceedingly well, he very wisely determined not to alter it. The work of putting together the bulkheads, lining the saloon, fitting up the staterooms, and generally completing her interior arrangements, was not laborious, but there was a great deal of it, and some of it came very awkwardly to their hands, due, no doubt, to a great extent, to the unaccustomed character of the work in the first place, and, in the second, to the confined spaces in which much of it was necessarily to be done; but at length there came a day when, after a most careful inspection of the craft, inside and out, Dick pronounced her hull complete and ready for launching. But at the last moment he decided that it would be more convenient to step her lower-mast ere she left the stocks; and, one thing leading naturally to another, an additional day was devoted to the job of stepping this important spar, getting the bowsprit into position, setting up all the rigging connected with these two spars, and getting the main-boom and gaff into their places. Then, with the remainder of her spars and all her sails aboard, they knocked off work for the night, with the understanding that the little craft was to be consigned to "her native element" on the morrow.

The dawn of that morrow promised as fair a day as heart could wish for so important a ceremony; and the three men were early astir and busy upon the final preparations. The most important of these was the greasing of the launching ways; and as Dick had foreseen this necessity from the very outset, he had not only adopted the precaution of bringing ashore from the brig every ounce of tallow and grease of every description that he had been able to find aboard her, but had rigorously saved every morsel that had resulted from their cooking during the whole period of their sojourn upon the island. Thus it happened that, when it came to the point, he found that he had what, with judicious and strict economy, might prove sufficient for the purpose. But he intended that there should be no room for doubt in so important a matter as this, and he therefore ruthlessly sacrificed almost the whole of a big case of toilet soap, with which he and the other two men went diligently over the ways, rubbing the soap on dry until a film of it covered the ways throughout their whole length. Then, upon the top of this, they plastered on their tallow and other grease until it was all expended; at which stage of the proceedings Dick declared himself satisfied, and marched off to rid himself of the traces of his somewhat dirty work.

And by this time breakfast was ready. Then, upon the conclusion of the meal, all hands adjourned once more to the yard, Flora being attired for the occasion in a complete suit of dainty white, topped off with a broad-brimmed flower-bedecked hat that, under other circumstances, would doubtless have graced some Valparaiso belle. Dick carried two bottles of champagne—the last of their scanty stock—in his hand, one of them being devoted to the christening ceremony, while the other was to be consumed in drinking success to the little boat.

Arrived alongside, Nicholls nipped up the ladder that gave access to the little craft's deck, and attached the bottle of champagne to the stem-head by a line long enough to reach down to within about six inches of her keel. Then he went aft and lashed the tiller amidships, which done, he announced that all was ready. Upon hearing this Dick placed the bottle of wine in Flora's hand, and, telling her when to act and what to say, stationed himself, with a heavy sledge-hammer in his hand, at one of the spur-shores, Simpson, similarly provided, going to the other. Then—

"Are you all ready?" shouted Dick.

"Ay, ay, sir, all ready!" answered Simpson, swaying up the heavy hammer over his shoulder.

"Then *strike!*" yelled Dick; and crash fell the two hammers simultaneously; down dropped the spur-shores, and a tremor appeared to thrill the little craft throughout her entire fabric.

For a single moment she seemed to hang—to Dick's unmitigated consternation, but the next second he saw her begin to move with an almost imperceptible gliding motion toward the water. Flora saw it too, and raising the bottle of wine in her hand, dashed it against the little craft's bows, shattering the glass to pieces and causing the wine to cream over the brightly burnished copper as she cried—

"God bless the *Flora* and grant her success!"

The speed of the handsome little clipper rapidly increased, and presently she entered the water with a headlong rush, curtseying as gracefully as though she had learned the trick from her namesake, ere she recovered herself and floated lightly as a soap-bubble on the water. (For although Dick had found an entire outfit of lead ballast for her, already cast to the shape of her hull, he had only put part of it aboard her, leaving out about six tons, in place of which he intended to stow the gold from the treasure-cave.) The little craft held her way for quite an extraordinary distance—showing thereby in the most practical of all ways the excellence and beauty of her lines—and when at length she came to rest Nicholls let go her anchor and waved his hand by way of a signal that all was well. Whereupon Dick and Simpson jumped into the canoe and paddled off to fetch him ashore.

The moment had now arrived when it became necessary for Leslie to come to some definite conclusion as to how far he would take these two men into his confidence. He had watched them both with the utmost keenness from the first moment of his connection with them, and everything that he had seen in their speech and behaviour had led him to the conviction that they were absolutely honest, loyal, and trustworthy. On the other hand, he had heard of cases wherein men even as trustworthy as he believed these two to be had succumbed to the influence of some sudden, over-powering temptation; and there could be no question that a treasure of such enormous value as that lying hidden in the cave constituted a temptation sufficient to strain to its utmost limit the honesty of any but the most thoroughly conscientious man. He therefore finally settled the matter with himself by determining upon a compromise; he would take Nicholls and Simpson into his confidence just so far as was absolutely necessary, and no farther.

Therefore, when they all landed on the beach, after taking Nicholls off the cutter, Leslie invited the two men to accompany him to the tent, there to empty their last bottle of champagne in drinking to the success of the new craft. And when this ceremony had been duly performed, Leslie turned to the two men, and said—

"And now, lads, the cutter having been successfully got into the water, I find myself in the position of being able to make to you both a certain proposal and offer that has long been in my mind. When I took you two men off your raft, and brought you ashore here in a dying condition, that tiny craft that floats so jauntily out there on the smooth waters of the lagoon was only in frame—a mere skeleton. But you saw of what that skeleton was composed; you saw that it was made of tough steel firmly and substantially put together with stout bolts and rivets. And since then you have assisted me to bring forward the little craft from what she then was to what she is to-day; you have seen and handled the materials that have been worked into her, and nobody knows better than yourselves what careful and faithful labour and workmanship has been bestowed upon the putting of her together. Now, I want you to give me your honest opinion, as sailors, of that little craft. You know that she was built for the sole purpose of carrying us all away from this island—which, I may tell you, lies well in the heart of the Pacific; I want you, as sailors of experience, to say whether you will feel any hesitation in trusting your lives to her."

Nicholls laughed heartily at the question; and Simpson grinned corroboratively.

"Why," exclaimed the former, "men have gone more than halfway round the world in craft that aren't to be mentioned on the same day as that dandy little packet! The last time that I was in Sydney—which was last year—there was a Yankee chap there that had made the voyage from

America in a dug-out canoe that he had decked over and rigged as a three-masted schooner—he and another chap—and they intended to go on and complete the trip round the world. I don't mind saying that I shouldn't have altogether cared about making such a voyage myself in such a craft; but yonder little beauty's quite a different story. I'd be as willing to ship in her as in anything else—provided that it was made worth my while. What say you, bo'sun?"

"Same here," answered Simpson, the man of brevities.

"You really mean it? You are both speaking in serious earnest?" demanded Leslie.

"I am, most certainly," answered Nicholls; "in proof of which I intend to sail with you when you leave the island—if you'll take me, Mr Leslie; and I don't think you are the man to refuse two poor castaways a passage, especially as you've got plenty of room aboard there for us both, and we can make ourselves useful enough to pay for our passages."

"Very well, then," said Leslie. "Now, this is the proposal that I have to make to you both. I have here, on this island, snugly stowed away in a cave, certain valuables that I am most anxious to personally convey to England; and for certain reasons with which I need not trouble you, I am equally anxious to get them home without bringing them under the notice of the authorities, and the only way in which this can be done is to take them home *in the cutter*. My plan is to make my way in the first instance to Australia, where Miss Trevor will leave the *Flora*. At Melbourne I shall revictual, and thence proceed to Capetown, where I shall do the like, sailing thence to England, with a call, perhaps, at some of the Canaries, if necessary. Now, if you have no fancy for such a long trip as that which I have sketched out, in so small a craft as the *Flora*, you will of course be perfectly free to leave her upon our arrival at Melbourne. But if, on the other hand, you are willing to ship with me for the whole voyage, I think I can make it quite worth your while, for I shall require at least two men whom I can absolutely trust, and I believe you two to be those men. Now, what amount would you consider to be adequate remuneration for the run home from here?"

"How long do you reckon the trip is going to take, sir?" inquired Nicholls.

"Um, let me see," considered Leslie, making a mental calculation. "We ought to do it comfortably in about one hundred and eighty days—six months; call it seven months, if you like."

Nicholls considered for a few minutes, and then looked up and said—

"Would sixty pounds be too much to ask, Mr Leslie, taking everything into consideration?"

"What do *you* say, Simpson?" asked Leslie, with a smile.

"Sixty pounds 'd satisfy *me*," answered the boatswain.

"Very well," said Dick. "Now, this is what I will do with you both. It will be worth a thousand pounds to me to get these valuables of mine safely home, as I said, without attracting attention. If, therefore, you will ship for the run home with me, rendering me all the assistance necessary to take the *Flora* and her cargo safely to some port, to be hereafter decided upon, in the English Channel, I will give you my written bond to pay each of you five hundred pounds sterling within one calendar month of the date of our arrival. How will that suit you?"

"It will suit me better than any job I've ever yet dropped upon, and I say 'done with you, sir, and many thanks,'" answered Nicholls, with enthusiasm.

"And you, Simpson?" demanded Dick.

"Good enough!" answered the boatswain, with his usual brevity.

"Very well, then; that is settled," said Leslie. "I will draw up an agreement in triplicate at once, which we can all sign, each retaining a copy; and that will put the whole matter upon a thoroughly ship-shape and satisfactory basis all round."

Dick prepared the agreement there and then, and having read over to the two seamen the first draft, and obtained their unqualified approval of it, he at once proceeded to make the two additional copies. All three were then duly signed, Flora also attaching her signature as a witness, and the transaction was thereupon completed.

"Now," said Dick, "that bit of business being arranged, I should like to take the cutter round to a little cove at no great distance from the cave where my valuables are concealed, and get them aboard her at once, before her decks are hampered up with gear and what not; we will therefore get the catamaran under way, and tow her round. We can leave the catamaran in the cove also, and walk back by way of change. Moreover, it will afford us the opportunity to stretch our legs a bit; we shall not get very much more walking exercise now until we arrive in England."

As the three men were wending their way down to the beach, Leslie's eyes happened to fall upon the case of rifle and revolver ammunition from which he had been drawing his supplies. It was the only case of ammunition that he possessed; and now, with a sudden fear that in the hurry of departure it might be forgotten, he said to Nicholls—

"See here, Nicholls, we might just as well be carrying something with us as go down to the catamaran empty-handed. If you and Simpson will lay hold of that case of ammunition, I will bring along half a dozen rifles, and we shall then be quite as well armed as there will be any need for us to be. We may not want them, but, on the other hand, we *may*, and if we should happen to want them at all, we shall probably want them very badly."

Upon taking the cutter in tow it was found that she towed very lightly, offering only a trifling resistance to the catamaran after both had fairly got way upon them; and in little more than half an hour both craft were off the entrance to the cove. Yet so cunningly had Nature concealed it that though Leslie knew almost to an inch where to look for it, he had the utmost difficulty in finding it, and had he not possessed a personal knowledge of its existence, and therefore persisted in his search, he would never have found it. But, after passing the opening no less than four times without being able to find it, he managed to hit it off at his fifth attempt, and, ten minutes later, both craft were inside and snugly moored to the rocky side of the basin, the catamaran being placed innermost to protect the dainty, freshly painted sides of the cutter from chafe against the rock.

Nicholls and Simpson betrayed the profoundest astonishment and admiration at the singularly perfect adaptation of the cove to the purposes of a harbour for small craft, and could scarcely be persuaded to drag themselves away from the water's edge. But when at length they had been induced to climb up the almost vertical face of the cliffs and found themselves at the mouth of the treasure-cave, their wonder at what they saw was greater than ever. They uttered loud exclamations of astonishment when they were invited to lift one of the hide-bound gold bricks, and felt the unexpected weight of it; but neither of them appeared to have the remotest suspicion of the real nature of the stuff they were handling, Nicholls merely commenting upon its excellence as ballast, and lauding Leslie's wisdom in having decided to so use it instead of those portions of the lead castings that he had rejected. Indeed, both men appeared to regard the queer little black leather—bound blocks as merely something especially suitable for ballast, and taken by Dick for that purpose and reason alone; it was the massive, ancient-looking, carved chests, with their elaborate binding of rusty metal-work that they appeared to regard as the receptacles of the "valuables" about the safety of which Leslie was so anxious.

They managed to get sixty of the gold bricks down aboard the cutter and stowed under her cabin floor that same afternoon, and by the time that they had accomplished this, the level rays of the declining sun warned them that the moment had arrived when they ought to be starting upon their march across country toward their camp.

The broken character of the country claimed a larger share of Leslie's attention upon this occasion than when he had last visited the cave. Perhaps it was because his mind was now more at rest than it had then been—for the cutter that was at the former period merely a possibility, was now an actuality; and, more than that, already carried a very respectable little fortune snugly stowed away in her interior; or, possibly—who can tell?—there may have been some vague, unsuspected mental prevision that ere long an intimate knowledge of every detail of those curiously shapeless earthquake upheavals would be of priceless value to him. Be that as it may, he now looked about him with the eyes of the warrior rather than the explorer, noting with astonishment the wonderful way in which the earthquake had split and piled up the rocks into the form of a natural impregnable fortress, including both the cavern and the basin. There was one point, and one only, at which this natural fortress could be entered, and upon his previous visit he had passed through it twice without noting this fact; now, however, he not only took notice of it, but saw also that a small rampart, composed of a dozen or so of stones, that could be arranged in five minutes, would enable a single man to hold the place against an army, or, at all events, so long as his ammunition held out. So strongly did this idea impress itself upon him that he could not resist the temptation to actually construct this small rampart then and there.

"Stop a moment, you two," he cried; "I have a fancy for trying a little experiment. Just bring me along a few of the heaviest pieces of rock that you can conveniently handle."

And, seizing a block himself, he carried it to a certain point, and threw it on the ground. Then on and about this he piled the others that were brought to him until, within ten minutes, he had constructed a breastwork of dimensions sufficient to efficiently screen one man from the fire of an enemy, while it enabled him, through a small loophole, to effectually enfilade the one only spot at which that enemy could possibly enter. He flung himself down behind the barricade and peeped through the loophole. The defence was now complete.

"There," he exclaimed, in tones of perfect satisfaction, "if anybody should ever come here in the future, and require a citadel upon which to retreat against overwhelming odds, this is the place. And so long as he can command the nerve to remain behind this barricade and maintain a steady rifle-fire upon that narrow gap—through which, as you may see, only one man can pass at a time—he will be absolutely safe. Well, thank God, *we* are not likely to need its protection, for we ought to be at sea on the third evening from now."

The following day was devoted by the three men to the task of putting the remainder of the gold bricks on board the cutter; and this they succeeded in accomplishing before knocking-off work for the day; but it meant that they had to work hard and late to do it. Meanwhile Flora was equally busily engaged upon the work of getting together, from the heterogeneous assortment of clothing that had formed part of the *Mermaid's* cargo, a sufficient stock to see her through her two months' voyage to the other side of the Pacific. Knowing that she was thus engaged, and would doubtless be fatigued by the time that she had arrived at the end of her day's work, Leslie was considerably surprised when, having traversed about half the distance between the cove and the camp, he encountered her; she having evidently walked out from the camp to meet him. Moreover he saw at once that this encounter was not merely the result of a natural desire on the part of a girl to meet her lover, it was something more momentous than that, for there was an excited look in her eyes that there was no mistaking. So, doffing his cap to her as she joined his little party, he said, with a smile—

"Well, dear, what is it? You have news of some kind for us, I see; but not bad news, I hope."

"Oh no," she replied; "it is not bad news at all—at least I should think not. It is simply that there is a ship approaching the island, and as I thought you would be glad to know it as soon as possible, I decided to come on and tell you at once."

"Thanks, very much," replied Dick. "This is indeed interesting news. Whereabouts is she, and how far off?"

"She is over there, in that direction," replied Flora, pointing to the north-westward. "It was by the merest accident that I happened to see her. I took the fancy to go up toward Mermaid Head to gather a bouquet of those lovely orchids that grow in that direction, thinking that probably it would be my last opportunity to get any of them, and it was while I was gathering them that I saw her. She is still a good distance away; and I might have thought that she was merely passing the island, for when I first saw her she was sailing in that direction,"—sweeping her hand from west to east; "but while I was still watching her she turned round, and now is coming nearly straight for the island."

"Ah," remarked Leslie, thoughtfully, "this is certainly interesting, and I am much obliged to you for coming out to tell us. Let us be getting on toward the camp; there may still be time for me to run up to the point and have a look at her ere nightfall." Then, following up his own train of thought, he added, "If she be as far off as you describe, she will hardly be near enough to hit off the entrance channel and come inside before dark—that is to say, if she really means to pay us a visit."

Nothing more was said upon the subject just then; but as soon as Leslie reached the camp he procured the telescope, and, hurrying away to the nearest point from which it would be possible to obtain a view of the stranger, subjected her to as careful a scrutiny as the circumstances permitted.

After all, however, there was not very much to be learned about her, for she was about twelve miles distant, dead to leeward of the island, and as the sun was already dipping below the horizon, the time available for observation was but short. He could distinguish, however, that she was barque-rigged, and apparently a very smart little vessel of about three hundred tons or thereabout. That she was beating up to fetch the island was obvious; for whereas when Leslie first sighted her she was on the port tack, heading south, she shortly afterwards tacked to the eastward, thus— in conjunction with what Flora had already observed—clearly indicating that her purpose was at least to pass the island as closely as possible, if not to actually touch at it. And that the latter was her intention Leslie had no manner of doubt; for if she had intended merely to pass it closely by, there would have been no need for her to have made that last board to the eastward; by standing on to the southward she would have slid down under the lee of the island quite closely enough to have made the most detailed observations that her commander might have deemed necessary. There was one peculiarity connected with her that for some inexplicable reason took hold upon Leslie's mind with a persistence that was positively worrying to him, yet it was a peculiarity of apparently the most trivial and unimportant character; it was simply that when she tacked he noticed—with that keenness of observation that is so peculiarly the attribute of the highly trained naval officer—that her yards were swung very slowly, and one after the other, as though she were very short-handed, even for a merchant vessel.

As Leslie closed the telescope and thoughtfully wended his way back toward the camp, he found himself perplexed by the presence within his mind of two strangely conflicting trains of thought. On the one hand, here was a ship approaching the island, and either intending to make a call at it, or to approach it so closely that it would be the simplest matter in the world for him to go out on the catamaran and intercept her. By acting thus he would be able, without any difficulty, to secure for his companions and himself transport to some civilised port from which it would be easy for them to obtain a passage to England, even though the barque herself should not be homeward-bound. And that transport would be at least of as safe a character as that afforded by the cutter, while it would be infinitely more comfortable, at all events for Flora, should they happen to encounter bad weather. Following this train of thought, it seemed to Leslie that the obvious commonsense course for him to pursue was to take the catamaran, go out to the barque, and, acquainting the skipper with all the circumstances relating to the presence of the little party upon the island, pilot her into the lagoon, with the view of coming to some arrangement for the shipping of himself and his companions on board her on the morrow.

But against this plan there was the thought of the treasure. What was to be done with it? Would it be prudent or advisable to entrust a property of such enormous value to a crew of absolute strangers, of whose characters he would have no time or opportunity to judge? Upon this point he had no doubt whatever; the answer to this question was a most emphatic negative. But if—so ran his thoughts—he was not prepared to ship the treasure aboard this unknown barque, and entrust it to her unknown crew, what was he to do with it? Was he to leave it concealed in the cavern that had already been its hiding-place for so many years, and return to fetch it away at some more convenient season? His recent experience of the great physical changes that may be wrought by an earthquake shock had already impressed upon him a strong conviction of the possibility that a second shock might at any moment bury the treasure irrecoverably; and this conviction was as strong an argument against the adoption of the alternative course as a man need wish for. No; he felt that it would be equally unwise for him to ship it aboard the stranger, and to leave it on the island until he could return to fetch it. If he desired to make sure of it—as he most certainly did—his proper course was to carry it away in the cutter, as he had always intended. And as to Nicholls and Simpson, he felt that, despite the appearance of this mysterious barque upon the scene, his liberal offer to them would quite suffice to hold them to their bargain with him. The ground thus cleared, there remained only Flora to be considered; and Dick very quickly arrived at the conclusion that she, and she only, was the one who could decide whether she would leave the island in the barque or accompany him in the cutter. But he had not much doubt as to what her decision would be.

Chapter Fifteen
The Mysterious Barque

When Leslie returned to the camp he found the tent lighted up, and Flora and dinner awaiting him. He was tired, for the day had been an unusually fatiguing one; and when a man is tired he usually prefers to be silent. Nevertheless, he recapitulated in detail to Flora all that had been in his mind during his walk home; and finally put the question to her whether she would rather leave in the barque, or in the cutter; the former, perhaps, offering her more comfortable—because more roomy—quarters than the latter.

"What have *you* decided to do, Dick?" she asked.

"Oh," he replied, "so far as I am concerned, I have quite made up my mind to adhere to my original plan of going home in the cutter, and taking our treasure with me."

"Then, of course, that settles everything," said Flora, simply. "Where you go, Dick dear, I go also—that is to say, if you will have me." This last with a most angelic smile.

There was but one reply possible to such a remark, so that matter was settled; after which, having lighted his pipe, he strolled over to the hut, to discuss with Nicholls and Simpson the unexpected appearance of the barque in their neighbourhood.

"If she means to touch here, as I feel pretty certain that she does," remarked Leslie, after he had related to the two men the result of his observations, "she will doubtless dodge off and on until daylight—as of course she cannot know the whereabouts of the channel through the reef—and then we can go out in the canoe and pilot her in. Meanwhile, what do you two men think of doing? Are you going to keep to your arrangement with me; or would you prefer to get the skipper of the barque to take you?"

Nicholls regarded Leslie with some surprise. "I hope, sir," he said, "that you don't want to cry off your bargain with us! I've already been planning in my mind what I'll do with that five hundred—"

"Certainly not," interrupted Dick, with a laugh; "*I* have no wish to cry off my bargain, as you term it. I merely wish you to understand that I will not attempt to hold you to it if you would prefer the barque to the cutter. The barque would doubtless be more comfortable than the cutter in heavy weather."

"May be she would, or may be she wouldn't," observed Nicholls. "Anyhow, the difference wouldn't be so very great, one way or the other. But there's no five hundred pound to be got out of the barque; and I'm bound to have that money, Mr Leslie—"

"Same here," cut in Simpson.

"All right," laughed Leslie. "Then that matter is settled for good and all; so we need say no more about it."

"Question is: What's she comin' here for?" inquired Simpson, volunteering a remark for the first time on record.

"Oh, who can tell?" returned Leslie. "She may be a whaler—although I do not believe that she is—putting in here in the hope of finding water. That is the only explanation that has occurred to me as accounting for her presence in this locality—which is really a long way out of any of the usual ship tracks. She is the first craft that I have sighted since my arrival upon this island. But no doubt we shall learn to-morrow—"

"Why, there she is," interrupted Nicholls, pointing. "By Jingo, just look at that; coming in through the channel as confidently as though she had been in the habit of sailin' in and out of it every day of her life! And with nothing better than the starlight to see her way by. Well, dash my wig, but that's a rum go, and no mistake!"

It was even as he said; for while the three men stood there talking together the shadowy form of the barque, under her two topsails and fore-topmast staysail, was seen gliding into the lagoon close past Cape Flora— her skipper evidently perfectly acquainted with the exact situation of the entrance channel—and presently her topsail halliards were let run and the sails clewed up, the rattle of the gear and the cheeping of the blocks being distinctly audible to the three on the beach. Then a minute or two later came the splash of the anchor and the rumbling rattle of the cable through the hawse-pipe, and the barque was seen to swing to her anchor.

"Well, it is perfectly clear that the man who has charge of her has been in here at least once before," remarked Leslie. "Evidently he knows the place quite well. Now, I wonder *what* it is that has brought him here; I would give a trifle to know. And, of course, I could readily find out by taking the canoe and paddling off aboard to ask the question. But I will not do that; and, furthermore, it may be just as well not to let those people know—until to-morrow morning, at any rate—that there is anybody on the island, therefore pleads take care, both of you, that no light shows from your hut to-night. And I will just step up to the tent and give Miss Trevor a similar caution. Good night, men. We had better be stirring by dawn to-morrow morning." So saying, Leslie turned away, and made his way to the tent, where he not only cautioned Flora against showing a light, but took such simple precautions as were required to render it impossible that the necessary lights in the tent should be seen from the barque. Then, this done to his satisfaction, he lighted his pipe and, taking the telescope—which was both a day and a night-glass—once more sauntered down to the beach to watch the proceedings aboard the strange vessel. For although he could find no legitimate reason or excuse for the feeling, it was an undeniable fact that the appearance of this barque upon the scene affected him disagreeably, producing within him a vague sense of unrest that almost amounted to foreboding. *Why* had she come to the island? That was the question that persistently haunted him, and to which he could find no entirely satisfactory reply. That her presence there was accidental he could not believe, else how came it that the person in charge of her knew so well where to find the channel giving access to the lagoon, and entered it so confidently, not even waiting for the daylight to enable him to see his way in? And as he mused thus he employed himself in intently watching the barque through the night-glass, again noting the fact that the vessel was curiously short-handed, for her people furled only one topsail at a time, and—so far as he could make out—had only four men available for the job, instead of at least twice that number. Furthermore, he noticed that, even for that small number of men, the time consumed in rolling up and stowing the sails was quite unconscionable, arguing the existence of an exceedingly lax discipline—if any at all—aboard the craft. He estimated that it occupied those four men fully two hours to furl the two topsails; and when it was at last done and the men had descended to the deck with exasperating deliberation, he came to the conclusion that, if the night-glass was to be trusted, the job had been done in a most disgracefully slovenly manner.

He patiently watched that barque until all visible signs of life aboard her had vanished, and then he walked thoughtfully back to the tent and turned in—Flora having retired some time before. But ere he could get to sleep he was disturbed by the sounds of a hideous uproar that came floating shoreward from the stranger; and, going again into the open air to hear more clearly, he presently recognised the sounds as those of discordant singing, finally recognising the fact that a regular drunken orgie was in progress aboard the craft—still further evidence of a singularly lax state of discipline.

Leslie's couch was a sleepless one that night; for the fact was that, taking everything into consideration, he could neither account satisfactorily for the presence of the barque at the island, nor convince himself that her errand there was an altogether honest one. Therefore, with the first faint flush of dawn he was again astir; and rousing Flora and the two men, he bade them get their breakfasts forthwith and make the best of their way out of the camp ere the barque's people should have had an opportunity to see them and become aware of their presence on the island. And he further gave Nicholls and Simpson instructions to proceed with and complete the rigging of the cutter and the bending of her sails, in readiness for getting under way at a moment's notice. Unfortunately the *Flora* had still to be provisioned and watered for her voyage; and it was just this fact, and the possibility that the strangers might be disposed to interfere with these operations, that discomposed him. But for this he would most cheerfully have marched himself and his little party out of the camp and left it, with everything it contained, to the mercy of the barque's crew—whom he had already, in some unaccountable fashion, come to look upon as outlaws. He gave the men the strictest injunctions that Flora was to forthwith take up her quarters aboard the cutter, while they—Nicholls and Simpson—were to camp in the natural fortress to which he had that same afternoon drawn their attention, holding it against all comers, and on no account leaving it altogether unguarded, either day or night. As for himself, he announced that he would remain, as sole occupant of the camp, to meet the strangers and ascertain the reason for their visit; after which his further actions would be guided by circumstances.

Leslie was of opinion that, after the orgie of the preceding night, the crew of the barque would be in no particular hurry to turn out; and his surmise proved to be quite correct, for although he kept a keen watch upon the vessel it was not until nearly nine o'clock that he detected the first signs of movement on board her, in the shape of a thin streamer of smoke, issuing from the galley funnel. He then watched for the usual signs of washing down the decks, the drawing of water, the streaming of the scuppers, and so on, but could detect nothing of the kind; neither was the bell struck on board to mark the passage of time—two additional indications of the absence of discipline that still further increased his fast-growing uneasiness respecting the character of his unwelcome visitors. As soon as the light was strong enough, it may be mentioned, he had taken a look at the barque through his telescope, and had read the words "*Minerva*, Glasgow," painted across her counter; he thus knew that the vessel was British, as, indeed, he had already suspected.

Now, it was Dick's purpose to learn as much as he possibly could about the strangers, and to let them know as little as possible about himself— and nothing at all about his companions—in return, until he had had an opportunity to get some notion of their true character. He had therefore determined to pose as a solitary castaway; and now, in that character, proceeded down to the beach, stepped into the canoe, and began to paddle laboriously off toward the barque. For he knew that one of the first things to be done by the skipper of that vessel would be to bring his telescope to bear upon the island, and this would immediately result in the discovery of his tent, his pile of salvage from the brig, the hut, and all the litter upon the beach; and as it was consequently impossible to conceal the fact of his presence upon the island, he judged that the natural action of such a castaway as himself would be to eagerly seize the first opportunity to communicate with a calling ship.

The canoe being a big, heavy craft for one man to handle, it took him a full hour to paddle off to the barque; but it was not until he was within a hundred yards of her that he was able to detect any open indication of the fact that his presence had been discovered. Then he saw a big, burly-looking individual come aft along the vessel's full poop, and deliberately bring a pair of binocular glasses to bear upon him. He at once ceased paddling, and, placing his hands to his mouth, hailed—

"*Minerva* ahoy!"

"Hillo!" came the response across the water, in a gruff voice that accurately matched the build and general appearance of the owner.

"May I come aboard?" inquired Dick resuming his paddle.

"Ay, ay; come aboard, if ye like," was the somewhat ungracious response.

Without further parley Leslie paddled up alongside under the starboard main channels, and, flinging his painter up to an individual who came to the side and peered curiously down upon him over the bulwarks, scrambled up the side as best he could in the absence of a side-ladder, and the next moment found himself on deck.

He cast an apparently casual but really all-embracing glance round him, and noted that the barque was evidently just an ordinary trader, with nothing in the least remarkable about her appearance save the extraordinary paucity of men about her decks. Under ordinary circumstances and conditions, at this hour all hands would have been on deck and busy about their preparations for the carrying out of the object of their visit to the island—whatever that might be; instead of which the man on the poop, the man who had made fast his painter for him, and the cook—a fat-faced, evil-looking man with a most atrocious squint—who came to the galley door and stared with malevolent curiosity at him—were the only individuals visible. It was not, however, any part of Leslie's policy to exhibit surprise at such an unusual condition of affairs, so he simply advanced to the poop ladder, with the manner of one a little uncertain how to act, and, looking up at the burly man who stood at the head of the ladder, glowering down upon him, said—

"Good morning! Are you the captain of this barque?"

"Ay," answered the individual addressed; "I'm Cap'n Turnbull. Who may you be, mister? and how the blazes do you come to be on that there island? And how many more are there of ye?"

"As you see, I am alone, unfortunately," answered Leslie; "and a pretty hard time I have had of it. But, thank God, that is all over now that you have turned up—for I presume you will be quite willing to give me a passage to the next port you may be calling at?"

"*Give* ye a passage?" reiterated the burly man, scornfully; "give nothin'! I'm a poor man, I am, and can't afford to give anything away, not even a passage to the next port. But if you'm minded to come aboard and *work* your passage, you're welcome. For I'm short-handed, as I dare say you can see; and it's easy enough to tell that you're a sailor-man. It you wasn't you wouldn't be here, would ye?" This last with a grin that disclosed a set of strong irregular, tobacco-stained teeth, and imparted to the speaker the expression of a satyr.

The conversation thus far had been conducted as it had started, with Leslie down on the main deck and Turnbull on the poop. The incongruity of the arrangement now seemed to strike the latter, for he added—

"Come up here, mister; we can talk more comfortably when we're alongside of one another; and you can spin me the yarn how you come to be all alone by yourself on yon island."

In acceptance of this graciously worded invitation, Leslie ran lightly up the poop ladder and, slightly raising his cap, said—

"Permit me to introduce myself, Captain Turnbull. My name is *Leslie*," — with emphasis—"and the recital of the chain of circumstances which ended in my being cast away upon the island yonder will be so lengthy that, with your permission, I will smoke a pipe as I tell it."

And therewith he calmly drew his pipe from his pocket and, filling it, lighted up. Meanwhile his manner, language, and appearance had been steadily impressing the other man, who insensibly began to infuse his own manner with a certain measure of respect as the interview lengthened itself out.

Having lighted his pipe, Leslie proceeded to relate the whole story of his adventure, beginning with his embarkation on board the *Golden Fleece*, and ending up with the stranding of the *Mermaid*, but carefully suppressing all reference whatsoever to Miss Trevor; and representing himself not as an ex-naval officer, but as an amateur yachtsman. He was careful also to mention nothing about the existence of the cutter, but, on the other hand, dwelt at some length upon the idea he had entertained of building a craft capable of carrying him and a sufficient stock of provisions away from the island. "I doubt, however, whether I should ever have managed it, single-handed. But your arrival renders all further trouble on that score unnecessary," he said, in conclusion.

"Well, yes," returned Turnbull, somewhat more genially than he had yet spoken; "there's no call for you to worry about buildin' a boat now, as you says, 'specially as you're a good navigator. You can come home with us, workin' your passage by navigatin' the ship. For a good navigator is just exactly what I happens to want."

"Ah, indeed! Cannot you rely upon your mate, then?" inquired Leslie, blandly.

"My mate?" ejaculated the burly man; "well, no, I can't. That's to say," he continued confusedly, "he's the only navigator I've got now, and—well, no, I *can't* depend upon him."

"Do you find, then, that your own observations and his yield different results?" asked Leslie, still in the same bland, quiet manner.

"My own observations?" reiterated Captain Turnbull. "*I* don't take no observations. Ye see," he added, looking hard at Leslie's impassive face to discover whether the latter had noticed anything peculiar in such an extraordinary admission, "my sight's a little bit peculiar; I can see ordinary things plain enough, but when it comes to squintin' through a sextant I can't see nothin'."

"Ah, indeed; that must be exceedingly awkward for you, Captain," returned Leslie. "I am not surprised at your anxiety to secure the services of another navigator. By the way, how long do you propose to remain here? I should like to know, so that I may make my preparations accordingly."

"Well," answered Turnbull, "there's no particular reason for you to hurry; I s'pose half an hour 'll be about time enough for you to get your few traps together and bring 'em off, won't it?"

"Oh yes," answered Leslie, nonchalantly, "that time will amply suffice. I will do so at once, if you like."

"There's no occasion for hurry, as I said just now," retorted Turnbull. "Now that we're here I think I shall give the men a spell and let 'em have a run ashore a bit. In fact, I think I could do with a week ashore there myself. Most lovely place it looks like, from here. By-the-bye, how long did you say you'd been on that there island?"

"A trifle over nine months," answered Leslie.

"Over nine months!" ejaculated the other in tones of intense surprise. "Well, nobody'd think as you'd been a castaway for nine months, to look at ye. Why, you look strong and healthy enough, and as smartly rigged as though you'd just stepped out of the most dandy outfitter's in the Minories!"

"Oh, but there is nothing very wonderful in that," laughingly protested Leslie. "Nine months of life, practically in the open air all the time, is just the thing to keep a man fit, you know; while as for my 'rig,' I found a big stock of clothes among the *Mermaid's* cargo, and I have drawn freely upon that."

"Nine months on the island," repeated Turnbull, still dwelling upon that particular fact; "why, I s'pose you know every inch of the ground ashore there by this time?"

There was a certain ill-suppressed eagerness in the tones of the man's voice as he asked this question that acted very much as a danger-signal to Leslie. It seemed to suggest that thus far the man had merely been fencing with him, but that he was now trying to get within his guard; that, in short, the object of the *Minerva's* visit to the island was nearing the surface. He therefore replied, with studied carelessness—

"No, indeed I do not. On the contrary, I know very little of it—not nearly as much as I ought to know. I have been to the summit once, and took a general survey of the island from that point, and I have wandered for a short distance about the less densely bush-clad ground on this side of the island; but that is about all. The fact is that I was much too keen upon saving everything I possibly could out of the brig to think of wasting my time in wandering about an island the greater part of which is covered with almost impassable bush."

"Ah, yes; I s'pose you would be," rejoined Turnbull, with an expression of relief that set Leslie wondering.

What on earth did it matter to Turnbull whether he—Dick Leslie—had explored the island or not? he asked himself. Turnbull's next remark let in a little light upon the obscurity, and distinctly startled Leslie. For, staring steadfastly at the island, the burly man presently observed—

"Yes; it's a fine big island, that, and no mistake. With a mountain on it and all, too. I should say, now, that that island would be a very likely place for *caves*, eh? Looks as though there might be any amount of caves ashore there in the sides of that there hill, don't it?"

Caves! Like a flash of lightning the true explanation of the *Minerva's* visit stood clearly revealed to Leslie's mind. That one word "caves," spoken as it was in tones of mingled excitement and anxiety, ill-suppressed, had furnished him with the key to the entire enigma. *Caves*! Yes, of course; that was it; that explained everything—or very nearly everything—that had thus far been puzzling Leslie, and gave him practically all the information that he had been so anxious to acquire. He had read of such incidents in books, of course, but had so far regarded them merely as pegs whereon to hang a more or less ingeniously conceived and exciting romance; but here was a similar incident occurring in actual prosaic earnest; and he suddenly found himself confronted with a situation of exceeding difficulty. For the mention by Turnbull of the word "caves"—careless and casual as he fondly believed it to be, but actually exceedingly clumsy—had in an instant driven home to Leslie's mind the conviction that somehow or other this man had become possessed of information of the existence of the treasure on this island, *and had come to take it away!* By what circuitous chain of events the information had fallen into the fellow's hands it was of course quite impossible to guess; but that this was the explanation of everything Dick was fully convinced. And now that he possessed the clue he could not only guard his own tongue against the betrayal of information, but could also doubtless so order his remarks as to extort from some one or another of his visitors all the details that he himself might require. So, in reply to Turnbull's last remark, he said carelessly—

"Caves! oh, really I don't know; very possibly there may be—unless the earthquake has shaken them all in and filled them up—"

"Earthquake!" roared Turnbull, in tones of mingled rage and consternation; "you don't mean to say as you've had a hearthquake here, do ye?"

"Certainly," answered Dick, with as much *sang-froid* as though an earthquake were a mere pleasant interlude in an otherwise monotonous life; "it occurred about three months ago, and gave the place a pretty severe shaking up, I can assure you. It also started that volcano into activity again after ages of quiescence."

"The mischief!" ejaculated Turnbull, with manifest discomposure. "I must go ashore at once!"

"I am afraid," said Leslie, gently, "that my mention of the earthquake and its possible effect upon the caves of the island has somewhat upset you. Are you going ashore in the hope of finding any particular cave? If so, I shall be most happy to assist you in your search."

"Assist! I'll be—I mean of course not," exclaimed Turnbull, beginning with a savage bellow and suddenly calming himself again. "What d'ye s'pose a man like me wants to go pokin' about ashore there, huntin' after caves for? I've somethin' else to do. I've come in here because our fresh water's turned bad, and I thought that maybe I might be able to renew my stock, I s'pose there's fresh water to be had on the island?"

"Certainly," answered Leslie; "there is a most excellent supply, and quite accessible to your boats. It lies over there," pointing toward Mermaid Head; "and falls over a low ledge of rock into deep-water. You can go alongside the rock and fill up your boats or tanks direct, if you like."

"Ah, that'll do first-rate," remarked Turnbull; "I'll give orders for the men to start the foul water at once. And now, as I see that the sun's over the fore-yard, what'll you take to drink? I s'pose you've been pretty hard up all these months for drink, haven't ye?"

"No, indeed," answered Leslie; "on the contrary, I found an abundance of wines and spirits aboard the brig. The only thing that I have lacked has been mineral waters; therefore if you happen to have any soda-water on board it will give me great pleasure to take a whisky and soda with you."

"I believe we have some sodas left," answered Turnbull, doubtfully. "You won't mind takin' it up here on the poop, will ye?" he continued. "Fact is there's a man lyin' sick in one of the cabins below, and I don't want to disturb him with our talk."

Of course Leslie, although he had his doubts about the genuineness of the "sick man" story, readily acquiesced in the suggestion of the other, and seated himself in one of two deck-chairs that were standing on the poop, while Turnbull retired ostensibly for the purpose of quietly hunting up the steward.

A few minutes later the steward—a young Cockney of about twenty-five years of age, who had the worn, harassed appearance of a man living in a state of perpetual scare—came up the poop ladder, bearing a tray on which were a couple of tumblers, an uncorked bottle of whisky, and two bottles of soda-water, which he placed upon the skylight cover. Then, taking up the whisky-bottle and a tumbler, he proceeded to pour out a portion of the spirit, glancing anxiously about him as he did so.

"Say 'when,' sir, please," he requested, in a loud voice, immediately adding under his breath, "Are you alone, ashore there, sir, or is there others there along with you?"

His whole air of extreme trepidation, and the manner of secrecy with which he put this singular question, was but further confirmation—if any were needed—of certain very ugly suspicions that had been taking a strong hold upon Leslie during the whole progress of his interview with the man Turnbull; Dick therefore replied to the steward by putting another question to him in the same low, cautious tones—

"Why do you ask me that, my man?" he murmured.

"Because, sir, there's— Is that about enough whisky, sir?"

The latter part of the steward's speech was uttered in a tone of voice that could be distinctly heard as far forward as the break of the poop, and, with the man's abrupt change of subject was evidently caused—as Leslie could see out of the corner of his eye—by the silent, stealthy appearance of Turnbull's head above the top of the ladder, and the glance of keen suspicion that he shot at the two occupants of the poop.

Dick took the tumbler from the steward's shaking hand and calmly held it up before him, critically measuring the quantity of spirit it contained.

"Yes, thanks," he replied; "that will do nicely. Now for the soda."

And he held the tumbler while the steward opened the soda-water bottle and emptied it's effervescing contents into the spirit. Turnbull glanced keenly from Leslie to the steward and back again, but said nothing, although the unfortunate attendant's condition of terror was patent to all observers. Dick waited patiently while the trembling man helped Turnbull, and then, lifting his tumbler, said—

"Your health, Captain; and to our better acquaintance."

"Thank 'ee; same to you," gruffly replied the individual addressed; adding to the steward, "That'll do; you can go back to your pantry now, and get on with your work."

The fellow departed in double-quick time, obviously glad to get away from the neighbourhood of his somewhat surly superior; and as he went Turnbull watched him until he disappeared down the poop ladder.

"Rum cove, that," he remarked to Leslie, as the man vanished. "Good sort of steward enough, but nervous as a cat. Did ye notice him?"

"It was quite impossible not to do so," answered Dick, with a laugh. "And I could not help feeling sorry for the poor beggar. I take it that he is the simpleton of the ship, and that all hands make a point of badgering him."

"Ay," answered Turnbull, eagerly, clearly relieved that Dick had taken this view of the man's condition; "that's just exactly what it is; you've hit the case off to a haffigraphy. Well, enough said about him. If you're ready to go ashore now I'll go with ye."

"By all means," answered Leslie, genially; not that he was in the least degree desirous to have the man's company, or even that he or any of his crew should land upon the island at all. Still, he knew that, the barque being where she was, it was inevitable that at least some of the ship's company would insist upon going ashore, and he could not see how he was to prevent them; meanwhile, it was much better to have the fellow alone with him than accompanied by half a dozen or more of his men.

As he spoke he rose from his seat and led the way toward the canoe, Turnbull following him. Upon reaching the gangway, however, Dick looked over the side, and then, turning to his companion, said —

"I think you would find it more convenient if your people rigged the side-ladder. My canoe is rather crank, and if you should happen to tumble overboard in getting into her I would not answer for your life; the lagoon swarms with sharks, and as likely as not there are one or two under the ship's bottom at this moment."

Turnbull grunted and turned away, looking forward to where two or three men were loafing about on the forecastle, hard at work doing nothing.

"For'ard, there!" he shouted; "rouse out the side-ladder and rig it, some of ye, and look sharp about it. Steward," he added, turning toward the cabin under the poop, "bring me out a handful of cigars."

The two men with the ladder, and the steward with the cigars, appeared simultaneously; and, pocketing the weeds, the skipper proceeded to the gangway to supervise the rigging of the ladder. As he did so, Leslie felt something being thrust surreptitiously into his hand. It felt like a folded piece of paper, and he calmly pocketed it, glancing casually about him as he did so. The steward was the only man near him, and he was shuffling off nimbly on his way back to his pantry.

Leslie took his time paddling ashore, and when at length the pair landed on the beach the sun had passed the meridian.

"Now, Captain," said Dick, "where would you like to go in the first place?"

Turnbull stood and looked about him admiringly. "Why," he exclaimed, "this here hisland is a real beautiful place, and no mistake. Dash my wig! why, a man might do a sight worse than settle here for the rest of his natural, eh?"

"Ay," answered Leslie, indifferently; "I have often thought so myself. Indeed it is quite on the cards that I may return here some day, with a few seeds and an outfit of gardeners' tools. As you say, a man might do worse. By the way, perhaps it will be as well to get lunch before we start out on our ramble. Will you come up to my tent? You will find it a very comfortable little shanty. I must apologise for the fare that I shall be obliged to offer you, but I have lived on tinned meat and fish ever since I have been here; and I have caught no fish to-day."

"Well, I must say as you've managed to make yourself pretty tidy comfortable," observed Leslie's guest as he entered the tent and stared about him in astonishment; "picters, fancy lamps, tables and chairs with swagger cloths and jigmarees upon 'em, and a brass-mounted bedstead and beddin' fit for a king! They're a blame sight better quarters than you'll find aboard the *Minerva*, and so I tell ye."

Leslie laughed lightly. "What does that matter?" he demanded. "True, I am fond of comfort, and always make a point of getting it where I can; but I can rough it with anybody when it becomes necessary."

Dick was obliged to leave his guest alone in the tent for a short time while he looked after the preparations for luncheon; and he had little doubt that during his absence the man would without scruple peer and pry into the other compartments of the tent. But to this contingency he was quite indifferent, for he had foreseen and forestalled it, before going off to the barque, by carefully gathering up and stowing away such few traces of a woman's presence as Flora had left behind her. That Turnbull had followed the natural propensity of men of his stamp was made clear immediately upon Dick's return, for, quite unabashed, the fellow remarked—

"I say, mister, you're doin' the thing in style here, and no mistake. I've been havin' a look round this here tent of yourn while you've been away, and I see as you've acshully got a pianner in the next room. And where's your shipmate gone to?"

"My shipmate?" repeated Leslie, staring blankly at him.

"Ay, your shipmate," reiterated Turnbull, severely. "You told me you was all alone here, but I see as you've got *two* bedrooms rigged up here. Who's t'other for, and where is he?"

"Really, Captain," said Dick, coldly, "I cannot see what possible difference it can make to you whether I have a shipmate or not, if you will pardon me for saying so. But," he continued, somewhat more genially, "it is perfectly evident that you have never lived alone on an island, or you would understand what a luxury it is to be able to change one's sleeping-room occasionally."

"Oh, that's it, is it?" returned Turnbull, with sudden relief. "You sleeps sometimes in one bed and sometimes in t'other, by way of a change, eh?"

"As you see," answered Dick, briefly. "And now, will you draw up your chair? It is not a very tempting meal that I can offer you; but you can make up for it when you return to your ship this evening."

It was evident to Leslie that Turnbull was much exercised in his mind about something, for he ate and drank silently and with a preoccupied air; and later on the reason for this became manifest, for when at length they rose from the table the fellow remarked with a clumsy effort at nonchalance—

"Look here, mister, I expect you've a plenty of matters to look after and attend to, so don't you worry about showin' me round this here hisland of yourn; you just go on with what you've got in hand, and I'll take a stroll somewheres by myself."

So that was it. He wanted an opportunity to go off upon an exploring expedition unrestrained by Dick's presence! But this did not at all chime in with Leslie's plans; for he felt certain that if he yielded to his companion's suggestion the latter would at once make his way in the direction of the treasure-cave, and endeavour to discover its locality, with the result that he would inevitably come into collision with Nicholls and Simpson. This, in any case, would doubtless happen, sooner or later; but Dick wished to acquire a little further information before it occurred. He therefore replied—

"Oh, thanks, very much. I was busy enough, in all conscience, before you arrived; but now that you have turned up, and have kindly consented to take me off the island, I have nothing further to do. So I may as well accompany you, since I know the shortest way to such few points of interest as the island possesses. Where would you like to go? The crater and the watering-place are about the only spots that are likely to tempt you, I think."

Turnbull glared at Dick as though he could have eaten him; and for a moment the ex-lieutenant thought that his guest was about to try violent measures with him. But if that thought was really in his mind he suffered more prudent counsels to prevail with him, and, after a few moments' hesitation, intimated that he would like to have a look at the watering-place. Dick accordingly piloted his morose companion to the spot, and pointed out how excellently it was adapted to the purpose of watering ships, drawing his attention to the deep-water immediately beneath the low cascade, and dilating upon the facility with which boats could be brought alongside. But it was clearly apparent to him that Turnbull was absolutely uninterested in the subject; and he was by no means sorry when, upon the return to the camp, the latter declined his invitation to remain on shore to dinner, and curtly requested to be at once put off to the barque. During the passage off to the vessel the man's surliness of demeanour suddenly vanished, and, as though a brilliant idea had just struck him, he became in a moment almost offensively civil, strongly urging Dick to remain aboard the barque and "make a night of it." But neither did this suit Dick's plans; the sudden change in the man's demeanour at once roused Leslie's suspicions; and as he had no intention whatever of placing himself in the fellow's power, he suavely declined the invitation, remarking that, as he would soon be having quite as much of the sea as he wanted, he would continue to enjoy his present roomy quarters as long as he could.

Chapter Sixteen
A Story of Mutiny

Not until Leslie was once more back in his own tent, and absolutely safe from all possibility of interruption or espionage, did he venture to open and peruse the scrap of paper that the steward had that morning so surreptitiously slipped into his hand. It was apparently part of the leaf of a pocket memorandum book; and, hastily scribbled in pencil, in an ill-formed and uneducated hand, it bore the following words:—

"Sir, for God's sake take care what your about, or your life won't be worth a brass farden. Turnbull aint no more the proper capten of this ship than I am. There won't be no anchor watch aboard here to-night so if youl come off about half after midnight I'll be on the lookout for yer and tell yer the hole bloomin yarn. For God's sake come.—Steward."

"Um!" meditated Leslie, as he held the document to the light of the lamp. "Now, what does this mean? Is it a trap to get me aboard the barque, or is it genuine? The latter, I am inclined to think, for several reasons; the first of which is that the poor man was obviously in a state of abject terror this morning. Secondly, he was so keenly anxious to open up communication with me that he made an unsuccessful attempt to do so while helping me to my whisky and soda. Thirdly, his statement that Turnbull is not the legitimate skipper of the barque is so evidently true that it needs no discussion. And fourthly, if Turnbull had seriously desired to make me a prisoner this afternoon, he could easily have done so by sending a boat's crew in pursuit of me—that is to say," he corrected himself, "for all he knows to the contrary, he could easily have done so. For how was he to know that I had two fully loaded revolvers in my pocket, equivalent to the lives of twelve men? Yes, I am strongly inclined to believe that this remarkable little document is genuine, and that there is something very radically wrong aboard that barque. What is it, I wonder? That Turnbull has somehow got scent of the treasure, and is after it, I am almost prepared to swear; his obvious vexation and disappointment at finding me here as 'the man in possession,' and his equally obvious efforts to shake me off to-day that he might have an opportunity to go away by himself in search of the cave, prove that; but there is something more than that, I am certain. I wonder, now, whether his story of the sick man in the cabin has anything to do with it? I should not be surprised if it had. And where were the crew this morning? Turnbull spoke of being short-handed; but surely there are more people aboard than himself, the steward, the cook, and the two or three men I saw? Oh yes, there is something very queer about the whole business; and this document is genuine. At all events I will go off to-night, and hear what the steward has to say about it."

In accordance with this resolution Leslie forthwith partook of a good hearty meal, and then, extinguishing his lamp, left the tent—to guard against the possibility of his being surprised there in his sleep—and, walking over to the pile of goods that he had accumulated from the brig's cargo, raised the tarpaulin that covered it, and, creeping underneath, stretched himself out as comfortably as he could to snatch a few hours' sleep, confident that the faculty which he possessed of being able to wake at any desired moment would not play him false. And a few minutes later he was fast asleep; for Dick Leslie was one of those men who, when once they have resolved upon a certain course of action, dismiss further consideration of it from their minds and allow it to trouble them no longer.

He had fixed upon half-past eleven as the hour at which he would rise, this allowing him a full hour in which to paddle off to the barque; and when by-and-by he awoke, and under the shelter of the tarpaulin cautiously struck a match and consulted his watch, he found that it was within five minutes of the half-hour. He next peered out from under the tarpaulin and carefully scanned the beach by the light of the stars, to see whether Turnbull had sent a boat ashore in the hope of "catching a weasel asleep;" but his own canoe was the only craft visible, and he accordingly made his way down to the water's edge, and, pushing her off, sprang noiselessly into her as she went afloat. Then, heading her round with a couple of powerful sweeps of the paddle, he pointed her nose toward the spot where the *Minerva's* spars made a delicate tracery of black against the star-spangled heavens, and with long, easy, silent strokes drove her quietly ahead.

That the crew had not yet retired to their bunks was soon evident to him from the fact that snatches of maudlin song came floating down to him occasionally upon the pinions of the dew-laden night breeze; but these dwindled steadily as he drew nearer to the vessel, and about a quarter of an hour before he arrived alongside they ceased altogether, and the craft subsided into complete silence.

Leslie deemed it advisable to approach the barque with a considerable amount of caution, not that he doubted the steward, but because, despite the silence that had fallen on board, it was just possible that some of the crew might still be awake and on deck; he therefore kept the three masts of the vessel in one, and crept up to her very gently from right astern. As he drew in under the shadow of her hull the complete darkness and silence in which the craft was wrapped seemed almost ominous and uncanny; but presently he detected a solitary figure on the poop, evidently on the watch, and a moment later saw that this figure was silently signalling to him to draw up under the counter. Obeying these silent signals, he found a rope dangling over the stern, which he seized, and the next instant the figure that he had observed came silently wriggling down the rope into the canoe. Leslie at once recognised him as the steward.

"It's all right, sir," whispered the man, breathless, in part from his exertions, and partly also, Leslie believed, from apprehension; "it's all right. But let go, sir, please, and let's get a few fathoms away from the ship, for there's no knowin' when that skunk Turnbull may take it into his head to come on deck and 'ave a look round; 'e's as nervous as a cat, and that suspicious that you can't be up to 'im. There, thank 'e, sir; I dare say that'll do; they won't be able to see or 'ear us from where we are now, for I couldn't see you until you was close under the counter. Well, you've come, sir, God be thanked; and I 'ope you'll be able to 'elp us; because if you can't it'll be a precious bad job for some of us." And the fellow sighed heavily with mingled apprehension and relief.

"You had better tell me the whole of your story," said Leslie, quietly. "I shall then be in a position to say whether I can help you or not. If I can, you may rest assured that I will."

"Thank 'e, sir," murmured the man. "Well, ye see, sir, it's like this. We sailed from London for Capetown a little more than four months ago; and everything went smooth and comfortable enough with us until we got across the line and into the south-east trades—for the skipper, poor Cap'n Hopkins, was as nice and pleasant a man as anybody need wish to sail under; and so was Mr Marshall, too—that's the mate, you'll understand, sir—although 'e kep' the men up to their dooty, and wouldn't 'ave no skulkin' aboard. The only chap as was anyways disagreeable was this feller Turnbull, who was rated as bo'sun, and give charge of the starboard watch, actin' as a sort of second mate, ye see. Well, as I was sayin', everything went all right until we got to the s'uth'ard of the line. Then, one night I was woke up some time after midnight by a terrific row in the cabin; and up I jumps and out I goes to see what was up. When I got into the cabin it seemed full of men; but I'd no sooner shown my nose than one of the chaps—it was Pete Burton, I remember—catches sight of me, and, takin' me by the collar, 'e runs me back into my cabin and says, 'You stay in there, Jim,'— my name's Reynolds—Jim Reynolds—you'll understand, sir. 'You stay in there, Jim,' 'e says, 'and no 'arm'll come to you; but if you tries to come out afore you're called, you'll get 'urt,' 'e says. Then 'e turns the key upon me, and I gets back into my bunk, and listens. The next thing I 'eard was a pistol-shot; then there was another tremenjous 'ullabaloo, men shoutin' and strugglin' together, followed by a sudden silence, and the sound of all 'ands clearin' out of the cabin. Then there was a lot of tramplin' of feet on the poop over my 'ead, with a good deal of talkin'; then I 'eard somebody cry out, there was a 'eavy splash in the water alongside, and then everything went quite quiet all of a sudden, and I 'eard no more until mornin'. But I guessed pretty well what 'ad 'appened; and when Turnbull come along about five bells and unlocked my door and ordered me to turn out and get about my work, I found I was right, for when I went for'ard to the galley, Slushy—that's the cook, otherwise known as Neil Dolan—told me that that skowbank Turnbull, backed up by the four A.B.s in the fo'c's'le and Slushy 'isself, 'ad rose and took the ship from the skipper, killin' 'im and Chips— that's the carpenter—puttin' the mate in irons and lockin' 'im up in 'is cabin, and compellin' the four ordinarys to help—whether they would or no—in workin' the ship. Then, by-and-by, when eight bells struck and I rang the bell for breakfast, along comes Turnbull, and says to me—

"'Well, Jim, I s'pose you've 'eard the news?'

"'Yes, bo'sun,' I says, 'I 'ave.'

"'Very well,' he says; 'that's all right. Now,' 'e says, 'all as you 'ave to do, my son, is to behave yourself and do your dooty, takin' care not to interfere with my arrangements. You'll give the mate 'is meals in 'is own cabin, regular; but you're not to talk to 'im, you understand, nor tell 'im anything that you may see or 'ear about what's goin' on. And don't you call me bo'sun no more, young man, or I'll knock your bloomin' young 'ead off, for I'm cap'n of this ship now, and don't you forget it! So now you knows what to expect. And, mind you,' 'e says, 'if you gets up to any 'ankypanky tricks I'll chuck you over the side, so sure as your name's Jim Reynolds, so keep your weather eye liftin', my son!'

"Later on, that same day, Turnbull 'as the mate out into the main cabin and spreads a chart of the Pacific Hocean out on the table; and, readin' from a paper what 'e 'ad in 'is 'and, says, 'Now, Mr Marshall, I'll trouble you to lay down on this 'ere chart a p'int bearin' latitood so-and-so and longitood so-and-so,'—I forgets what the figures was. 'And when you've done that,' he says, 'you'll navigate this 'ere barque to that identical spot. I'll give yer two months from to-day to get us there,' 'e says; 'and if we're not there by that time,' 'e says, 'I'll lash your 'ands and feet together be'ind yer back and 'eave yer overboard. So now you knows what you've to do if you want to save yer bloomin' life,' 'e says.

"That same a'ternoon, while I was for'ard in the galley, Slushy—who was in 'igh spirits—tells me as 'ow Turnbull 'ave got 'old of a yarn about a lot of buried treasure on a hisland somewhere, in the Pacific, and that we was bound there to get it; and that when we'd got it, Turnbull and them as 'ad stood in with 'im 'd be as rich as princes and wouldn't need to do another stroke of work for the rest of their naturals, but just 'ave a good time, with as much booze as they cared to swaller. And I reckon that this 'ere's the hisland where Turnbull thinks 'e'll find 'is treasure."

"No doubt," agreed Leslie. "Well, what do you want me to do?"

"Well, sir, it ain't for the likes of me to say just exactly what you ought to do," answered Reynolds. "I thought that maybe if I spinned you the whole yarn you'd be able to think out some way of 'elpin' of us. There ain't no doubt in my mind but what you bein' on the hisland 'ave upset Turnbull's calculations altogether. As I makes it out, 'e reckoned upon comin' 'ere and goin' ashore with 'is paper in 'is 'and, and walkin' pretty straight to the place where this 'ere treasure is buried, and diggin' of it up all quite comfortable, with nobody to hinterfere with 'im. But you bein' 'ere makes it okkard for 'im, you see; because 'e's afraid that where 'e goes you'll go with 'im, and if 'e goes pokin' about lookin' after buried treasure you'll drop on to 'is secret and p'rhaps get 'old of the stuff. And that's just where the danger to you comes in; because, d'ye see, sir, if 'e'd kill one man for the sake of gettin' 'old of the barque to come 'ere on the off-chance of findin' the treasure, 'e ain't the kind of man to 'esitate about killin' another who'd be likely to hinterfere with 'im."

"Just so," assented Leslie; "that is quite possible. But I will see that he does nothing of the kind. Now, tell me, how many of the ship's company are with Turnbull, and how many are there against him?"

"Well, first of all, there's Turnbull 'isself; that's one," answered the steward. "Then there's Burton, Royston, Hampton, and Cunliffe, the four A.B.s; that's five. And, lastly, there's the cook; 'e makes six. Then, on our side, there's Mr Marshall, the mate; that's one. I'm another; that's two. And there's Rogers, Andrews, Parker, and Martin, the four ordinary seamen; that's six again. So there's six against six, as you may say; only there's this difference between us: Turnbull 'ave got two revolvers, one what 'e found in the skipper's cabin, and one what 'e took from the mate, while the four A.B.s 'as their knives; whereas we 'aven't nothin', they 'avin' took our knives and everything away from us."

"Still," argued Leslie, "the belaying-pins are always available, I suppose, and they are fairly effective weapons in a hand-to-hand fight, to say nothing of handspikes and other matters that you can always lay your hands on. But of course Turnbull's brace of revolvers gives him an immense advantage, should it come to fighting. But I can plainly see that if the slip is to be recaptured at all—and I believe it can be managed—it must be done without fighting; for you are not strong-handed enough to risk the loss, or even the disablement, of so much as a single man. Now, tell me this. Turnbull informs me that your water is bad, and that he intends to re-water the ship, here. Is that true, or is it only a fabrication to account to me for the presence here of the *Minerva*?"

"Why, just that, and nothin' else, sir," answered the steward. "Our water's good enough. But certingly we're runnin' rather short of it; and I don't doubt but what 'e'll fill up, if there's water to be 'ad 'ere. But it's the treasure as 'e's after, first and foremost, and don't you forget it."

"Quite so," agreed Leslie. "Now, no doubt he will go ashore again soon after daylight; and as I shall not come off to the ship he will be compelled to come ashore in his own boat. How many men will he be likely to bring with him, think you?"

"Not more'n two, sir, certingly," answered the steward; "and p'rhaps not any at all. Likely enough when 'e finds as you don't come off 'e'll scull 'isself ashore in the dinghy. Because, you see, sir, 'e don't trust none of us 'ceptin' the four as is standin' in with 'im, and them four 'as their orders to keep a strict heye upon us to see that we don't rise and take back the ship from 'em. So I don't think as 'e'll take any o' them ashore with 'im if 'e can 'elp it. And 'e won't take none of the others either, 'cause 'e'd be afraid to trust 'isself alone with 'em."

"Very well," said Leslie. "I think I can see my way pretty clearly now. If Turnbull should go ashore by himself to-morrow, I will look after him and see that he does not return to the barque. But if he should take any of his own gang with him—say two of them—that will leave only two and the cook aboard against six of you, which will make you two to one. In that case you must watch your chance, and, if you can find an opportunity, rise upon those three and retake the ship. And if you should succeed, hoist the ensign to the gaff-end as a signal to me that the ship is recaptured. But do not run any risks, mind; because, as I have already said, you cannot afford to lose even one man. If you cannot see a good chance to retake the ship, we must watch our opportunity, and think of some other plan. That is all, I think. Now I will put you aboard again. But look out for me to come off again about the same time to-morrow night."

With the same caution as before Leslie now again approached the barque, but this time he took the canoe up under the craft's mizzen channels, from which it was a much easier matter for the steward to scramble aboard again than if he had been compelled to shin up the rope dangling over the stern, by which he had descended; and having seen the man safely in on deck, he softly pushed the canoe off the ship's side with his bare hand, and allowed her to be driven clear by the wind; and it was not until he was a good hundred yards astern of the *Minerva* that he took to his paddle and returned to the camp. It was nearly two o'clock in the morning when at length he once more entered his tent and stretched himself upon his bed to finish his night's rest.

Leslie was habitually an early riser, and, notwithstanding the fact that the previous night's rest had been a broken one, he was once more astir by sunrise, taking his towels and soap with him to a little rocky pool in the stream where he was wont to indulge in his morning's "tub;" and by eight o'clock he was seated at table in his tent, enjoying his breakfast, and at the same time keeping an eye upon the barque.

It was not, however, until close upon half-past ten that Dick detected any signs of a movement on board the *Minerva*; and then with the aid of his telescope, he observed that they were getting the vessel's dinghy into the water. Ten minutes later he saw Turnbull climb down the ship's side, and, throwing over a short pair of sculls, shove off and head the little craft for the beach. Dick waited only just long enough to make quite sure that the man was really coming ashore, and, this presently becoming evident, he at once started for the treasure-cave. Knowing the way by this time perfectly well, an hour's easy walking took him to the spot, where he found Nicholls and Simpson on the watch. A few terse sentences sufficed to put the men in possession of the material facts of the situation, and he then hurried down aboard the cutter to see Flora and assure her of his safety, and that everything was going well. Then, returning to the cave, he made his final arrangements with the two men, and set out on his way back toward the camp. He did not go very far, however, for he knew that, finding him absent, Turnbull would at once seize the opportunity to institute a search for the cave; and he knew, further, that—since the man was undoubtedly possessed of tolerably complete information, including, probably, a map of the island—he must sooner or later make his appearance in the neighbourhood; he therefore selected a spot where, himself unseen, he could command a view of the ground over which the fellow must almost inevitably pass, and sat down to patiently await developments.

At length, after Leslie had been in ambush for nearly three hours, he saw Turnbull approaching among the trees, carrying what appeared to be a map or plan in his hand, which he consulted from time to time, with frequent pauses to stare about him as though in search of certain landmarks. As the burly ruffian drew nearer, Dick took a revolver from his pocket and finally scrutinised it to make absolutely certain that it was in perfect working order. Slowly the fellow approached, muttering curses below his breath at the unevenness of the way and the unsimilarity of the landscape with that described in the document which he carried. Presently he went, stumbling and execrating, close past the spot where Leslie remained concealed, and the latter at once rose to his feet and followed him noiselessly, at a distance of some fifteen paces. In this fashion the two men covered a distance of about a quarter of a mile, when Turnbull once more paused to consult his map.

"IT IS NO GOOD, TURNBULL, YOU WILL NEVER FIND THE PLACE WITHOUT MY HELP. THROW UP YOUR HANDS."

At the same moment Leslie halted, and, levelling his revolver at the boatswain's head, said—

"It is no good, Turnbull; you will never find the place without my help. No, you don't! Throw up your hands. Over your head with them, quick, or I'll fire! Do you hear what I say, sir? Well, take that, then, you obstinate mule, as a hint to do as you are told in future!"

And as Leslie spoke he pulled the trigger of his revolver, and sent a bullet through the man's left arm, shattering the bone above the elbow.

For, with the sound of Dick's voice, Turnbull had faced about, and, with a bitter curse, made as though he would plunge his hands into the side-pockets of the pilot jacket that he was wearing. As the shot struck him he gave vent to another curse that ended in a sharp howl of anguish as he flung his uninjured arm above his head.

"What the blazes are ye doin' of?" he yelled in impotent fury. "D'ye know that you've broke my arm?"

"Sorry," remarked Dick, nonchalantly, "but you *would* have it, you know. I distinctly ordered you to throw up your hands, and you immediately attempted to plunge them into your pockets to get at your revolvers. If you compel me to shoot again I shall shoot to kill, so I hope that, for your own sake, you will make no further attempt to do anything foolish. Now, right about face, and march. I will tell you how to steer. And be very careful to keep that right hand of yours well above your head."

"Ain't you goin' to bind up this wound of mine for me, then?" demanded Turnbull. "And what right have you got to shoot at me, I'd like to know?"

"All in good time," answered Leslie, airily. "Now march, as I told you, and be quick about it, or I shall be compelled to freshen your way for you with another shot. I know all about you, my good man, and I am therefore not at all disposed to put up with any nonsense. Forward!"

With a further volley of curses of extraordinary virulence, Turnbull turned on his heel and resumed his way in the direction of the treasure-cave, with Dick at his heels directing him from time to time to "port a little," "starboard a bit," or "steady as you go," as the case might be.

A few minutes of this kind of thing sufficed to bring the pair close to the treasure-cave, the entrance of which had been considerably enlarged by Nicholls and Simpson for their own convenience. They were, however, absent for the moment when Dick arrived with his prisoner; and the latter stared in wonderment at the cave and the chests in front of it, which the two men had removed from the interior prior to transference to the cutter.

"So," exclaimed Turnbull, savagely, "that's what you're at, is it? Stealin' my treasure! Very well; if I don't make you smart for this my name ain't

Robert Turnbull, that's all. What d'ye mean, I'd like to know, by comin' here and stealin' treasure that don't belong to ye, eh?"

"To whom does it belong, pray, if not to me?" demanded Dick, blandly, curious to learn what kind of claim this ruffian would set up.

"Why, to *me*, of course," howled Turnbull, clenching his right fist and shaking it savagely at Leslie.

"Keep that right hand of yours over your head," ordered Dick, sharply, again covering him with lightning-like rapidity. "That's right," he continued. "Now perhaps you will kindly tell me how it came to be yours."

"Why, I got it off a former shipmate of mine," answered Turnbull. "He give it to me when—when he—died."

"What was his name?" asked Dick.

"His name?" reiterated Turnbull, "what do his name matter? And anyhow I've forgot it."

At this moment Nicholls and Simpson made their appearance upon the scene, much to Turnbull's amazement, and turning to them Leslie said—

"Here is your prisoner, lads. Have you your lashings ready? And is the cave empty of everything that we intend to take away with us? Very well, then; march this fellow in there and bind his two feet and his right hand together securely—his left arm is broken and useless, you need not therefore trouble about that. And when you have done that I will set his broken arm and dress his wound for him. Keep him in the cave until I give you further instructions concerning him, and meanwhile give him a sufficiency of food and water to keep him from starving."

For a moment Turnbull, wounded as he was, seemed very much disposed to make a final struggle for his liberty; but although he was a strong man, Simpson would have been more than a match for him even if he had been unwounded, and presently, recognising the futility and folly of resistance he sulkily entered the cave and submitted to be bound, growling and cursing horribly all the while, however. Then Leslie, assisted by Nicholls, dressed his wound and set the broken bone of the arm; lashing it firmly with splints hastily cut out of small branches from the nearest trees. Satisfied now that the fellow was absolutely secured, and quite incapable either of escaping or of inflicting any very serious injury upon himself, the three men at length left him to his; own devices, and proceeded to get the remainder of the treasure aboard the cutter and snugly stowed away—a task that they accomplished early enough to enable Dick to get back to the camp ere nightfall. Arrived there, Leslie at once set to work to prepare himself a good substantial meal, which he subsequently devoured with much gusto—having eaten nothing since breakfast; and, this important matter being disposed of, he immediately turned in, desiring to secure a few hours' sleep ere setting out upon his nocturnal trip off to the barque.

When, at about half an hour after midnight, he again approached the *Minerva*, observing the same precautions as before, he found the steward awaiting his arrival with considerable trepidation. The man again descended into the canoe by way of the rope over the stern; and again Leslie allowed the little craft to drive with the wind to a perfectly safe distance before opening the conversation. At length, however, he said—

"Now I think we are far enough away to permit of our talking freely without being either heard or seen; so go ahead, Reynolds, and give me the news. Has Turnbull's failure to return to the ship caused any uneasiness to the others of his gang?"

"Well, it 'ave, and it 'aven't, if you can understand me, sir," answered the man. "What I mean to say is this," he continued, by way of explanation, "the chaps—Burton and the rest of 'em—seems a bit puzzled that 'e 'aven't come off aboard to sleep to-night; but so far as I can make out, they thinks 'e's stayin' ashore with you, chummin' up with you, in a manner of speakin', and tryin' to get to wind'ard of you. They seems to think that Turnbull—who thinks 'isself a mighty clever chap, but ain't nothin' of the sort—'aven't been able to hinvent an excuse to get away from you, and that you've been goin' about with 'im all day, showin' 'im round the hisland and such-like; and that 'e's stayin' ashore to-night 'opin' to be able to give you the slip early in the mornin' and get off by 'isself to 'ave a look for 'is treasure-cave. That's what they thinks; but of course it ain't nothin' of the sort. *You* knows what 'ave 'appened to 'im, sir; no doubt?"

"Oh yes," answered Leslie, with a laugh; "I know quite well what has happened to him. He is alive; but he will not come off to the barque again."

"Thank God for that!" ejaculated the steward, piously. "Well, sir," he resumed, "what is to be the next move?"

"That," answered Leslie, "will depend upon circumstances—or, in other words, upon the action of Turnbull's accomplices. It would no doubt be easy enough to recapture the barque without further delay, if I were willing to risk a fight. But I am not, for two very good reasons; one of which is that my own party is so small that I cannot afford to have either of them hurt; and the other is that your party is also so small that if even a single man should happen to be disabled in a fight it would be exceedingly difficult for the remainder of you to handle the barque. Therefore I would very much rather spend a few more days over this business, and recapture the vessel without any fighting, than rush the matter and perhaps get somebody badly hurt. By the way, what sort of men are these accomplices of Turnbull's? Are they of the resolute and determined sort?"

"Ay," answered the steward, "you bet your life they are, sir. Turnbull took 'em in with 'im just because 'e couldn't 'elp 'isself. 'E 'ad to 'ave 'elp to take the barque, and naterally 'e chose the chaps as 'e thought would be most useful to 'im, 'specially as 'e didn't want to 'ave more 'n 'e could 'elp to go shares with 'im. Now these 'ere four—Burton and the rest of 'em—are big, strong fellers, all of 'em. Either of 'em could tackle any two of the rest of us in a stand-up fight and make mincemeat of us; so I reckon that's the reason why Turnbull chose 'em. With they four and the cook on 'is side, and the mate safe in irons and locked up in 'is cabin, 'e could laugh at the rest of us, and do just ezactly as 'e liked."

"I see," assented Leslie. "But what sort of a man is your mate, then? Could he not devise some scheme whereby, with the assistance of the rest of you, he could get the better of these fellows?"

"Mr Marshall?" responded the steward. "Oh, 'e's all right; 'e's smart enough, 'e is; not much of a chap to look at—bein' a small man and not over strong—but 'is 'ead's screwed on the right way. But 'e can't do nothin', because, ye see, sir, they keeps 'im in irons and locked up in 'is own cabin, 'cept when 'e was let out twice a day to take the sights and work up the ship's reckonin', and then either Turnbull or one of 'is gang was always alongside of 'im, and nobody else was hever allowed to go anigh 'im; whilst at other times—when I was givin' 'im 'is meals, I mean—either Pete Burton or one of the other chaps what was in with Turnbull was always about to see as 'e and I didn't 'ave no talk together. So, ye see, the poor man 'adn't no chance to do anything 'owever much 'e might 'ave been minded."

"Poor beggar!" ejaculated Leslie; "he must have had an awfully rough time of it. And, evidently, Turnbull and his pals do not mean to take any chances—which makes the recapture of the barque without a fight somewhat difficult. However, I believe it can be done; and, anyhow, I intend to try. Now, as I suppose you know these fellows pretty well, I want you to tell me what you think will happen when they find that Turnbull does not return to the ship."

The steward carefully considered the matter for some moments. At length he said—

"Well, sir, if Turnbull don't come off by to-morrow night, it's very likely as they'll begin to suspect that you knows somethin' about it. Then, what'll they do? They daren't all four of 'em leave the barque, with only Slushy to take care of 'er, because they knows very well that the rest of us 'd pretty soon tie up Mr Slushy and have the barque back again. And they knows, too, that if all four of 'em was to come ashore, we could slip the cable, make sail, and take the 'ooker out to sea afore they could pull off to 'er. No; they won't do that. What they *will* do, I expect, is this. If Turnbull don't come off by sunset to-morrow—which I s'pose he won't, eh? No. Well, if he don't, I expect as they'll wait till some time a'ter midnight, and then two of 'em 'll quietly drift ashore in one of the quarter-boats, leavin' the other two to take care o' the ship. And the two as goes ashore 'll reckon upon catchin' of you calmly asleep in your tent, there, and makin' you tell 'em where Turnbull is."

"Y-e-s," assented Leslie, thoughtfully, "it is quite likely that they may do some such thing as that. Yes; no doubt they will do that, sooner or later; if not to-morrow night, then the night after, or the night after that again. Very well; if they do, I shall be ready for them. And on the succeeding night, steward, you may look out for me again, about this time, unless, meanwhile, I see any reason to alter my plans. Now, that is all for the present, I think, so I will put you aboard again. I suppose, by the way, these men have no suspicion that you and I are in communication with each other?"

"Lor' bless ye, no, sir," answered Reynolds, cheerfully. "Why should they? They don't dream as you've any idee of the real state of affairs—at least not up to now. They may p'rhaps 'ave their suspicions if Turnbull don't come aboard some time to-morrow; but at present they believes as 'e 've bamboozled you completely. Then, they drinks pretty freely every night, and sleeps sound a'ter it, which they wouldn't do if they 'ad a thought as I was up to any game."

"So much the better," remarked Leslie. "What you have to do is to leave them in the same comfortable frame of mind as long as possible. Now, here we are. Good night!"

As Leslie paddled thoughtfully ashore again he pondered over the foregoing conversation with the steward, and after carefully weighing the several *pros* and *cons* of the situation, finally arrived at the conclusion that the steward's surmise as to the mutineers' line of action would probably prove to be a very near approach to the truth. In any case he thought it in the highest degree improbable that they would attempt so exceedingly risky an operation as that of leaving the barque in broad daylight, when all hands would be awake and about; he therefore partook of a leisurely breakfast next morning, and then fearlessly left the camp to take care of itself while he sauntered over to the cove to see how Nicholls and Simpson were getting on. And as he passed the treasure-cave he looked in, just to satisfy himself that Turnbull was still in safe keeping, and also to examine his wound. He found the fellow still bound hard and fast, and in a state of sullen fury at his helpless condition, but otherwise he was doing fairly well, except for the fact that his wound presented a somewhat inflamed and angry appearance, due, no doubt, to the man's unhealthy state of body through excessive drinking. Leslie dressed the wound afresh, and then passed on to the cove, where he found Nicholls and Simpson busily engaged in getting the cutter ataunto. They had already got her mainsail bent, set, and flapping gently about in the small currents of wind that eddied round the cove, the idea being to allow it to stretch uniformly before exposing it to the regular strain of work. And when Leslie came upon them they were busy upon the task of bending the foresail; and Nicholls reported that they would be easily able to complete everything, even to getting the topmast on end and the rigging set up, before nightfall. As for Flora, she had gone off upon a ramble, leaving a note for Dick which contained instructions as to how he might find her. This he did, without difficulty; and as the whole of the treasure was now loaded on board the cutter and the little craft herself was in condition to leave the cove at an hour's notice, there remained little or nothing to be done prior to the recapture of the *Minerva*. Dick therefore felt himself perfectly free to devote the remainder of the day to his sweetheart.

About an hour before sunset, however, the pair turned up at the cove, and while Flora went on board the cutter, Leslie instructed Nicholls to accompany him back to the camp, which they reached just as darkness fell. Arrived there, the two men at once made their way to the great pile of bales and cases that Dick had, with such a tremendous expenditure of labour, brought ashore from the wrecked *Mermaid*, and, rummaging among these, found the big case of firearms from which Leslie had provided himself. The case was opened and a brace of good, serviceable revolvers withdrawn therefrom for Nicholls' use, after which the two men leisurely partook of their evening meal. By the time that this was finished and cleared away it was close upon eight o'clock, and as Leslie rather anticipated the possibility of a visit from some of the mutineers that night, and had no fancy for being taken unawares by them, he directed Nicholls to lie down and sleep until midnight, when he would relieve him, it being Dick's purpose that the two men should take watch and watch through the night.

Chapter Seventeen
The Recapture of the Minerva

The camp being in complete darkness, Dick took his station just inside the tent-flap and, with the aid of his night-glass, maintained a close watch upon the barque. Hitherto there had been something very much in the nature of a carouse carried on aboard her every night since her arrival, the revel usually lasting up until nearly midnight. But on this particular night there was a difference, the singing and shouting coming to an end before four bells, or ten o'clock, a circumstance that further confirmed Dick in his impression that the mutineers meditated some step of a more or less decisive character. Yet when, by the carefully screened lamp in the tent, he consulted his watch and found that the hour of midnight was already past, he had entirely failed to detect any sign of life or movement on board the *Minerva*.

He now called Nicholls, and when the latter appeared he said to him—

"If you will sit here, where I have been sitting, you will be able, by using the night-glass, to keep a very perfect watch upon the barque without being yourself seen, and the moment that you detect anything like the appearance of a boat coming ashore, please wake me. And be especially careful not to light your pipe where you can be seen, as I am particularly anxious not to scare those fellows from coming ashore. And, in their present state of mind, I am afraid that anything which might excite within them the suspicion that they are being watched would suffice to scare them back to the ship again."

Then he, in his turn, stretched himself out and was presently sound asleep.

It seemed as though he had been asleep scarcely five minutes, although it was really more than an hour when Nicholls shook him by the shoulder and said—

"Mr Leslie, wake up, sir, please. There's a boat of some sort coming ashore from the barque. She's been in sight for the last quarter of an hour, but she's coming along very slowly, and I expect it'll be quite another quarter of an hour before she reaches the beach."

"Where is she?" demanded Leslie, seizing the night-glass. "Oh, there she is," he continued, as he brought the instrument to bear. "I see her. She appears to be one of the barque's quarter-boats, Nicholls, and, so far as I can make out, there are only two men in her."

"It's difficult to tell by starlight, sir," replied Nicholls, "but I should say there's about that number. There can't be less, for she is pulling two oars, and one man wouldn't be likely to attempt the job of pulling a heavy boat like a gig ashore, much less pull her back again against the wind. And I don't think there's likely to be more than two of 'em, otherwise they wouldn't be pulling only two oars."

"Just so," agreed Leslie. "Now where are those seizings? Oh, here they are! That's all right; we must have them where we can put our hands upon them at a moment's notice. And are your pistols all ready, in case you should need to use them? That's well. Now all that remains for us to do is to quietly await the arrival of those gentlemen here, in the darkness of the tent. They will be pretty certain to come here first. And when they do, I will cover them with my revolvers while you lash their hands behind them. And take care that you lash them so securely that there will be no possibility of their getting adrift again."

"Ay, ay, sir; never fear. You may trust me for that," answered Nicholls, cheerfully.

And with that the two men seated themselves well back within the deepest shadows of the tent, and quietly awaited the approach of their nocturnal visitors.

The boat was by this time so close to the beach that it was apparent that the men in her were pulling with muffled oars; and presently she glided in upon the sand so gently that she grounded without a sound. Then the two figures in her silently rose to their feet, and, laying in their oars with such extreme care that the deposition of them upon the thwarts was accomplished with perfect noiselessness, stepped gently out of her on to the yielding sand. They conferred earnestly together for a minute or two and then, turning, came cautiously up the beach, each of them carrying a short length of rope in his hand.

"By Jove," whispered Leslie to his companion, "they are determined to leave nothing to chance; they have actually brought along with them the lashings wherewith to bind me!"

Nicholls chuckled quietly. "So they have, sir," he whispered. "It'll be a joke to see the way that they'll be taken aback presently."

Treading carefully and using every precaution to avoid the slightest noise, the two men slowly made their way up the beach and on to the thick grass of the little savannah upon which the tent stood. They now seemed to think that the necessity for such extreme caution was past, and advanced much more rapidly, until they arrived within about twenty yards of the tent, when they again paused for a moment to confer together.

"Now!" whispered Leslie; and, at the word, he and his companion rose to their feet and stepped forward into the open. The new arrivals did not see them at once, for their heads were close together as they whispered to each other, and there were perhaps never two more surprised men than they were when Leslie's voice smote upon their ears with the words—

"Don't move an inch, or you are both dead men. And throw up your hands! If you dare to move I will fire; and, as you may see, I am covering you both!"

As Leslie spoke the two men started guiltily apart, and then stood staring in stupefaction at the two figures that had so suddenly appeared before them.

"Up with your hands, both of you," reiterated Leslie, sharply, for the strangers had apparently been taken too completely by surprise to fully comprehend all that was said to them. "And," he continued, "listen carefully to me, both of you. You are my prisoners, and I intend to make perfectly sure of you. I know all about you; I know you to be two men who are engaged in a desperate enterprise, and are likely to stick at nothing. Now, understand me well: I am just as resolute as you are, and if you give me the slightest trouble I will put a bullet through you, as surely as you stand there; so do not attempt any nonsense if you value your lives. Now you," indicating one of them with his levelled revolver, "move three paces to your right—so; halt! that will do. Now, Nicholls, lash that fellow's hands firmly behind his back."

"Well, here's a pretty go," yelled one of them to the other in an access of impotent fury. "A dandy old mess you've made of this job, Mister bloomin' Peter Burton, haven't you? and dragged me into it along with yer! I wish I'd never had nothin' at all to do with the cussed business, now, I do; I *knowed* it was boun' to go a mucker, from the very fust! But you and that bloomin' skowbank of a Turnbull *would* drag me into it, temptin' me with your yarns of treasure, and bein' as rich as a Jew, and a lot more rot o' the same sort, and now, here I am, landed—"

"There, that will do, my man," interrupted Leslie, sharply, as Nicholls deftly proceeded to lash the fellow's hands behind him; "your repentance comes just a little too late to be of any use to you. You are a mutineer and a murderer, and you must take the consequences of your evil deeds."

"What do *you* know about it?" growled the man who had been addressed as Burton. "Who's been blowin' the gaff to *you*? If it's Turnbull that's been doin' a split, I'll wring his neck for 'im!"

"There, sir, number one is all right," exclaimed Nicholls as he stepped away from his victim. "If he gets adrift I'll give him leave to eat me, body and bones! Shall I go ahead with this other chap now?"

"Yes," assented Leslie; "truss him up, and let us have done with them both as quickly as possible."

Burton, who was an immensely powerful fellow, poured forth a volley of the most horrible curses and threats as Nicholls approached him; but Leslie stood but half a dozen paces from him, with his revolver levelled straight at the fellow's head, and a stern word of caution sufficed to quell the fast-rising inclination to resistance that shone in the man's eyes; he subsided suddenly to a state of sullen silence, and submitted in his turn to be bound. The whole episode had not occupied more than five minutes, at the outside. Then, with their hands firmly secured behind them, the two men were marched off to the hut that had been built by the savages, where they were compelled to lie down and submit to a further process of binding, upon the completion of which they found themselves absolutely helpless; for now both their hands and their feet were lashed together so tightly and securely that it was quite impossible for them to move otherwise than to give an occasional feeble, impotent wriggle.

This accomplished to their complete satisfaction, Leslie and Nicholls returned to the tent, and resumed their alternate vigils until the morning; for they knew not what arrangements these men might have made with their fellow-mutineers, and deemed it wisest not to relax their vigilance now until the entire adventure had been brought to a successful issue.

The remainder of the night passed, however, without further incident, and at daybreak the occupants of the tent were once more astir and preparing breakfast. Then, having satisfied their own appetites, they took a good liberal supply of food to the hut and, loosing their prisoner's bonds sufficiently to allow them the use of their hands, bade them eat and drink freely.

Then, when at length Burton and his companion—whose name, it transpired, was Samuel Cunliffe—sullenly acknowledged that they had eaten and drunk all that they desired, their hands were once more lashed securely behind them, their feet released, and they were bidden to follow

Leslie, who went ahead while Nicholls, as rear-guard, walked close behind. And thus they all proceeded until the cave was reached, where the two new arrivals were forced to join their fellow-prisoner, Turnbull. And there, in that gloomy cavern, the exigencies of the situation demanded that, for a time at least, they should be once more subjected to the extreme discomfort of being lashed, hands and feet together, as they had been in the hut on the previous night, in order to avoid all possibility of their getting together and releasing each other.

Having satisfied himself that his prisoners were absolutely secure, and dressed Turnbull's wound afresh, Leslie, accompanied by Nicholls, next made his way to the cove, where he found the cutter lying at anchor in the centre of the little basin with all her canvas set and gently flapping in the light breeze. And a marvellously pretty picture the little craft presented with her snow-white hull, surmounted by a broad expanse of scarcely less white cotton canvas, sitting daintily and jauntily upon the water, the white of her hull and sails, and the ruddy sheen of her copper sheathing brilliantly reflected upon the smooth, dark surface of the element she rode in such saucy fashion. Dick stood for some minutes feasting his eyes upon the pretty picture she presented against the dark-brown background of scarred and riven rock that formed the sides of the basin, and then he and Nicholls quickly descended the precipitous slope to where the catamaran lay moored, and, jumping on board her, paddled off to the *Flora*, whose namesake fortunately happened to be on board her at the moment, but was just preparing to go ashore for another ramble.

"I am afraid, dear, you cannot go just now," said Dick, "unless indeed you would like to walk over to the camp, for we are about to return there at once, preparatory, I hope, to sailing for home to-morrow."

"Do you think Dick, it would be quite safe for me to take the walk alone? Because, if so, and we are actually going to sail to-morrow, I should so like to do it. It is a lovely walk; and there are associations connected with it that endear it to me," she said shyly.

"Very well, little girl," responded Dick. "Then take the walk, by all means, for it is perfectly safe. Only be very careful not to look in at the cave on your way, for I have three prisoners stowed away there, now, and although they are too firmly secured to be able to hurt you, they may say things that would offend your ears."

Flora promised that she would most carefully avoid the cave, and was set ashore by the catamaran, Dick instructing Nicholls and Simpson to afterwards proceed round to the camp in that craft while he himself undertook to work the cutter round to the same point single-handed. While, therefore, the two seamen were conveying Flora to the landing-place, Leslie busied himself in taking a pull upon the halliards all round and getting up the cutter's anchor. He was still thus engaged when the catamaran pushed off, under sail, and, passing close under the cutter's stern, hailed, inquiringly which way she was to steer.

"Keep the land close aboard on your starboard hand all the way, and you cannot go wrong," answered Leslie, adding: "But I shall be after you in a few minutes, and will give you a lead."

The catamaran stood out of the cove, and headed away to the eastward on the starboard tack; and a few minutes later Dick followed in the cutter. Within the cove, the breeze that came in over the overlapping headlands was light and baffling, yet the *Flora* gathered way quickly and glided along at a pace that rejoiced Leslie's heart. But when she passed outside beyond the shelter of the heads, and felt the full strength of the briskly blowing trade wind, her solitary navigator found that he would have his hands full when it presently came to working her. For Simpson had hoisted the big jack-yard topsail, to give the sail a good stretching, and Dick had been too preoccupied to notice the fact; the little craft therefore made her first essay *in* the open ocean under precisely the same canvas that she would show to the most gentle of breezes, whereas the trade wind was piping up quite fresh. The breeze struck her with something of the suddenness and violence of a squall, with everything creaking and twanging to the violence of the strain, and the little craft heeled to it until her lee rail was buried and the water was halfway up the deck to her tiny skylight; but with a plunge, like that of a mettlesome horse to the touch of the spur, she darted forward, burying her sharp bows deep in the heart of the first sea that came sweeping down upon her, and in another moment she was thrashing along in the wake of the catamaran like a mad thing, leaping and plunging with long floaty rushes over the sharply running sea that overran the ponderous Pacific swell. Within the first five minutes it became quite clear to Leslie that the catamaran was nowhere compared with this smart and handsome little ship, for to Dick the former craft seemed to sag away to leeward like an empty cask, while the cutter walked up to her as though the other had been at anchor. By the time that the *Flora* had overtaken the catamaran, the two craft had gained a sufficient offing to enable them to fetch the entrance channel on the next tack, and they accordingly hove about, the cutter whisking round with a celerity that gave Leslie as much as he could do to trim over the head sheets in time to catch a turn with them as she paid off on the other tack. And now the *Flora* ran away from the catamaran at such a rate that she had reached her anchorage and was just rounding into the wind to bring up when the other craft passed through the channel and entered the lagoon. This little trip round from the cove to the lagoon had not only given the cutter's sails a nice stretching, but it had also stretched her new rigging to such an extent that Dick saw it would be quite necessary to set it up afresh all round before he started on his voyage, if he did not wish to risk the loss of his spars. This, however, was a matter that would have to wait; he had something of an even more pressing nature that called for his immediate attention.

By the time that the catamaran had arrived alongside the cutter, the latter's anchor was down and the jib and foresail taken in. The big gaff topsail was next hauled down and carefully stowed away, and finally the mainsail was lowered, stowed, and the coat put over it.

Then Dick jumped aboard the catamaran. "I suppose you both have your revolvers?" he said to Nicholls and Simpson. "Are they fully loaded?" The two men replied in the affirmative. "Then up with your canvas," he commanded; "and we will be off to the barque and settle this business forthwith. I will explain my plans to you as we go."

With the cutter no longer sailing alongside her, the catamaran once more took rank as a fast-sailing and weatherly craft, and soon worked out to the spot where the *Minerva* rode at anchor. Dick, of course, by this time knew the curious craft well, and handled her with such consummate judgment that when at length he luffed her into the wind's eye and ordered her sails to be lowered, she just handsomely slid up alongside the barque and came to a standstill abreast her starboard gangway.

"Look out there and catch a turn with this 'ere painter," exclaimed Simpson, tossing a rope's-end to a couple of men who peered down from the *Minerva's* bulwarks upon the catamaran and her crew with mingled astonishment and dismay; and at the same moment Leslie and Nicholls made a spring for the barque's side-ladder, and, shinning up it, tumbled in on deck to the further discomfiture of the two men aforesaid, leaving Simpson to follow, which he promptly did. The whole thing was done so smartly that the only two visible members of the barque's crew—who seemed to be quite slow-moving and slow-thinking men—were completely taken by surprise, and evidently knew not what to make of it.

Meanwhile Leslie, with a single glance about the ship's deserted decks, seemed to grasp the situation intuitively.

"Are you two men named Royston and Hampton?" he demanded.

"Ay, ay, sir; that's us, sure enough," answered one of the two, with a visible appearance of relief for some reason best known to himself.

"Unbuckle your belts and throw them down on deck," commanded Dick, quietly drawing a brace of revolvers somewhat ostentatiously from his side-pockets.

"What for?" demanded one of the fellows. "Who be you, mister, to come aboard here and order—"

"Come, no nonsense," interrupted Leslie, sternly. "You will do exactly what I order you to do, at once, and without hesitation, or it will be the worse for you. You understand?" And he levelled a pistol at the head of each man.

Thus gently persuaded, the two men grumblingly did as they were told. And when the discarded belts were flung savagely to the deck, it was seen that attached to each was a formidable sheath-knife.

"That's right," commented Nicholls, as he stepped forward, also with a brace of revolvers in his hands, and with a kick swept the two belts far along the deck beyond the reach of their owners. "Now, come here, my joker, and let me tie you up," he continued, addressing one of the men as he flung a coil of the fore topgallant brace off its belaying-pin.

"I'll be shot if I do!" exclaimed the man addressed, with a furious oath.

"You will be shot if you *don't*" retorted Leslie, in a quiet, concentrated tone of voice that made the man addressed involuntarily shudder. "It is no good, men," he continued, "your comrades are prisoners ashore and utterly powerless to help you. The game is up. We are here to regain possession of this ship, *and we mean to do it*. And if either of you is foolish enough to offer resistance, you will be badly hurt."

Leslie's stern and uncompromising manner had its effect; and the two men, realising their utter helplessness, sullenly and with many curses submitted to be bound—an operation that Nicholls performed with much gusto and an effectiveness that left nothing to be desired. Then, leaving Simpson to mount guard over the grumbling pair, Dick and Nicholls went forward to the forecastle to call the remainder of the crew on deck, noticing, as they passed the galley door, that the Irish cook was busying himself inside with his pots and pans, and it was not difficult to discern that he was in a state of extreme mental perturbation. Arriving at the forecastle hatch, they found the cover on and secured with a bar and padlock, whereupon Dick returned to the galley and, putting his head inside, said—

"Dolan, I see that the fore scuttle is locked. Who has the key?"

"Sure, and it's Jack Hampton that has that same, sor," answered the cook with alacrity, and some surprise at Leslie's unaccountable familiarity with his name. "And by the same token he also has the key of the main cabin and of Misther Marshall's stateroom, your honour's honour," he added.

"Which of those two men is Jack Hampton?" demanded Leslie.

"It's the fellah that's triced up so nately to the port rail, sor," answered Dolan.

"Then go you and take the keys out of his pocket," commanded Dick. "I have no doubt you know which they are."

"Ay, ay, sor; faith and I do that same," replied the man.

And with ready officiousness he bustled out of the galley and, walking aft, to the spot where Hampton was lashed up, thrust his hand unceremoniously into the man's trousers pocket, withdrew a bunch of keys secured together upon a ropeyarn, and offered them to Leslie.

Dick looked at them as they lay in the fellow's hand.

"There are four keys there, I see," he said, "What are they?"

"This," answered Dolan, "is the key of the forecastle hatch. This, the key of the main cabin, which is locked. This is the key of Misther Marshall's cabin. And this is the key of the irons that's on the same gentleman's hands."

"Very good," said Leslie. "Now come forward with me, and unlock the forecastle."

The man obeyed, and presently, in response to Dick's call, four very decent-looking young fellows came up on deck and stared about them in some bewilderment at the sight of three total strangers on board, and two of the mutineers in bonds. From the forecastle Dick proceeded aft, still with the cook in company, and compelled the latter to unlock first the main cabin in which Reynolds was found confined, then the mate's cabin, and finally the irons on the latter's wrists.

The mate of the *Minerva*, who proved to be a very smart-looking young fellow, with a keen, resolute expression, but drawn and haggard with anxiety, stared in amazement at the apparition of a total stranger in his cabin, who was evidently acting with authority. But Leslie did not leave him much time for wonderment.

"Mr Marshall," he said, "permit me to introduce myself. My name is Leslie. It has been my misfortune to be cast away on the island, a glimpse of which you have perhaps occasionally caught through your cabin port. I have been on that island nearly ten months, and my preparations for leaving it were practically complete when your vessel entered the lagoon. Naturally, I came off aboard to make the acquaintance of your skipper, and found the man Turnbull in command. Knowing the fellow so well as you must, you will not be surprised to learn that, from what I saw, I quickly guessed there was something very seriously wrong aboard here; and a little judicious investigation soon enabled me to arrive at the actual facts. I am now glad to inform you that, aided by my two companions, I have managed to recover possession of the ship for you, and have much pleasure in turning her over to you. You will find Royston and Hampton, two of the mutineers, securely lashed to the rail, on deck, and doubtless you will lose no time in clapping them in irons. The other three—Turnbull, Burton, and Cunliffe— are prisoners ashore, at present, and if you are disposed to maroon them, they can, of course, remain there, as the island possesses ample resources in the shape of fruit, fish, and water, for their sustenance. But if, on the other hand, you prefer to take them with you, I will bring them off aboard at any time that may be most convenient to you."

"Thank you, Mr Leslie," answered Marshall, fervently, as he rose and stretched himself with obvious delight in his recovered freedom, "I am sure I don't know how I am to express my gratitude for the service that you've done me and the owners of this ship. I'm afraid I shall have to leave it to them to do when we get home. But I can repay you in a measure by offering you and your companions a passage to England, which I do now, with the greatest of pleasure. And I'll do my level best to make the trip comfortable and pleasant for you. As to Turnbull and the other two that you've boxed up ashore, of course I must take them along with me and hand them over to the authorities upon our arrival at Capetown, because, d'ye see, they're all guilty of the murder of poor Cap'n Hopkins. So you can bring them off—or I'll send ashore for 'em—whenever you like. And now, if you've no objection, we'll go out on deck, for, to tell you the truth, I'm just pining for a breath of fresh air."

The poor fellow looked about him in amazement when, a minute later, he stood on the barque's poop and gazed thence at the lovely island, rich in verdure of every conceivable tint of green, and glowing here and there with patches of the vivid scarlet blossoms of the bois-immortelle, the whole bathed in the brilliant sunshine of a tropical day. Nor was he less astonished at the sight of the handsome little cutter lying at anchor close in with the shore. For this was the first time that he had ever been on deck since the day on which the island had been "made" from the barque's fore-yard; and everything was therefore absolutely new to him, save such slight glimpses as he had been able to catch through the port-hole of his cabin. He was most anxious that Leslie and his two companions should remain on board and take dinner with him; but Dick was by this time quite as anxious to get back ashore and satisfy himself as to Flora's safe arrival. So a compromise was made, and Marshall, having seen the two mutineers safely clapped in irons, gladly accepted Leslie's invitation to go ashore and take lunch with him. They were still some distance from the beach when Flora was seen flitting busily about the camp; Leslie's anxiety therefore on her account was at an end. And, after lunch, while Nicholls and Simpson went blithely to work upon the job of provisioning and watering the cutter, and stowing their several personal belongings on board, Leslie and Marshall took the catamaran and sailed round to the cove, from whence they proceeded to the cave, where they found Turnbull and his two companions still bound hard and fast, and by this time thoroughly subdued. With some difficulty they succeeded in getting the three prisoners down the face of the cliff and aboard the catamaran; and, this done, their transference to the *Minerva* and their confinement in irons was an easy matter. The owners of the barque had made the grave mistake of sending her to sea without so much as a single weapon of any kind to aid her officers, if need be, to maintain order and discipline among the crew; but this was an omission that Leslie was fortunately in a position to easily remedy by a simple application to the case of firearms that had formed part of the *Mermaid's* cargo, and he willingly supplied Marshall with a brace of revolvers and a sufficient quantity of ammunition for all practical purposes. The party from the island—that is to say, Flora, Leslie, Nicholls, and Simpson—accepted a very pressing invitation from Marshall to dine and spend the evening on board the *Minerva* in celebration of that vessel's recovery from the mutineers; and before they left again for the shore Captain Marshall made a long entry in the ship's official log, detailing the circumstances of her seizure and recapture, with full particulars of the part played by the steward in the latter—much to

Reynolds' gratification; and Leslie attached his signature to the entry, in attestation of its truth. Leslie also seized the opportunity to compare the chronometer saved from the *Mermaid* with those belonging to the *Minerva*, and was much gratified to find that it was absolutely to be relied upon. They returned to the camp about midnight, and turned in highly elated with the joyous knowledge that on the morrow they would actually be starting for home.

As may be supposed, the whole party were early astir next morning; Nicholls and Simpson wending their way to the woods to collect a stock of fruit for the first few days of the voyage, while Flora prepared breakfast, and Leslie overhauled the entire camp to satisfy himself that he was not leaving behind him anything that would be of material service to him. There were a few trifling matters that, at the last moment, he decided to take; and these he put into the barque's dinghy and thus carried off to the cutter. By the time that he was back the two men had returned, laden with quite as much fruit as could be conveniently stowed away aboard so small a craft as the *Flora*; and this also they carried off and put on board. Then came breakfast—their last meal on the island, and a happy, hilarious meal it was.

Then, leaving everything just as it was, they all went down to the beach and stepped into the barque's gig, in which they pulled alongside the cutter. Arrived there, they dropped overboard a heavy "killick" of rock which they had previously attached to the boat's painter, and thus anchored her in readiness for the *Minerva's* crew whenever they might choose to fetch her. To set the cutter's canvas was the work of a few minutes, and, this done, the anchor was quickly hove up and the little craft got under way. On their way out of the lagoon they tacked close under the *Minerva's* stern, receiving a cheery farewell hail of "A quick and pleasant passage to you!" from Marshall, who was walking the poop while his scanty crew were getting some water-casks into the longboat; and ten minutes later they dashed through the entrance channel, and found themselves riding buoyantly over the long undulations of the Pacific swell, as Leslie bore away to pass to the northward of the island and thence west over the interminable miles of water that lay between them and home.

My story is told; for with the voyage of the *Flora*, adventurous though it was, this narrative has nothing to do; suffice it to say that having called at Tahiti and Tongatabu the little cutter safely passed Port Phillip Heads and arrived at Melbourne on the fifty-third day out from the island. Here Leslie duly cashed his draft for one hundred pounds, and with the proceeds thereof secured for Flora a passage to Bombay, that young lady having decided to go on at once to her father—without waiting to visit her Australian friends—in order that the judge's natural anxiety to see his daughter after her singular adventure might be gratified with as little delay as possible. And further to curtail that anxiety to its lowest limit, she despatched a cablegram to her father within an hour of her arrival in Melbourne. As for Dick, he allowed his affairs to stand during the two days that elapsed between their arrival and Flora's departure, devoting himself entirely to her.

But as soon as he had waved his last good-bye to her, he went to his hotel and wrote a long letter to his father's lawyers, detailing at length the events that had transpired subsequent to the wreck of the *Golden Fleece*, including the discovery and appropriation of the treasure, and of his intention to take it home in the cutter; leaving to their discretion the decision whether or no they would communicate the information to his father. And, thin done, he forthwith re-victualled and re-watered the *Flora*, and cleared for Capetown, which was to be his next port of call.

It was drawing on toward three o'clock in the afternoon of a glorious spring day when the cutter-yacht *Flora*, from Funchal, homeward-bound, came sliding unobtrusively into Weymouth harbour, where, having taken in her thin and almost worn-out sails, she modestly moored among a number of other yachts under the Nothe. Perhaps it was her somewhat dingy and weatherworn appearance that caused her crew to avoid attracting to her any unnecessary attention, or possibly it may have been some other reason; at all events, to all inquisitive inquiries the bronzed and bearded trio who manned her merely replied that they had "been cruising to the south'ard." To the custom-house officers they had of course to be a little more explicit; but even they were satisfied when, after a careful search of the craft's tiny cabins and forecastle, they were invited to sample a bottle of choice Madeira, on some four or five dozen of which Leslie willingly paid duty. The next day her sails were unbent and she was taken up the Backwater and laid up, in charge of Simpson; and a month or two later her ballast was taken out of her and stowed away in a shed under which she also was hauled up. A certain portion of this ballast was soon afterwards packed up somewhat carefully and conveyed to London by train; and eventually the little craft was sold.

Meanwhile, however, Leslie had despatched a wire to his father's solicitors, announcing his arrival home; and that same evening he received a reply requesting him to go to town and call at the office of the senders on the following day without fail, as they had intelligence of the utmost importance to communicate to him.

Of course he went; and upon his arrival was at once ushered into a private room. There was but one individual in the apartment, a tall, handsome, grey-headed old gentleman of most aristocratic appearance, who rose to his feet in much agitation as Dick entered.

"Father!" cried the younger man, in the utmost astonishment. "My son!" exclaimed the elder; and their hands locked in a grip that was far more expressive than many words.

"Dick, my son," at length exclaimed the Earl, when he had sufficiently overcome his agitation to speak, "let me be the first to congratulate you. Your innocence has been fully proved!"

A month later the man whom we have known as Dick Leslie was once more afloat, and on his way to Bombay on board a P. and O. liner.